SHADOWS

The Rephaim

BOOK I

SHADOWS

PAULA WESTON

TUNDRA BOOKS

Copyright © 2013 Paula Weston
Published by arrangement with The Text Publishing Company, Australia
Published in North America by Tundra Books, 2013

Published in Canada by Tundra Books, a division of Random House
of Canada Limited, One Toronto Street, Suite 300, Toronto, Ontario
M5C 2V6

Published in the United States by Tundra Books of Northern New York,
P.O. Box 1030, Plattsburgh, New York 12901

Library of Congress Control Number: 2012947613

Library and Archives Canada Cataloguing in Publication

Weston, Paula
    Shadows / Paula Weston.

"Book one in the Rephaim series".
ISBN 978-1-77049-547-0. – ISBN 978-1-77049-549-4 (EPUB)

    I. Title.

PZ7.W5266Sha 2013   j823'.92   C2012-905829-7

We acknowledge the financial support of the Government of Canada
through the Canada Book Fund and that of the Government of
Ontario through the Ontario Media Development Corporation's
Ontario Book Initiative. We further acknowledge the support of
the Canada Council for the Arts and the Ontario Arts Council
for our publishing program.   ONTARIO ARTS COUNCIL
                                    CONSEIL DES ARTS DE L'ONTARIO

Cover designed by obroberts
Cover image: © Mark Owen/Arcangel Images

www.tundrabooks.com

Printed and bound in the United States of America

1 2 3 4 5 6   18 17 16 15 14 13

FOR MURRAY

INTO THE TREES

I'm running along the boardwalk, wind and sand stinging my arms. It's after work and I have the track to myself. A handful of surfers are battling the choppy waves, and the Williamsons are walking on the beach like they do every morning and afternoon in their matching track outfits and orthopedic shoes. Their silver heads are bowed against the wind, but they're still holding hands. It makes me feel emptier than usual.

Dark storm clouds scud across the sky. Next to me the palm trees shake and creak. I keep running, away from town, towards a fork in the track. The main path continues along the beach. A smaller trail heads into the rainforest and turns to dirt underfoot. I know before I reach the fork which way I'm going, even though it will further punish my leg.

I can live with the pain. It wasn't that long ago I couldn't run at all. And then I could, and didn't want to. But sharing the bungalow with Maggie and watching her lace on running shoes every day finally got me off the couch. For a while we ran together, but I was too slow that first month or so. She was adamant she didn't mind, but she'd never tell me if she did. I made the decision for her by running in the afternoons. Turns out I like the solitude.

In the rainforest, there's little hint of the gale blowing on the beach. It's cooler in here, and quieter. Ferns taller than me crowd along the track, and the fronds brush my arms when I stray too close. Fig trees stretch overhead, branches so thick they almost blot out the sky.

I concentrate on the sound of my feet hitting the hard-packed dirt. A butterfly flitters ahead of me, a flash of electric blue near the dark forest floor.

Pandanus Beach is tucked away, well off the highway, bordered by the ocean and closed in by mountains and rainforest. Being able to run along this lush, sheltered path is one of the reasons I'm still here.

I climbed off the Grayhound bus nine months ago alongside a bunch of dreadlocked surfers, not too long after my eighteenth birthday. My plan was to hang around for a few weeks and then move on. It took me a while to find the right place, a place where I wouldn't be noticed. Almost everywhere reminds me of Jude.

Jude would have loved it here. He'd go anywhere as long as there was a beach and a decent bar. He would have owned Pan Beach in a fortnight.

The pain hits my chest so hard my knees buckle. I stumble, barely managing to keep my feet. I try to catch my breath. But it's not a lack of oxygen that's my problem, it's the weight. The cruel, crushing weight.

I lean against a fig tree, the trunk rough with dried moss. My chest heaves, my throat burns and I let the tears come. For a while, that's all I do, sob and breathe in cool forest air, fighting the urge to scream. I have to pull it together. I'm stronger than this.

As I straighten, something moves to my left. A flicker. I turn my head and peer into the dense trees, wiping my cheeks with the back of my hand. There's only a spider web strung between tree trunks, glinting silver. Nothing. Another flicker, at the edge of my vision. It's gone by the time my eyes track it. I wait, hold my breath. There. A shadow, gone again before I blink. It's not a wallaby. Way too tall.

'Hey,' I call out, but my voice is still thick from crying. If someone *is* here, I need to sound less pathetic. 'Stop fucking around.'

The silence is unnatural now. I can't hear the surf or the wind. The afternoon light is fading quickly around me.

'Fuck this.' I make my voice hard and sharp, and scan

the vines and trees. Then I take off. My plan is to look like I'm casually jogging back the way I came but, two steps on, adrenaline kicks in and I'm running flat out.

I've never noticed how much this trail twists and turns. How close the trees are. The rainforest is full of shadows, so when I see a dark shape flitting between the ferns to my right, it takes a moment to realize there really is someone in here. Shadowing me. With ease.

I can't turn to look. I can't take my eyes off the track or the tree roots that sprout out of it. I'm fifty meters from the tree line, ferns and webs slapping against my arms and legs. Thirty meters. A vine hits my face. Blood pounds in my ears and my lungs burn. Ten meters. Almost there. I strain to hear footsteps behind me, but the wind muffles everything now.

I burst out of the trees.

Where are the surfers? I take the beach track, ignoring the jarring in my bad leg. I hit the sand and my feet sink, but I keep going. Halfway to the waterline, my legs finally turn to jelly. My breath is ragged and my chest is about to explode. I collapse to my knees and look back.

No one has followed me out of the rainforest.

'Hello, love.'

I look up to see the Williamsons on their way back towards town.

'Are you all right, dear?' Mrs Williamson has to shout

to be heard over the wind. Her straw hat is clutched between her arthritic fingers.

I hold up a hand. I still can't speak. I offer a thumbs up, and they both smile, probably chalking up my bizarre behavior to some new fitness craze. The run-for-your-life-and-collapse-in-the-sand workout.

I stay on my knees, eyes on the trees. As the sun drops lower in the sky, the spiky shadow of a palm tree lengthens across the sand.

No one is coming out of the forest. I feel stupid.

I wish it was all I felt.

NOT SO SWEET DREAMS

Maggie and I are in the red laminate kitchen of our bungalow. Mottled shadows from the jacaranda tree flicker across the bench, hiding the scratches and red wine stains. Maggie has pushed her knitting aside while she reads. Outside, the surf is constant, muffled; the beach is down the hill, a block away.

Yesterday's gale is forgotten. I wish I could say the same about what happened in the rainforest. I keep turning it over, trying to figure it out. I was on edge before the figure shadowed me out of the trees. It's like my body sensed a threat before I saw that dark shape. But was there a threat, really? It seemed impossible this morning, waking up with the sun in my eyes and a clear blue sky outside. Unreal. Now I'm not sure the figure was even there.

Maggie has been staring at the laptop for a few minutes, her muesli untouched. I move into a patch of sunlight and rinse the dishes in the sink. I can't help myself—I check over her shoulder to see what part she's up to.

She looks around at me. 'You really wrote this?'

I nod, wary.

She sips her coffee. 'Gaby . . . this stuff's in your head?'

'I have weird dreams.'

'But what made you put it online?' She gestures to the screen. 'Why this website?'

'Dark Thoughts?' I wipe my hands on a damp tea towel. 'The short story with the most votes wins a thousand bucks.'

She stares back at the screen, clicks the mouse, and then looks at me again. I'm wearing old jeans and a yellow T-shirt. At least I look harmless. Maggie doesn't seem so sure anymore. Whatever happened in the rainforest yesterday, I can't tell her about it. Not now.

She gets up from the table and puts her cup on the bench. She's still in her running gear, her streaky blonde hair in a neat ponytail. Her skin looks so healthy she's almost glowing. Maggie is just about an official local attraction, alongside the surf beach and the annual beer and wine festival. She works at the Green Bean, an organic café on the esplanade run by her mother. Tourists go there because they've read about it in glossy foodie magazines.

For the locals, Maggie is as much of a drawing card.

'Don't look at me like that,' I say. 'Maybe I like this stuff because it's not real.' I run a hand through my hair, which is not blonde or neat. It's dark and hard to manage. A bit like me.

'I'm not saying there's anything wrong with it. It's just a little gory, that's all. I didn't even know you liked to write.' Her smile is easier now. This is firmer territory. 'Have you got any other stories?'

She means any others not involving hell-beasts and beheadings. I give her a lopsided grin. 'It's all right, Mags, I won't make you read any more.'

Her face falls. 'Oh, babe, I didn't mean—'

'Stop that,' I say, catching her eye.

'No, really, if you want to talk about, you know, stuff.'

I *really* don't want to have this conversation. 'Margaret Jane,' I say in my best impression of her mother. 'It's not that big a deal.'

'But it's getting close, though, isn't it?'

I keep smiling. 'It's okay.' It's a lie, but it's the easiest thing to say.

In eight days, it'll be a year since Jude died. He was my twin.

'Don't you have to work this morning?' I ask.

Maggie glances at the clock on the microwave and sighs. 'I'd better get moving.' She takes two steps towards the hall and stops. 'You know you can talk to me, though, right?'

'I know. Thanks.'

I like Maggie. She's the only person I've felt normal with since the accident. And I know she's had her own share of loss. But this isn't something I'm going to chat about over coffee.

She leaves the kitchen slowly, in case I change my mind. I go to turn off the laptop. I know every word, but I have to read the story again, try to see it through Maggie's eyes. The nightclub draped with corpses. The hell-beast with the glistening teeth and toaster head. Me, cutting that head off with a sword, alongside a guy who has vivid green eyes and smells like sandalwood.

I'm surprised Maggie made it through as far as she did. I'm glad she didn't ask me how much of it I'd actually dreamed, or how often the guy with the green eyes turns up to fight monsters at my side. Morning after morning, I wake up with him lingering in my thoughts and I feel guilty without any idea why.

I've named him Matt. In the end it was a relief to get him out of my head and onto paper.

HAPPY HOUR

It's late Friday afternoon and Rick's is starting to fill up. It's the only place to be this time of the week. The bar opens onto the street and Maggie and I are sitting at the window, chatting to people we know as they walk past outside. The sun has dipped behind the headland, leaving a soft purple glow in the sky over the ocean. Down the esplanade, fairy lights shimmer in the old poinciana trees. I love those trees. When I got off the bus last year, I stepped onto their carpet of orange blossom. I felt safe underneath those branches. Protected.

'Hello, ladies.' Simon stacks glasses together and puts them on his tray, then wipes down the open window ledge we're leaning on. 'How are we this fine evening?'

'Glad the week's over,' Maggie says.

Simon looks at me, waiting. He's Rick's younger brother, working shifts to pay his way through uni.

'Thirsty,' I say, holding up my empty beer bottle.

He leans around Maggie to grab it. 'Let me rectify that.'

I let him take it, and pretend not to notice him checking me out. Simon meets my gaze, knowing he's been caught. He's the sort of guy most girls find sexy: close-cropped tawny hair, Japanese-style tatts on his arms, and long eyelashes. Easy company. Hot body. And still hopeful I'll go home with him some night.

'Imagine what he'd do if you wore a short skirt,' Maggie says when he heads back to the bar. 'He'd probably have a heart attack.'

I look down at my T-shirt and cargoes and then at her. 'We can't all pull off *that* outfit.'

Maggie is wearing a short denim skirt and a black tank top. 'You could,' she says, grinning. 'You're just not brave enough.'

'You've got that right.' I might be toned again, but I'm still not flashing too much skin—for a number of reasons.

After our second beer, Maggie leans in close. 'Check out the new arrival at the bar. He hasn't stopped staring at you.'

I turn and skim the faces. Nothing of interest, as usual. But then I see him and stop breathing.

'Don't gawk.' Maggie nudges me, her beer sloshing.

I turn back.

It's impossible.

He looks like the guy I keep dreaming about. *Exactly* like him: short dirty-blond hair, messy like he's just woken up, a face too masculine to be pretty, and a lean, muscular body. T-shirt and jeans.

I look again. He's facing me now, elbows behind him on the worn timber bar like he owns the place. All he needs is a sword in one hand and a severed head in the other.

He's watching me watching him. He can't be more than twenty.

I finish my drink. 'My shout. Ready?'

'You're going to talk to him?' Maggie's eyes widen, mocking me.

'Yep.'

'Wait up.' She empties her beer and covers her mouth to hide the smallest of burps. 'Let's go.' She heads straight for him.

I follow her, not really sure what I'm doing.

Maggie props her arms on the bar and waits to be served. I position myself between her and the Matt look-alike, and pretend I'm trying to get Rick's or Simon's attention.

'Interesting place.' The voice next to me is low, with a slight growl to it. He even sounds like Matt. Or how Matt sounds in my head.

I turn to him, trying hard to be casual about it. He's

studying me, almost wary. His eyes are green, eyelashes long . . . god, it *is* Matt. This guy is real.

There's only one explanation.

'Do I know you?'

His laugh comes from somewhere deep in his chest. 'Are you seriously chatting me up?'

'What? No.' I bite my lip and turn away.

Somebody shoot me, please. I haven't given anyone a second glance since well before the accident. And here I am blushing because this guy happens to resemble someone I see in my increasingly violent dreams.

He looks past me. 'Friend of yours? She's cute.'

Maggie is working hard to pretend she's not listening, but her lip twitches and gives her away. I take a step back. 'Don't let me get in the way.'

'But I came all this way to see you, Gabe.'

I stiffen. 'How do you know my name?'

He frowns and looks at Maggie again before his attention settles back on me. He measures his words. 'I knew your brother.'

'What?' The chatter in the room spikes. Loud voices, laughter, clinking glasses: a wall of noise. The shelf of cocktail bottles behind him blurs. I grip the bar.

'Tell me what happened,' he says.

I breathe in and out. In. And out. Someone calls Simon's name.

'Tell me,' he says again. 'You were there, right?'

All the guilt and grief and anger are back in the space of a heartbeat, suffocating me. 'Of course I was there.' I clench my teeth. 'I was in the car.'

Maggie puts her arm around my waist. 'Back off,' she says to him with as much venom as I've heard from her.

It's his turn to stare. 'The car? What car?'

I give him a black look. 'I don't need this.' I push away from Maggie.

I make it a few paces before he grabs my arm. 'Gabe.'

I jerk away from him. 'Fuck off.'

He lets go, and glances at the faces around us. A few drinkers are watching with interest. He takes a deep breath then smiles like nothing has happened. 'Come on, let me buy you a drink.'

'Why?'

'To talk.'

'About Jude?' I hate how much my voice still cracks when I say his name.

'Yeah.'

'Why?'

His smile fades. 'Because I miss him.'

And that's all it takes.

Of course I've seen him almost every night for a year, but I'm not telling him that.

He watches me for a moment and then pulls out his phone. He flips through a few images, and then turns it to me. My breath catches. It's Jude, smiling, with a box of beer on one shoulder. He's walking towards the camera, wearing a Led Zeppelin T-shirt, untucked. I can't see past his knees, but I'd put a week's wages on him wearing combat boots. He has—*had*—dark hair like me, and it's threatening to fall into his eyes. He looks different from how I remember him. Wilder somehow.

Rafa flicks his thumb across the screen and another image comes into view. This time it's the two of them, shoulder to shoulder, with a packed stadium behind them. A football match. They're both laughing. Another, Jude and Rafa again, pretty blonde girls either side of them, trying to force their way into the frame. The girls are posing, Rafa's brooding at the camera and Jude's laughing at him.

I don't realize I'm touching the screen until the image flicks off and another appears. Rafa hesitates and then lets me take the phone. This one is of Jude sitting at a table, outdoors somewhere. There's an orange-streaked sky behind him and a calm sea. He's wearing a beanie; his hair is sticking out underneath. His head and shoulders fill the frame, but he's not looking at the camera. Something offscreen is holding his gaze. He's thinking, trying to figure something out. It's the quiet Jude most people never got to see. He looks about seventeen, not long before the accident, but I can't work out when any of these could have been taken.

I can't look away. Seeing new images of Jude . . . I know it's going to rip my heart out sometime soon, but right now it feels like a gift.

'Can you send me these?'

'If you want.'

I can't place his accent, which is rare for me.

'When did you last see him?'

He's measuring me again, like it's a trick question. He swigs his beer. 'Just before you two took off.' He looks me over. It's not subtle. 'Were you hurt?'

I nod.

'How bad?'

'Bad enough.' I'm glad my hair's down. It's long enough to cover the back of my neck.

He raises his eyebrows.

I sigh. 'Broken leg, two busted ribs, twenty stitches in my neck, bruised spleen, huge lump on my head.' My fingers go to the spot where the lump was. It's long gone, but the habit remains. 'How come I've never heard of you?'

He runs his thumb down the length of his beer bottle. It's very distracting. 'You tell me.'

I look straight at him, at those green eyes, and I'm taken

aback again by how familiar he is. I must have met him before. How else could I have pictured him so clearly? But why have I been dreaming of him?

'I lost some things, after the accident. There's a few gaps here and there.'

In truth, the details of my life before the night of the crash are still in a fog. Leaving school, all the shit with my parents, it's all sitting there under a layer of numbness I'm not ready to deal with.

Rafa leans forward, and I smell sandalwood, the faintest trace of it.

'So, what are you doing'—he looks around—'here?'

'It's peaceful,' I say without thinking. 'I like it here. Everything's simple.'

'And how long do you plan on keeping things simple?'

'As long as I can.'

'I find that hard to believe.'

He settles back and the sandalwood is replaced by beer and wood-fired pizza, and a hint of frangipani blossom from somewhere outside. I watch, fascinated, as he tears the label off the bottle without looking. He rips neat long strips and then absently pastes them on the table in a row, like soldiers. Exactly how Jude used to.

For once, I'm thinking about Jude without it feeling like I'm swallowing wet cement.

'You wanted to talk about Jude?'

He nods. 'Your shout, though.'

I raise my eyebrows, but go to the bar. Maggie is still with the surfer. He's pulled on a T-shirt and tied back his bleached blond hair. She's always polite to the guys who hit on her, but she actually seems interested in whatever he's saying. She touches his arm when she speaks, her eyes bright.

Simon serves me. 'Who's that?' he asks.

I follow his gaze and meet Rafa's. 'Friend of Jude's.'

I go to pay, and find Simon staring at me. He's never heard me say Jude's name before, though Maggie told him the story, and I guess it's taken him by surprise. 'You okay?'

'I'm fine.' I avoid his eyes and take the beers back to the table.

'New boyfriend?' Rafa asks.

'He's on the short list.'

'Brave man.'

I fold my hands on the table and wait.

'You seriously want me just to talk about Jude?'

The truth is, I don't know if I want him to or not, but I nod anyway. Rafa regards me. It takes him a few seconds to begin speaking.

'We were in Egypt once,' he says, 'and Jude ate kushari from a roadside stall. Typical Jude, you know. Eat anything.'

I picture it as the story unfolds: an explosive stomach bug on a donkey ride. I'm listening, but the distance between me and Rafa is so much wider than the table separating us. I can't stop thinking: I don't remember Jude ever going to Egypt.

Rafa breaks into a grin as he describes Jude paying a couple of Egyptian pounds for a handful of toilet paper in a Third World washroom, and Rafa having to pay extra so Jude could stay in there until it was safe to come out.

'He was pale and sweaty. God, I laughed. But he cleaned himself up and still managed to pick up that night. The man had a gift. Here—'

With a few flicks of his thumb, Rafa brings up a photo of two tall guys on tiny donkeys in a dry landscape. A boy in a white dishdasha robe stands next to them, a huge smile on his face. They look ridiculous with their legs almost touching the ground. Both are wearing caps and sunglasses, but I'd know Jude anywhere, and the other rider is unmistakably Rafa. It doesn't make any sense. Just how much did I lose in that car wreck?

I can't focus. I need space. 'I'll be back in a minute,' I tell Rafa. I go to the ladies and splash water on my face. It doesn't help.

Rafa watches me walk back through the crowded room and I feel heat climbing up from my chest. 'You're really going to keep this up?' he asks when I sit back down.

I have no idea what he's getting at, and when I don't answer, he leans in closer.

'What about if I do this?' He runs his fingers through my hair, not quite far enough to discover the scar at the nape of my neck. It feels good. So good, I sigh.

With his hand still in my hair, he brings his lips down to my ear. 'You're not going to hit me?'

'Not yet.'

'What about if I do *this*?' He kisses my neck, just under my ear, his warm tongue against my skin. I can't help myself. I shudder with the pleasure of it. It's been so long since I let anyone touch me. I don't even mind that it's my neck.

He pulls back, watches my eyes. He's the type of guy who never goes home alone, but it's as if he's expecting rejection. From me. It's endearing. I put my glass on the table and touch his lips with cool fingers. They're as soft as they look.

I kiss him.

He kisses me back, but he's not really committed. It's like he's waiting for something. I run my fingers over his arms, pull him to me. His grip tightens on my hair and his arm comes around my waist. He's not waiting anymore. It's all heat and breath and tongue. I've never been kissed like it.

Finally, after what feels like an indecently long time, we pull apart. His eyes are ocean-dark.

'I had no idea you were this good.' He's breathing fast,

but then so am I, and my head is a little swimmy, between the beer, the noise of the bar, and the heat in my body. The night air is heavy with blossom and sandalwood.

'I think it's time to get you home.' Maggie is beside me, pushing a half-full bottle out of my reach. I didn't notice her coming. 'Big day tomorrow. You have to work, remember?'

Rafa takes his hands from my waist. It's not what I want. What I want is to take him back to my room and see what else I might be good at.

He finishes my beer. 'Work where?' He's still watching me closely.

'The library,' Maggie says, steering me off the bar stool.

'You work in a *library*?'

'Certainly do.' My legs are a little shaky so I keep hanging on to Maggie.

He throws his head back and laughs. 'That's priceless.' He leans in and kisses me again, tongue and all, right in front of Maggie. I feel him smiling before he pulls back. 'See you soon, *Gaby*.'

He disappears into the crowd, every girl he passes checking him out.

'Oh, babe.' Maggie squeezes my arm. 'What's gotten into you?'

I don't answer because, honestly, I don't know.

I KNOW WHAT
YOU'RE THINKING

I wake up seedy. The pain in the base of my skull is a dull throb rather than a steady pounding, so I guess I should be grateful.

Maggie is in the kitchen when I shuffle in, reading the paper and drinking dark juice. Beetroot and carrot. My stomach turns.

'So this is what tall, dark, and handsome would have woken up to? You definitely owe me.'

I look down. I'm wearing gray track pants, a baggy white T-shirt with some sort of food stain down the front—probably spaghetti sauce from two nights ago—and my hair's a bird nest. 'He was blond,' I say, slipping into the chair across from her, 'not dark.'

'I wasn't talking about his hair.' She smiles, but she's not as playful as she's making out. Maggie isn't good at conflict, but if she's got something to say, she'll find a way to say it. It usually takes her a while to get the words right in her head, so I'm guessing she's spent the last hour stewing over whatever it is she wants to say to me. It's a wonder she hasn't pulled out her craft bag—not that she needs to knit another scarf she'll never wear in this climate.

'Every second guy in that bar has made a play for you over the past nine months,' she starts. 'You show no sign of interest. And then along comes this guy, and you go from snarling at him to sticking your tongue down his throat in the space of an hour. In front of Simon!'

She's known Simon since kindergarten. It's no secret she hopes we'll hook up.

'What's going on, Gaby?'

I shrug. 'It just happened.'

She closes the newspaper, folds it, and pushes it aside. 'Is this a grief thing?'

'Maybe. I don't know.'

'But why him?'

Thinking about Rafa brings a flush of warmth across my chest. God, I was ready to drag him home last night. I don't even know his last name, or where he's from. Or, now that I think about it, how he knew where to find me.

I shrug again. 'Did you *see* him?'

She nods. 'Oh, he's got it all happening, all right. I just think you might want to ease yourself back into the dating pool. Not throw yourself in the shark tank.'

I laugh. I can't help it. She so rarely gets this annoyed.

'Does this have anything to do with that story of yours?'

I stop laughing. 'What are you talking about?' I get up and go to the espresso machine.

'You've been writing that violent stuff, and now you're all over some guy we've never seen before. I didn't know that was your type.'

'It's not.' I scoop coffee out of the tin and pack it down in the basket.

'But you're going to see him again?'

'It's a small town, and you did tell him where I work.' I start frothing milk, and the noise ends the conversation for a while. I make us each a cappuccino and then sit down again. Maggie doesn't even notice the fern leaf I've made in the foam.

'Is it because he knows Jude? Is that why you could talk to him?'

Finally, the light comes on. Maggie isn't worried about my sex life; she's hurt that I can talk about my brother with a complete stranger, and not with her.

I met Maggie on my second day at Pan Beach, when she dropped a plate of scrambled eggs on the floor beside me in the Green Bean. Instead of losing it, she just laughed. I helped clean it up and she gave me breakfast on the house. Before I knew it, we were talking about travel and books and she was loaning me her well-worn copy of *The Book Thief*. Then she put in a good word for me at the library and talked me into moving out of the backpackers and in with her. I know it was tough for her to leave her mum. Her dad had died only the year before, quickly and horribly from cancer. But she needed to breathe. She told me she couldn't afford to move out on her own, which I knew wasn't true, even back then. We got the bungalow and didn't care about the minor annoyances: how tiny it was, the showerhead with the pressure of a soak hose, the front door that sticks every time it rains, and the stove with only three working gas burners. I've always been grateful.

I take a deep breath, wanting to give her something.

'Every time I think of Jude, it's like someone's stabbing me in the heart.' I tap my breastbone with two fingers. I feel the tears coming and for once I don't force them away. 'I can't stand it, so I avoid it. But Rafa . . . he knows Jude, and he misses him and, I don't know, it was a bit easier because he's grieving too.' I turn away before the tears spill down my cheeks.

Maggie comes over to my side of the table and puts her arms around me. She and her mum are mad huggers. I don't remember being hugged all that much before I came here. It used to make me uncomfortable when they did it, but now I don't mind so much. Even so, Maggie keeps it short, giving me a tight squeeze, and then letting go.

'I'm sorry. I'm such a crap friend,' she says.

I pull myself together. 'Maggie, you are many things, but a crap friend is not one of them.' I smile at her, and I mean it. I need for us to be okay.

'Really?'

'Absolutely.'

She smiles.

I check the clock. 'We'd better get ready.' I throw down my coffee and race her for the shower. It's only when I'm under the dribbling hot water that it hits me: I slept through the night without dreaming of hell-beasts. Or Matt.

FINGERNAILS

The Pan Beach library and gallery looms over the esplanade, its gleaming glass façade reflecting the sky and rolling surf across the road. A towering wave sculpture on the roof casts an abstract shadow over the beach every afternoon. The center opened just before I hit town, and it still sparks arguments about whether it has put Pan Beach on the cultural map or sold its soul to the sea-change millionaires whose mansions dominate the headland. It's my haven. All those books downstairs, the art upstairs, and the smell of freshly ground coffee coming through the window that connects the Green Bean to the library.

But this morning I sense the panic as soon as the automatic glass doors close behind me.

All but one of the couches around the window to the

Green Bean have been pushed aside, and about thirty-five people are sitting in plastic chairs, waiting. On the lone couch is Jacques, whose exhibition opened upstairs last night. He's not supposed to be sitting alone.

I find Jane, our pregnant head librarian, with her head in the toilet.

'You have to take the session,' she says.

'Uh-huh. Jacques is a freak. Find someone else.'

She rests her cheek on the toilet seat, her face pale and sweaty. 'You know more about art than anyone else here.'

'No, I don't.'

'Last week you debated the differences between the Uffizi and Accademia galleries like you'd spent a year in Florence.' Jane wipes her mouth with the back of her hand. 'Just do it, please.'

Normally, I'd stand my ground, but if there's no way she can interview Jacques without throwing up all over him, as entertaining as that might be . . .

I refill her water bottle. 'Where are your questions?'

Two minutes later, I'm on the couch with Jacques. Mid-sixties. Lanky. Makes objects from human hair. And toenails and fingernails. Pretty much anything discarded from the human body, even dead skin. Upstairs is a bizarre array of items—cups, a birdcage, parchment, soap, and most disturbingly, a wedding dress—all made from things that were once part of the human body.

The gathering is a mix of familiar faces—all wearing more black than is usual in Pan Beach, some with note-pads and pens—and a few backpackers attracted by the free orange juice and muffins. I clear my throat, welcome Jacques, and everyone settles down.

'So, Jacques,' I begin. 'How do you source your materials?'

He nods, expecting the question. 'My niece has a day spa. The things I use to create my objects are all a by-product of her work.'

'A local day spa?' There are three in and around town. A perfectly manicured woman in the front row looks ill, probably wondering if she's inadvertently featured in Jacques's creations.

'No, no. It's in the city.' He sits forward, wanting a tougher question. But I'm not done with this one yet.

'Was she at all concerned about what you planned to do with the materials?'

He smiles and eases himself back against the couch. 'It's interesting you assume she would be repulsed by the request. That goes to the very heart of the nature of my work.'

'I think it's a valid question.'

'Of course you do. But you are young, and perhaps you can't see beyond your limited experience to think laterally.'

I smile back at him. 'So, my question isn't legitimate because I'm young? I thought your work was meant to speak to everyone, not just those *experienced* enough to understand it.'

Jacques sits back up. 'That's not what I meant.' He touches his bald head.

'Is there any of *you* in your work?' I glance up at his head and there are a few muffled laughs.

'Would it upset you if I said yes?'

I write about disembowelment and beheadings. What do I care what some creep does with his nail clippings? But what I say is, 'Not at all. It's one of the great things about being young: having an open mind.' Although, quietly, I hope that if he's used his own hair, it's come from above his navel.

I check the audience. Definitely engaged, which is better than them staring off into space, wishing they'd just gone to the Green Bean and read the paper.

A movement to my right catches my attention.

It's Rafa.

He's leaning against the end of the nearest stack. It's as much of a jolt seeing him now as it was in the bar. I'd started to wonder if I'd imagined his likeness to Matt. But it's broad daylight, I'm completely sober, and Rafa is still a dead ringer for him. All broad shoulders, toned arms, and short, mussed hair. I don't know how long he's been there, but he's been waiting for me to discover him. He gives me a slow smile.

I've lost track of what Jacques is saying.

'. . . and it makes all the difference, don't you agree?' Jacques is looking at me, eyebrows raised. I give a non-committal nod.

'Good,' he says, and I hope I haven't just given him the upper hand in the conversation. 'Human hair has been used in artwork and in other objects of beauty for thousands of years,' Jacques continues. 'I've simply taken the notion a step further. As humans, we can hold something of value for generations, and then discard it as worthless. We throw away what no longer has meaning or purpose for us—often with feelings of disgust—ignoring the fact that it may still thrive in another form. My work is a metaphor for how society turns its back on the things that were once integral to its existence, like religion and philosophy, or understanding the stars and the elements.' Jacques's face is alive now, his hands in the air.

Rafa picks up a pencil and feigns stabbing himself in the eye. My nostrils flare from the effort of not reacting.

'These things that we reject . . . they don't just disappear. Many of them may even outlast us.'

The session ends. I direct Jacques and a few curious hangers-on back to the muffin table so I can pack up the chairs. I half-expect Rafa to help, but he stays leaning against the bookshelf, hands in his pockets.

When I stack the last chair, he comes over. He's dressed

more like a local today, in a white cotton shirt and light-weight cargoes, but he'd never be mistaken for a surfer.

'I didn't realize you were a fan of Jacques's work.' I fuss with the last chair to avoid making eye contact.

He gives a short laugh. 'What a tool.'

I check to make sure Jacques hasn't overheard, but he's too busy talking about himself. 'What are you doing here?'

'Just wanted to see you in action.'

I don't know what to say to that, so I head to the Green Bean window and he follows. The smell of coffee and fresh blueberry cakes makes my mouth water.

'You distracted me last night,' he says, close to my ear to be heard over the clattering cups. 'Caught me off guard.' He's not that much taller than me, but for a moment I feel dwarfed by him. 'We still need to talk.'

'About what?' I catch Maggie's eye in the cafe and she comes over before he can answer. Her smile falters when she sees Rafa.

He steps around me and rests his elbows on the counter. 'I should have introduced myself last night. I'm Rafa.' His smile is all warmth and charm. He may have licked my neck last night, but he didn't give me *that* smile.

'Oh,' she says, completely thrown. 'I'm Maggie. Gaby's housemate.' They shake hands. 'What can I get you?'

'*I'll* have my usual,' I say.

She grins. 'I know what you'll have. I was asking Rafa.'

'I'll have an espresso, thank you, Maggie.'

Maggie looks from me to Rafa and back to me again. I know that look.

'What time are you knocking off?' she asks me.

'Four-thirty.'

'Why don't you bring Rafa home for dinner? Jason's coming over.'

I lift my eyebrows at her. 'Who's Jason?' Maggie has a steady string of admirers, but few of them make it past our front door.

'He's a law grad who's taken a year off to have some fun.'

'And when did you meet him?'

She gives me a sly smile. 'Last night.'

'The shirtless six-pack?'

'I keep telling you, all sorts of people come here to surf.'

I glance at Rafa. I'll admit, I'm equal parts fascinated and disturbed by him. I don't understand why I have no memory of Jude knowing him, or why he acts like he knows me.

'Well?' Maggie sets out cups for our coffees.

'You want to try out Maggie's cooking?' I ask Rafa.

He shoves his hands back in his pockets. 'Sure.'

I leave Maggie at the fish market on the way home, and walk up the hill, awkwardly holding a bottle of white wine. I'm breathing heavily when I reach our front gate and preoccupied with the latch, so it takes a second to see him.

Rafa is standing in our tiny front yard under the jacaranda tree. The last of the purple blossoms disappeared a few weeks ago, and the tree is now a dense canopy of green. Rafa is dead still, watching me intently. The afternoon light has turned orange.

'Hey,' I say. 'You're not due here for another half-hour.'

He doesn't move and something quivers in my stomach.

'Just drop this shit, Gabe.' He says it softly, as if it saddens him. 'As much fun as last night was, I really don't have time for games.'

I stand there, the bottle ice-cold against my chest. My fingers are numb.

'You're supposed to be dead,' he says.

I cross the yard and put the wine down on the front steps. When I face him again, he has turned a little to the side and is flexing his fingers. 'I didn't come here to fight, but that doesn't mean I won't.' His smile is wry. 'I reckon I could take you in record time. You've gone soft.'

The power of speech finally returns to me. 'What the *fuck* are you talking about?'

He paces under the tree, in the leafy shadow, his eyes on me. 'You can drop the act. Your little friend's still down the street.'

'I don't know who the hell you think I am—'

'Fuck, Gabe, if you didn't want to be found, why'd you

post that story on a website you'd know I'd read?'

My mouth falls open. 'You read that?'

'How do you think I found you?'

I step back and grab on to the railing of the front deck. The flowering shrubs by the fence blur and my legs feel weak. Pressure builds in my head. 'You need to go.'

'Just tell me how he died. Tell me what you did. If you and Jude got yourselves into trouble, I can help—'

I slam my fist on the railing. 'We weren't into anything! We were arguing over music and he took his eyes off the road. We rolled and went through a fence. A post came through the window and took his head off. Is that what you want to hear?' I'm shouting at him, and I can't stop. 'His blood was all over me and I couldn't find his head. I don't know why I'm still alive—I wish I wasn't!'

I'm shaking. From grief and rage and shock. Nothing feels real except this. Nothing ever feels as real as this pain. Except the loathing I have for Rafa right now. I've never spoken about the accident. Not when they cut me from the car, not when I was in the hospital, not when I was in rehab.

Rafa has stopped pacing. 'His head?' He swallows and looks away.

I'm taking deep breaths, trying to hold back tears. I am *not* crying in front of him.

Rafa rubs a hand over his face and his shoulders fold.

'I wish I knew what the hell was going on here.' He glances towards the road and sighs. By the time I look at the front gate and back to where he's been standing, he's gone. Dead leaves and a stray dandelion settle to the ground. I blink. Nobody moves that fast.

I don't want Maggie to find me like this, so I go inside and lock myself in the bathroom. I sit on the edge of the tub, staring at the pale blue tiles on the floor. If I let go now, I won't be able to stop. I run the shower and get in, shaking, and wait for the warm water to calm me.

What the hell *is* going on?

WHAT LURKS IN THE DARK

By the time I've showered and dressed, I've convinced myself I'm fine. Jason turns up on time with a bottle of wine worth more than the entire contents of our fridge. He seems keen to impress Maggie, but he doesn't talk in riddles, kiss her fiercely, or demand to know why she's not dead. So how serious about her can he be?

'Is Rafa still coming?' Maggie is pouring a second round of drinks. Her fish is in the oven and the kitchen smells of ginger and lime. Newton Faulkner is strumming out a tune from the speakers on the bench.

'I doubt it.'

She puts the bottle down. 'What happened?'

'We had words.'

'Gaby,' she chides. 'You hardly know him. How can

you be arguing already?' But I can see in her eyes that she has an idea, and it's not as comforting to her as I thought it would be.

Jason is sitting on a stool by the bench, relaxed and easy in our cramped home. 'Men,' he says and smiles.

He's certainly easy on the eyes. His hair is even fairer than Maggie's, and hangs to his shoulders in soft curls. He's got an open face, with startlingly blue eyes. All this and a lawyer? Maggie may have hit the jackpot. She obviously thinks so—she can't stop looking at him.

'Shame they're all bastards,' I say to Jason and raise my glass.

He chokes on his drink, and then recovers. 'So young, and yet so jaded.'

I shrug, and give him my best jaded smile, forcing myself to be sociable for Maggie's sake.

'So where are you from, originally?' he asks.

Small talk. Great.

'All over.'

'Really?'

'Yeah, my parents traveled a lot.'

'Where are they now?'

Clearly Maggie didn't cover every taboo topic with surfer boy here. 'No idea. We lost touch a few years ago.'

His brow creases. 'But what about when . . .' He stops. 'Sorry. None of my business.'

How can I go almost a year without talking about Jude and then have this many conversations about him in less than twenty-four hours? 'They had Jude's funeral while I was in intensive care, and they took his ashes with them.'

Jason opens his mouth and then closes it without speaking. I don't blame him. What can you say to that?

My glass is empty, so I take it as my cue. 'Look, I might just leave you two to it.'

Maggie blocks me on the way to the door. 'Gaby. You need to eat, and I've made enough food to feed an army.'

Jason smiles. 'And then maybe after dinner, we can head down to Rick's and see who's around town.'

Maggie gives him a look that says he's heading in the right direction to make it well beyond the kitchen tonight. And on his first attempt too. I'd cheer for him if I wasn't so preoccupied with my own troubles.

'We could do that,' I say. Part of me wants to see Rafa and punch him in the head. Part of me wants to beg him to tell me what's going on. Only a very, very small part doesn't want to see him at all. 'But don't come crying to me if it ends badly.'

The fish is delicious, and I'm glad Maggie made me stay for it. Jason helps her clean up as I push my wine glass around the table. They have an easy way with each other that makes my chest ache. He's been asking her about organic food, telling her about a time he drank a fifty-dollar cup of coffee made from berries that passed through some Asian cat's stomach. She says it sounds disgusting. They laugh a lot. Maybe if I'd shown more interest in Simon I'd be enjoying that sort of uncomplicated attention myself right now.

We take a shortcut through the park halfway down the hill on our way to the esplanade. With the sun now behind the headland it's deserted. The lamps have come on under the camphor trees, and the barbecues are squat silhouettes beyond the playground. The smell of burnt sausages lingers in the air.

My stomach is churning at the thought of seeing Rafa at the bar. Will he pretend nothing's happened? Will we talk? What if he's not there? What if he is?

I'm still stewing over it when a figure emerges out of the trees and steps onto the path ahead of us.

'I don't believe it.' The voice is deep, male, and surprised. I look at Maggie and Jason, assuming one of them knows him, but they're looking at each other and me with the same expectation.

I step forward. There's enough light from the dusk sky to see that he's in his mid-twenties, with straight dark hair to his shoulders and a goatee. His long-sleeved shirt and heavy-duty jeans suggest he hasn't been in town long.

'Gabriella.'

I freeze. Nobody calls me that. Ever.

He's shaking his head, slowly. 'I would have sworn this was a trap. I never expected to find you here.' He runs a hand through his hair. 'I can't believe you're alive. Why didn't you just come home?'

A coldness settles in my stomach. I've never seen this guy before.

'Friend of yours?' Jason asks, moving in front of me in an oddly protective gesture.

'No. And I'm getting sick of being told I should be dead.'

Goatee lets out a small laugh. 'It's just a shock to see you.'

A breeze stirs behind me, caressing my hair. Goatee's face hardens. 'So, it's true then.' All friendliness is gone from his voice.

I turn and stumble. Rafa is standing close by, not looking at me. 'Finders keepers,' he says.

'Rafael, you have no claim here.'

'How can you be so sure? You didn't even know she was alive.' Rafa moves closer to me, and even though Goatee is a few meters away, he steps back. 'You don't know what happened, do you?' Rafa asks.

'Do you?'

Rafa ignores him. 'How did you find her?'

'Followed you.'

'Bullshit. You can't track me any more than I can track you.'

Goatee smiles. 'You need to get with the times, Rafa. We tracked you online. Honestly, we thought you were bored and planted that story to draw us into a fight.'

I look from one to the other. This has to stop. 'Will somebody please tell me what the *fuck* is going on here?'

Goatee tsks. 'I see you haven't lost that foul mouth.'

Maggie is beside me, linking her arm through mine. 'Let's just go. We'll get to Rick's and then we can sort out all of this inside.' She pulls me across the path towards the playground and, beyond it, the bright safety of the supermarket. We've taken only half a dozen steps when something flashes out of the trees and slams into us.

Maggie cries out and we both hit the grass. Pain jolts through my shoulder and I raise my head to see a girl roll past me and spring back up. She's about my age, dressed in a dark shirt and jeans, like Goatee, her black hair tied in a severe ponytail. She's already crouched, ready to attack again. Her head whips around to Jason, who's helping Maggie back to her feet.

'Don't even think about it,' she says to him. 'Just stay there and you won't get hurt.'

I scramble back, the grass cool and slick under my fingers, and she follows, more cautious now.

'What do you want?' My voice is hoarse.

'Taya,' Goatee says, flicking nervous glances at Rafa, but moving closer. 'Be careful.'

Taya hasn't taken her eyes from me. 'I want to know why you betrayed us.' Another step. 'Was it worth it? Did you find Semyaza?'

I back up against a tree with nowhere to go. Panicked, I look for Rafa. I try to stand, but my legs don't want to work.

'You know they'll do what they have to, Gabe, to take you back,' Rafa says. He's still on the other side of the path, his face in shadow. 'I suggest you drop the bullshit right now. Get up and fight.'

'You bastard.' Jason glares at Rafa, and then charges across the path at Goatee. Goatee doesn't flinch. He spins around and kicks Jason in the chest, hard, sending him flying.

'Stop it!' Maggie rushes over to him. 'Rafa, what's going on?' She helps Jason sit up. There's blood trickling from her knee.

Rafa doesn't move.

There's grass and a piece of broken glass under my fingertips. In the distance, bass thumps from somewhere on the esplanade. The dusk has slipped out of the sky and the dark is hunkering down. As I crouch there, it occurs to me this may be my last twilight. I may actually die here. A few months ago, I might have welcomed it. But not now. And not here, like this.

A jolt of adrenaline launches me to my feet, but before I can swing at Taya, she smashes her fist into the side of my head. The park reels around me and I reach for a branch to steady myself as she grabs the back of my shirt. I'm airborne. And then I slam into a tree. I bounce off it. Face-plant into the dirt. My ribs are in serious trouble. There's blood in my mouth and on my face. I'm still trying to work out if I can move when someone kicks me in the kidneys. White light explodes behind my eyelids. I grunt and curl into a ball, but the kicks keep coming. Dimly, I hope Maggie has got away.

'You're a traitor.' Taya is panting as she lays her boot into me, this time to my spine. 'You're going to tell us—' But she doesn't finish. There's a yelp, and then silence. I lie there, every breath like a knife in my lungs.

And then Rafa is kneeling down in front of me. He touches my face and tries to roll me over, but my whimpering stills his hands.

'Oh, shit,' he says. 'Shit. Shit.' He stands, and all I can see are his boots as he paces in front of me. I'm losing consciousness when he crouches down again, his warm fingers back on my face. *'Fuck.'*

LOST IN CONFUSION

'Gaby.'

Maggie's voice is far away, indistinct.

'Don't touch her,' Rafa says. 'I've got this.'

Maggie's strappy sandals come to a halt near me and Jason's canvas shoes limp behind her.

'What was that?' It's Jason. 'Why didn't you get involved before that madwoman threw her into a tree?'

'Because Gabe should have been able to handle them both in her sleep.' Rafa brushes dirt from my cheek.

'Are you insane? She was terrified and you just stood there.' Maggie tries to move around him. 'Let me see to her.'

Rafa blocks her.

Sounds of her fumbling in her handbag.

'Then I'm calling an ambulance—'

'You're not.'

The anger in his voice cuts through my pain. I try to move, but all I do is whimper some more.

Rafa is next to me again.

'Look,' he says. 'I can help her, but you two need to get away from here.'

'No chance.' It's Jason again. 'We're not leaving her with you.'

'Don't think I won't hurt you if you get in the way.'

Nobody moves.

Rafa lets out an impatient sigh. 'Fine. But you're not calling an ambulance. I'll get her inside.'

'You can't pick her up. What if her neck's broken?'

His fingers gently probe under my hair. 'It's not.'

Before Maggie or Jason can stop him, he scoops me up in his arms. Pain rips up my spine and forks through me like lightning. I cry out. Then Maggie is there, pushing hair out of my bloodied face.

'Oh, Gaby.' She's crying.

Jason is close by, his mouth set in a grim line.

'Sorry, Mags,' I whisper and swallow another mouthful of blood. I hang limply in Rafa's arms, my head resting against his chest as he walks.

'At what point are you going to explain what just happened?' Jason asks.

Rafa doesn't answer.

'I mean it.'

Rafa keeps walking.

'Maggie's place isn't this way.'

'Mine's closer.'

I fade in and out. And then a door opens and a light flicks on. I see Rafa's face above me and, beyond that, a bare bulb hanging from the ceiling, spindly shadows on the wall.

'You two stay out here.' We move further into the house.

'What are you going to do?' Maggie is panicked. Her sandals slap on the floor behind us.

'Just give me a minute. One fucking minute.' Rafa slams a door behind us, not bothering to turn a light on. He kicks something in front of the door, maybe a chair.

A fist thumps against the door. 'That's it, I'm calling the police and—'

But I don't hear the rest of Jason's threat because my ears are filled with the sound of a howling gale. And I'm so cold, I can't draw breath. My body feels like it's being stretched and compressed at once, and my head swims. At last, I pass out.

I wake in a bed that's not mine. The blankets are rough and the pillow smells like sandalwood. I open my eyes to find Rafa sitting in a chair not far from me, elbows on his knees. It's still night.

'Don't freak out,' he says.

The reading lamp on the bedside table is the only light. In its soft glow, the room is almost bare but for a pile of clothes on the floor.

'I don't understand.'

He sighs. 'Yeah, I get that.'

'Where are we?'

'Safe. For now.'

'Mags?'

'She and Goldilocks are in the other room. They're fine.'

I've never felt so exhausted in my life. I close my eyes, feel the rough wool of the blanket against my skin. And then the realization hits: I'm exhausted and I ache all over, but I'm not in pain anymore. 'Did you drug me?'

'Of course I didn't.'

Under the blankets I probe my ribs. They're sore, but there's no way I could touch them if they were broken— and they felt broken after I hit that tree.

'Have I been out for a while?'

'Not long. An hour or so.'

'Then how . . . ?' I throw off the blankets and sit up. I'm in a T-shirt two sizes too big, but aside from that all I'm wearing is my undies. My legs are pale from lack of sun, and the deep scars from the crash stand out in stark contrast to my skin. I pull the bedding back over myself.

Rafa straightens. 'Just let me figure a few things out.'

'Like why you didn't help me?'

He shrugs, unrepentant. 'I thought it was an act. It didn't cross my mind you wouldn't fight.'

'If I knew how to fight, Rafa, you wouldn't still be conscious.'

That brings a quick grin to his face. 'See, now that gives me hope all's not lost. You're still in there somewhere.'

'Who's still in here? Who is it you and those psychopaths think I am?'

His smile fades. 'You really don't know.'

'I know exactly who I am. It's everyone else who seems to be having a problem.'

'All right then, *Gaby*. Tell me who you are.'

I eyeball him. 'I'm Gaby Winters. I don't know how to fight. I like to run. I read a lot. I love Thai food and Turkish delight. Not the chocolate kind, the real stuff, from Turkey. Jude and I went there when we were backpacking.'

'How long were you two traveling?'

'About fifteen months.'

'And that was up until a year ago?'

I nod.

'And how old are you?'

'Nearly nineteen.'

He gives me a pointed look. 'You were both only sixteen when you hit the road?' He doesn't wait for an answer. 'Tell me again how he died.'

My chest constricts. 'In the accident.'

'Where?'

'Outside Melbourne. We'd just arrived in Aust—'

'He was driving?'

I nod, swallowing.

'But you were backpacking, weren't you? Where did the car come from? How did he get a license?'

I blink. I know the answer to this, but it's somewhere in the fog. 'I . . . I can't remember.'

'You told Goldilocks your *parents* came and had Jude cremated.'

'How did you hear—'

'How do you know Jude was cremated?'

'A nurse told me.'

Rafa lifts the blankets to look at my legs. I draw my knees up, away from him.

'I've seen what's under your hair.'

My fingers instinctively touch the thick scar on my neck.

'You think a car accident did all that?'

I snatch the blankets from him and cover myself again. As usual, I don't know what he's talking about. But I do notice he looks pretty wrecked himself. His hair is sticking up at strange angles and there are dark circles under those green eyes.

'Fine. Give me your version of my life.'

He blows his breath out. 'Okay, how do I explain this?' He drums two fingers against his temple. 'You and Jude had a difference of opinion and fell out for . . . a while. Last year, you patched things up and started hanging out again. Then you both just took off. Jude rang me to say you were sorting some stuff out, but then, nothing. I didn't hear from him again. Rumors went around that you'd done something really stupid. And that you'd both been killed.'

I blink. He may as well be talking about people I've never met.

'The life you remember is a lie. I've never heard of anyone powerful enough to wipe memories and create new ones, but someone's done it to you, and they've done a hell of a job. They've taken your memories and, I don't know, *twisted* them somehow.' He gets up and walks over to the window. The night sky outside is cloudy, starless. 'You're estranged from your parents and you feel guilty about Jude's death, right?'

I don't even bother to answer.

'But you're not estranged from your parents. Your mother's long dead and your father . . . well, he's not dead, but you've never met him.'

I open my mouth to argue but he goes on before I can speak. 'So, if your memory of them is so distorted, then your memory of what happened to Jude might be just as inside out.' He bites his lip. 'Do you really remember seeing him lose his head?'

I look at the worn floorboards, but I'm not really seeing them. I remember what it *felt* like. Is there a difference? My head is pounding again.

'What did Jude and I argue over?'

Rafa uses his thumb and forefinger to rub his eyes. 'Does it matter?'

I wait.

Another sigh. 'For the moment, let's just say you, me, and Jude, we're part of a very large and dysfunctional . . . *association*. Within our ranks, there's a difference of opinion about how to tackle a particular problem, and you and Jude chose different sides.'

That makes no sense. 'And you and me?'

'Not on the same side. The last time you saw me, you broke my nose.'

I study his face. His nose looks pretty straight to me, but there's a flush creeping over his cheeks; he's embarrassed. 'Then why did you kiss me last night?'

A half-smile. 'I thought you were messing with my head with all that "do I know you?" crap. I assumed you didn't want to start trouble in front of your new little friend. I was seeing how far I could push you before you snapped.'

His behavior finally makes sense. Humiliation sweeps over me. I feel my skin reddening. Rafa didn't want me.

He just wanted to bait me. What the hell would have happened if I'd taken him home?

'What?' he asks, searching my face, and then he understands. 'Oh . . .'

I slide under the blankets and draw my knees to my chest. 'I need to sleep.'

'There's more,' he says, but doesn't meet my eyes.

'It can wait.' I turn my back so I face the wall, stare at the flaking paint that looks like cracked eggshells. I can feel him behind me. 'Leave me alone.'

'I can't. Not now.'

'At least tell Maggie I'm okay.'

The chair creaks as he stands up. Otherwise the room is silent.

'Just so you know,' Rafa says quietly, 'Jude really was my best friend. And I really do miss him.'

'Me too,' I say, and then quietly cry myself to sleep.

MORE THAN A LITTLE ALARMING

The smell of toast and bacon rouses me. I sit up. The chair beside the bed is empty. Early morning sunlight filters through the window, showing up the cracks in the walls and clumps of dust on the floor. I probe my side again. I'm not in pain, but I feel strangely hollow, and fragile, like my ribs are bird-bone thin.

There's a gentle knock on the door and it opens a fraction. 'Gaby, are you awake?' Maggie peers in. 'Should you be sitting up?' She's at the bed in three steps.

'I'm fine, really.'

'How are you fine? I mean, I'm so glad you're okay, but you were in really bad shape last night.' She sits on the bed. 'Your face, it's almost healed.'

I check my lips and then my cheek. I'm sure I felt my skin split last night.

Maggie studies me. 'What did Rafa do in here?'

'I let her rest, which is what you should be doing.' Rafa is standing in the doorway, still dressed in last night's clothes. A tea towel is slung over his shoulder and he's holding a spatula. He looks at me. 'Unless you're hungry.'

'Yeah, I am.' I swing my legs over the side of the bed and carefully stand up. 'I'm also curious as to how I can walk today.'

His eyes stray to my bare legs. 'I guess it wasn't as bad as it looked.'

'She threw me against a tree.'

'You're tougher than you think.'

I felt my ribs break, but I'm not going to push the point. For now. 'Where are my clothes?'

Rafa grabs my cargoes off the floor and hands them to Maggie. 'Your shirt was covered in blood. Keep that one.'

I look down. I hadn't noticed before, but it's familiar—the Led Zeppelin T-shirt Jude was wearing in one of Rafa's photos. I pull it up to my face. Somehow there's still a hint of Jude there. He always smelled like he'd just come from the beach. My breath comes out in a sigh.

'What?' he says.

'You like keeping me off balance.'

'You can talk.'

I almost forget how pissed off I am with him. 'Yeah, well, I'm not doing it intentionally.'

Rafa takes another look at my bare legs. 'Breakfast is nearly ready,' he says and leaves the room.

'Here,' Maggie says. 'I'll help you get dressed.' She's looking at me. Differently.

I take the pants from her. 'I have no idea what that was about, last night.'

'I didn't say anything.'

'You didn't have to.'

In the kitchen, Jason is cooking bacon and Rafa is doing the eggs. They don't speak or acknowledge each other as they stand side by side at the grimy gas stove. They're almost the same height, but Rafa's shoulders are broader.

I drag out a chair from the table and they both turn.

'Good morning,' Jason says.

'That smells good.' I sit down. Maggie sits opposite me. Her fingers are drawn to a scratch in the table. She traces it, a long curved line.

We're in a house not much bigger than our bungalow, but a lot older. The paint's peeling out here too, and the laminate on the bench is gouged and discolored. Aside from the table, there's a fridge chipped with rust and a frayed couch. That's it. On the couch is a scrunched up blanket and a single pillow—obviously not the end to the evening Maggie and Jason had hoped for. I can see Maggie redecorating the house in her mind—she's always trying to make things more beautiful. But this place is beyond even her talents. Through the filth of the kitchen window is the parking lot at the back of the supermarket. No beach views from here.

We eat breakfast in a strained silence. Jason looking at Maggie. Maggie looking at me. Rafa not looking at any of us. Jason starts stacking the plates when we're finished. He's moving gingerly.

'Are you okay?' I ask.

He rubs a palm over his chest where Goatee kicked him. 'The bruise is starting to come out, but I'll live.' He puts a hand on the back of Maggie's chair and looks at Rafa. 'Are we going to talk about what happened in the park?'

Rafa pushes his chair back from the table and stretches his legs out on my side. 'Go for it.'

'Let's start with who those two were and why they were so obsessed with Gaby.'

Rafa eyes him. 'Lawyer, right?'

'You can tell me what's going on or I can go to the police. Your choice.'

'Knock yourself out.'

I lean forward. 'Well, I'd like to know, seeing as it was me they were trying to kill.'

Rafa's laugh is shallow. 'They weren't trying to kill you. Taya just wanted to incapacitate you,' He glances at Jason and Maggie and then back to me, as if to check that I want him to keep going.

'Why were they here?' I ask.

He taps a finger on the edge of the table. 'You and Jude upset a few people when you disappeared.'

'But Gaby doesn't know them,' Maggie says and then to me, 'Do you?'

'No.'

'But Rafa does,' Jason says. 'And they were scared of him.'

I hadn't given much thought to why Taya suddenly stopped kicking me. Jason meets my questioning look.

'He threw that girl off you like she weighed nothing. Then he chased down the guy and dragged him into the trees. Neither of them came back.' He faces Rafa. 'Who's Semyaza?'

Rafa's eyes narrow. 'What makes you think Semyaza's a *who*?'

'Am I wrong?'

Rafa ignores him and looks at me. 'Those two, they won't be the last to come looking for you. You need to get that crap offline.'

It takes me a few seconds to realize what he means.

'Are you talking about that horrible thing Gaby wrote?' Maggie says, and then quickly, 'Sorry, babe, you know what I mean.'

'That's exactly what I'm talking about,' Rafa says.

'But it's a *story*.'

'With her name on it and where she's from. It won't stop them coming back, but there are worse things to worry about.'

Worse than the beating I took last night?

'I'm going now,' I say, not wanting to know what else I should be worrying about.

'Just give me a second to have a shower—'

I stand up too quickly and my head swims. 'I don't need you to babysit me.'

Rafa doesn't move. 'Yeah, you did so well on your own last night.'

'He's right,' Jason says, wiping his hands on a tea towel. 'He brought them here, so he should protect you. The question is,' he says to Rafa, 'is she safe with you?'

'You seem to be taking all of this in your stride, Gold-ilocks.'

'Is that a no?'

'Of course she's safe with me.'

I've had enough of this pissing contest. I'm in pain, I don't know what's going on, and potentially there are more psychopaths headed my way, for reasons no one's explained.

'Come on, Mags. Let's go.'

I limp out the door, half-expecting Rafa to try to stop me. Instead, I find myself out on the street with Maggie and Jason. The air is fresh and clean, and the morning sun warm on my face. We climb the hill to the bungalow in silence. Jason's car is still parked outside. It looks too new next to all the old houses on the street.

'Thanks for everything,' I say to him at the gate. I'm not sure if I mean for getting hurt, for sleeping on a couch, or for copping being called Goldilocks by Rafa.

He glances back down the hill, hesitates, then says, 'Rafa knows more than he's telling.'

'I know.'

'You need to find out what it is.'

Maggie touches his arm. 'Do you want to come over later?'

'Do you mind? I don't like the idea of the two of you being alone after last night.'

She steps closer and puts a hand on his chest. 'As long as that's not the only reason you're coming over.'

'Hardly.' He leans in and kisses her gently on the cheek. Her hand goes to his neck, and they stay like that for just a moment. It's so tender, I have to look away.

The car starts up as we go inside. I head straight to the kitchen where my laptop is still on the bench.

'Coffee?' Maggie asks as I ease myself onto a stool.

'Absolutely.'

I send an email to Dark Thoughts and ask for my story to be taken down from the site. The coffee is ready by the time I'm done. We sip slowly, neither of us speaking. Finally, it gets too much for Maggie.

'Show me your injuries.'

'What, you're a doctor now?'

'Seriously, Gaby.'

I head to the bathroom and she follows. I pry off my shirt and examine myself under Maggie's watchful eye. My ribs are bruised, and so is my back where Taya kicked me, but the bruises are yellow, like they're a few weeks old. Not black and purple like they should be.

'That's impossible,' she says at last. 'How did he do that?'

I sit down on the tub. 'I need to tell you something.'

'Anything. You know that.' She sits beside me, her hands tucked between her knees.

'Those dreams I told you about, and the story I wrote . . . That guy Matt. It's Rafa.'

Maggie frowns. 'I don't get it. You know him?'

'No. But I've been dreaming about him ever since the accident, and it's always in that nightclub fight.'

'That fight . . . with demons?'

I know if it wasn't for what she's seen in the last twelve hours, Maggie would be slowly backing away from me about now.

'Yeah.'

I tell her Rafa's version of my relationship with Jude.

'But that makes no sense at all.' She picks at her fingers,

the pale nail polish. 'You'd know more about your brother than he would.'

'I know.' I shake my head. I can't think. 'I need air.'

I stand up and Maggie gets between me and the door. 'Gaby, you just about passed out coming up the hill.'

'I'm fine. I need to clear my head so I can work this out.'

'I'll come with you.'

'No. I'll just go to the lookout.'

'Gaby, please. It's not safe.'

I put up a hand. 'I need *space*, Maggie.'

'Oh.' She steps aside and finds a stray thread on her shirt to fiddle with. 'Of course.'

I don't want to hurt her feelings. I wish I knew what to say, how to explain that I work better on my own.

But I don't, so I walk away.

SINKING

The lookout is at the top of our street, around a bend: a small viewing platform, perched on the edge of the cliff. It's not a tourist spot—underage locals come here after dark. There are no trees or houses close by, and the drop-off overlooking the town is dizzying. It's a dead end. I'll be able to see anyone coming.

There's a gentle breeze, and it carries a hint of the cooler weather not too far away. The sky is hazy but the sun bright and comforting. It takes a few minutes to reach the lookout and I'm really feeling it by the time I ease myself onto the bench there. I brush my fingers over familiar scratchings in the wood railing: *AA 4 SL 4EVA, Rat 1986, Pan Beach sux*. The town sits below me, nestled between the rainforest and the ocean. Looking at it relaxes me. I've always felt safe up here. It's the closest I've felt to being grounded.

Something tells me Rafa might not be lying about my life before the accident. There is something prickling at the edge of my memory. It's not just the photos on Rafa's phone, or even what happened last night. It's that my memories of my life before Jude's death have never been clear or sharp. Any time I've tried to concentrate on a particular moment, the memory skitters away. It's like a speck in my eye: there at the edges, out of focus.

A residual effect of the crash, I thought—either because of the trauma or some brain injury the doctors never found. But now . . .

Now I have to go back to Rafa and find out what he knows. Maybe, if it is the truth, this hollowness I carry around every day will ease.

'Hey.'

I turn so fast I almost fall off the bench. A tall redheaded girl is walking towards me. She must have come up the road while I was staring out at the sea. Two days ago I didn't bat an eyelid at strangers—Pan Beach is full of them—but now I'm gripping the bench like it's the only thing keeping me from tumbling over the cliff.

She's about my age, dressed like Taya in dark jeans and a T-shirt. Her skin is fair, her arms toned. She studies me intently as she comes closer.

'You okay?' she asks.

I nod. 'I didn't hear you coming.'

She's watching me closely. Her face is freckled, friendly. 'Mind if I join you?' She points back down the road. 'Tough hill.'

There's only one bench. I hesitate, and then nod. She leaves room between us when she sits down. Most people who climb our hill end up red-faced and dripping with sweat. She doesn't even look puffed.

'Nice spot.'

I shrug, forcing myself to let go of the bench.

'Are you staying around here?' she asks.

I run my tongue across my teeth so my lips will work. 'Just passing through.'

'Good place for a break.' She looks out over the town and ocean. Her chin-length hair is styled straight, and moves with the breeze. 'It's gorgeous here.' She twists her bottom lip between her thumb and forefinger. 'This is so weird.'

I stay completely still. How am I going to protect myself if she can fight like Taya?

'The view?'

'No, you having no idea who I am.'

I have zero chance of playing this cool.

'Or that you're so wary of me.' Her smile is sad. 'It's just . . . wrong.' She hasn't made any move to attack, but that could just be a trick. Goatee started out friendly too.

But this girl's wearing ballet flats—surely nobody heads off for a fight in those?

'I heard what those two idiots tried to do last night. If I'd known you were really alive—'

'Did you know Jude?' I blurt.

She blinks, and then nods, slowly.

'Did he and I fall out?'

'Yeah. For about a decade.'

I stare at her. A *decade*?

'What has Rafa told you?'

I don't answer. A decade? How is that possible?

She shakes her head. 'So, you don't know anything about yourself? Or the Rephaim?'

A *decade*?

'And you don't know what happened to you and Jude?'

She has my full attention again. 'Do you?'

'Nobody knows, Gabe, that's the point.' She brushes her fringe back. 'You don't remember who you are, but you know an awful lot about what happened at the Rhythm Palace.'

'The what?'

'The nightclub blood-fest Mya's crew got into a few years back with a pack of hellions. Absolute debacle.'

I'm trying to digest this, but it's just too big.

'I know you weren't there, because you were with us in Morocco.'

The image of a decapitated monster flashes in my mind. 'It's all real?'

The redhead regards me. 'This is a freaking tragedy, Gabe.' She swings a leg over the bench so she's straddling it, facing me. 'Listen, I can't stay long. We're in lockdown, so someone's going to notice I'm gone, but I had to come and see you for myself.'

'Why?'

She blinks. 'Because you're my friend.'

'I don't remember you.'

'You will. I don't know who's done this to you, but we'll find a way to fix it.'

Who says I need fixing?

I rip a splinter from the bench. 'What's your name?'

'Daisy.' She smiles. She's got tiny dimples. 'I know. But it's better than the one I started out with.' She laces her fingers together and turns them inside out, stretching her arms. 'You need to keep your head down. Nathaniel will send others, and god help us when Daniel gets back and finds out.'

Who are Nathaniel and Daniel? I don't get a chance to voice the question.

'Has Rafa called for backup?'

'Not that I've seen.'

'Oh, you'd see those posers if they were around. So, he's still on his own? That's interesting.'

I stand up and move away from the bench. Maybe if I can get some distance, her words will make more sense.

'I don't know what Rafa's game is,' Daisy continues, 'but you're safe enough with him for the moment. He can be a dick, but he'll look after you—for Jude's sake if nothing else.' She springs to her feet. 'And tell him to get some balls and explain the facts of life to you.' A smile, wider this time. 'I wish I could be there for *that* conversation.'

'Why don't you just tell me?'

'Trust me, you'll have a mountain of questions, and I have to get back. Plus, it won't kill Rafa to do something useful for a change.'

I manage a small laugh. 'He seems to enjoy watching me stumble around in the dark.'

'I bet he does. But the longer he screws with you, the more trouble he's going to be in when you get your memory back—and he knows it.'

A gust of warm wind blows my hair across my face and I push it back without taking my eyes off her.

'Listen,' Daisy says. 'Give me a few days, and I'll come back. We'll work this out.' She pulls a piece of paper from her jeans and holds it out to me. 'Don't lose this.'

'What is it?'

'My number.' She steps clear of the bench. 'God, Gabe, it's so good to see you.' She regards me for a few seconds, and then runs to the edge of the cliff and jumps off.

STRANGER THINGS HAVE HAPPENED . . . RIGHT?

I scramble to the cliff. There's no sign of Daisy below. The rocks are clear.

'What the . . . ?' I don't even bother finishing the question. It's too ridiculous. About as ridiculous as the idea hellions exist and people fight them with swords. In nightclubs.

Maybe I'm losing my mind. But I wasn't on my own last night, so that at least must have been real. I walk back towards the house. I don't want to be out here alone anymore.

Maggie is at the kitchen bench, hunched over my laptop. 'That was quick,' she says, barely raising her head. When I don't answer, she takes a longer look. Her fingers stop moving on the keyboard. 'Are you okay?'

'I met this girl. Daisy. One of them.'

I tell her what happened but not what Daisy said about Jude, only that she knew him. I write down the names she said: Nathaniel, Daniel, and something about Mayans.

'She really jumped off the lookout?'

I hesitate. 'Yeah.'

Maggie bites her lip, shakes her head, and goes back to typing. I can usually read her, but I've got no idea what she's thinking right now.

'What are you doing?' I ask.

'Research. What was the name that girl said last night?' She closes her eyes in concentration. 'Samyarzi?'

I get goosebumps down my arms, even though the room is warm. I remember it clearly: 'Semyaza.'

She types and clicks a few times. 'Check this out.'

I pull up a stool. 'Wikipedia? Really?'

'Just read it.'

She points to a section titled 'Sins of Semyaza and his associates'.

In the Book of Enoch he is portrayed as the leader of a band of angels called the Watchers, who are consumed with lust for mortal women and become Fallen Angels.

And Semjâzâ, who was their leader, said unto them: 'I fear ye will not indeed agree to do this deed, and I alone shall have to pay the penalty of a great sin.' And they all answered him and said: 'Let us all swear an oath, and all bind ourselves by mutual imprecations not to abandon this plan but to do this thing.'

I take the mouse and scroll back up to click on 'Watchers'. Another page appears.

The Watchers, or Grigori, are a group of fallen angels told of in Biblical apocrypha who mated with human females, giving rise to a race of hybrids known as the Nephilim . . . According to the Book of Enoch, the Watchers numbered a total of 200 but only their leaders are named.

'That can't be what she meant,' Maggie says. 'Maybe we misspelled it.'

'Or it's someone else with the same name.'

'Or we heard it wrong.'

I click on 'Nephilim'. A new page appears. This one says that the hybrids were wiped out by a flood. I keep reading. I'm not sure what I'm looking for until a highlighted word jumps off the screen.

Rephaim.

It's something Daisy said: *So, you don't know anything about yourself? Or the Rephaim . . .*

It's not how I would have spelled it, but here it is, on a page detailing the story of fallen angels and their offspring.

'What?' Maggie says.

'Rephaim.'

She frowns as she reads it. 'This says they were a race

of giants in early biblical times, maybe descended from the Nephilim. I'm confused.'

'*You're* confused?' I rub the scar on my neck, wait for the pieces to fall into place. They don't. 'Have you got a bible?'

Maggie blinks. 'No.'

'You're still Catholic, aren't you?'

'About three times a year.'

'Do you remember a Book of Enoch?'

She frowns. 'Genesis, Exodus, Leviticus . . .' She counts them off on her fingers. 'I can't remember what comes next. There could be an Enoch in there somewhere.'

'Your mum would have one, right?'

'I am not going home to ask for a bible. It's taken me two years to get her used to the idea I'm not going to Mass anymore.'

Maggie stopped going to church after her father died. The closest she gets now is the cemetery.

'Who else do we know who would have one?'

She breaks into a knowing smile. 'How about the library?'

'You're a genius.' I climb off the stool.

'Come on, we're not going now. It's Sunday. Let's just google it.'

I grab my staff swipe-card off the bench.

'Gaby, you're exhausted. And you need a shower.'

I smell my shirt. 'Yeah, fair call. Back in a minute.'

I'm wrestling my damp hair into a ponytail when I come back into the kitchen, still trying to figure out how a myth about fallen angels relates to me.

'Hey, do you think—'

I stop. Jason is at the bench, reading over Maggie's shoulder. So close they're almost touching.

'You're back early.'

'I called him,' Maggie says, before he can respond. 'You won't make it down and up that hill again today, and you shouldn't be alone in case you get another visitor.'

'You told him about Daisy?'

She nods, measuring my mood. 'All of it.'

I grab a bottle of water from the fridge. 'I'll be fine. Don't waste your day.'

'It's no trouble,' Jason says.

'Then just drop me off.'

'It'll be quicker with three of us.'

'Plus,' Maggie adds, 'we want to know what's going on as much as you do.'

I seriously doubt that.

I weigh up what I need more right now: efficiency or privacy. Rafa said more people would come for me. Efficiency wins out.

———

In the reference section the sun throws rectangles of light across the carpet. I grab the first bible I come to, the New King James, and run my finger down the names of the books listed under the Old and New Testaments.

'There's no Book of Enoch.'

Jason is further along the stack. 'Try the apocrypha.'

'The what?' I slide the bible back onto the shelf.

'Books written by prophets and other people, not kept as official Jewish or Christian texts.' He grabs a hardcover, checks the contents and then turns the open page to me. 'See, Book of Enoch.'

'How do you know this stuff?'

'I studied religion for a year.'

'You did not.'

He flicks through the pages, head down. 'I got mixed messages about religion when I was younger. I wanted to find out a few things for myself. A year was enough. It's not like I went into the seminary.' He gives Maggie a quick smile. 'It was just a couple of subjects at uni.'

Maggie is sitting on one of the tables, swinging her legs. 'I think it's sexy.'

'Wow,' I say. 'Religion as foreplay.'

They both blush.

'Anyway . . .' I gesture to the book.

Jason skims the page. 'This says the Book of Enoch is an ancient Jewish text. Enoch may have been Noah's great-grandfather . . . The Ethiopian Orthodox Church is the only church that includes it in its official canon.' He flicks through the pages. 'Here.' He hands the book to me, pointing to where I should start.

I read aloud:

> *And the Lord said unto Michael: 'Go, bind Semjâzâ and his associates who have united themselves with women so as to have defiled themselves with them in all their uncleanness. And when their sons have slain one another, and they have seen the destruction of their beloved ones, bind them fast for seventy generations in the valleys of the earth, till the day of their judgment and of their consummation, till the judgment that is for ever and ever is consummated. In those days they shall be led off to the abyss of fire: (and) to the torment and the prison in which they shall be confined for ever.'*

I toss the book on the table next to Maggie. 'Noah's *great-grandfather* wrote that? Seriously?'

Maggie clicks her fingernails on the table. 'Noah, as in Noah's Ark?' She frowns. 'Wasn't there something about Nephilim and a flood in that stuff we read online?'

'Yeah. Some theory about God sending the flood to kill them as well as the wicked.'

'Who is Michael?'

'My guess—the archangel,' Jason says.

'What's an archangel?' I ask.

'From memory'—Jason squints in concentration—'they're part of the upper echelon of heaven. I think Michael was the most important.'

Maggie's forehead creases. 'Do you think this is all real, about the fallen angels?'

He picks up the book, rubs his thumb on a corner. 'I think there's more to the world than what we can see.'

'But they're just stories. Aren't they?'

'Most stories are based on something real.'

I go over to the window. A couple is walking past on the esplanade, away from the beach, carrying plastic buckets and shovels. Two young girls skip along behind them, laughing. They're sunburnt, and trying to eat gelati before it runs down their sandy arms.

'But what's any of that got to do with me?'

'I have no idea,' Maggie says.

I go back to her and Jason, tapping my finger along the reference shelf. I can work this out. I just have to get my head around it.

'All right. Let's pretend I have this whole other life I know nothing about. And that angels really were kicked out of heaven because they couldn't keep it in their pants. Why would I be looking for their leader if he and the rest of them are in hell?'

'That story is a couple of thousand years old,' Jason says. 'Older even. Maybe that wasn't the end of it.'

'Do you seriously think a story about fallen angels has something to do with me?'

Jason shrugs. 'Hard to say. But we all know who can shed some light.'

All roads lead to Rafa. There's no getting around it.

TRUTH AND CONSEQUENCES

His house is two blocks away. A little weatherboard with bright pink bougainvillea growing up a ratty trellis around the front door. One of the dozens of holiday rentals scattered around town. This one has seen its fair share of backpackers, given the burnt-out forty-four-gallon drum in the front yard and the rusty deck chairs clustered around it.

The front door opens before we're out of the car. Rafa has changed since this morning. He's wearing a faded blue tank top, pants, and combat boots that he hasn't bothered to lace up. He leans against the doorframe and watches us approach.

'I had another visitor,' I say, stopping whatever smart-arse comment he was about to make.

He stands up straight. 'At your place?'

'No,' Maggie says, and brushes past him. 'She went for a walk.'

'Shit, Gabe. Some things never change. When are you going to listen?'

'I'm in one piece, aren't I?'

He checks me over and then steps aside so Jason and I can go in.

'Who was it?' He follows us into the kitchen. He's been busy since we left: our breakfast dishes are washed and drying on the rack and the place smells of disinfectant.

'She said her name was Daisy.'

'Tall, red hair?

I nod.

'Was she armed?'

'No. She said she just wanted see me.'

Maggie, Jason, and I sit at the table, all of us where we sat this morning, and Maggie begins tracing the scratch in the table again.

Rafa leans against the sink. 'What else did she say?'

'That you're a dick.'

'She's called me worse. Anything else?'

'That you'd take care of me.'

His eyebrows go up. 'A vote of confidence from the gingernut. That must have hurt her.'

'She also said you needed to grow a set and tell me the

truth—that it was about time you did something useful.'

His lips twitch but he doesn't smile. 'Did she ask you to go back with her?'

I shake my head. 'She asked if you had backup.'

'What did you say?'

'Not that I was aware of.'

He pushes off from the sink. 'What did you do that for?'

'Ah . . . because I didn't know not to?'

'If she tells Nathaniel I'm here alone, he'll send another pack of dogs after you.'

Maggie's hand stops moving.

'She won't.'

'What, you remember Daisy? You *know* her?'

'No, but I don't think that's why she asked.'

He runs a hand through his short hair and it sticks up. 'We have to go. You need to be long gone before they come. I can't hold them off on my own.'

'No.'

He leans on the table across from me, blocking the light from the window. 'Gabe, for once in your life would you just do what you're told.'

'Not until you tell me what connection I have to a mythical gang of fallen angels.'

He falters. 'What did Daisy tell you?'

'Nothing!' My voice is too loud in the small kitchen.

'And I'm sick of everyone keeping me in the dark.'

Jason is watching Rafa intently.

Rafa stands back from the table, looks at the wall behind us and then stretches his neck until there's a cracking sound. 'Fine. But you might want to have this conversation in private.'

I shake my head.

'Gabe . . .'

I cross my arms and wait.

'If I tell you this, will you come with me?'

'Probably not.'

He breathes out heavily and moves back against the sink. 'Where do I start . . . ?'

'How about with Semyaza?'

'We know he was the leader of the fallen angels,' Jason breaks in, 'and that they were all sent to hell.'

Rafa cracks a knuckle. 'Pity they didn't stay there.'

Jason seems surprised by the answer, even though his instincts were right.

'They broke out about a hundred and forty years ago,' Rafa says. 'Nobody knows how they did it. They spent forty-eight hours on earth, amusing themselves with willing virgins, and then disappeared off the face of the planet. Popular theory is they're hiding out somewhere. Or trapped.'

'Hold on a minute,' Maggie says. 'They were originally

sent to hell because they hooked up with human women, and then as soon as they saw the light of day, they did the same thing again?'

'Guess they were slow learners.'

Jason's chair creaks as he shifts position. 'What makes you think they weren't caught and dragged back to hell?'

'Because the demons are still looking for them,' Rafa says.

'The demons?' Maggie swallows. 'God, you're serious, aren't you? You really believe this stuff?'

Rafa ignores her.

I dig my fingers into my arms. 'And where do Jude and I fit into this?'

'Like I told you, we're all part of an association.'

'The Rephaim?' The word brings a flutter to my chest. 'Daisy mentioned it,' I say, before he can ask.

'Yeah,' Rafa says slowly. 'We hunt for Semyaza and the two hundred.'

'Why?'

He looks at me like I've just asked why he's wearing pants. 'What else are we going to do?'

'But, you said . . .' I'm trying to remember our conversation in his room.

Rafa shrugs. 'There's a difference of opinion about what we should do if we find the Fallen.'

'What's that got to do with—'

'The story doing the rounds is that you and Jude disappeared because you'd found them, and it cost you both your heads.' He pauses. 'So, you see, now that you're back from the dead, everyone's going to be more than a little curious about what happened. Your crew, our crew, the demons . . .'

'But I don't know anything.'

'And I'm sure if you politely explain that to the hell-spawn, they'll just leave you alone.'

Daisy wasn't kidding about the questions I'd have.

'So, Taya and the other one last night . . . they're on *my* side?'

Rafa scoffs. 'No, you were on *theirs*. When you and Jude took off, your crew thought you'd joined us. And ours thought Jude had joined you. Everyone's been a little twitchy ever since. You reappearing like this . . . Let's just say there'll be a frenzy going on at the Sanctuary right now.'

The only noise in the kitchen is the slow drip from the tap over the sink. Maggie's attention has drifted to the window. Her face is pale, eyes distant. I rub my temples.

'Gabe,' Rafa says. '*Gaby.*' He waits until I'm looking at him again. 'Demons exist. The hell-spawn you wrote about, they're real. And sooner or later all this chatter about you being alive is going to reach their deformed ears and they'll come for you. I can't protect you here.'

It's hard for me to argue with him when I have no idea what he's talking about. That doesn't mean I'm not going to try. 'But why do I care about fallen angels? And who the hell are the Rephaim?'

Rafa glances at Jason and Maggie. I'm not sure she's even listening, but Jason is hanging on every word.

'Just spit it out,' I say.

'Those forty-eight hours the Fallen spent on earth, they got busy. They seduced about a thousand women between them.' He waits, as if that should mean something to me. It doesn't so he continues. 'More than a few of them fell pregnant. To the Fallen.'

'But what does that have to do with me or Jude, or these *crews* you keep talking about?'

The corners of Rafa's lips turn up just a little. He's enjoying this.

'Because, Gabriella, we're the result. We're the offspring of the Fallen.'

AND EVERYTHING KEEPS SPINNING

'You are such a prick.'

'What?' he says, laughing. 'You wanted to know.'

I shove my chair back from the table and walk out of the house. When will I learn? Every time I start to trust him, he makes me the punch line of a joke. I expect Maggie and Jason to follow, but I'm out the gate now, and I'm alone. Disappointment flares. I push it away.

It's only anger that gets me back up the hill.

I throw our front door open so hard it slams into the hallway wall and the whole house shudders. I walk in to my bedroom, ready to slam another door, but I don't get the chance. Rafa is standing on the other side of my bed.

'How . . . ?'

He's not even sweating.

'Enough,' he says.

The only way to our house from his is up the hill. He could easily outrun me, but he would have had to pass me.

'You've got to get past this shit,' he says, his hands resting lightly on his hips.

I open my mouth. Close it. Try again. 'You just told me I'm descended from fallen angels. How did you think I'd take it?'

'Now you understand why Daisy was too gutless to tell you.'

I glare at him.

'Look, I can show you. But you have to come with me, now.'

I look longingly at my bed. The sun streaming on the striped quilt. Maybe everything will make sense after some more sleep.

'The other two don't know I'm gone yet. As soon as they figure it out, they'll come straight here.' He moves around the bed and stands in front me. Sandalwood, a hint of cinnamon. 'You don't need them for this.'

For once, his green eyes are completely serious.

'I don't trust you.'

'I know.' His hands come up to my arms. They're cool, even though the morning is warm. A shiver runs through me. 'Come on. It won't take long.'

I can't look away. 'Where?'

'You'll see.'

'And we'll come straight back?'

He sighs. 'I'd rather not, but for what it's worth, I'll bring you back here if that's what you want.'

I'm so tired, I don't know what to do. Nothing in my bedroom brings me comfort. None of it is mine. A bright shawl of Maggie's hanging over an old armchair her mum gave me. A beat-up desk from the market, piled with secondhand books. Faded curtains from the thrift shop. Nothing of Jude's either. What was left of our lives was destroyed in the accident. Nothing in my life is clear. That needs to change.

'Okay.'

His shoulders relax. 'Thank you.'

He gently pulls me to him. My body responds before my mind does, and I wrap my arms around him. He murmurs in surprise and draws me closer. I mold myself against him, not caring about anything except the promise he might kiss me again. I can't help it when he's this close. He breathes in, and the air around us turns wintry. The floor drops out beneath me. We're moving. *Fast.* I try to lift my head but there's a hurricane pressing down. I can't move. I can't even open my eyes. It's terrifying . . . and exhilarating.

It lasts only a couple of seconds, and then the ground

is solid under my feet again. I catch my breath and try to lift my head, but everything around me is still spinning. Wherever we are, it's dark. And cold. Rafa is still holding me tight.

'Don't freak out.'

'What did you do?' I whisper. My pulse is still skittery.

He pries my arms from his waist. 'Give me a second to light the fire.'

My eyes adjust to the light and I track his silhouette towards a wall. We're in a house, I think. It smells stale. I shuffle towards the window, checking for hazards on the stone floor. I look out, and forget to breathe.

It's night here. We're on a hill, and there are town lights speckled below. It's not Pan Beach.

A match strikes, and I jump. Rafa puts the flame to a stack of scrunched up newspaper and kindling in the fireplace. It catches. He walks off into the darkness.

I am not going to panic. I am *not* going to panic.

Rafa comes back carrying blankets. He moves as if to wrap one around me, but I duck away from him.

'Where the fuck are we?' I'm surprised by how steady my voice is. Everything else is shaky.

He drops the blankets on the floor. 'Your mood swings are starting to wear a little thin.'

'You want me to *apologize*?'

'I want you to stop acting like a teenager.'

I back away from him. 'I *am* a teenager!'

'No, you're not. You're a hundred and thirty-nine years old.'

I stumble backwards, feel rough fabric against the back of my legs, lose my balance, and sprawl onto something wide and hard. A couch. It smells as musty as the room.

He kicks a blanket over to me. 'Put that around your shoulders.'

I want to defy him, but it's bloody cold in here, so I wrap myself in it.

'This is where Jude and I used to come when we'd had enough of all the bullshit.'

Jude was here . . . My fingers are still trembling. I hide them in the blanket. 'It smells,' I say.

He cricks his neck. 'Yeah, well, housekeeping hasn't been a priority lately.'

'Why am I here?'

'Some of Jude's stuff is still in his room. I thought if you saw it, you might accept I'm not a complete liar.'

'How can I see anything? It's dark.'

'It won't be forever.'

He adds fuel to the fire. It's cracking and popping, and starting to throw out serious heat.

I still resent the accusation that I've been the unreasonable one. 'I thought you were going to drive wherever we were going.'

His face dances with shadows from the bright flames. 'Even after you found me in your room?'

I don't answer.

'So, what, you thought I just wanted a hug?'

And yet again, I feel like a fool.

'I'm not complaining,' he says. 'I'm still getting used to the idea you don't want to punch me every time you see me.'

'I wouldn't go that far.'

He gives a short laugh and picks up the other blanket. 'Move over.'

I do.

I have a thousand questions. 'Tell me about the Rephaim.'

He rubs his eyes. 'In a minute. You thirsty? There'll be something to drink here somewhere.'

I almost ask where *here* is and decide I don't want to know just yet. One surprise at a time. 'Like what?'

Rafa rattles around in a cupboard behind the couch and comes back with a bottle of water and two glasses. He fills the glasses and hands one to me. I hold it for a few seconds, surprised how cold it is.

'It's just water,' he says, misreading my hesitation. 'If I wanted to hurt you, I would have done it that first day in the rainforest.'

My breath catches. 'That was you?'

He lifts his glass to his lips.

'Rafa.'

He seems startled to hear me say his name.

'Yeah, that was me. I was about to get closer when you started crying. It kind of threw me. And then you *ran* . . . It made me curious. So I did a bit more reconnaissance, and figured my best option was to come at you again when there was safety in numbers.'

'The bar.'

'Yeah.' He smiles. 'Not at *all* what I expected.'

I feel my skin heat up and I take a sip of water.

'Okay,' Rafa says, stretching his free arm along the back of the couch. 'The history of the Fallen and their bastard children.' He lifts his glass as if to make a toast. 'So, the Fallen break out of hell, roam the globe for two days, and leave behind a couple of hundred pregnant women. Except not all of the Fallen disappear. Nathaniel got left behind.'

The guy Daisy mentioned.

'Why?'

'The way he tells it, he didn't want to repeat the sin that landed him in hell in the first place, so he *abstained* in the hope of scoring points with the archangels.'

'You know him?'

Rafa laughs without humor. 'He's the one who brought us all together and called us the Rephaim.'

'Why not just call you the Nephilim, like the others?'

'The Nephilim have such a bad name. Nathaniel didn't want God doing anything drastic to wipe us out—you know, like a global flood—so he called us after a dead race, and tried to convince the angelic host we're not a threat to mankind.'

'The who?'

'Angelic host. Host of Heaven. You know, the rest of the angels.'

'Oh.' I pick at the label on the water bottle. 'How did Nathaniel find everyone?'

'He spent a few years looking for us.'

'But how did he know which babies belonged to the Fallen?'

Rafa puts his back to me. 'Look under my hair.'

I lean over. 'There's nothing there.'

'Touch it.'

I run my thumb over the skin near the base of his skull. There's a rough area there, like an old burn. 'What is that?'

'The mark of the Rephaim. It's a crescent moon. We all got branded during conception.'

I'm still stroking his skin with my thumb. I stop. He turns around and I slip back to my corner of the couch. 'So I should have one?'

'You did. Right where your scar is.'

I reach up under my hair. 'Convenient.'

'The only way we can be killed is decapitation, and the

blow has to sever the mark. It makes perfect sense that someone wanting to kill you would try to take your head.'

I think of Jude. And his missing head. I can't deal with that yet.

'Nathaniel found all of them?'

Rafa glances out at the sky beyond the window. A lone cloud blots out the moon. 'There are a hundred and eighty-two of us that we know of. A chance, maybe, that there are more half-angel bastards out there, keeping their heads down, doing their own thing. Nathaniel found the majority of us in those first few years and took care of—'

'Hang on. What about their mothers?'

'All died in childbirth.'

'All of them?'

'Yep.' He swirls the water in his glass like it's expensive whisky.

A log on the fire ignites. I watch the flames caress it until it's completely engulfed.

'What does it mean to be . . . like you?'

Rafa stretches his legs out. 'We're stronger and faster than humans. And we can shift. That's how we got here. It's one of the *gifts* we've inherited from our fathers—the ability to shift from one place to another in the blink of an eye.'

That's impossible. Even if I have just changed time zones without boarding a plane.

'And we're immortal—unless we lose our heads, of course.'

I clutch my glass to my chest. He's messing with me again. Right? 'Shouldn't you be old and wrinkled if you're a hundred and thirty-nine?'

'We all stayed whatever age we were the first time we shifted. For most of us, it was late teens. There are a couple of exceptions—'

'Is that what you did after I got the crap kicked out of me last night? *Shifted*?'

'When we shift, we can exchange energy. You were hurt. I helped you heal quicker. It's why we usually travel in pairs.'

My fingers stray to my ribs. 'Where did you take me?'

'Here. Just for a second. The place wasn't important, just that we shifted. Maggie was hammering on the door, so I didn't have long.'

'That's why you were so wrecked this morning?'

He nods.

'So why haven't you shifted us before now if you're so keen to get me out of Pan Beach?'

'Force you to leave?' He yawns. 'That only works on humans. A Rephaite must consent—unless we're unconscious or incapacitated. That's why Taya ambushed you. You were with me, so she figured she'd have to knock you out before she could take you with them.'

'Take me where?'

'To the mothership.'

I pause. 'What?'

He laughs. 'God, this is too easy. To the Sanctuary. Rephaim HQ. It's an old monastery in the Italian mountains. Not a spaceship.'

'I knew that.'

'No, you didn't.' He grins. 'Your head hurt yet?'

'Like it's going to explode.'

He puts his glass down. 'Let's get some sleep. I'll show you Jude's room when the sun's up.'

'What about Mags? She'll be worried.'

'No, she won't. You get snarky, you disappear. Don't tell me she hasn't seen that before.'

I straighten the blanket around my shoulders. That was just a good guess—he can't know me that well.

'Your turn for the fire.' Rafa gestures towards the wood pile beside the hearth.

I use a log to flatten the coals and then toss it on. Sparks shower up the chimney. When I turn back to the couch, Rafa has stretched out, filling its entire length. He's got one blanket around him and the other in front of him spread out. He pats it.

'Don't you have a bed?'

'Sure, but the fire's in here.' He gives me that slow smile.

I take a breath. I am *not* making a fool of myself again.

He watches me wrestle with his offer. 'I may have the hormones of an eighteen-year-old, but I can control myself. Unless you don't want me to.'

'What I want,' I say, walking over to him, 'is a night where you don't harass me in my sleep.' The best form of defense is attack, right?

I lie down on the couch and pull my blanket around me, careful not to touch him. Rafa has positioned a cushion as a pillow and I jerk it forward so there's enough for me.

'Doesn't sound like me.' His mouth is close to my ear. 'I prefer my women awake when I harass them.'

'No, smartarse, you keep showing up in my dreams. And not *those* sort of dreams either. The kind where you're cutting the heads off hellions.'

He's quiet for a few seconds. 'Is that how you know about the Rhythm Palace? You dreamed it?'

'Yep.'

'That story, it's like it was Jude's version of what happened. We got there late and came in through the back door, just like you wrote, and we helped turn the tide in the fight. But you didn't write it like he would have.'

'In what way?'

'Well, for starters, he would have called them hell-turds, not hellions. And, secondly, he wouldn't have noticed my aftershave.'

I close my eyes. There's just no way I can throw this guy off balance.

'And that website—Dark Thoughts—how did you know it existed?'

'I don't know. I must have heard about it somewhere.'

He moves around behind me, getting comfortable. 'I figured Jude must have told you about it. He's the only person who knows I read that stuff.'

'If you fight real demons, why would you want to read made-up stories about them?'

'Some of it's hilarious. And not all of it's made-up.'

I pull the blanket tighter around me. It's the middle of the day at home, but I'm tired enough to sleep.

'You still having those dreams?'

'Not since you showed up at the bar.'

We're quiet for a moment. And then: 'Why did you call me Matt?'

'It seemed like a good idea at the time. Now that I know you, I realize I should have called that character Dick.'

He laughs, and the couch shakes. 'Honestly, Gabe, I forgot you could be this much fun.'

FILL ME WITH EMPTINESS

Church bells wake me. Loud, clanging bells that sound like they're inside my head. I don't even have the brief luxury of disorientation. I know exactly where I am. Well, sort of.

Rafa's arm is draped over me, his body pressed against mine. There's no way he can be sleeping through this noise, but he's giving no signs of being awake. Maybe he's pretending to sleep so he can keep holding me. But that kind of thinking will only lead to me feeling stupid again. Rafa's got his own game going on here. If I had more experience with men, I could work it against him. But no matter what he says, I'm only eighteen. And while I've come close, I've never actually been with a guy. Before the accident, there were plenty of close encounters, but afterwards, I didn't want anyone to touch me. And then along comes Rafa . . . But if what he says is true, and I'm a hundred and thirty-nine years old, then clearly I'm not a virgin.

I've only been awake a few minutes and I've managed to tie my brain in a knot again.

The bells finally stop. Behind me, Rafa stirs and draws me closer.

'Morning, Gabriella,' he says, his voice still heavy with sleep.

'Where are we?'

'Same place we were a few hours ago.' He nuzzles the back of my neck.

I push his arm away and sit up.

'Hey.' He grabs me. 'Come back here and keep me warm.'

His grip is light, so I slap his hand away and stand up. The room might be musty, but it's a vast improvement on Rafa's shack in Pan Beach. The walls are white and clean, and the couch looks antique-expensive. No wonder it was so uncomfortable. Above the fireplace is a school of fish made from beaten copper, each stuck to the wall individually, and there's an ornate silver plate propped up on the mantelpiece. The fire is down to a few flickering coals. I throw more wood on and go to the window.

I stand there for a good five minutes, taking in the view. It's a town of whitewashed buildings with flat roofs.

Beyond the houses, the sea stretches out in all directions. Is that a cruise ship in the distance? I press my face against the cold glass. Down the road is a church with a white dome and arches hung with bells.

'Worked it out yet?' Rafa is behind me.

My breath fogs the window. 'We're in Greece somewhere, aren't we?'

'Patmos.'

I turn. He's still got his blanket wrapped around his shoulders, his hair's mussed and the first signs of stubble have appeared. For a second, I wish I was back lying next to him on the couch.

'It was Jude's idea to get a place here. He liked the irony.'

Patmos. The name is familiar. 'The Apostle John was exiled here.' Strange I can remember that, but not that I'm descended from fallen angels.

'Back in the days before the place was crowded with tourists and cruise ships.'

I run my fingers through my hair. 'I don't suppose there's a brush here somewhere?'

Rafa nods in the direction of the hallway. 'Second door on the left is Jude's room. There are a few things in there. Help yourself.'

The door is plain timber. It's not latched. All I have to do is nudge it. On the other side is a room that supposedly belonged to Jude. A room I never knew existed—in a house my brother shared with a man I don't remember. My stomach twists. I don't know what's unsettling me more: the idea I might discover something new about Jude, or the fear I won't.

'You need a hand there?' Rafa asks, watching me from the window.

I ignore him and push open the door.

Inside, there's a bed, a wardrobe, a chest of drawers, and a floor-to-ceiling bookcase, all made from dark, heavy timber. Out the window is a hill dotted with olive trees. The bed has been stripped of its blanket, but the rest of the room is strangely neat. I pick up a pillow and inhale deeply. Is there a hint of Jude there, or is that just wishful thinking?

The bookcase is crammed with paperbacks and hard-cover books. I run my finger over the spines. Two whole shelves are dedicated to books about angels and demons. Volumes on Judeo-Christian and Islamic theology, and a brightly illustrated tome on Hindu teachings. Essays on the concept of the human soul. I count ten bibles and six volumes of apocryphal writings. Copies of the Talmud and the Koran. In Hebrew and Arabic. I pull a few out and flip through them. One after the other is peppered with underlining and handwritten notes. Jude's spidery scrawl.

There's also a smattering of crime novels by various writers in English, Italian, and German, and what might possibly be first editions of *The Lord of the Rings*. Cracked, leather-bound covers.

I open the wardrobe, expecting to find clothes. Instead, I find swords and knives. *Dozens* of deadly weapons of all shapes and sizes. The shelves have been removed and the weapons hang on hooks on the sides and back of the wardrobe. It's a mass murderer's tool shed. I close the doors and stand there for a few seconds, just breathing.

I go to the drawers, almost afraid to open them. I start with the bottom one. A few stray socks and a pair of combat boots. Of course the boots are in a drawer—it's not like you'd put them in your weapons cupboard.

I open the second drawer: T-shirts and light-knit sweaters. I recognize a few of them from our backpacking days . . . or at least my memories of those days. Below that, jeans and track pants, all folded with military precision.

Finally, I open the top drawer. Socks and underwear are neatly folded and lined up. Ordered. It doesn't feel right. Jude was always tidy, but not like this. This seems *disciplined*.

I rummage through his things, not sure what I'm looking for. And then my fingers touch the edge of something under a pair of woolen socks. I pull it out, and it takes me several long moments to accept what I'm seeing.

It's a photograph of Jude, smiling, with his arm slung over a young woman's shoulder. She has long dark hair, hanging past her shoulders, and she's laughing. They're in Istanbul, in front of the Blue Mosque. They're both wearing clothes that haven't been in fashion for at least two decades. The photo itself has seen better days—it's slightly discolored, and folded at the edges. I feel like I'm being dragged through the air by Rafa again.

The woman in the photo is me.

I carry it over to the bed and sit down. I can't take my eyes off that impossible image. It's only when the tears come that it blurs out of focus.

It's too much.

All of it.

More tears fall, and I don't have the strength to stop them. I don't care anymore. Jude is gone. And the brother I'm mourning is a lie. A memory someone else has given me. I have a whole other lifetime with him I don't remember.

I ball my hand into a fist, pull the bed sheet free from its neat hospital corner. Grief wraps itself around me. I can barely draw breath. My throat burns and tears spatter onto the crisp linen. I sob and shudder and make a low noise like a wounded animal.

After a while, a weight settles next to me on the bed. Rafa tilts the picture in my hand so he can see it, but he doesn't try to take it from me.

'I never said you didn't go to Turkey with Jude. It just wasn't recently.'

My face is hot and wet and my whole body aches. I stare up at him, empty. Lost.

'Gabe . . .' His voice catches.

I wait for him to lob another grenade but, for once, he's got nothing to say. He scoops me up and carries me back out to the couch. He sits me across his lap, and draws me to his chest, dragging the blanket around my shoulders. His hand makes slow circles between my shoulder blades.

'I'm sorry,' he whispers. 'I didn't think it would be like this.'

'Did he hate me?' It's hard to form the words.

'Of course he didn't.' Rafa's voice is sharp. 'You were both as stubborn as each other, that's all. You were so pissed at him for leaving the Sanctuary, and he was so pissed at you because you wouldn't listen to him.' His hand comes to rest on the small of my back. 'He grabbed that photo when we left the Sanctuary. It's one of the few things that ever meant anything to him.'

I wipe my cheeks with my thumb. 'Why do you care what happens to me? Is finding Semyaza that important?'

Rafa looks at me. All his usual attitude has fallen away. 'I couldn't give a shit about Semyaza anymore, or any of the Fallen. But Jude's the one person I've been able to trust in the last century and I want to know what happened to him.'

I take a ragged breath, and he pauses to brush a stray hair out of my eyes.

'And . . . ?' I ask.

His fingers linger on my face.

'You shouldn't be alive, Gabe, but you are.' He swallows, and it seems to take an effort to get his next words out. 'And I can't help but wonder if you're not the only one who survived.'

IN THE DARK,
I OPEN MY EYES

I stare at him with sore eyes. 'Is that possible?'

The idea is so huge, so shattering, I can hardly bear to think about it.

'It makes as much sense as you being here,' he says.

Jude may be alive somewhere.

All this time I've been lounging around Pan Beach and Jude may be alive.

My breath comes quickly. Too quickly. Black spots explode in my vision.

'Hey, hey,' Rafa says. 'Settle down. Take a deep breath.'

I do, and it catches half a dozen times on the way in. I let it out and take another. And another. Eventually my pulse settles.

'The thought never crossed your mind?' Rafa asks. He hasn't let me go.

'But what I saw? The way he died?'

'A lie, like everything else you remember.'

What if there really was no accident? No screeching tires and hot metal. No crushed windshield and shattered glass. No smell of blood and fuel. My mind is doing laps and I have to get moving so I can keep up. I get up—Rafa makes no attempt to pull me back—gently slide the photo into my pocket, and start to pace. It's a short track I make back and forth, between the fireplace and the window.

'If there's even the faintest chance he's alive, we have to look for him,' I say.

'I know.'

I stop in front of him. 'You came looking for me because you thought I knew what happened.'

'I still think you do. You just don't remember.'

'What do we do then?' I'm ready to go anywhere with him, do anything. Everything I've tried to absorb in the last few hours is nothing compared to this possibility.

Rafa can't hold my gaze. He's looking at the rectangles of sunlight across the stone floor.

'You have no idea, do you?'

'I need to know what the two of you were doing. If we can figure that out, we'll at least have a starting point.'

The buzzing in my chest fades. 'I need that other life back.'

'Agreed.' Rafa looks up. 'Of course, if you remember who you are, you're just as likely to kneecap me and go off on your own.'

It's so weird to hear him speak about this other person. This other me. 'Am I different now?'

A half-smile. 'Yeah, and it's a big improvement.'

I chew my lip. He knows I want more, but he still takes his time.

'You're still you, trust me,' he says, finally. 'Just without the baggage.' He pauses. 'Make that *different* baggage. And with only two decades' worth instead of a century and a half.'

'But if my memory of Jude isn't real, does that mean the way I feel about him isn't either? Or how I think he feels about me?' My lungs constrict. I shouldn't have said that out loud.

Rafa rubs his jaw with the back of his fingers. 'No. I think the feelings are real—it's just the details that have been screwed with. You two have always been tight.'

'Except for that decade or so where we didn't talk?'

'Yeah, but even then you were both obsessed with knowing what the other was up to.'

'I still don't understand what it was we fought over.'

He stands up. 'Long story, and not relevant.'

'But—'

'It's more important we find out who messed with your mind, and why.' He wanders over to stand in the sunlight at the window. 'I think you and Jude found something you weren't supposed to—something to do with the Fallen—and someone wanted to make sure you didn't remember it.'

'But why not just kill us? And why didn't we tell someone what we were doing if it was that big?'

'I don't know. I wish to hell I did.'

'Jude didn't tell you?'

Rafa has his arms over his head now, stretching. His shirt rides up and I see a flash of bare stomach. It's flat and hard with a thin trail of fine hair running south from his navel. He drops his arms and the view is gone. So is the distraction.

'. . . Some things to sort out with you. That's it. You'd only been talking again for a few weeks. I figured it was family stuff. You're the only twins we've got, so what went on between you was always a bit of a mystery to the rest of us.'

I rub my palms together and press them against my eyelids, soaking in the warmth. 'We have to go back.'

'To the Sanctuary?' Rafa's voice hardens.

I drop my hands. 'Pan Beach.'

'But there's nothing there.'

'I have to let Maggie know I'm okay.'

'Ring her. We can stay here until we work out what to do.'

A few minutes ago, I would have agreed to anything, but Rafa has no plan and I'm no good at sitting still.

'I have a life there. It's the only one I know, and I'm not giving it up until we know what we're doing.'

'If you go back, Nathaniel will manipulate you into going to the Sanctuary. He'll send others—Daisy, probably. Or Daniel.'

There's that name again. 'Who's Daniel?'

Something shifts in Rafa's expression and he pauses before answering. 'A prick.'

'But who—'

'And I'm serious about the demons,' he presses. 'They'll come for you if they think you know something about the Fallen.'

'I have to work tomorrow.'

'Are you serious? It's a fucking library!'

I fold my arms. 'You said you would take me back when I asked. You promised.'

'So? It's not like you trust me.'

'I trusted you enough to come here.'

'And why did you do that?'

'Because you asked me to.'

Rafa's nostrils flare, but he doesn't say anything. He looks away first. Outside, the sky is growing brighter.

'You want to go right now?'

I glance at my watch. It's early evening back home. 'Please.'

'I won't be able to be with you every second of the day.'

I cross the floor. 'I didn't ask you to.'

'That's because you have no idea what's coming.'

He holds me tight when we shift. When I open my eyes, we're in the garden at the side of the bungalow. I keep my arms around him until my stomach stops fluttering and my skin warms. I'll never get used to that.

It's almost dark here, the sky smeared pink. We're hidden out of sight of the road, just beyond the kitchen window—the perfect place to materialize out of thin air. And a good place to eavesdrop. This isn't the first time Rafa's been here; it's where he must have stood when he overheard me telling Jason about my parents.

'What are we going to tell Mags?' I ask when I finally unwrap myself from him.

'What's this "we"? She's your friend. Tell her what you like.'

Whatever moment we shared before has well and truly passed. 'What's up your arse all of a sudden?'

'I just don't get what's so important here.'

'I told you—'

'Daisy's coming back for you, isn't she?'

I stare at him in the dying light. 'What?'

'You think she'll be more use than me in finding Jude.'

Unbelievable. He's nearly a hundred and forty but not too old to sulk. 'I've had one conversation with Daisy and it lasted less than five minutes. Why would I trust her any more than I do you?'

'Because that's what you've always done. Stuck with the safe option.'

'For fuck's sake, Rafa, I have no idea what the safe option is.' I grab the scrap of paper from my pocket. I've already put the number in my phone. 'Here. Sort your shit out with her, not me.'

He tucks the paper in his jeans. 'Are you going to call her?'

'I haven't thought about it.' And I don't have the energy to fight. 'Look, I'll come with you when we know what we're doing. Until then, I'm not leaving Pan Beach. With anyone.'

He exhales. 'Fine.'

And then he disappears. Like a light going out. The air stirs where he was, and a few dry leaves swirl back to the ground.

I can't believe I let him have the last word.

In the kitchen, Maggie is lining up knitting needles on the table. 'Oh my god.' She stands up, sweeping a needle to the floor. 'Where have you been? Are you okay?'

She hugs me so fiercely I forget to lie. 'No.'

'Are you hurt?' Her eyes search me. 'Gaby, you can't . . . I thought . . .' She steps back, says 'demons' under her breath. 'I've been worried *all day*.'

I wipe my face. 'I'm sorry, Maggie.'

'Have you been crying?'

I shake my head, fighting back fresh tears.

Maggie looks as tired as I feel. The sink is filled with dirty coffee cups, and skeins of wool are scattered across the table. A half-finished red scarf is draped over a chair.

Her nose wrinkles. 'Why do you smell like a campfire?'

I pull the photo from my back pocket and hand it to her.

She glances at it, starts to look away, and then brings it close to her face. 'Is that Jude? God, you look alike. I never knew you had hair that long.'

I sit down at the table. 'Me either.'

'When was this taken?

'By the look of those clothes, sometime in the eighties.'

The fridge kicks in behind us. 'Rafa wasn't lying?'

'It seems not.'

I tell her everything—where he took me, and how we got there. When I finish, she's still staring at me, her mouth slightly open.

'He took you to *Greece*?'

'*That's* the most interesting thing out of what I just said?'

She blushes, and her fingers stray to the balls of wool.

'So, was he charming Rafa or jerk Rafa?'

'A bit of both.' I count the cups in the sink. 'Where's Jason?' No way did he leave her sitting here on her own all day.

'He's gone to get fish and chips. You hungry?'

I haven't eaten anything since breakfast at Rafa's this morning, but I'm not in the mood to tell the story again. 'Nah, I'm good.'

Maggie follows me into my room. She watches as I kick off my shoes and climb into bed, fully clothed. I don't want to talk anymore. I've shared more with her in the last twenty-four hours than I have in the last year. Now I just want to hide in the dark, not talk to anyone. Sleep again. We say goodnight. She closes the door and my room sinks into darkness. A minute later, a sliver of light cuts across my face.

'Gaby?'

'Yeah?'

'It'll be okay.'

Only Maggie could actually believe that. Because, really, there's nothing about my life that's going to be okay.

TALK TO THE HAND

Piercing beeps wake me.

I slap the alarm, sending it skittering out of reach on the bedside table, and drift back to sleep. Back to the dark, murky dream I was in: shadows flickering across a distant pinprick of light. The stench of moldy leaves and blood. Life draining out of me.

The alarm goes off again.

I drag myself down the hall to the bathroom, my body leaden. Water dribbles out of the showerhead. The shampoo bottle offers barely enough to make a lather, and I hurl the empty container over the shower screen. It clatters on the tiles and comes to rest against the door. My towel is damp. My hair won't sit down, no matter how vicious I am with the blow-dryer and brush. My stomach won't stop churning. At least the nightclub dream hasn't come back. Yet.

I stare at the mirror, which is black in one corner from age, and chipped in a couple of places. I've always known who I am. My reflection is the same: hair, skin, eyes, lips, all familiar. So who is this person I'm staring at if it's not me?

Jason is making a cup of tea in the kitchen.

'You fucking live here now?'

Maggie looks up from buttering toast. 'Gaby—'

I hold up my hand. 'Let's not.'

I leave the house, my stomach still empty.

Outside, the sky is clear and the ocean flat. The glare on the water is blinding. I walk down the hill, my sandals slapping on the asphalt and bag banging against my hip.

Every step jolts.

I'm not who I think I am.

How am I supposed to deal with that?

At the juice bar on the esplanade I grab breakfast. There's a band flyer on the table. I tear off a corner. Then another.

I half-expect Rafa to pull up a chair, but there's no sign of him. *He's* the one I should be unloading on. He brought this circus to town. I was happily living in oblivion until he turned up. And because of him, I can't shake the one thought that threatens to suffocate me.

Jude might be alive.

The table is littered with confetti and I've run out of things to tear up. Time for work.

The day passes slowly. I avoid the Green Bean, stack books, check my email.

There's only one message: from the editor of Dark Thoughts. It comes in late in the afternoon.

Gaby, are you sure you want to pull the pin? Your story is on fire! 105 hits in the last 12 hours. Seriously dude. Let me keep it up a bit longer. You could win this thing.

It's too late.

I doubt those hits were from regular bloggers. That's around a hundred people who now know I'm in Pan Beach. Some of them could be here already. How am I supposed to recognize them? The old lady with stooped shoulders and tissue-paper skin? Unlikely. The pack of teenagers in tiny skirts and platform shoes? Doubtful. The guy in his twenties wearing designer sunglasses, holding a stack of books? Maybe.

I don't bother replying to the email. What's the point of taking the story down now? Let them come. The sooner they realize I've got nothing they want, the sooner they'll leave me alone. I go upstairs to clean the gallery.

Gaz, the other junior, is meant to help, but as usual, he's out on the deck with his hands in his pockets. He might have a penchant for piercings, army fatigues, black hair, and pale skin, but he doesn't mind checking out the talent. He's slouched against the French doors, staring down at a group of blondes in bikinis. No one's up here looking at Jacques's hair and fingernail birdcage, but that's not the point; the empty cups scattered around the gallery aren't going to pick themselves up.

'You planning on doing anything useful today?' I ask.

He turns his head, managing to make even that look lazy. 'I got you a coffee, didn't I?'

'Well, shit, Gaz, you'd better knock off early then. Don't want you to strain yourself.'

'You've been a bitch all day. That time of the month?'

I have the urge to walk over there and slam the side of my hand into his windpipe so he can't talk. Then I want to punch him in the gut until all the air rushes out of him. And then I want to grab a fistful of that greasy black hair and ram his face through the plate glass window—

I blink. I've never imagined doing that to someone before.

'You're off your game, Gaby,' Gaz says. 'Maybe all that tofu at the Green Bean has started to rot your brain.'

My annoyance fades and, with it, the violent urges.

'Gaz, I know *your* brain is even smaller than your dick, so every now and then you get a charity shot. That was your freebie today. Don't push your luck because there won't be another one.'

He gives a happy nod. 'Thank you. For a while there I thought the love was gone.'

I don't mind Gaz—when I'm not having an existential crisis. He's a bit weird, but who am I to talk?

'Just help me tidy up,' I say.

He strolls over to the cupboard and grabs the broom, and I straighten the promotional flyers strewn across the information table.

'Is that Foo Fighters?'

'What?'

'What you're humming. Is that "All My Life"?'

'I wasn't humming.'

'Yeah, you were. You've been doing it a bit lately. Didn't pick you as a Fooey fan.'

'I'm not a fan. My brother was, though. I don't even know that song—'

But even as I speak, I can hear it running through my head. We were fighting over music before the crash. Was that what was playing when we left the road?

'I love "Monkey Wrench",' Gaz says, and bursts into song, completely out of tune. I silently mouth the words along with him, amazed I know them. It's like discovering I can speak a foreign language. And like everything else, I have no idea what it means.

We go downstairs to close up. Maggie is waiting for me at the service desk.

'Hi.' She's smiling, all cautious optimism.

'Hey.'

'You heading home now?'

'Guess so.'

She waits while I grab my bag. 'You know it's Tommo's last night in town tonight?'

Tommo is one of her high school buddies who treks south to uni every semester. Maggie should be going with them: she's meant to be going to some elite fashion design school. When I first met her it was all she talked about after a few drinks and she was lit up for days when she was accepted a few months back. But she deferred it, decided to stay in town another year—she never brings it up.

'A few of us are heading to the falls for a send-off. Do you want to come? Should be fun.' She's talking quickly, constantly repositioning the strap of her handbag on her shoulder. 'We don't have to talk about anything you don't want to.'

We're out on the street. The air is fresh and salty.

'Pretend like everything is normal? Like I'm normal?'

'You *are* normal, Gaby.'

I'm not, but I appreciate her saying it.

The sun is still warm, but huge thunderheads are building out over the sea.

'Do I hum the Foo Fighters a lot?' I ask as we head for home.

'Is that what it is? I can never pick it.' She gives me a curious look. 'You didn't know you did that?'

I shake my head.

'It's only when you're really lost in thought.'

'It's weird. I didn't realize I even knew their songs.'

'Maybe you used to like them. You know, before.'

Of all the things to linger, you'd think music would be low on the list.

Conversation stops as it always does when we reach the steepest part of the hill. Tall coconut palms dot the footpath, punctuating red-roofed Queenslanders on one side and the sprawling park on the other. A pot-bellied man in a blue tank top and shorts mows his lawn. Grass clippings carry on the breeze and stick to my sunbaked arms. We keep climbing until we round the bend. There's no car outside the bungalow.

'Where's Jason?' I ask, between breaths.

Maggie looks at me. 'He got the message.'

Oh. Right.

'Is he going to the falls?'

'I asked him, yes, but he won't come unless you want him to.'

'It's a free country, Maggie. He can go where he likes.'

She opens the gate and steps through. 'Really? That's not the impression I got this morning.'

We reach the front door and I pause. 'Look, I like my

privacy—I'm only just getting used to sharing stuff with you. I'm not quite ready for a group hug.'

Her face softens. 'It's just . . . he already knows so much, and he wants to help you figure out what's going on.'

'Why?'

She smiles, coy. 'Maybe he's just a good guy.'

'Maybe he just wants to get in your pants.' I bump her with my elbow and she laughs.

'I can live with that.' She opens the front door but doesn't go through. 'Come with us tonight. Jason won't bring up anything you don't want to talk about, I promise. It'll be fun. Have a night off worrying.'

I don't know if that's even possible. But her smile is full of hope, and there are worse things to do than have a cold beer at the falls on a warm afternoon.

I'm willing to give it a try.

MAKE ME FORGET

By the time we arrive, the party is well under way. Tommo's built a campfire and set up the keg next to his mud-splattered four-wheel drive. Reggae blasts from the car, almost drowning out the sound of the falls.

Tommo is a short, wiry guy and he's so pumped about his last night in Pan Beach, he hugs everyone as they arrive.

'Looking good, Gaby.' He lays a wet kiss on my cheek before slapping my backside. He skips away before I can take a swipe at him. 'Come on, it's my last night in town!'

'It'll be your last night on earth if you do that again,' I say, but he knows he's got away with it and comes back to scoop Maggie into a big hug. 'Gorgeous!'

She laughs and hugs him back as he swings her around. It's hard to believe this guy's in his third year of medicine.

Tommo sets Maggie down and manages to stand still while she introduces Jason. Tommo drags him into a backslapping man-hug, gives him props for his taste in women, and then goes off to get us beers. True to Maggie's promise, Jason hasn't uttered a word about fallen angels, dead brothers, or fake memories.

I accept a huge plastic cup of beer and move closer to the falls, away from the music. Cool mist kisses my skin. The sun is still in the sky somewhere above us, but here in the rainforest, the light is turning a hazy purple. There are no walking tracks up here; the forest is too thick. Dragonflies buzz around me, and a few lyrebirds call to each other on the other side of the river. There's a low rumble of thunder in the distance, but the storm is still a while away.

About a dozen of Tommo's closest mates have turned up for his send-off. I recognize most of them: Pan Beach's best and brightest. The girls are all in short skirts and tight tops, showing off their toned bodies. Maggie still stands out, in tiny denim shorts and the silk halter top she tie-dyed in our laundry. I'm wearing the skinny jeans she made me spend almost a week's wages on last month. They look good, but they're not easy to sit down in, so once I get comfy on a blanket, I stay put, listening to the chatter and letting the beer drain the tension from my body.

Simon arrives as the light fades. Everyone except

Tommo left their car at the gravel car park out of sight around the bend, but Simon rides his motorcycle into the clearing. The gathering gives him a cheer when he pulls up, engine rumbling. He kicks down the stand and takes off his helmet, scanning the group. He doesn't always show off his tatts, but tonight the ink is clearly visible. One of his upper arms has a tiger and the other a koi fish. He's got a huge dragon on his back—apparently. I'm yet to see it. Simon registers me, salutes Maggie, and heads for the keg.

My thoughts stray to Rafa. Where is he right now? What if he's so pissed off he's left town? What if I never see him again? I take a sip of beer, not sure if it's relief or anxiety flooding my chest.

The music gets louder, alternating between heavy metal and dance tracks, depending on who gets to Tommo's car first. Almost everyone is dancing around the fire now, including the man of the hour, who's cheerfully grinding against his girlfriend. She throws her head back and laughs, her fingers laced around his neck.

I've reached comfortably numb. Maggie and Jason are next to me, distracted.

'Refill?' Simon is standing over me.

'Shouldn't you get the night off?'

He shrugs. 'A barman's work is never done.'

I hold out my hand. 'It's okay, I need to wake up my backside. Give me a hand?'

'To wake up your backside?'

'To help me up.'

The fire is behind him, so I can't see his face as he helps me to my feet.

Maggie breaks away from Jason to smile, bright and encouraging. I follow Simon to the keg, where he fills our cups.

'Your brother's mate still in town?' he asks as we move away from the others.

I shrug. 'I'm not his keeper.'

Simon clears his throat. 'I just thought . . .'

I can see his face now. Its strong lines. His hair is mussed from his helmet, and it looks cute. He turns to me, the firelight catching the contours of his arms. Above us, the darkening sky rumbles again, closer now.

'I don't want to talk about him.'

'Oh, so you're not . . . ?'

'No.'

He glances at me, and then studies the fire, waiting for something—probably an explanation for my behavior in the bar.

'So he's all yours if you want him,' I say.

He bites back laughter.

'And there was a time I thought you were sweet . . .' He smiles.

I go to bump him with my shoulder, but I end up

leaning against him. His arm comes around my waist and I hold him to steady myself. He smells citrus-fresh. No trace of sandalwood.

I have to stop thinking about Rafa. But that kiss, and how he held me when I fell to pieces, I can't get it out of my head. I need to.

I tilt my head back. Simon is watching me closely. He's not leaving town with Tommo because his university is only an hour away, which means he's home most week-ends. Maybe what I need is—

Simon kisses me. His lips are cold from the beer, and his touch is gentle, uncertain. He draws back a fraction, checking he hasn't misread the situation. If it was Rafa, he'd have me pinned against Tommo's car by now, hands in my hair . . . I give Simon the hint of a smile. Our lips meet again.

'Come with me,' he whispers, and keeps his arm around me as we walk out of the firelight to the forest edge.

'Tommo says you're trouble,' he says. His lips brush my collarbone.

I close my eyes. 'You have no idea.'

He strokes my cheek with his thumb, so close his breath warms my skin.

'You're so beautiful, Gaby.'

I kiss him before he can go on. I don't want to talk. I don't want to think.

This time I find Simon's tongue, and the connection lights a fire in him. He pushes me back against a tree and leans into me, his breath coming quickly. My body reacts to his touch, even though I'm vaguely aware it's not him I'm responding to, but the memory of another set of lips and hands. I don't care; this is my entire world right here. His hand drops to my breast and he runs the back of his fingers lightly over my T-shirt, lifting his face from mine to watch my reaction. Then he's kissing my neck and the ecstasy of it almost buckles my knees. I forget whose lips they are for a moment.

He slides his hands under my shirt and brings his leg between mine. My hands are on his back, pulling him to me. He can do what he wants; just let me stay lost in this sensation.

And then he's wrenched out of my arms.

I hear a grunt as he hits the ground. 'What the fuck—' He jumps to his feet.

Rafa moves in front of me.

'Back off, arsehole,' Simon says. 'She's with me.'

Simon runs at him, and Rafa collects him with two palms to the chest. He hits the ground again. Harder this time.

Rafa turns on me and I can feel the anger rolling off him. 'What the hell are you doing out here?'

'Enjoying myself.' My heart is still racing.

'You enjoy getting felt up by the barman?'

'What's it got to do with you?'

Rafa checks to see if Simon is getting up again, but for the moment he's not moving. The music from Tommo's car is loud. No one has noticed the scuffle.

'Do you have any idea what's at stake?'

'Yeah,' I say and wish I'd had less to drink, because that glow I was enjoying so much a moment ago is putting me at a severe disadvantage now. 'But there's nothing I can do, so I'm pretending I'm normal.'

'You're *not* normal,' he says. 'And being out here is reckless. Jude would kick your arse for this, and I'm tempted to give you a lesson myself.'

I step forward. 'Do it! I don't care anymore. About any of it.'

'What about Jude?'

'You mean the brother I don't *know*? Even if he's still out there somewhere, he's not *my* Jude, so what's the point?' My fingernails bite into my palms. I didn't want to share that.

'For fuck's sake, Gabe, you're acting like a child!'

'And you're acting like someone who cares about me.'

Rafa checks on Simon again. He's gone. Can't blame him really. I'm not worth the hassle.

Rafa moves in closer, blocking out the fire. 'Get your shit together; it's not safe here. And do up your pants.'

I'm about to tell him to grow up when I check my jeans

and find them undone. He's good with his hands, Simon, I'll give him that.

Rafa gives me no privacy while I get myself sorted. 'So, what, you like the barman?' His tone is prickly.

'Simon's a good guy.'

Rafa leans in. 'Does he kiss like me?'

I ignore the heat that flares at his nearness. 'No. Like I said, he's a *good* guy.'

'So good he got your pants undone without you noticing. You really know how to get that testosterone firing.'

'Would you just leave it—'

'Gaby!'

I stop. It's Maggie. Something's wrong.

'GABY!'

I push past Rafa. Everyone is watching something on the other side of Tommo's car. I'm running now, searching for Maggie. Jason is staggering to his feet, a hand pressed to the back of his head. I clear the car, and that's when I see it: Taya leading Maggie into the trees, her arm around her. Maggie is straining to look back over her shoulder, not putting up a fight. Taya must have a weapon.

'Hey!' I rush towards them, trying to give Rafa time to do something. But Taya is deep in the forest now, out of sight of the others. She sees me and smiles. And then she disappears, taking Maggie with her.

THE SECRETS WE KEEP

'Bitch,' Rafa says under his breath, catching up to me. He grabs my elbow. 'Act like it's a prank, or this is all going to turn bad, real quick.'

'She took Maggie.' My heart is smashing against my rib cage. I might also be hyperventilating.

'And we're the only ones who can get her back. We don't want the cops here.'

Jason and Tommo reach us at the same time.

'What just happened?' Tommo looks Rafa up and down. 'And who are you?'

Without Maggie, I'm completely exposed. 'This is Rafa. He's a mate of my brother's.' But Tommo is more interested in an explanation for Maggie's departure, so I say the first thing that pops into my head. 'That girl was Jason's ex.'

Jason blinks.

'Wow.' Tommo turns to him. 'What's her drama?'

Jason doesn't miss a beat. 'Not enough attention from her parents.' He's already got his car keys out.

'Yeah, but—'

'Seriously, this is what she does. She tried this with my last girlfriend too. I found them at the pub half an hour later trading stories about me.'

Tommo looks back at the track where they disappeared. 'That didn't look like she was inviting Mags for a drink.'

'It's all show. She's just making sure I got the message.'

Tommo tosses the dregs from his plastic cup. 'I'd call that overkill.' Someone calls out to him. He half-turns towards the fire.

'We'll sort this,' I say. 'Leave it with us.'

Rafa catches my eye, nods in the direction of the forest. 'I'll go this way, see if I can catch them before they get to the car park. You should come with me.'

Yeah, because I'd trust him right now not to shift with me, and leave me on the other side of the planet.

'I'll go with Jason.'

Rafa mutters something I don't catch and then veers off into the trees.

Tommo stews for a few more seconds, then nods and goes back to the party.

On the way to the car, I look around for Simon. He's

sitting by the fire, watching me. Hurt. Angry. I look away.

The music is muffled as soon as we slam the doors.

'What the hell happened?'

Jason jams the key into the ignition and starts the car.

'We had our backs to the trees. She came out of nowhere.' He drives onto the dirt track and guns the engine. 'I think she hit me with a rock.' He holds his hand out to me; his fingertips are covered with blood.

I dial Maggie's number. 'Straight to voice mail.'

'What are we going to do?'

'I've got a few ideas,' Rafa says from the backseat.

I nearly jump through the windshield. Jason jerks the steering wheel, and gravel sprays up from the tires. Trees loom dangerously close. He brings the car back to the center again and glances at Rafa in the rearview mirror.

'How on earth can you do that in a moving vehicle?'

'Practice.'

I twist around in my seat. 'Where have you looked?'

'Your place, mine, and the park. Nothing.'

'She shouldn't be caught up in all this,' Jason mutters.

I shake my head. 'Neither should you.'

'I told you being out here was reckless,' Rafa says. 'If you'd stayed with me none of this would have happened.'

'Bullshit,' I all but spit at him. 'Taya could have grabbed Mags while she was asleep. The end result's the same.'

The black forest falls away as we reach the asphalt. Jason puts his foot down and we're at the bungalow in minutes. I know Rafa's already been here, but I still check everywhere, calling Maggie's name. I leave her room till last because I know she's not in it. Her bed and work table are strewn with bolts of cloth and half-finished projects. An unfinished scarf is draped over her chair. Cherry red. A sketchbook is open on the floor next to a dirty coffee cup and a chewed pencil. Pages alive with fuchsia and gold, summer dresses and skirts. I haven't seen these designs before. I flick the page. Men's clothes. A lightweight suit. Color swatches are stuck to the page. Notes made neatly. Then, in a messier hand as if she's revisited the page later, there are wings drawn on one of the models. Rough, beautiful wings. My breath catches.

In the kitchen, Jason is in Rafa's face. 'Where is she?'

'How would I know? I'd take a step back, Goldilocks, if you don't want to bleed some more tonight.'

Jason holds his ground for a few seconds, his chest rising and falling. And then he steps away.

'How about an educated guess?' I ask Rafa.

He shrugs. 'Somewhere sanctioned by Nathaniel.'

'The Sanctuary?'

'Probably.'

Sheet lightning momentarily flares in the roiling sky. The storm is almost on us.

'Then go there.'

He laughs without humor. 'To the Sanctuary? No chance.'

'Why not?'

A large rumble shakes the house.

'I haven't set foot there in ten years, and I'm sure as hell not changing that now.'

'Then take me.'

'No.'

I stare at him. 'You're a selfish prick, you know that?'

'And you're naive. You don't even know what the Sanctuary is, do you?'

'Well, here's a thought: explain it to me.'

His fingers flex. Almost a threat. 'It's an old monastery,' he says. 'In the Piedmont mountains. It's got a dozen buildings and hundreds of rooms over three floors. If she's there, she could be anywhere. I wouldn't know where to look.'

'You could ask someone. You must still have *some* friends there.'

His eyes harden. 'I'd never give Nathaniel the satisfaction. I'm not groveling to him—or anyone else.'

'Then what *are* you going to do?'

Rafa pushes off from the bench. 'You two stay here. I'll be back.'

'Don't you dare disappear or I'll—'

He's gone before I finish my threat. '*Shit!*'

I throw open the kitchen window. A gust of cool air hits me, and the smell of rain. It's close by. This time the lightning is forked, and the thunder that follows rattles the plates stacked on the sink.

'Taya wants me, not Mags. She won't hurt her.' I'm trying to convince myself as much as Jason. I tap my fingers on the dish rack, my mind racing. 'Daisy!'

Jason is right behind me. 'You have her number?'

I'm already scrambling to get my phone out. The call goes straight to voicemail. I tell her what happened, leave my address, and then hang up.

'That's it. I'm out of ideas.' I collapse at the table.

Jason goes to the sink, drinks a glass of water, and comes back to the counter. Then he moves past me to the door. Then back to the sink, then the counter, and the door again.

'That's not helping.'

He nods, and pulls up a chair next to me.

'I can help,' he says.

'What are you talking about?'

He swallows. 'Give me your hand.'

I blink. 'Why?'

'Please, just give it to me.'

He guides my fingers under his hair to the nape of his neck. To the shape of a crescent moon.

OFF BALANCE. AGAIN

'I can go after her. I just need to know where the Sanctuary is. Exactly where it is.'

I open my mouth. Close it. Try again. I've got nothing.

Jason lets my hand drop. 'I wasn't found with the others. No one knows I exist.'

I vaguely remember Rafa saying something about the possibility of other offspring.

'But you can shift?'

'Not with as much precision as the others, but I get by.'

I stare at him. Really see him for the first time.

'Why did you come to Pan Beach?'

'To find you.' He holds his palms up by way of apology. 'I'd heard about you and your brother and—'

'What do you *want* from me?'

'I'm just looking for my father like everyone else.'

'You lied.'

'No. I don't tell *anyone* what I am. I've hidden from Nathaniel for nearly a century and a half because I don't want to get dragged into his apocalyptic politics. But if it means getting Maggie back—'

'You used Mags.'

'No, it's not like that. I didn't know I could still feel this way about a woman.' He rubs his hand over his eyes. 'This is a mess.'

I let him stew.

'You've never been to the Sanctuary?' I finally ask.

He shakes his head. 'I've heard about it, and know roughly where it is, but it's difficult for me to shift somewhere I haven't physically been.'

'What does that mean?'

'If I get somewhere normally—plane, train, whatever— I can shift there again. It's like I bookmark it.' He shrugs. 'I've been able to shift blind over small distances if I know enough about the location. If you can get Rafa to give you details about the Sanctuary, I'll go there myself and bring her back. He doesn't need to know.'

'What about Taya? Can you fight?'

'Not like them. I wasn't raised and trained with the others. I've kept to myself—'

'Are you even a lawyer?'

'Among other things. I've had time to pick up some qualifications over the years.'

Something's still missing here. 'How do you know about the Fallen and the Rephaim then, if you never joined them?'

'My mother told me about my father—'

'I thought all the women died.'

'Not true.' He pauses. He's struggling with something. 'I grew up in Italy in a tiny fishing village. When I was five, I climbed the tallest sycamore tree in our garden, and got stuck. Mamma stood underneath for hours, trying to talk me down. She finally lost her patience and yelled at me. I lost my grip and fell. I landed on my feet without a scratch, let alone a sprained ankle. I wanted to tell everyone I could fly, so she had to tell me the truth about who I was.' Jason taps the table. 'She said an angel appeared to her when she was walking along the beach at dusk. Mamma was the daughter of a fisherman—a good Catholic girl. She figured it wasn't a sin if she gave herself to an angel, and she didn't plan on telling anyone about him. But then a month later she found out she was pregnant.' The cracking of thunder booms above us. 'She said I couldn't tell anyone because there were other angels who would find me and hurt me.'

There's a knock at the front door.

'Gaby, please,' Jason whispers. 'Don't say a word to anyone.'

It's dark on the front deck and the breeze coming through the screen door is stronger now, and cooler. I flick on the front light and find myself staring at the most beautiful man I've ever seen.

I open the door, utterly distracted. He's got the cheek-bones of a model, soft lips, and short, dark, styled hair. In the dim light, he looks like he's come from a photo shoot. I'm taking all this in, which is my excuse for staring. I don't know what his excuse is because he's just as fixated by me.

'Gabriella.' His voice is deep, and breaks a little as he says my name.

I shouldn't be surprised he knows who I am, but it still rocks me. I rest a hand on the doorframe.

'And you are?'

Something passes across his face. Disappointment?

'Daniel.'

I close my mouth. The guy Rafa hates. Another Rephaite.

'Do you know where Maggie is?'

'Yes.'

'Is she all right?'

'She's unharmed.'

'Bring her back. Now.'

'We need to talk.'

'Make it quick.'

I step back and direct him down the hall. He hesitates,

and then moves ahead of me. He smells woodsy, musky. Like Rafa, he looks about twenty. He's dressed like he's on his way to dinner: expensive jeans, collared shirt, and square-toed boots. He's not as tall as Rafa, or as broad-shouldered, but he walks like he doesn't expect to fail. He falters, though, when he sees Jason.

I introduce them. 'Jason is Maggie's boyfriend.'

Their handshake is brief. Daniel turns his back to Jason. 'Is there somewhere we can talk in private?'

Another crack of thunder. The sky lights up.

'This is as private as it's going to get.'

'But—'

'Jason knows about the Rephaim.'

Daniel's cool expression doesn't change. 'How is that possible?'

I move around him, forcing Daniel to face both of us. 'Taya and her idiot mate weren't very subtle. She threw me into a tree with inhuman strength, broke my ribs. Mentioned someone called Semyaza—so we did some research. And then she showed up at a party, snatched up Mags, and disappeared into thin air. All in front of Jason.'

Daniel is watching me with unnerving intensity. 'But who told you about the Rephaim?'

When I don't answer, he twists his lips. 'Rafael. And where is he now?'

'Looking for Maggie,' I say. 'Is she at the Sanctuary?'

'You remember it?'

I pick up a damp tea towel and hang it on the hook over the bench. 'Until two days ago, I thought I was a backpacker, so, no, I don't remember it.'

'Can you still shift?'

'I wouldn't know how.'

'But you *have* shifted recently?'

'I had to, after Taya worked me over the other night.'

He waits.

'I was in bad shape. Rafa took me.'

'Where?'

I shrug. 'I passed out.'

I don't tell him about the second trip. I don't know him and he doesn't fit the picture I've been putting together of the Rephaim. He's more controlled than Rafa and Taya, guarded.

'Do you know where Maggie is or not?'

He nods. 'You have to come with me.'

'Why not bring her here?' Jason says.

Daniel doesn't take his eyes from me. 'Because it's up to Gabriella to secure her freedom.'

'Why?'

'Because this is all about her.'

Of course it is. My stomach flips.

'Why should I trust you?'

'You used to, with your life.'

Heat flares in my chest. 'Did I? So you must know what Jude and I were doing when we went missing.'

'You remember him?'

'Answer the question.'

Daniel takes a step closer. 'Do you remember what happened with your brother?'

'All I remember is a car accident, which apparently never happened. So, again, no, I don't remember. Now answer my question. Did I tell you what Jude and I were planning to do?'

He watches me, impassive. 'No.'

'Then I couldn't have trusted you that much.'

We eyeball each other. He wins.

'I want my friend safe and sound.'

'Then come with me.'

Jason touches my arm. 'Maybe you should wait for Rafa.'

I frown at him. A minute ago, he was in Rafa's face, and now he thinks Rafa's our best option? Rafa had his chance to take me.

'I don't have time to wait.'

'Make sure you tell him she's with me,' Daniel says.

I have a blinding urge to punch his perfect nose.

'Gaby, don't go. We've got more to talk about.'

'I'm coming back.' I want to sound confident, but my throat is already closing up.

Daniel waits for me to look at him. 'Come to me,' he says.

It's an order. I don't move.

He sighs, and it's the first sign of real emotion since his brief lapse at the front door. 'Please.' He holds out a hand.

I take it, surprised to find his fingers a little clammy. Did I do that, or is it just the storm?

He laces his fingers through mine. 'Don't let go.'

'This is it?' I panic, remembering the wild sensation of shifting with Rafa.

'As long as we're in contact, I won't lose you.'

I close my eyes. So, no need for intimate embraces then? Rafa's really been having fun with me. I grip Daniel's hand as huge rain hits the tin roof, drowning out everything else.

PLEASED TO MEET YOU. NOT.

Shifting with Daniel is nothing like shifting with Rafa. It's less extreme for starters, no worse than being on a roller coaster. Then there's a change in the temperature. It's still warm, but the air feels more artificial.

I'm in what looks like a pricey hotel room, everything stainless steel and polished timber. The carpet and walls are beige, soulless. There's a bed, a desk, and a flat-screen TV on the wall. But no Maggie.

'Where is she?'

Daniel lets my hand go. 'In a moment.'

'Let me see her.'

He walks to the door and I follow.

'I need to speak to some people first. Be patient.'

'This *is* me being patient.'

He turns to me. 'I need you to wait here.'

'Why?'

'We're at the Sanctuary. There are rules.'

'Didn't I used to live here?'

'And now you're a guest.'

I know the door is locked before I turn the handle, but I try anyway, then press my ear against the cool timber. Faint voices. I can't make out words but Daniel is talking to at least one other person. Male. The voices fade. Tell me I haven't done something incredibly stupid.

The windows are the oldest things in the room, three of them, rectangular with timber frames. A white muslin curtain obscures a bleak sky outside. I pull it back and draw in my breath. It's not the sky that's gray. It's the side of a mountain. There are snow-covered peaks high above. Three stories below is a wide piazza with a fountain in the middle and, beyond that, a church with a domed roof.

Rafa said the Sanctuary was an old monastery. I'm in the right place. I push open a window and a cold blast drives me back. *Much* colder than Pan Beach. I slam it and rub my bare arms to warm up.

Fuck. I'm in Italy.

I pull my phone out, thinking I'll call Daisy again. But there's nothing where the signal bars should be. Which is when I remember I stopped paying for international roaming six months ago. Shit.

A bell tolls. Monks in dark robes move along a cloister on the far side of the piazza, towards the church. I'm trying to figure out why monks live with the Rephaim when the door opens behind me.

Daniel places a top on the bed, black, a light knit.

'That won't be enough to keep you warm,' he says, gesturing to my T-shirt. He seems to be making an effort not to look at my breasts. I make it easier for him by folding my arms.

'I don't want hand-me-downs. I want Maggie.'

His mouth quirks a little, but it's far from a smile. 'It's your jumper. You left most of your things behind when you went.'

'Where. Is. Maggie?'

'I told you, she's safe. As soon as you tell me what happened with you and Jude, she'll go home.' He could easily pass for an Italian with his dark hair and brown eyes. There's even a hint of an accent.

'Is she here?'

'She's safe.'

For a second I can't feel my legs.

She's not here.

I've given myself over to them for nothing. I knew this was a trap, but I still thought I'd find Maggie in it somewhere. 'You lied to me . . . I trusted you and you lied to me.' I lower myself onto the edge of the bed. The mattress is hard.

'I never said she was here.'

'You're an arsehole.'

'I didn't lie.' It seems important to Daniel that I believe him.

'No, you just let me believe a lie.'

'Your friend is safe, and your cooperation will keep her that way. That's not a lie.'

I focus on the thick beige carpet, blood throbbing at my temples. I may be caught here, but that doesn't mean I have to play nice. I get up and move towards the desk, my eyes still down.

'Gabriella.' Daniel's voice is soft. 'You have to prove your loyalty. You've been hiding on the other side of the world with Rafael. You have to understand how that looks. Taya is not your enemy. Neither am I—'

I grab the chair and swing it at his head, hard and fast. But he's faster. He dodges sideways, barely making a sound as he blocks the strike. Before I can turn to swing again, the air beside me shimmers. I have time to recognize Goatee before he knocks me onto the bed and straddles me. I thrash wildly. He shifts his knees until they're on my shoulders, and pins my wrists over my head with one hand. His other is around my throat.

'Malachi, enough!'

The pressure immediately eases.

'Get off her.'

He does as he's ordered. I spring to my feet, backing away until I hit the wall beside the bed, all the while dragging in oxygen. Daniel is by the window, straightening his clothes. He's not calm anymore. 'I told you to stay out of this.'

'But she attacked you—'

'You don't think I can look after myself?' Daniel's tone is dangerous, and Goatee lowers his eyes.

'Of course, Daniel. I'm sorry.'

How did he know what was going on in here? I scan the room and see a small black dome over the door. Like the ones you see in supermarkets and service stations.

The door opens. Taya. Her black hair is tied back and she's still wearing the dark jeans and shirt she's had on both times I've seen her.

'Look who's come home,' she says, walking calmly into the room.

Bitch.

I leap on the bed and launch myself at her.

'Taya, no—' Daniel says. But her fist catches me while I'm still in the air. I have no idea how hard I hit the floor because the world goes black before I get there.

END OVER END

When I come to, there is blood in my mouth and ropes cutting into my skin.

I'm still in the beige room, but now I'm tied to a chair. Not the flimsy wooden one I tried to break open Daniel's head with, but something sturdier. Antique, by the feel of it. What is it with the Rephaim and old furniture?

My tongue finds split flesh inside my cheek. My face aches. I'm wearing the sweater Daniel brought for me; it's a good fit, so maybe he wasn't lying about it being mine.

My back is to the door. Like I'm not vulnerable enough strapped to a chair.

'Arseholes,' I say, and wish it didn't come out as a croak. There's no response but I know I'm not alone. 'I'm thirsty.'

There's movement behind me, followed by clinking

glass and the sound of liquid pouring. Daniel steps in front of me, holding a heavy tumbler.

'Are you going to sit still?' he asks.

I give him a black look.

He puts one hand behind my head and lifts the glass to my mouth. I part my lips, and he cradles my head while I drink. When I'm finished, his hand lingers under my ponytail, and then his fingers trail down to the thick scar.

I jerk out of his reach and his fingers don't follow. He sits on the edge of the bed, which was remade while I was out cold.

'So, Taya's not my enemy?' I find the cut in my cheek again.

Daniel rests his elbows on his knees, watching me through thick eyelashes.

'How many days was Rafael with you?'

This is what he wants to know?

'I don't know. A couple.'

'Did you sleep with him?'

'What the hell would that have to do with you?'

'Nothing at all.' He's as unreadable as ever. 'But Gabriella would never forgive you.'

My hands ball into fists. 'Stop talking like there are two different people involved here.'

'All right. *You* won't forgive yourself.'

'And why is that?'

'Didn't he tell you?'

'All he told me was that I broke his nose the last time I saw him.'

He pauses. 'Well, that's something.'

I can't tell if he means the fact Rafa told me, or that I broke his nose.

'Did he tell you you're the only Rephaite woman he hasn't been with? No?' A pitying smile. 'He's seduced all of them except you, Gabriella. And before he left here, he was obsessed with having you, so I find it hard to believe he hasn't taken advantage of the current *situation*.'

My smile is bitter. 'You'll be happy to hear my record is untarnished.' He can thank Maggie for that.

His shoulders relax a fraction. How important was that answer?

'You need to remember, lust is what made our fathers fall,' he says. 'Lust is part of our nature. Even when you didn't know what you were, you must have felt it?'

Heat spreads across my cheeks and I turn my face away. I actually hadn't felt it until Rafa walked out of my dreams and into Rick's that afternoon. Correction: until Rafa ran his hands through my hair and kissed my neck . . .

'Nathaniel has taught us control. It's what separates us from those like Mya and Rafael.'

'And Jude?'

He nods. 'It's why you didn't follow him, no matter how

much he wanted you to turn your back on the Sanctuary. You understood the need for discipline and restraint.'

'Who's Mya?'

Daniel's lips harden. 'The worst example of what we can be. Obsessed with sex and power and incapable of respecting authority.'

'And she left with Jude?'

'She manipulated him beautifully.'

I can't imagine my brother being manipulated by anyone. 'Was he in love with her?'

Daniel lets out a low laugh. 'No. Rafael was.'

I ignore the faint sting behind my ribs. 'So, why did Jude leave?'

'For the same reason the other twenty-one did. To do as they pleased. And because your brother and Rafael were incapable of independent thought. Whatever one did, the other followed. Your brother chose him over you. You owe him no loyalty.'

'I'm not protecting him. The brother I remember was a high school dropout who loved tequila and surfing—not the guy you're talking about.' The ropes are biting into my wrists. I can move my arms a little, but there's no relief. 'Help me understand this. Jude, Rafa, and the others—they left here, but they still fight demons?'

Daniel laces his fingers together. 'It's not the same. We fight demons to keep them from the Fallen. The Outcasts provide a mercenary service. They track and kill demons with no regard for human collateral damage. They hire themselves out to the highest bidder to solve *problems*.' He regards me for a moment. 'But you already know that. You wrote about it. And that particular bit of recklessness cost sixteen human lives.'

'I dreamed it. I had no idea it was real.'

'You dreamed about fighting with Rafael?'

I grit my teeth. 'When I wrote about it, *I had no idea he was a real person*.'

Daniel takes a slow breath. Good to know I'm getting under his skin. 'Please, Gabriella, tell me what you remember.'

'Will you let me out of these ropes then?'

'Perhaps.'

I don't believe him, but I've got nothing to lose.

So I tell him what I told Rafa: about backpacking with Jude, the crash, and what happened when I was in hospital. I don't get choked up talking about it this time—either because I've said the words out loud before, or because I'm starting to believe they might not be true—but it still drains me.

'And you knew nothing about the Fallen or the Rephaim until a few days ago?'

'No.'

He rolls his shirtsleeves up over his toned forearms.

He doesn't dress like he's about to commit violence, but I get the feeling he's capable of it.

'What's your story?'

The question catches him off guard. 'What do you mean?'

'Well, you don't seem to be a meathead like Taya and Melchezedick—'

'Malachi.'

'Whatever. You're different, so what do you do?'

'I'm one of the Council of Five. The governing council of the Rephaim.'

'I thought Nathaniel ran the show.'

'He's our leader, not a dictator. We elect our own council every five years.'

That explains a lot. He's a politician. 'I hope you don't think you're getting my vote.'

He dips his head but I think I catch a smile.

'What?'

When he speaks, his voice is warm. 'You're like my Gabe in so many ways. I miss her.'

My Gabe?

I'm trying to work out how to ask the obvious question when there's a rap on the door. Daniel stands up, his face again composed in that infuriatingly calm expression. He talks to someone in the hallway and then comes back into my line of sight.

'I have to attend to something. You should drink some more before I go.'

He pours another glass of water and again slides his fingers into my hair to hold my head. It makes me think of Rafa.

And then Daniel's gone and I'm alone, tied to a chair in a monastery in Italy. I'm exhausted. Every muscle in my body aches and my eyelids are too heavy to keep open. Warmth floods across my chest, and as I give in to the pull of sleep, the realization hits.

The bastard has drugged me.

LIVING IN MY HEAD

As usual, I wake to pounding guitars and screaming vocals. Bloody Jude and his need for continuous noise, even at this hour of the day.

'Turn that down!' I call out and drag the quilt up to my neck.

My bedroom door opens and the music blasts even louder. Jude stands there in torn jeans and a faded T-shirt. 'What?' He grins at me. 'You love it.'

I throw a pillow at him. He catches it in one hand and saunters over, kicking the door shut behind him with his bare foot. The wall of noise is again muted. Jude holds the pillow like he's going to use it as a weapon, but when he reaches the bed he tosses it aside and sits down.

His thick dark hair is a mess but, as usual, it looks good.

We have the same crazy hair, but I can never pull off that level of cool dishevelment. Kids at school used to mistake us for each other from a distance, at least until I grew my hair to my shoulders and filled out my bra.

'What?' I ask.

'I think we should do it.'

I sit up against the headboard, drawing my knees to my chest. 'Do what?'

'Hit the road.'

A smile spreads across my face. 'Hoo-fucking-ray.'

Jude laughs. 'Some guys mightn't want to kiss a mouth as dirty as yours, you know.'

'Lucky I'm interested in culture then, not foreign tongues.'

'Glad to hear it.'

I give him a gentle shove. We sit there, grinning at each other. Where will we go first? We've always talked about Machu Picchu . . .

'They're going to lose it,' I say, nodding in the direction of the kitchen, where our parents are eating their homemade eggs Benedict and sipping freshly squeezed organic juice.

'They'll find a way to spin it. They always do.'

Our parents have high hopes for us. Our father is a big deal in legal circles. He married beneath him when he fell for our mother, and his parents never let him forget it.

They'd hoped having exceptional children would justify the choice. Unfortunately, Jude and I haven't lived up to expectations.

We've inherited our parents' good coloring and bone structure, we have above-average grades, do well at sport, and have thriving social lives. But it's not enough. Jude loves music but doesn't play. I love to read, but my writing's never going to set the world on fire. Neither of us have a gift worth bragging about at dinner parties.

We should be planning for our futures in law or medicine or literature studies, not watching bands on weekends, reading fantasy, and daydreaming about Machu Picchu, Abu Simbel, and the Colosseum. I wish I had a dollar for every time one of them told us what a disappointment we were, more often than not in front of their friends. Or ours. We could have left years ago.

'Are you sure we've got enough cash?'

Jude nods. 'For a couple of months at least, especially if we start in countries with a kind exchange rate. Say, Peru?'

'You read my mind.'

'And when the money's gone, we'll look for work.'

'Good enough for me.' I smile. 'They're off to Paris again next month . . .'

Jude nods. 'We can get organized by then. We've got money, maps, and passports—'

'Our charm and wit.'

'Now all we need is an itinerary, and a brilliantly crafted letter that makes them think we're finally taking some initiative, which they can take credit for.' He collapses back on the bed and stares up at the patched ceiling, a reminder from our father that tennis is not an indoor sport. 'We're going to do this, aren't we?'

I nudge him with my foot. 'You bet your arse we are.'

Jude turns so he can look me in the eye. 'You're not worried about what could happen?'

I shrug. 'Nope. You?'

'Shit, no. It's you and me against the world, kid. Who's gonna get in our way?'

It's the best dream I've had of Jude since he died, and I can still hear his voice when I wake up. About a second before someone shoves my head into a tub of freezing water.

WEARING BLACK AND BLUE

I claw at the fingers that are clamped around my neck, holding me under. My throat has closed over, but water rushes up my nose. My lungs are on fire. Air . . . Any second now I'm going to pass out.

I thrash and kick, striking something that feels like bone. My head is ripped out of the water and I'm flung backwards, hitting something hard. A wall. I make horrible noises trying to get air back into my lungs. The floor under my hands is tiled and cold. Tremors rip through my body. I'm soaking wet, tasting blood.

'Come on, Gabe, you've got to have more than that.'

Through strands of wet hair, I see Malachi standing with his leg up on an enamel bath, rubbing his shin.

We're in a gleaming bathroom with fresh white towels

and a thick bath mat I'm possibly about to throw up on.

'What's happening?' I manage to rasp.

'I'm trying to help you.'

I choke. 'What, drown?'

He sits on the edge of the bath. His goatee and straight hair are jet black under the heated lights. 'Come on, you know you can't die unless you lose your head.'

I stare at him, more interested in breathing than speaking.

'We don't kill each other, Gabe. There's not enough of us left as it is.' He checks me over. 'Ready?'

I scramble sideways as he comes at me, wondering where Daniel is and why Malachi's been let loose on me. But the door is shut and Malachi grabs me by my hair before I reach the handle and drags me back towards the tub.

'You know how to get out of this,' he says, keeping clear of my fists. I search for purchase on the tiles, but he's too strong. I have time to inhale before he plunges my head under again.

Back in that wet, muted world, the panic is overwhelming. I can't die. I could drown for hours. I open my eyes. Black spots flicker against white enamel. I reach out, fingers scraping for the plug. But the bath is too big; I can't reach it.

The thought comes again. *I can't die.* This isn't about

killing me—this is about hurting me. And by thrashing I'm making Malachi's job easier.

I stop struggling, but his grip doesn't loosen. He must know how long he's got before I slide into unconsciousness. I grip the bath again and push back with all my strength. Malachi presses down harder to keep me under. When he's right over me, I let my arms go limp. He loses his balance, stumbles, and I slam my elbow upwards. From the way he lets go of my hair, I've found the target.

Again I stagger back, gasping, but this time I keep my feet. I look around for a weapon, but there's nothing close by except a plastic toilet brush.

'Shit, woman.' Malachi's leaning against the wall, clutching between his legs but still blocking my way to the door.

What would badass Gabe do in this situation? I lunge for the brush. Surprise registers on Malachi's face just before I fling it at him. I wrench open the door and stumble through.

Daniel is standing with his back to the room, looking out the window. He turns when he hears me and I race for the outer door. I'm moving too fast and hit it hard with my shoulder. I grapple for the door handle, and then my breakout attempt is over. It's still locked from the outside. Of course.

Daniel hasn't moved from the window, but he's watching

me, his face bleak. It's darker outside—late afternoon. How long was I out?

I sink to the floor. 'What the *fuck*?'

Daniel glances at the bathroom and runs a hand through his dark hair. 'The easy way didn't work.'

I push my soaking fringe out of my face. 'For what?'

'Getting to the truth.'

'I've told you the truth.'

'No, you haven't, because you don't remember it.'

I sit there, dripping water all over the carpet. 'You think drugging and drowning me will help?'

'I gave you something to open your mind, but it's a mess in there. Everything bleeds together.'

'So the next option is to let that arsehole hold my head underwater?'

Something in the bathroom catches Daniel's attention and he holds up a hand to stop Malachi from whatever he was about to do. 'It's not just your mind that's forgotten things—your body has too. If we can get your instincts to kick in, then maybe your mind will follow.'

I wring out my hair. 'Did I pass?'

He moves closer.

I wish I had something to throw at him. 'Don't touch me.'

'Gabe, this is not the way I wanted to do this. But whoever did this to you left us with no choice.'

'Of course there's a choice—you could choose *not* to hurt me! You could accept my memories are gone. Whatever I may or may not have known about your precious Fallen no longer exists.' I stop to catch my breath again.

Daniel has paused halfway across the room. 'The Fallen are as important to you as they are to us. Your father is among them, and your fate is as tied to them as ours.'

Malachi emerges from the bathroom, his jaw set. Daniel gives him a cursory glance. 'Go,' he says.

Malachi raises his chin, as if he's not quite ready to walk away from his work.

'Now,' Daniel says.

Malachi eyes me, and then he disappears in a blink. I should have known he wouldn't leave the room like a normal person.

Daniel offers me a dry towel. I snatch it and wipe my face and neck, and then drape it around my wet shoulders. He sits on the bed and gestures for me to join him.

I don't.

'Gabriella—'

'It's Gaby.'

A sigh. 'Gaby. The Fallen are the scourge of heaven and hell. They're hunted by angels and demons, reviled for their weakness. We're their illicit offspring—the product of their sins.'

'So?'

'The archangels despise us—they've only let us live because of Nathaniel.'

'How does finding them change any of that?'

'It shows we're loyal to heaven.'

'Why don't you just leave it to the demons to find the Fallen and take them back to hell? Find something else to do with your lives.'

Three lines crease his smooth forehead. 'The only way we can redeem ourselves is to deliver Semyaza and the Fallen to the Angelic Garrison, show that we're willing to hand our fathers over.'

'And then what?'

'And then the archangels will accept us among them.'

'How do you know that's what they want? Or that they'll give you anything?'

Daniel's face darkens. 'What crap has Rafael been telling you?'

It's the closest he's come to profanity. I'm tempted to keep pushing, but I have a more important question.

'Where's God in all this?'

'God's covenant with mankind has nothing to do with us,' he says. 'We're neither angel nor human. We're something in between.'

I hold out my arms. 'Really?' I'm trying to mock him, but the idea I'm something other than human deeply unnerves me.

'Appearances can be deceiving.'

'How can you be so sure you're not just a human with a few special gifts?'

'Humans grow old and die. Humans have children.'

I pick at the carpet, breaking his gaze. Not that I was planning on having kids anytime soon, but I'd assumed I'd be able to if that day came.

'We're hybrids, Gabriella, we can't procreate.'

Is that a hint of bitterness?

I stretch out my bad leg. My knee protests. 'But God created angels and humans. Angels were there at the virgin birth, and they were there when Jesus rose from the dead, after dying for *humans*. You can't separate the two. So how can we be nothing?'

Daniel stands up. He rotates his wrist until it cracks—further evidence he was something other than a politician not so long ago. 'We leave the existential questions to our priests and philosophers. And you forget, we have Nathaniel.'

'An actual fallen angel.'

'An actual *angel*.' The edge in his voice warns me I'm heading into territory that may lead to my head in a bath again.

I shiver. I'm wet and cold. The adrenaline has gone now, and my muscles ache. 'Any chance I could have a hot shower without someone trying to drown me?'

He regards me for a moment and then nods. 'Of course.'

I use the door handle to pull myself up, then limp across the room. I pause before I go back into the bathroom. 'Why is everyone so convinced that what happened to me has anything to do with the Fallen?'

Daniel closes his eyes for a second and sighs. 'Do you believe a car accident is responsible for giving you new memories?'

I rub my neck. Malachi's fingers have left more bruises. 'No. But do you really think Jude and I found the Fallen when no one has been able to in over a century?'

'It's possible.'

'You think two hundred angels are just hiding out somewhere in the world?'

'We're not convinced they're in this dimension.'

It takes me a second to absorb that. 'Then how is anyone going to be able to find them?'

Daniel picks a tiny piece of lint from his shirt. 'Wherever they are, they got there from somewhere in this realm, and if we can find that location, Nathaniel can track them.'

'Oh.' My brain is now officially full.

The door closes behind Daniel. No flashy shifting like Malachi.

I shut myself in the bathroom and stand there for a good minute, staring at the water in the tub and the twisted bath mat. And then I dash to the toilet and throw up.

THE LIE IN THE REFLECTION

In spite of everything, or maybe because of it, the shower is the best I've had for a long time. The water pressure is so fierce it almost drives me against the glass screen. I withstand it, letting the heat seep into my bones.

Emptiness gnaws at me.

I can't ignore it any longer. The sense that something's missing. I've always assumed it was Jude, but maybe what I've been missing is me.

I help myself to expensive-looking shampoo and conditioner. When I finally get out of the shower, smelling like aloe vera and vanilla, I drag my forearm across the steamy mirror and look at myself. Still the same Gaby. Somehow, I keep expecting to see someone different—the person everyone else seems to know.

Wet hair drips down my back. I run my fingertips over the lumpy tissue on my neck. It feels the same, but it means something else now.

Someone tried to cut my head off.

I had stitches and recovered the slow, painful way. Nobody shifted and healed me. Does that mean Jude really is dead? Because if he survived, surely he would have healed me like Rafa did. I exhale. I need to run to make sense of this. What are the chances Daniel will let me take a few laps around the grounds?

I open the bathroom door and let the steam out ahead of me. The room is empty. On the bed is a selection of T-shirts and sweaters, all gray or black and all designed for function over style. No designer labels here. Maggie would be appalled.

Maggie.

Rafa must be back at the bungalow by now, probably tearing Jason a new one for letting me leave. Not that he could have stopped me.

I put on two T-shirts and a long-sleeved shirt and feel more grounded. I go to the window. The sky is almost completely dark now and hanging lamps have come on around the piazza. Shadowy figures hurry along the cloister. The need to be moving is almost unbearable. I can't run, so I pace, flipping the bird to the camera in the corner, once or twice.

All right, so what do I know? I make a mental list.

I'm the bastard child of a fallen angel.

I used to live here.

Jude left a decade ago and I stayed; we stopped talking as a result.

Something happened a year ago and we made up.

We didn't tell anyone what it was that ended our rift.

We went missing together, presumed dead.

I survived and someone wiped my memory.

I pass by the window, see my reflection in the dark glass, my nervous pacing.

Let's say Jude and I somehow found the Fallen. It makes sense they would wipe my memories. But why would they give me the fake life I remember? Whoever altered my memory wanted me to remember Jude. Wanted me to think I had a normal childhood. That I was okay with not having a relationship with my parents. They made sure I grieved deeply for my brother.

Why?

Steam drifts out of the bathroom and I go over to shut the door. Someone's standing on the bath mat.

'Fuck!'

'Sorry,' Daisy says. 'You okay?'

My heart thumps again and then settles. She's injured. Her cheek is bruised and her top lip is swollen and split.

'Me? What happened to you?'

She shrugs with one shoulder. 'I went to see you without permission.'

'Today?'

'No, on Sunday.'

'How did they find out?'

A half-smile. 'You rang.' Her red hair looks dull today, tucked behind her ears. Her skin is even paler than when we met at the lookout.

'Shit.' I'd forgotten all about my panicked call a few hours ago. 'Sorry.' I glance up at the camera, step into the bathroom. 'You know I'm being watched, right?'

She smiles and then winces. 'Everyone's in a briefing right now.'

'Why aren't you there?'

'I don't get to know what's going on—at least for a day or so.' She closes the toilet lid and sits on it. 'But just to be on the safe side, I'll stay in here.'

'Do you know where Maggie is?' I ask.

'Sorry, I don't.'

I want to believe her.

'I had an argument with Taya over what happened the first time she went to see you, so there was no way she was telling me the plans today. Nobody thinks I can be impartial.' She sighs. 'Sorry I couldn't answer your call. Daniel was handing out surveillance jobs when you rang. I turned it off as soon as I saw it was a new number, but he doesn't miss a trick. He asked to borrow my phone as I was heading out. Nobody says no to Daniel.'

'Did he do that?' I gesture to her lip and cheek.

She touches her face. 'That was Malachi. But only after I busted his nose.'

'Excellent. I smashed his balls.'

Daisy's green eyes light up. 'Why?'

'He tried to drown me.'

'*What?*'

I tell her about the bathroom session.

'Daniel let that happen?' She's studying me, a frown changing the pattern of her freckles. 'Why did you agree to come with him?'

'He let me believe Mags was here.' I'm embarrassed at how easily he manipulated me.

'Ah, well, there's a reason he's one of the Five.'

'So, it's not just because of his perfect hair? It's a wonder he's got time to do anything that doesn't involve a mirror.'

Daisy snorts. It's not a delicate sound. 'Ow,' she says, and presses her fingers to her lip, trying not to laugh. 'Oh, I *like* the new you.'

'Yeah?' I don't mean to sound so hopeful.

She manages a lopsided smile. 'It's just . . . you're seeing everything with fresh eyes.'

'What do you mean?'

'Well . . .' She pauses. 'Daniel likes to look sharp. Everyone knows that. But nobody makes jokes about it. Especially you.'

'Why not?'

'Well, for a start, you two only broke up a little while before you disappeared.'

I blink. And gape.

'He didn't tell you?'

I shake my head. Parts of our earlier conversation make a *lot* more sense. 'He asked me if I'd slept with Rafa.'

'I hope you said yes, even if it's not true.'

'No, and no,' I say. 'Daniel says I'm the only Rephaite woman Rafa hasn't slept with.'

She shrugs. 'True enough, but that's Rafa.'

'So you've been with him?' The question's out before I even know I want to ask it.

'Yeah, but it was a hundred years ago. We were teenagers. Actual teenagers. I was one of his earlier conquests.' A small smile. 'Not one of my prouder moments, but he wasn't such a cocky bastard back then.'

I really shouldn't care about any of this, but . . . 'How did he and I get along?'

'That's complicated.' A frown. 'You and Rafa were always our best fighters—when everyone was still together. You led every major operation, and no one went into even a bar fight without one or both of you.'

'Why didn't I sleep with him, then?'

'I don't know. On principle? He was Jude's best friend. And of course he's a prize smartarse. You two fought with each other almost as much as you fought beside each other, but it was never anything serious. Until Mya came along.'

I'm so sick of that name. 'What's her story?'

'She managed to make it on her own for nearly a hundred and thirty years before Nathaniel tracked her down. She wasn't a big fan of our way of life here. Too many rules. Plus, she wanted to be one of the Five. Rephaim have waited decades for that chance, and she just waltzes on in and wants to run the place. When she worked out how long she'd have to wait, she stirred up a lot of trouble, questioning Nathaniel and telling us we should think for ourselves. Anyway, she finally left and took twenty-two of our best fighters with her.'

'Including Jude and Rafa.'

'Rafa followed his dick—big surprise there. Jude followed Rafa, and everyone else followed Jude.'

I pick up a damp towel, toss it on the edge of the bath. 'Were Jude and Daniel friends?'

'They were civil to each other, at least until Daniel became interested in you. Then it all went bad.'

'How come?'

'Jude didn't like how you were when you were around Daniel.'

I wrap my arms around my knees. I'm not sure I want to know what that means.

'They were never buddies, even when we were kids,' Daisy continues. 'Daniel was always a bit threatened. Jude could have been one of the Five in a heartbeat if he'd wanted it, but he stayed on the front line with us.' She straightens the bath mat. 'Everything changed after Hurricane Mya.'

I glance back at the camera. I hope that briefing is still going. 'Can you take me to Pan Beach?'

She looks down at the empty bath. 'I can't. They'll know it was me.'

I push down my frustration.

'I'll figure something out,' she says. 'I know I've said that before . . .'

'Thanks.' I gesture to her face. 'How come you're still injured?'

She wrinkles her nose. 'No one's allowed to shift with me at the moment.' She checks her watch and stands up. 'I'd better get out of here.'

I nod, and get to my feet too. 'Thanks, you know, for coming.'

Daisy catches sight of herself in the mirror and probes her bruised cheek until she winces. 'My pleasure. Gabe—' She turns to me. 'Trust your body. You might not remember how to fight, but I don't believe Daniel's theory that your body's forgotten.' She cracks her neck. 'And Gabe?'

'Yeah?'

'Fight hard, because we *will* keep hurting you.'

And then she's gone. All the warmth in the bathroom leaves with her.

HOW MANY TIMES DO I HAVE TO SAY IT?

My stomach growls. I haven't eaten for hours. I'm still staring out the window, not seeing anything. I'm thinking about my parents. Not the self-righteous pair who it now seems never existed, but the two people who gave Jude and me life: a woman from another place and time, and a fallen angel.

Did she know what he was? Was it the best night of her life, or did it just leave her knocked up without a husband? There weren't too many places on the planet last century where being a single mother was a good thing. And did her life slip away giving birth, or did she somehow survive, like Jason's mother? And if she survived, what made her give up her babies when Nathaniel came calling? Was she scared? I almost can't bear to think about her.

I stare at my reflection in the window. Do I look like her? Do we have the same cheekbones? The same dark eyes? Am I like her in other ways? Even if I remember who I used to be, I'll never know. If she survived Nathaniel's visit, she's still been dead for a century.

I almost hope she didn't care about Jude and me. I could bear that. But a mother who loved me, who lived a life searching for me—or who died protecting me . . . My throat closes over and I shut my eyes. A tear still slips out.

What about my father? I try to imagine him. I can't.

Does he know I exist? Do any of the Fallen know they left behind a legacy of bastards now hell-bent on destroying them?

My breath fogs up the window and I use my finger to draw a crescent moon. It fades almost instantly. All I have to do is *remember*. Then Maggie is safe. Then at least some of these questions will have answers.

There's a knock on the door. I tense, ready for anything, but it's only Daniel carrying a tray of food. My traitor stomach greets him with enthusiasm.

'Is that drugged too?'

Daniel has changed into a fresh shirt, less dressy than before, but still crisp. He puts the tray on the desk. The plate is covered with a stainless steel cloche, like in a hotel. There's a sealed bottle of water beside it and some thin breadsticks.

'Your food is fine.' He sits on the edge of the bed and gestures for me to eat at the desk.

I don't move.

He lets out the smallest of sighs. 'Opening your mind that way didn't work, so there's no point trying it again.'

'Who opened my mind?'

'Nathaniel.'

I swallow. 'He was here? He can read minds?'

'Nathaniel can see into our thoughts if we submit ourselves to him.'

'Or if we're off our face.' I tuck a stray hair behind my ear. 'What did he see?'

'Memories of a life you never lived.'

'No shit.'

The room now smells like cheese and mushrooms—and my stomach rumbles again.

'Eat your dinner before it goes cold.'

The benefits of a full stomach outweigh the fear of being drugged again. I lift the lid. Risotto. It looks plain enough, just mushrooms and onions, stirred through with parmesan, but when I taste it . . .

'This is pretty good.'

'It's the truffle oil.'

I don't get it. One minute they're drowning me and the

next cooking me gourmet meals. Must be some kind of Rephaite interrogation method. I pick up the pace. The meal could be ripped away before I finish it. Or I could.

'Good god, you even eat like him now.'

Daniel is watching me, fascinated.

'Who?'

'Your brother.'

The Jude I remember loved food, but he rarely lingered over it. Apparently the real Jude wasn't all that different. I lick my fork and smile.

Daniel clears his throat. I look over at him, but keep eating.

'What does Rafael want with you?' he asks.

It's oddly satisfying, how much he hates acknowledging I've been with Rafa.

'He wants what you want. To know how Jude died.' I don't tell him Rafa's theory that Jude might still be alive, but it must have crossed Daniel's mind. I don't think too many things get past him.

'That's all?'

'Isn't that enough?'

It's not a question he answers. I scrape the last of the rice onto my fork and try to make my deal. 'Let's assume my old memories are never coming back. You must have a plan B?'

He doesn't answer, so I keep going. 'Why can't you treat

me like I'm another long-lost Rephaite? If you let Maggie go, I'll stay. Train me.'

I'll stay until I learn to shift.

'No.'

'Why not?'

He sighs and wets his lower lip with his tongue. If he didn't have such a huge stick up his arse it might be sexy. 'Because we have to know what happened.'

'But if you retrain me, that other life might come back. I might remember.'

'We don't have time, Gabriella. It might be too late. You and your brother could have already changed the course of history.'

'How could we have possibly done that?'

'If you found the Fallen and made some pact with them it will condemn us all.'

I scowl at him. Everything is so freaking life and death with these people.

'Maybe we just wanted to find our father, ask for child support, and move on with our lives.'

Daniel stands up, but not before I see a muscle twitch in his jaw. 'You need your memory back for no other reason than to stop this childish behavior.'

I wrench the cap off the water and take a long drink. I belch, as childishly as I can, and then meet Daniel's gaze. 'When do I meet Nathaniel?'

He scoffs, forgetting himself for a second. 'You have to earn that right.'

'Or be unconscious.'

Daniel drums his fingers against his thighs. I've pushed him too far.

'Have you finished eating?'

'Why?'

'Because your time's up.'

READY OR NOT

Daniel signals to the camera, and Malachi and Taya materialize about two seconds later. I'm already scrambling for the window in slow motion, like I'm running underwater. How much would falling three stories hurt? But they're already between me and freedom.

I get a flash of Rafa standing under the jacaranda tree in my front yard. I mimic him, turning side-on and balancing my weight on my toes. I flex my fingers and raise my eyebrows at Taya and Malachi.

They falter.

And then they remember I'm harmless.

It takes them all of ten seconds to contain me. Taya pins my wrists behind me and Malachi's fingers dig into my neck as he pushes me forward.

I struggle against them. 'You'd better hope I don't get my memory back.'

'No, Gabe, you'd better hope you don't.' Taya jerks my arms up behind me. It hurts like hell. 'When the truth comes out, you're going to die. For real this time.' Her voice is low so Daniel can't hear her trash-talking.

We're in the hallway, more beige carpet, acres of it. We reach a tiny lift and only the three of us squeeze into it. Daniel is gone. The lift groans and jerks, then starts down, slowly. I close my eyes. Would Jude be going through this if he'd survived instead of me? What would he do if he was here in my place?

The lift shudders then stops. The temperature has dropped a couple of degrees. We must be underground. Malachi and Taya frog-march me down a dim passage. The walls are stone and the floor is bare concrete. Fluorescent lights sheathed in wire punctuate the low ceiling, and the place smells old and dank. We pass through two sets of iron gates before we reach a solid door. It's green and mottled, like tarnished bronze. Malachi yanks me to a standstill. He presses a buzzer and looks up. Another camera. A few seconds later, electronic bolts slide back. What do they have down here that needs this level of security?

The door swings open, slowly, like it weighs a ton. My pulse thuds in my temples. Malachi shoves me forward into a cavernous gymnasium. Before me, punching bags hang from long chains that are bolted to the high ceiling. There are two makeshift boxing rings, and weights and barbells scattered around the floor. But what takes the air from my lungs is the room's centerpiece.

It's a cage.

A towering, fully enclosed steel cage, made of chain-link wire, with sawdust on the floor, linked by a walkway to another heavy-duty bronze door. It looks like it belongs in a back alley in Bangkok. Bile rises in my throat.

Please don't let me be going in there.

The door behind me closes, and the electronic bolts slide back.

There's no one else here. But from the stench of sweat hanging in the air, it hasn't been empty long. Malachi propels me across the stone floor, towards the cage, my wrists still pinned behind my back. I struggle against him.

'I wouldn't waste any more energy if I was you,' he says.

Taya's already at the cage. She throws open the door, her sleek black ponytail swishing behind her. She gestures for me to step inside.

'No fucking way.' I dig in my heels. But we're close enough now that it only takes a rough shove and I'm in the cage. I hit the sawdust on my hands and knees.

Taya grins and snaps a padlock over the bolt. 'Don't blame me. You got yourself into this.'

I fling a handful of sawdust at her. As she's flicking it out of her hair, her attention locks on to something behind me. 'Oh, *come* on.'

I look over my shoulder. Daisy is standing there, carrying a sword, her face still bruised and busted, her red hair pinned back from her face.

'You don't think I'm letting her face this alone, do you?' She gives me a quick nod.

'Get out of the cage, Daisy,' Taya says, her tone flat.

'She'll get torn up in here on her own.'

'*Or* her instincts will kick in.'

'You haven't even given her a weapon.'

'We will. So get out. Now.'

Daisy spins the sword in her hand. She looks dangerous, even with those freckles. 'Make me.'

Taya's face lights up and she reaches down for something at her feet.

'Stop!'

Taya freezes. Daniel crosses the floor from the other side of the gym.

'Enough,' he says, his voice tight. 'Taya, stay where you are.' He looks into the cage, avoiding eye contact with me. 'Daisy, get out of there.'

There's no mistaking his tone for anything other than a command, but Daisy holds her ground. 'Daniel, this is wrong.'

His face is pinched. 'It is what it is.'

'But does it have to be *this*?'

I'm turning from one to the other as they speak.

'I'm not asking again,' Daniel says.

She holds his gaze for a few long seconds, and then her shoulders drop and I know I'm on my own. 'Sorry, Gabe,' she says quietly, and disappears.

My eyes linger on the imprint of her boots in the sawdust.

'But I'm not leaving the room,' she says behind me. She's on the opposite side of the cage to Daniel, Taya, and Malachi, her fingers hooked through the wire.

Daniel pretends not to hear. He nods at a camera across the room. A signal. All this time I've been crouched down, so I stand up on shaky legs and face the only other access point to the cage: the bronze door at the end of the walkway. It groans and slides open.

Something thuds at my feet, and I flinch. A sword.

Its blade is long and slightly curved, like Daisy's—and the one in my dream.

I try to shake the tension from my limbs. The bronze door is fully open now, but there's only darkness on the other side. I test the weight of the sword. It's lighter than I thought it would be. The leather hilt feels vaguely familiar against my palm. I've dreamed about fighting with a sword like this almost every night for a year. I know how to grip it, maybe even how to use it. For a heartbeat, I think I might be okay.

And then I see what shuffles out of the darkness into the cage.

LIKE RIDING A BIKE

It's a hellion.

With yellow eyes and leathery skin. A head disfigured by lumps. Long muscular arms and bony fingers, talons for fingernails. It's more than seven feet tall.

And it's so much more terrifying that those in my dream.

The hellion stops a few steps beyond the door. Its thick nostrils flare. It *smells* me.

My legs dissolve. Somehow I keep my feet.

'Just take the head,' Daisy says quietly from outside the cage.

I give a short, hysterical laugh. I can't swallow.

The hellion's misshapen ears prick up at the sound of my voice. It gives a deep, throaty snarl, baring long teeth.

I stagger back against the wire mesh of the cage, my heart hammering against my ribs.

'You have the advantage,' Daisy says. 'It's unarmed.'

I'm still staring at those teeth, unconvinced.

'Didn't Rafa teach you anything?'

I shake my head, afraid to take my eyes off it. 'Can it shift?'

'Not without help. It's one of Zarael's brainless foot soldiers. Be glad it's not a demon.'

I don't care that I don't know who, or what Zarael is, or that there's a difference between hellions and demons. I'm too busy remembering to breathe.

The hellion is taking in Daisy, Malachi, Taya, and Daniel. It's not quite as brainless as Daisy wants me to believe. Those yellow eyes fix on me again and my breath shortens. The stench of sweat and sawdust is choking me.

'Don't get pinned against the cage.' Daisy nudges me through the wire. 'Always have room to move.'

The hellion snarls again, louder this time. I turn side-on and grip the sword with both hands. I inch towards the middle of the cage, blood rushing in my ears.

The hellion lowers its head and charges.

The floor vibrates as it thunders towards me. I raise the tip of the sword.

Oh, fuck. I roll my wrists and sweep the blade back and forth through the air. It's halfway across the cage.

What did I do in the dream? It's almost on me. Come on, come on . . . *think* . . . And then I remember.

I throw myself sideways, at the same time slashing at its heel. The blade finds flesh, and it takes all my strength to hang on to the hilt as the hellion stumbles, roaring in pain. My knees hit the hard floor. I pull back on the blade. It comes free, along with a gush of thick, dark fluid. The hellion hits the chain wire, and spins around, snarling. It tests its injured foot, throws its head back and roars again.

I'm on my feet. If I can hamstring the other leg, force the hellion to its knees, maybe I can take its head off. I flinch. Who am I kidding? *Take its head off?* I can't even set a mousetrap at the bungalow.

It snarls. And charges again.

I will myself to stand still. Wait . . . Wait . . . *Now.* I dive to the left. As soon as my feet leave the ground, a searing pain rips along my side. I bury the blade in its thigh before I meet the sawdust. This time, though, I can't hold on to it.

The ground shakes when the hellion falls. I try to sit up, but my body hurts like the hellion's claws are still in me. I probe below my ribs. Everything there is wet and torn.

Unarmed, my arse.

We both lie there, me whimpering and it snarling. And then the hellion wrenches the blade out of its leg and hurls it across the cage. It may as well be in the next room for all the chance I have of getting to it. My limbs are lead and every old injury hurts. My leg, my ribs, even the wound on the back of my neck. All throbbing in time with my heart.

'Get the sword!' Daisy yells at me. Her voice is strange, distant.

The hellion is sitting up now, slumped against the side of the cage, watching me. Dark blood pools in the sawdust around its legs. Its slashed pants are soaked. I haven't done nearly enough damage to stop this thing.

I press both hands against my injured side. I'll pass out in a minute if I don't stop the bleeding. I put my weight on one elbow. My breath catches. I grunt and roll onto my hands and knees. For a second, I rest my head on the sawdust, catching my breath. Then I force myself to sit up, wait till the fluorescent lights wheeling above the cage settle and still. I grab the hem of my sweater, brace myself, and pull it over my head. A few ragged, nauseated breaths later, I'm still upright. I tie the fabric as tightly as I can bear. Daniel is just beyond the wire, his expression unreadable.

A snarl pulls my attention back to the hellion. It's using the chain wire to haul itself up. I have to find a way to stand. If I stay here, it's going to tear me to pieces. I'm going to die.

I swallow blood and fear, stagger to my knees. The hellion is almost upright.

The sword is lying impotently in the sawdust by the

walkway. The hellion looks from me to the weapon and back. It pushes off the cage and lumbers towards me.

'RUN!' Daisy screams.

I take off.

My leg jars but I keep going. The floor shakes. Nearly there, *nearly there*. I hear panting, right behind me. I'm not going to make it.

I dive for the sword. Pain tears at my side—I've opened the wound wider—but I get my hands around the hilt, roll over, and bring up the blade. The hellion has already left the ground. Too late it sees the sword. It roars, and then lands on the blade. The steel pierces its leathery skin and slides in. It slams its hands into the sawdust either side of my head to stop its fall. I'm pinned, straining to stop the hilt driving into my chest. I twist the blade. The hellion roars, and the sound vibrates down my spine. Its face is so close I can see the veins in its skin and taste the fetid stench of its breath. Its eyes flare with pain as I twist the hilt again, but I'm fast losing feeling in my arms. If the hellion collapses, its weight is going to crush me.

I'm screwed.

My arms are pinned, the hellion's are free, and it's just worked that out. Holding its weight on one hand, it grabs a handful of my hair and reefs my head so my neck is bared. I scream, but the weight on my chest holds all sound. Where is everyone? Do they want me to die?

Razor-sharp teeth puncture the skin above my collarbone. White spots flare across my vision. I'm frozen, waiting for the hellion to rip flesh from me. But it's not tearing at me. It's . . . drinking.

The bars on the cage blur together.

My blood is pumping into its mouth. This is wrong. This is so *wrong.*

And, oh god, it hurts.

I close my eyes.

I'm not human. I'm *not human.* I'm the offspring of an angel. The pulling at my throat. The sound of it. My blood. Nothing from hell should *ever* be free to feed from me. What makes me Rephaite? My blood.

Is the hellion feeding on me for strength?

But it's *mine.*

Warm blood runs down my neck and soaks into my shirt. I can't feel the wound on my side now. My fingers are numb.

Focus.

I picture my heart, pumping Rephaite blood through my limbs. It has to be powerful. I'm meant to be immortal. I need it to pump harder.

Heat spreads across my chest. Adrenaline.

It courses through me.

I tighten my grip on the sword hilt, feel my fingers again, and imagine drawing all that energy into my shoulders.

I twist the blade. The hellion unclamps its teeth to snarl. I shove it as hard as I can, with everything I have.

It lands next to me on its back. I don't know who's more surprised: it or me. But I recover first. I spring to my feet and jerk the gore-soaked blade from its gut. The hellion convulses as it comes free.

I swing the sword hard and fast.

The blade slices through the hellion's neck—through flesh, muscle, tendon, and vertebrae. It's impossible. No way am I strong enough to do that. But the hellion's head is no longer attached to its body. Dark blood gushes onto the sawdust. A couple of fingers on the beast's left hand twitch, and its legs spasm. And then . . . nothing.

I drop the sword and turn away. My body burns. For the moment the adrenaline is stronger than the pain. I face my audience. Daniel is watching me, his expression still unreadable. Taya and Malachi have stepped back from the cage.

'Gabe?'

I look across to find Daisy, her eyes hopeful. The pain is rushing back now, filling me.

'Sorry,' I say to her. 'Just me.'

And then her face and the wire diamonds of the cage are spinning. I pass out before I hit the sawdust.

DROWNING

I fade in and out. I'm rolled onto a stretcher and carried from the cage. I catch pieces of conversation.

'Just let me shift with her.' Daisy's voice, tight and angry.

'No.' Definitely Daniel.

'But she'll take weeks to heal from these injuries. I don't understand why you're being so—'

'Daisy, go to your quarters and stay there until you're summoned.'

If Daisy argues with him, I miss it, because I pass out again.

When I next come to, I smell antiseptic. My body feels cased in cement and the skin on my neck stings like a bastard. Even through closed eyes I can tell the room is brightly lit.

'I'll guard her.'

'No, Taya, you go.' Daniel's voice is close. 'Tell the Council I'll be there shortly.'

'But there are no cameras in here. What if—'

'Gabriella isn't going anywhere.'

'But Daisy—'

'Won't disobey an order.'

Any further exchange is silent. The air beside me stirs. Taya is gone. The only sound now is the faint buzzing of a fluorescent light. Daniel must be alone.

Fingers gently move hair out of my eyes. Daniel sighs. 'I wish I knew what you did.'

I don't have the strength to move my head away.

'I just . . . I can't take the risk.' He strokes my cheek with the back of his finger, slowly, softly. 'If you really betrayed us, and I show you mercy . . .' Another sigh, and then the touch is gone. A door opens and closes. As usual, Daniel leaves the old-fashioned way. Maybe shifting creases his shirts.

I pry open my eyes. I'm in a treatment room. Stark white. Clinical. I touch my side, gingerly, to find that the sweater's gone and the wound is bandaged. There's a dressing taped over the bite on my neck. The pricks haven't even given me fresh clothing. I'm sticky with my own congealing blood. And I stink of hellion.

There's a door across the room. A plain door, no locks

or keypads. No voices or footsteps on the other side. If I can get over there . . . Can I even sit up? I grit my teeth, try to lift myself on my elbow. A thousand knives twist below my ribs. I whimper and sink back to the bed, wait for the waves of nausea to pass. My eyes close and I let sleep drag me back into the comfort of oblivion.

I wake with goosebumps. My aching skin tingles. I'm not alone.

'I'm so sorry, child.'

The voice behind me is rich, masculine. Nathaniel.

I stay on my side, my pulse quickening. The air in the room is cooler now.

'This was not the path meant for you.'

I swallow loudly, letting him know I'm awake.

'Be still, Gabriella. Submit to me.' His voice is like balm. 'Let me see if anything has changed.'

I should fight him. I should make this hard. But the memory comes, unbidden.

Jude and I have raced each other up a steep hill and we're standing, hands on knees, catching our breath.

We're in a vineyard in Monterosso al Mare. Every new place in Italy becomes my favorite, but the Cinque Terra may last. I love the fishing villages on the cliffs and the vineyards defying gravity above them. We've spent the last few days walking between villages, sometimes on the cliff tracks, sometimes through the hills.

We collapse in the grass between the vines. The sea is before us. Usually, it's flat, but today it's choppy, and the sky is pensive. Endless clouds dull the multicolored buildings in the village below. Jude stares out at the horizon.

'Don't hurt yourself,' I say.

He gives me a playful shove.

'What are you thinking about?'

'Nothing much.'

We've been backpacking for over a year now, and lately he's been drifting in and out of melancholy.

'Are you thinking about home?' It's not something we talk about, but here, today, on the side of this hill, it seems okay to.

'Not really.'

'You miss the guys, though, don't you?'

Jude makes friends everywhere we go, but he had a tight group of mates back home. It was tough for him to leave them behind.

He turns to me. 'Sometimes.' His brown eyes, so much like mine, study me closely. 'Have you got any regrets?'

I answer without hesitation. 'No.'

'But you left friends behind too.'

'But now we're *living*.'

A gentle breeze lifts the dark hair from his face. 'You know I'll always look out for you, right?'

He's never said anything like that before. I've always known how protective he is of me, but it's another one of those things we don't talk about.

'Likewise,' I say. 'Even when you don't want me to.'

He grins. 'Cock blocking doesn't count.'

'Ugh!' I shove him. 'You know I hate that phrase. It's revolting.'

'And it still gets a reaction every time.' His smile fades. 'Seriously, though. I know I let you down sometimes, but never doubt you mean more to me than anything else in the world.'

I nod, not speaking. The feeling in my chest is so big I can't name it.

'I'd die for you, you know.' His voice is quiet. I barely catch the words.

'Jude . . .' I stop. Swallow. 'What's going on?'

'I just want to make sure you know that.'

I do something I almost never do: I put my arm around him and lean against his shoulder. He is so strong, so permanent. I can't imagine life without him. I don't want to imagine it.

'I've always known that,' I say.

'Whatever happens, don't forget it.'

'I won't.'

'Promise?'

'I promise.'

It ends abruptly. A tear slides over my nose.

'Impossible. Gabriella, did you meet Semyaza? Did he do this?'

I don't answer because I'm too busy clinging to this memory of my brother. I know it's not real but I don't care. The weight of what I feel for Jude, these fabricated memories, they must be based on something.

'It cannot be Semyaza.' Nathaniel is talking to himself. 'Too much power involved.'

I want to see him. I know it's going to hurt, but I roll onto my back. A low moan escapes my lips, and in the moment it takes to absorb the agony, Nathaniel disappears. There's a flash of blue-white light and then there's just me, and the empty room.

I close my eyes as the air in the room stirs again.

'Leave me alone,' I whisper.

'Ah, fuck, Gabe.'

I know that voice, but I open my eyes, just to be sure.

Rafa.

He stands there, taking in the wreckage. A muscle twitches in his jaw. 'I thought she was exaggerating. What the hell were they thinking?' His voice cracks. 'Hey, hey . . . Don't cry.'

Through my tears, I see he's not alone.

Jason is hiding under sunglasses and a bucket hat. His

tanned face is pale and his blond curls nowhere to be seen.

'Is Mags here?'

I shake my head. I know his presence is significant, but I can't grasp why.

'You done with this place?' Rafa asks.

'I'm sorry I didn't—'

'Just tell me I can take you out of here.'

I answer by trying to sit up. His arms come around me, taking my weight. 'Slow down or you'll do more damage.'

'I don't care,' I whisper.

Rafa lifts me off the bed and Jason steps in to take the weight of my legs.

'Just like we talked about,' Rafa says to him. 'Ready?'

The door swings open and Daniel walks through. He stops in his tracks. 'You . . .'

Rafa tenses. I feel him hesitate. Oh, please, no.

But before Daniel can gather himself, the room disappears, and the only noise is rushing wind.

WAKE ME WHEN THIS
IS OVER

I feel it this time, the sense of being stretched and compressed. I bury my face in Rafa's chest and smell the sandalwood on him.

It's all over in seconds, and then Rafa is laying me on a couch, in a dark room that smells of old dust and smoke. We're back on Patmos. The fire's already lit, and blankets are piled up on the floor beside the couch. Rafa covers me and puts a pillow under my head.

'This is why I didn't want you to go there,' he says, straightening the end of the blanket. The effort of healing my wounds hasn't burned off his anger.

I sink deeper into the pillow. 'Can we argue about this later?'

He doesn't answer, but the line of his mouth softens.

'Where's Jason?' I ask.

'Over here.'

He's leaning against the wall, bathed in firelight. The hat is gone and his sun-bleached curls are loose around his shoulders.

'Get some sleep,' Rafa says to him. 'You look like you're about to pass out.'

Jason crosses the room and crouches so his face is level with mine. 'Are you okay?'

My body still aches, but it's nothing compared to a minute ago. 'I'll live. You?'

'I'll be better when we get Mags back. Was she there, at the Sanctuary?'

'No. I don't think she ever was.'

He glances at my bandaged neck. 'Would they do this to her?'

'Why would they?' She's not one of them. She's not me.

'Who knows what they're capable of.' Jason runs a hand over his face. He's tired and agitated, and won't look at Rafa.

I glance from one to the other, and the pieces fall together. 'You told him.'

'It seemed wrong not to, under the circumstances.'

Rafa sits on the arm at the other end of the couch.

'What happened?' I ask him.

'Goldilocks found Daisy's number in my phone and rang her while I was out of the room.'

'There was no answer,' Jason says. 'I didn't leave a message, but she rang back anyway.'

'She didn't know it was my number,' Rafa says, 'but when she got me, she told me what happened in the cage. She didn't *exactly* suggest I come get you, but she let me know where you were, and when you'd be unguarded.' He unlaces his boots. 'I didn't know if she was lying about the hellion, but there's no way I could heal you on my own if you'd been drained. I was about to call for backup when your buddy here dropped his little bombshell.'

Jason stands up. 'I need to sleep. Have you got another pillow?'

'Try the second door on the right,' Rafa says. 'The bed's made if you want it. And Goldilocks?' Jason pauses at the door. 'I'm not finished with you.'

Jason disappears into the shadows. Somewhere in the dark, a door opens and closes and then bedsprings squeak.

'I only found out tonight,' I say. 'He told me about two minutes before Daniel turned up.'

I instantly regret mentioning Daniel's visit. I don't want to have *that* conversation. 'Daisy got in the cage with me,' I say. 'Did she tell you that?'

Rafa kicks his boots off. 'Daisy said you fought that hell-turd on your own.' He doesn't look at me.

'I did.' There's a small, belated spark of pride. 'Actually, Daisy got in the cage but Daniel ordered her out. She stood her ground for all of a minute, and then left me in there on my own.'

Rafa shrugs. 'That's what happens at the Sanctuary. Everyone obeys. You used to be like that.'

'Bullshit.'

He shakes his head. 'You have no idea how ironic this is.'

'But she just caved in. I don't get it. What's the worst thing that could have happened?'

'If you disobey one of the Five? You get cut off.'

'Cut off from what?'

'From Nathaniel. From your family. Not everyone's in a hurry to get kicked out of home.'

'You left. So did Jude.'

'Yeah, but we all paid a price.'

As usual, everything he tells me about the Rephaim brings more questions, but I'm too tired to ask them.

Rafa yawns. 'Got room for me under there?'

I roll onto my side so there's space for him at the back of the couch. He gets under the blanket and eases me back to where I was so he can look at me. There are dark circles under his eyes.

'You're a mess,' I say.

He laughs. 'You can talk. You stink like a hell-turd.'

'I know. It's revolting.'

'We'll get you cleaned up in the morning.' He touches the dressing on my neck. 'The Five must be desperate, to let a hellion feed on you. I can't believe Pretty Boy stood there and watched.' He runs his thumb along my collarbone, almost absently. 'And you cut its head off?'

I flinch at the memory. 'Yeah.'

'So you still know how to swing a sword.'

'I just remembered what I dreamed.'

'It takes a lot of strength to cut through a neck that thick.'

I have no idea how to describe what happened when that thing drank from me. 'I had a moment.'

'A moment?'

'A burst of strength. It lasted long enough to save me. Then it went.'

'You haven't felt it since?'

'If I had, Daniel wouldn't still be in possession of his balls.'

'Now *that* I'd like to see.' He gives me a long look that I can't quite read, and then settles down behind me.

'Thanks for coming for me,' I say, quietly.

He tightens the blankets around us. 'I should have done a better job of convincing you not to go there.'

'Is that an apology?'

His lips move against my ear. 'As close to one as you're getting at this hour. Now, stop talking and go to sleep.'

'Hiding out here isn't getting Mags back.'

'Neither is shifting when you're shattered.'

I'm alone on the couch. Rafa and Jason are talking quietly in the room. It's still dark and the fire is down to embers.

'I'm fine,' Jason says.

'You won't be when we shift with Gabe again. Hellion bites are hard work. What is it with you and Maggie? You've known her for, what, five minutes?'

'No shorter than you've known Gaby, and don't tell me you weren't torn up two hours ago.'

'That's different. We've got a century or so of history.'

'Not anymore, you don't.'

Rafa ignores him. 'You're one of us, so I get why Maggie is so into you—humans can't help themselves. But what's up with you? I mean, she's hot, but so are a thousand other women.'

'How many women do you know who could see and hear what she has in the last few days and be cool with it?'

'Is that it? You've been waiting to find that special girl who can cope with the fact you're not human?'

A sigh. 'Yeah, well, we're not all walking cocks.'

'God, Nathaniel's going to love you.'

'That'll be hard, given he's never going to have the chance. I have no intention of joining him—or anyone else.'

'Is that right?' The fire spits and hisses. 'You're going to crawl back to that rock you've been hiding under all these years?'

'We're not talking about any of this until Mags is safe.'

It takes some effort, but I sit up. 'What time is it at home?'

A green light radiates from Jason's wrist as he checks his watch. 'About ten in the morning.'

My shirt is stiff with dried blood. I stand up. 'So, I can't be forced to shift, even if I'm sleeping? You said if you were unconscious . . .'

'I didn't mean asleep. If someone grabbed you, you'd wake up. Unconscious as in knocked out.'

'Then there's no reason we can't go home.'

'Apart from Taya turning up and kicking the shit out of you again.'

I touch the bandage on my neck. The wound is tender, but it doesn't feel like the skin is broken anymore. 'I'm hoping you might stop that from happening.'

'Oh, you *want* my help now?'

I wish I could see his face. I can't read his mood from his voice alone. 'Yes.'

'Please tell me this isn't about your job at the library.'

'I don't work Tuesdays.' I run my fingers through my hair and don't get far. 'But we're not going to find out where Mags is unless we go back to Pan Beach. Daniel has to negotiate now, and to do that he has to be able to find me. And Mags is due to start work in an hour.'

Rafa moves closer. 'So?'

'Her mum will come looking for her if she doesn't show. Mags never bails on a shift, not since her dad died, and there's no way I'm telling Bryce her only child is missing. I'll cover her shift.'

'Will that work?' It's Jason who asks the question.

'It'll have to.'

JUST ASKING

'Your place or Rafa's?' Jason asks.

The fire is completely out and we're ready to go.

'Mine,' I say.

'Which room?'

'It doesn't matter.' Rafa takes me by the elbow. 'I'll look after that. You worry about healing her. I can manage both, but you don't have the skill.'

As he has every time, Rafa pulls me to him and, almost out of habit, I slide my arms around him. We shift to the bathroom at the bungalow, to the smell of cherry blossom shampoo and Maggie's Chanel No. 5. The room settles around us, and the sound of the ocean replaces the wind.

Home.

Jason looks at me, and slips away.

I lean against Rafa while the feeling comes back into my body.

'Gabe,' he says, and swallows. 'It's okay. Please don't cry.'

'I'm not.' I brush my face against his T-shirt.

He rubs my back, sighs. 'You never used to do this, you know.'

'What, I didn't cry?'

'Not in front of me.'

I'm still hanging on to him. His hand settles in the small of my back.

'You never cared this much about people either, apart from Jude.'

I look up at him. 'What do you mean?'

'It usually took you a decade or so before you decided you liked someone, let alone got close to them.'

'Yeah, well, I'm not that person. I'm not Gabe.'

He raises his eyebrows at me.

'Okay, so maybe I don't make friends as easily as some people. But with Mags, it's different. We just clicked. It's like I've known her forever.' I rub my eyes, weary again. 'How was the shift? Easier that time?'

He nods. 'You feel just about mended. But you've ruined my shirt.'

I look down and see the cotton is flecked with dried blood. 'You're the one who insists on keeping me close.'

His lips twitch and he stands back to get a better look

at me. All traces of playfulness disappear. 'Let me see.' He reaches for the hem of my ruined shirt, but waits for me to nod before lifting it. He examines the dressing and then sits on the edge of the bath. I hold up the tattered fabric as he carefully removes the bandages from my side.

'That doesn't look too bad.' He runs his fingertips lightly over the wound. The claw marks have healed closed, and black sutures stick out of the puckered flesh. Rafa takes tweezers and small scissors from a chipped mug on the sink. 'This'll feel weird, but it won't hurt.'

'I've had stitches before.'

He glances up.

'From the accident.'

'Oh, yeah.' He works quickly and soon has them out. 'Sixteen.' He holds out his palm to show me. 'Let me see your neck.'

Again he peels off the bandages with studied care. How many times has he done this over the years? How many times has he done it for me?

He makes a small noise of disapproval. 'This is going to scar pretty bad.'

I touch the spot above my collarbone where the hellion fed from me. I can't make sense of what I feel, so I go to the mirror. It looks like I've been bitten by a shark—a small shark with two rows of sharp teeth. The yellow bruise has two arcs of punctures, all of them closed over but still red and angry.

'I guess I should be glad it didn't bite through.' I join the dots with my fingertip, completing the circle.

Rafa comes up behind me. 'It'll fade. You'll just have to grow your hair to cover it.'

Like my hair doesn't already have a big enough job covering that other monstrosity on my neck.

'I need a shower.'

'You really do.' Rafa gives me a half-smile in the mirror. 'You want a hand?'

'I'll be fine.'

He doesn't move. Is he going to touch me again?

'I hear you've been with every Rephaite in a skirt.'

Crap. Where did that come from?

'Who told you that?' His smile shifts into something less amused. 'Daniel. Who else? The prick.'

'Is he a liar?'

Rafa leans against the pale wall. 'I haven't been with *everyone*.'

'What about Taya?'

'Hell, no. I'm no monk, but I have standards.'

I wonder what else Daniel was wrong about. 'What about me?'

Rafa's teasing smile doesn't quite reach his eyes. 'You had standards too.'

I turn away so he can't see the heat climbing my cheeks. 'I won't be long. See you in the kitchen.'

I wait until I hear the door shut but still turn to check he's on the other side of it. Then I peel off my clothes and throw them in the corner for burning at the first opportunity. The water pressure is as weak as ever, but I'm okay with gentleness. I rest my head against the tiles and let its warmth wash over me. Slowly, I come back into my body again. Here, in this old bathroom, I'm more myself than at any point at the Sanctuary. The water circling down the drain finally runs clear instead of reddish-brown.

I put on a white T-shirt and black skirt. For once, the long scar across my knee seems inconsequential. I have to tie my hair back—Bryce won't have it any other way if I'm serving food—so I grab a lime-green silk scarf from Maggie's collection to cover the bite marks.

The guys are in the kitchen. Rafa is reading the paper and Jason is rummaging in the fridge, pulling out our collection of almost empty jam jars. The smell of fresh toast makes my stomach rumble.

'You could have told me they keep hellions at the Sanctuary,' I say to Rafa, but not with any accusation. I put the scarf aside to help Jason butter toast.

'I didn't know they did. It makes no sense. They're useless as prisoners because they've got the vocabulary of a warthog and the brain function of a slug, and only an idiot would use them for training.'

'Why's that?'

'It's not worth the risk. If they get a taste of one of us and manage to escape, they can track us—' His face changes. 'Son of a bitch.'

'What?'

Rafa shakes his head slowly. 'That's why they let it in the cage. The Five didn't want the hell-turd to kill you, just to get a taste of you. They must have been planning to let you go, and then get it to track you, although I don't know how they thought they were going to control it.'

'But why? They have to know this is the only place I'd come.'

'They think you're going to lead them to the Fallen. But now you've gone and cut the head off their bloodhound.' He gives a short laugh and flicks through the paper to the sports section. 'God, I wish I could've seen Pretty Boy's face.'

I try to absorb this theory. I can't.

'Why do they still want Mags?' Jason asks.

'They never wanted her,' Rafa says. 'She's just a way to Gabe.'

'Then they don't need her anymore.'

'They need her now more than ever. Your little girl-friend is the only bargaining chip they've got.'

He's right, but I don't want to think about what that means.

'Aside from Daniel, who else is part of the Five?' I pick up the scarf and loop it around my neck. It won't sit the way I want it to.

'As far as I know, it's still Zeb, Calista, Uriel, and Magda. Daniel and Calista used to be soldiers, and Uriel still goes on a few missions. Zeb's a priest and Magda's a professor of psychology or philosophy or some such shit. Nathaniel likes to have all three Rephaite disciplines covered.' Rafa counts them off on his fingers. 'Military, religious, academic.'

I fiddle with the scarf again. Accessories are not my thing. Maggie would have me sorted in no time. Even Daniel would have more of an idea about how to wear a scarf than I do.

I toss it on the table.

Rafa raises his eyebrows. 'I bet Goldilocks can fix that for you.'

Jason snatches it up. 'It's not rocket science.' He loops the scarf over my head, twists it inside itself, and turns it so it sits over the bite.

'Let me guess—a semester at fashion school?'

'I've spent a lot of time around women.'

I want to ask which women in particular, but I know he's not going to talk about his past in front of Rafa.

'Did Daniel get a good look at you at the Sanctuary?' I ask.

'It doesn't matter anymore. Not now I know they can't force me to shift.'

Rafa flicks the paper shut. 'How the hell have you managed to keep a head on your shoulders all these years?'

'By keeping a low profile.'

'More like dodging responsibility.'

I sigh. 'Are you two going to bicker the whole time I'm gone?'

'What are you talking about? I'm coming with you,' Rafa says.

'Me too,' Jason says. 'I want to be there if Taya shows up.'

I fiddle with the silk, trying to figure out how Jason looped it.

'And what's the plan when she—or anyone else— arrives?'

Jason and I both look to Rafa. He's picking at a spot of dried blood on his shirt.

'I'll think of something.'

I'd kind of been hoping for more than that.

COLORS BLEED TOGETHER

Jason parks the car on the beach side of the esplanade and they watch me cross the road to the Green Bean.

The outdoor tables are packed with sunburnt tourists, sipping lattes and watching the surf roll in. The only locals I recognize are the Williamsons, already done with their morning walk. They look up from their croissants and wave. I check my hair and my story, and go inside. Maggie's mum spots me from behind the counter.

'Gaby, where is Margaret Jane?'

I force a sheepish grin. 'Hi, Mrs. Bailey. Sorry for the late notice. I've pinched a shift today if that's okay.'

She gives me her best I-wasn't-born-yesterday look. Bryce Bailey is blonde, like Maggie, with the same fine bone structure and huge brown eyes. Her fingernails are polished and her designer white linen dress is pristine. Bryce wears her grief like an old scar: it's always there, but you have to look for it.

'I know Thomas had his party last night, but Margaret is well aware she has responsibilities.'

I straighten the sugar packets on the counter. A chair scrapes behind me. 'To be honest, I'm a bit short on cash this week, so she's really doing me a favor.'

'You're not working in the library today?'

I shake my head.

She purses her lips. 'Clear the outside tables. Then you can help Connie. Have you been using that espresso machine I gave you?'

'Every day.' With Maggie hanging over my shoulder, giving me instructions.

I bury the memory before it gives me away. The only thing I can do to help Maggie right now is cover this shift.

It helps that everything in here is so familiar: the smell of coffee and croissants, shelves crammed with organic tea and scented candles, and the world music Bryce plays all day.

I dump my bag, tie on an apron, and start clearing dirty crockery from the recycled timber tables outside. By my third trip, a couple of tables have emptied, and I stop to wipe them down. The sun is deliciously warm. I close my eyes and turn my face to it. It's hard to believe it was only a few hours ago I thought I was never going to feel that comfort on my skin again.

The beach is busy, but not as packed as it was in the height of summer. A few puddles on the road are the only signs of last night's storm. I breathe in deeply, tasting the salt on the back of my tongue.

In the life I remember, Jude and I explored the world. The other me, the real me, must be as well traveled, probably more so—I can't quite get my head around how old I am. But Pan Beach is one of the few places I *know* I've been, the closest thing I have to a home. How could I not come back? How could I not come back when I know the trouble I've brought here?

A loud wolf whistle snaps me back to the moment. It's the hoodie brigade outside the greasy takeout a few doors down. They live on the far side of town in fibro houses with car wrecks in the front yards. One day they'll join their tattooed older brothers at the Imperial Hotel, on the next street over. In the meantime, the esplanade is their domain.

One of the boys grabs himself and licks his lips in my direction. I shake my head and discreetly give him a middle-finger salute—which they all cheer—and go back inside with my dirty plates. Bryce points me to the library service window, where Gaz is waiting.

'Hey, Gabzilla, you're on the wrong side.' Gaz gestures

to my neck. 'You get a little action up at the falls last night?'

'Jealous?' I check the scarf is still covering the bite and wonder if anyone's been talking about Maggie's dramatic departure from the party. 'Caramel latte?' I ask Gaz.

'Puhlease . . .' He taps his black fingernails on the ledge. 'Flat white. Double shot. Two sugars. Fat milk.'

I write it down and stick it in front of Connie, the barista. She gives a curt nod and pours a long line of cappuccinos, each with a perfect heart in the foam.

'Table seven,' she barks at me.

I take two steps and stop. Simon is at the counter, placing an order with Bryce.

So much has happened since Rafa threw him aside last night. But all he's going to see is a girl who left a party with another guy.

He gets his change, turns, and stops. I stand there, holding the tray of coffee. 'Hey,' I say. I shouldn't have kissed him last night. It was selfish and stupid, and it's created yet another mess I have to clean up.

'Hey.' He mumbles it more to my shoes than me. He can't even look at me. 'What are you doing here?'

'Oh . . . Mags wanted a day off.'

'Is she all right?' His gaze lifts for a second and mine shifts.

'Just a bit seedy.'

Simon gestures to the tray. 'Someone probably wants those.'

I nod. Not only am I a dud date, I'm also a dud waitress. I take the order to table seven, and get back inside in time to put the lid on Gaz's coffee and hand it to him. He points at my neck.

'Did *Simon* do that to you?' he asks, way too loud.

I shoot him a foul look. 'Get back to work before Jane kicks your arse.'

'Ooooh, touchy.' And then he's gone, but his taunt lingers like cheap perfume. On the other side of the counter, Simon is staring accusingly at my neck.

'What's under there?' he gestures to Maggie's scarf. Any embarrassment he felt about last night seems to have taken a backseat to something stronger.

'Nothing,' I say, willing Connie to hurry up with his coffee so he can go before Rafa or Jason arrive. But she's got another order ready, so I pretend he's not there and head outside.

Most people wait for takeout coffee on one of the Balinese day beds, but Simon stands right in my path when I go back inside. I can't get behind the counter without walking by him. Given the black look on his face, there's no chance he's going to step aside.

'I have to work,' I say. 'Can we talk later?'

He blocks me. 'You made me look like an idiot last

night.' To his credit, his voice is low so only I can hear. 'Was I just bait to make that dickhead jealous?'

I glance around, but no one's paying attention to us. 'There's stuff going on that I can't begin to explain,' I say, 'but I promise you I did not intend last night to end the way it did.' *That's* the understatement of the year. 'I'm really sorry for the way I left the party, but I can't talk about it here.'

I go to move past and, before I can stop him, those quick hands lift the scarf from my neck.

'Hey!' I pull away from him, but not fast enough.

'What the fuck . . . ?' Simon's hand drops to his side.

I put the scarf back in place, and look into his eyes. *Let it go.*

'Did he do that?'

'Of course not.' I push past him, and he follows, taking my arm.

'What did that?' Simon says in my ear.

I spin around. 'Back off.'

He takes a step back, almost involuntarily.

'Just let me do my job.'

His coffee is ready. I jam the lid on and slide it towards him.

'Gaby . . .'

A flash of blond hair catches my eye. It's Jason. He glances our way, gives me a casual nod, and then joins the short queue at the counter. Simon follows my gaze.

'What's he doing here without Mags?'

'They're not joined at the hip.'

Connie thumps the milk jug on the counter to settle the froth, getting my attention long enough to glare at me.

'Didn't he stay at your place last night?' Simon presses.

'So? Maybe he feels like coffee and he's letting Mags sleep in.'

I grab the next order and head out again, catching Jason as he leaves the counter.

'Simon's seen the mark on my neck,' I say, walking with him.

'What did you tell him?'

'Nothing. But he's not going to let it go.'

'Leave it with me.'

Jason leads Simon to a table against the wall. They pull up chairs under a watercolor of a yacht on wild seas.

I've delivered skinny mocha-lattes and chocolate éclairs to a table of flushed women in cycling gear, when I spot Rafa walking towards the cafe. He's scanning both sides of the street, his hands in his pockets.

I catch his eye and shake my head to warn him off, but of course he just keeps coming. I meet him halfway.

'Simon's inside.'

'So?'

'He saw my neck.'

'How the hell did that happen?'

'He grabbed this.' I lift the scarf to demonstrate.

Rafa stares at me. 'You managed to decapitate a hellion, but you can't stop a barman from touching a *scarf*?'

'Slightly different circumstances,' I say, stung. 'Jason's in there trying to handle the situation.'

'Well, then, we can all rest easy. No chance that'll go pear-shaped.'

'What's your problem with Jason?'

'You mean aside from the fact he's been swanning around for decades without a care in the world? How about the way he lied to both of us about who he was? Or the way he's still lying?'

'What are you talking about?'

'How does he know so much about us if he's never mixed with Rephaim? He's too cagey about his past. I don't trust him.'

I squint against the sun. 'Well, I do.'

'And your judgment has worked out so well this far.'

I'm tempted to smack him across the side of the head with my empty tray. 'Yeah, well, I trust you too. Is that bad judgment?'

His lack of a comeback is immensely satisfying.

Rafa follows me back to the café and sits outside, at a table against the window. It's tucked behind a pot plant, but he'll be able to see inside.

One of the other waitresses, Nicky, grins at me when I pass her.

'Who's the hottie?'

'Trouble,' I say.

She winks. 'Half your luck.'

I take two more orders out before Jason's is ready.

'You could have just told me,' Simon says when I reach the table.

'Told you what?'

'The truth, Gaby,' Jason says, holding my gaze with enough intensity that I let him finish. 'About Jude finding out something he shouldn't have before he died. About the people looking for you, and how they took Maggie to get at you. How you said you'd go with them if they let Maggie go.'

'And what they did to you.' Simon's eyes flick to my neck. His anger has diffused a little. His anxiety hasn't.

'We just let that girl take her,' he says to Jason. 'You lied to us, and we all let it happen.'

I bang Jason's cappuccino down on the table; the coffee spills into the saucer. 'If he didn't, everyone at the party might have had a night like me.'

Simon studies his cup, turns it around a few times, takes the lid off. 'How does he fit into all this?'

He means Rafa.

'Like I told you, he's a mate of my brother's.' I wipe my

hands on my apron. 'A lot of people thought I died with Jude. When Rafa found out I was alive, he came looking for me. So did the people who took Maggie.'

'Do you know what it was Jude found out?'

'Not a clue.'

'Order up!' Connie shouts at me from behind the machine.

'I'll be back.'

I take an espresso outside to Rafa and fill him in. He completely misses the cleverness of Jason's half-lies.

'This is bullshit. Now the barman's going to want to play hero, and I'm telling you right now, I'm not baby-sitting your little boyfriend.'

'I didn't ask you to,' I say, wishing for once he would act his age. 'I have no intention of involving him. And he's not my boyfriend.'

Rafa begins to stand. 'I'll sort this out.'

I put a hand on his shoulder. 'Just give Jason a chance.'

Rafa lets me push him back into his seat. His green eyes are unnaturally bright in the sunlight.

'He's got till I finish this coffee.'

I make my way inside.

'You have to tell the cops,' Simon says to me.

'No,' I say. 'And neither can you.'

'But—'

'You'll get her killed.'

I'm about to push the point when a throat clears behind me.

'Excuse me, do you offer table service here?'

I turn, annoyed at the interruption—and come face to face with Malachi.

CROSS MY HEART

'You bastard.' Jason stands up so quickly his chair tips and smacks on the timber floor. All heads in the Green Bean turn to us.

Malachi is still dressed in dark jeans, although he's remembered Pan Beach's climate and worn a T-shirt. He's a few paces away, out of swinging range.

'Calm down, kids, I've just come for the espresso. I hear it's good here.' He folds his arms and flexes his biceps. Like I need a reminder of how strong he is.

Simon's eyes dart from me to Malachi and back again. Jason's chest is rising and falling quickly.

'What do you want?' I risk looking outside. Rafa's table is empty.

'Honestly?' Malachi sighs. 'I want for none of this to have

happened. For life to go back to the way it was. I'd like to not have to worry about you smashing me in the *coglioni*.'

Jason stands his chair back up. He slides it under the table, giving a quick, reassuring smile to three middle-aged women behind us. Slowly, people turn back to their coffees and food. There's a flash of white linen as Bryce leaves the counter and goes back to the kitchen.

'You mean you want it to be like it was before, when Jude and I weren't talking to each other?' I ask.

Malachi shakes his head and looks at me like I should understand. 'Before that, when we were all still one big happy family.'

'Come on, Malachi, we were never that.'

He turns to find Rafa a couple of meters away from him. It's taken all my concentration to not look at Rafa. He's come from the toilet; he must have shifted there as soon he saw what was going on.

Malachi steps back, raises his hands, says under the cover of the music, 'Rafael, let's not make a scene in this nice *public* place.'

'Like Taya last night?'

'That wasn't exactly how it was meant to go down. She may have gone in a little early.'

'And what about Gabe in the cage? Was that meant to happen?'

'I just follow orders, you know how it goes.'

Rafa is relaxed, conversational. No matter how strong Malachi is, Rafa is the better fighter, and both men clearly know it.

'It's a wonder Gabe could find your balls at all. Sounds like you still haven't grown a pair.'

Malachi's lips draw together. 'And I suppose you're here out of the goodness of your heart?'

'Nathaniel's the only one kidnapping her friends.'

Malachi's eyes light up. 'Ah, Maggie . . . *Amazing* body. That sweet arse and those beautiful—'

The table screeches as Jason pushes it aside and flies at him. I should have been ready for it, but I was too busy thinking about going for him myself.

Jason might not be trained, but he's still Rephaite. Malachi goes to swat him away, only to find Jason's hands clamped around his throat, driving him into the wall.

'Hey, HEY.' Bryce is back at the counter again. 'Take it outside.'

Malachi doesn't fight back. He's probably under orders not to.

'Where is she?' Jason says. 'I *will* kill you if you hurt her.'

'Take it outside or I'm calling the cops,' Bryce says. A few customers have stood up, unsure.

Rafa holds up a palm to Bryce. 'No need, I've got this.'

Simon grips the top of his chair, his fingers threatening to push through the flimsy wicker.

'Calm down,' I mouth at him.

'Come on, boys,' Rafa says, like this was a bit of fun gone too far. He grabs Malachi and Jason by the neck and squeezes until he gets Jason's attention. 'Not here,' he says, and breaks them apart.

Simon and I follow as Rafa walks them through the cafe, and outside, down the street. He shoves Malachi and Jason into a laneway and follows them a few meters in, still keeping them separated.

I'm close behind, but Simon hangs back, keeping one eye on the street and the other on us.

'What did you come here to tell Gabe?' Rafa asks.

Malachi readjusts his shirt and stretches his neck. Jason tries to push past, but Rafa blocks him.

'Think,' Rafa says, and gestures to Simon at the end of the laneway. 'You want to explain it if Malachi disappears in front of him?'

I duck under Rafa's arm while he's distracted, and he does nothing to stop me.

'What do you want?' I ask Malachi.

'You made an offer to Daniel.' He waits for me to nod that I understand. 'He's accepted your terms.'

My heart stutters.

'That was before the cage.'

'Wait,' Rafa says. 'What offer?'

I ignore him, my eyes locked on Malachi.

'How else do you think the lovely Maggie is coming home?' he says.

'No more torture,' I say. As if I'll have any say in it once I'm back at the Sanctuary. 'And I want Mags back here before tomorrow. I'm not going anywhere until I see she's okay.' My voice shakes.

Rafa is beside me. '*What* offer?'

'I'll explain later.' I'm not game to look at him.

Malachi nods. 'I'll be back before sunset to give you a place and time for the exchange. Be home.' He looks past me. Simon must be out of sight because he shifts, right there, in the sunlight.

Rafa grabs me by the arm, rougher than he's ever been with me. 'What have you done?'

THAT BUZZ INSIDE YOUR BRAIN

After work—after telling Simon that Malachi was negotiating to bring Maggie home, after a dozen lies and apologies and reassurances to Maggie's mum—I find solace in the late afternoon sun.

I'm a few steps from the cafe when Bryce calls to me. I stop and wait for her. 'Before you go,' she says. 'You know I'm not blaming you for what happened earlier.'

I nod. I just want to go home.

'Gaby.' She puts her arms around me. There are orange blossoms in her perfume. 'I know how much your friendship means to Margaret. She was a little lost after her dad died. And then you came along . . .' She squeezes me. 'I'm so glad she's got you looking out for her.'

I don't trust myself to speak, so I stand there and take the hug.

'But you need to make sure you keep company with the right people.' She pulls back to look at me. 'Okay?'

I nod.

'Now, go and tell that girl of mine I expect her to work her own shift tomorrow.'

She gives me one last squeeze. I walk away.

The sky is vivid blue, the breeze so gentle it barely disturbs the leaves in the poincianas. How can my life be such a mess when the weather is so perfect?

There's no sign of Rafa or Jason, so I head for home through the park. I think I'm safe from Malachi—at least for the moment.

Lorikeets shriek in the wattles, waiting for dusk. Somewhere a dog barks. It's all perfectly normal. Except nothing is normal to me anymore, not even this park. Its landmarks have all changed. There's the place I first saw Malachi. Here's where Taya knocked me down. Which of these trees did she throw me against? I'd be able to find my blood if—

'Tell me about this deal you've struck with Daniel.'

I flinch. Rafa is leaning against a tree at the edge of the path. The startled birds take off from the branches above him.

'Don't you walk anywhere?'

'Not if I can help it.'

I keep moving, forcing him to follow.

'We could get there quicker if we—'

'No.' I don't look at him. 'I'd like to enjoy this last small slice of normality.'

Rafa grabs my elbow. Not roughly, but it brings me to a standstill. 'What have you agreed to?'

'I offered myself as a trade for Mags. I told Daniel I'd stay at the Sanctuary. Let them train me.'

'Please tell me you're not naive enough to think anything has changed.'

'No.'

'Then why?'

'I'm not planning on staying. I'll go with them when I know Mags is safe, and then I'll shift straight back.'

He raises his eyebrows. 'How are you going to do that?'

'I was hoping you'd teach me.'

He stares at me for a good five seconds. 'You're joking, right?'

'Can't you do it?'

'Of course I can. With time. What you're asking, it's like . . . It's like a ten-year-old asking to fly an F1-11.'

'I'm like a ten-year-old now?'

'Shit, Gabe.' He runs his hands through his hair. 'Okay, so maybe it's not quite as bad as that, but it's not something I can teach you in an hour.'

Without shifting, I have no plan. The cage flashes into my mind, the diamond-shaped wire, the blood-soaked sawdust.

'There's a hundred different things that can go wrong when you shift. For a start, the first few times you end up in places you don't expect. You think you're crossing the room and you end up in the middle of a herd of goats in Afghanistan.'

'Then why haven't you started showing me already? My voice rises. 'You've never offered to teach me a thing.'

His voice flattens. 'How was I to know you'd go all weak-kneed at the sight of Pretty Boy? If you'd listened to me—'

'Listened to you about what?' The anger comes easily. 'You've kept me blundering around in the dark, and don't act like you haven't been enjoying yourself—'

'I'm not the one who put you in a cage with a hellion.'

'But you've been having fun at my expense.'

His eyes darken. 'Yeah, it was a blast going back to the Sanctuary.'

'That's not what I—'

'It doesn't matter that I told Nathaniel I'd never set foot there again. It's not like it cost me my pride or anything. And yeah, it was so much *fun* to find you torn up like that.'

'Rafa . . .' I rub my eyes. 'That came out wrong.'

He stares past me.

'I don't want to go to the Sanctuary,' I say quietly. 'So what do I do?'

I watch the birds resettle in the cluster of trees across the path, flashes of red and green between the branches.

'We need to know Nathaniel's next move,' Rafa says finally. 'Let's get back to your place and wait for Malachi.'

He doesn't look at me, and I think he's going to shift and leave me to walk home alone. But then he moves off on foot.

I fall into step with him. There's a strained silence until we're well clear of the park, only the noise of the birds and the wind. Finally, I can't stand it any longer. 'How do you think Jason learned to shift?'

We're crossing a small footbridge. The creek beneath is racing after last night's storm, rubbish caught at its edges.

'No idea. But I've had enough of his ducking and weaving.'

'Have you ever considered you might get more out of him if you're actually pleasant, instead of bitching at him all the time?'

He looks at me. 'You've got a short memory.'

'Are you trying to be a smartarse?'

He almost smiles. 'You know what I mean.'

'Not really.'

'It's just, you're so much like *you* sometimes. I keep forgetting you're not, you know, *you*.'

I can't tell if it's a compliment or not, but at least his mood is improving.

'Yeah, well, I'm starting to wish I was.'

'I don't know.' Rafa puts his hands in his pockets. 'Maybe we shouldn't be in such a hurry.'

Rafa goes through the gate first and scans the yard. Jason is probably inside, but I'm not ready to face a kitchen without Maggie again yet, so I sit on the top step. It's the best spot to enjoy the view. Two freighters dot the horizon, so far out they look stationary. I lean back on my hands and watch a yacht motoring into the marina.

'You and Jude have never been happy unless you're near the sea,' Rafa says, sitting down beside me. 'He had this theory that your mother came from a family of fishermen.'

I frown. 'Didn't we know?'

'Nathaniel said he found you somewhere around the Mediterranean. He never gave specifics.'

'What about you?'

'French Alps, apparently.'

'You don't believe him?'

'It's like everything Nathaniel says, there's no way to know for sure. But it doesn't matter where we come from, does it? Just who.'

A smattering of small clouds drifts across the sun and mutes the glare off the water.

'You could've gone anywhere,' Rafa says. 'Why here?'

'I don't know. I wanted to get away from everything that reminded me of Jude.' I untie the scarf around my neck. It's hot and making me itch. I rub the bite mark. 'And I still ended up at the beach.'

'What else do you remember?'

'Nothing. God, how many times do I have to say it?'

'Since the accident. What do you remember about being in hospital?'

'Oh.'

How do I dredge up those memories without the weight that comes with them?

'Where were you?' he presses.

'Melbourne.'

'Are you sure? How do you know that was real?'

'The pain.' My fingers go to the old scar under my hair. 'Everything before is hazy, even the crash. But the hospital, and everything since—it's clear.'

Every day of rehab. Every night, screaming for Jude.

'Did anyone visit you?'

'No.'

'You told Jason a nurse broke the news about the funeral. It was a woman?'

I nod. 'I can't remember her face.'

'There must be something.'

'I remember her accent—Irish or Scottish, I think.'

A vague memory surfaces. The ward at night. The nurse

talking to me, telling me I'm doing well, that I'll be all right. The dark room smelling of hospital and grief, her uniform faintly of menthol cigarettes.

'That's a start,' Rafa says. 'We'll find her and see if she remembers who delivered the message. I'd like to know how you turned up at that hospital. Someone really went out of their way to hide you.'

'Shifted, you mean?'

'Yep.'

'Then how come I was so busted up?'

'Maybe you started off worse.'

I was in agony that first month in hospital. I find it hard to believe it could have been worse.

'So, that's the plan,' Rafa says. 'We go to Melbourne.'

'Maggie first.' I hug my knees. 'Can I see those photos again?'

He gives me a blank look.

'Of Jude. My phone's in Italy, remember? I didn't get the chance to collect it when I checked out of the Sanctuary.'

'Right.' He hands his phone over.

I close my eyes, feeling the weight of it in my palm. And then I look at my brother for the first time with open eyes.

It should be different, knowing this Jude is more real than the one in my memories, but it isn't. I linger on the last image, where Jude is staring out at the water.

'Is that Patmos?'

'Yeah,' Rafa says. 'We went back around the time you two started talking again. I've looked at that shot a thousand times.' He leans closer. 'He's thinking about you there.'

I touch the screen. 'Not me. Gabe.'

'Same thing.'

'Is it?'

Rafa's eyes roam my face: my hair, my eyes, my lips. He doesn't answer.

A throat clears behind us.

'Ah, Goldilocks,' Rafa says, standing up. 'Got the coffee machine on in there?'

PATIENCE IS OVERRATED

Jason has found the ingredients for a date and walnut cake, and it's cooling on the rack in the kitchen. It smells amazing. I don't know if he overheard our conversation, and I don't ask. I make coffee and cut the cake.

'What do you think is going to happen this afternoon?' I ask Rafa.

He's seated at the bench, too busy buttering his slice to answer.

'You know how much cholesterol is in that?' Jason stares at the soaked cake.

Rafa slaps another layer on, just to annoy him. 'So? Unless it makes my head fall off, it's not going to kill me.'

'But—' Jason glances at me and lets it drop.

'Malachi will turn up at some point,' Rafa says through

a mouthful of cake, 'and tell you the place and time for the big *exchange*. It'll all be very dramatic.'

'And then what?'

He wipes his bottom lip with his thumb. It distracts me for a second. 'Depends on the where and when.'

'That's not very helpful.'

'Best I can do at this point.' He absently wipes his buttery fingers on the side of his hoodie. 'Look, Jude was the planner. I'm the doer. And when the time comes, I'll do what needs doing.'

I nod, but I hate not having a plan.

Rafa gestures to my neck. 'Give me a look at that.'

My hand comes up to cover the scar. My skin is still warm, and the scar is lumpy. I go over to him and offer my neck. He runs his fingertips over the wound.

'Still hurt?'

'A bit.'

'You want to shift again?'

I shake my head.

His fingers linger on my skin. 'You should put some-thing on it so it doesn't get too dry. I bet Goldilocks has a nice range of moisturizers in a man bag somewhere.'

'Give it a rest,' I say, leaning in to him.

Jason's knife clatters to the table. His face is flushed. 'Is all this because I managed to avoid your little cult?'

'It's because you've avoided responsibility.'

'To do what? The bidding of a religious zealot?'

'To sort through the endless shit of our existence, like the rest of us.'

Jason glares at him. 'Tell me you wouldn't have done exactly what I did if you'd had the chance?'

Rafa's eyes narrow. 'And what exactly did you do?'

'I chose to stay on my own.'

'How did you know there was any other way—and don't give me your bullshit about having no contact with the Rephaim.'

'I—'

There are three loud thuds on the front door.

Jason stands up. 'Malachi.'

'Just fucking spit it out,' Rafa says.

'It's not a simple answer and we don't have time.'

'I'll go,' I say.

The hallway is full of shadows. Rafa materializes a few steps ahead of me, and doesn't look back until he reaches the front door. He signals for me to open it. I pause for a heartbeat, and turn the handle. As usual, the rain has made the timber swell. The door sticks, then jerks open.

There's no one there.

Rafa makes a noise—something between a grunt and a laugh. He points to a blank envelope nailed to the door.

'I told you,' he says. 'Dramatic.'

I take it to the kitchen, opening it as I go. Three words

written neatly on a piece of notebook paper.

Il ritiro. All'alba.

I turn it over, but there's nothing on the back. I shove it at Rafa. 'It's obviously meant for you.'

He skims the page. 'Retreat, at dawn.'

'What does that mean? We have to leave in the morning?'

'No,' Jason says, reading over Rafa's shoulder. 'It's a noun, not a verb. It's *the* retreat.'

'Does that mean something to either of you?' I ask.

'It means Daniel wants me to know you've made the deal,' Rafa says. 'Why else write it in Italian? He knew you'd have to show it to me.'

'But what's the point if we don't know what he's talking about?' I push my hair off my face. 'What if we can't work it out?'

I need fresh air. I go to the window on the other side of the bench. Like the front door, it's stiff from the recent rain. I push against the pane. It gives without warning, and I lose my balance. I'm half in, half out. Far enough out to see someone standing in the place where Rafa and I arrived not two days ago.

'What the—'

Simon's palms come up. 'I know I shouldn't be here, but listen for a second before you go off your brain. I think I know where Mags is.'

BITTERSWEET AFTERTASTE

We wait in silence while Simon comes inside. Did we say anything we shouldn't have in the last few minutes? Rafa listened in on our conversations from that spot before. Hopefully Simon's hearing isn't as good as his.

The front door opens, and steps echo in the hallway. I tie the scarf back around my neck.

'I thought you had to work,' I say as soon as Simon appears.

'And I thought I told you to stay out of this,' Rafa says.

Simon stops near the fridge, wary. 'I've known Mags longer than the three of you put together, so don't tell me this is none of my business.'

'Have you told anyone?' Rafa's eyes are dark, dangerous.

'Not yet.'

Rafa smiles. It's not friendly. There's every chance he's about to launch across the kitchen and take Simon somewhere far, far away. 'Are you involved in this? Did you put this on the door?' He holds up the note.

Simon balks. 'Of course I didn't! God, dude, you're paranoid.'

'You just happened to be stalking Gabe at the same time someone leaves us a note?'

'I was trying to find out what you're doing to get Mags back. *Excuse* me for not trusting you. I was about to come around the front—'

'Do you know what the Retreat means?' Jason interrupts.

Simon nods. 'There's a place way up in the hinterland, a really exclusive, high-end resort. It's a bunch of fancy cabins scattered through the rainforest. Each one's completely isolated from the others. All your food is brought in before you get there and no one comes near you unless you call for something.'

'Why would they stay so close?' I ask.

Jason answers. 'Why not? I mean, was there really any reason to take Maggie to'—he catches himself—'further away?'

No, there wasn't. Not when I took the bait so easily. They only needed me to believe she was at the Sanctuary. She didn't have to actually be there.

Rafa stares out the window at the orange sky. A muscle in his jaw twitches. 'Pricks.'

Jason hands Simon a piece of cake. 'How many cabins are up there?'

'Six maybe—eight tops.'

'How far away?'

'A good hour by car. It's a pretty windy road up the range.'

'Why do you know it?'

'Rick supplied the wine for a bunch of surgeons and their wives last year. We had to stock each of the cabins before they got there.'

Jason opens drawers until he finds a piece of paper and a pencil. He slaps them on the table. 'Can you draw a map to show where they are? And the general layout of the cabins?'

'It'll be rough, but, yeah, I think so.'

I move away from the table, my back to Simon, and catch Rafa's eye. 'Can we just *go* there?' I flick my palm in front of my chest in a lame attempt to demonstrate shifting.

'Too risky.' Rafa checks Simon is still busy drawing. 'With maps and a good description of the terrain we could get close, but I can't risk arriving on Daniel's lap by mistake. We need to take them by surprise.'

Something flutters in my chest. It could be hope. 'You have a plan?'

'Kind of.' Rafa beckons me into the hallway, where we can still keep an eye on the table. 'They're not just going to hand Maggie over—not until they've got you back at the Sanctuary. So we'll have to create a distraction. They don't know about Goldilocks. He might be able to get her out before they work out what's going on.'

Jason looks up from the table at his nickname.

'But Mags doesn't know about him either.'

'So? He can still grab her and get the hell out of there.'

He means shift. 'That's going to be a nasty shock.'

'She'll get over it.'

I glance at Jason and he nods. Then the rest of Rafa's plan registers. I draw him further down the hallway. 'So, you and me, we're going to take on whoever's there?'

'Wouldn't that be something.' Rafa half-smiles. 'Back in the day, we could have taken down half the Sanctuary on our own. But given you're not quite yourself, we're going to need some back-up.'

I swallow. Please don't let it be Mya. I've never met her, but I already know I don't want her help. 'Who?'

'A couple of people who are very handy in a scrap.'

'Are they Outcasts too?'

Too late, I wonder if the term is offensive, but it rolls right over Rafa.

'Two of the best.'

He takes out his phone, and I close the kitchen door.

Rafa watches me as he dials and waits for an answer. He turns away to speak. 'It's me . . . Hang on, I'll tell you in a sec. Look . . .' He sighs. The voice on the other end is loud, but I can't make out the words. 'For fuck's sake, Zak, I'm fine. And I'm not apologizing . . .' His shoulders tighten. 'I don't give a shit what she thinks.'

My pulse picks up.

He glances at me. 'Yeah. I'm looking at her right now . . . Trust me, it's weirder here.' He looks away again. 'I'll explain when I see you . . . No. It's complicated.'

Whoever he's talking to knows me. I'm never going to get used to that.

'I'll come to you and Ez . . . No, just me. She won't leave.' He raises his eyebrows at me.

I shake my head. I'm curious, but not enough to risk getting stuck somewhere on the other side of the Equator.

'Hey, Zak. Don't tell anyone you've heard from me.'

Rafa ends the call and walks down the hallway. I follow. He stops before the front door and puts his hands on my shoulders. 'Stay. Here.'

'I'm not a dog.'

'I mean it. I don't care who else turns up and what they tell you. You wait for me to get back. Jason's got my number, so call me if you get twitchy.'

'Where are you going?'

'Mexico.'

Mexico in the blink of an eye. He'll be so far away. 'But you'll be back in a few minutes, right?'

A hint of a smile. 'You can always come if you can't live without me.'

'Oh, please.' I don't like the idea of him not being here. But he doesn't need to know that. And I'm not sure how I feel about meeting more Rephaim—especially Outcasts. 'You really trust them?'

'With my life. So did Jude.' He looks at me. His eyes are a paler shade of green now. 'So did you at one point.'

'Not fair. I can't argue with you about stuff I don't remember.'

He grins. 'I know.' And then he disappears.

I stand there alone, feeling the void he's left behind. Then I go back to the kitchen.

'Where's he gone?' Jason asks.

'To get help.'

He closes his eyes. 'Wonderful.'

Simon tosses the pencil onto the table. 'So I've got time to duck home and grab Rick's jeep?'

'You're not coming with us,' I say.

'Do you know someone else familiar with the hinterland?'

'We'll make do.'

'No, you won't. Not if they have eyes on the road coming in. But if we go the back way—'

'You didn't mention a back way.'

'I just told Jason about it.'

Jason nods. 'It sounds like a bit of goat track. We'd need a four-wheel drive, and then we'd have to hike the rest of the way, but it could be our best option.'

'How are we going to see what we're doing once we're on foot? It'll be dark by the time we get up there.'

'I've got a good torch and it's almost a full moon,' Simon says. 'If it's a clear night, it won't be too bad.' He digs his bike keys out of his pocket. 'Let me help.'

I push a stray hair out of my face. 'This isn't a game, Simon. You could get killed—'

'So could you.'

'Rafa and the people he's bringing know how to handle this kind of thing. You don't.'

'I'm just offering to get you up there. Your mates can knock themselves out being heroes.' He stands up. 'And if it goes bad, I'll call the cops.'

I know Rafa's not going to like the plan, but I'm tired of arguing. I step out of the way and he narrows his eyes. 'I'm going up the mountain whether you wait for me or not.'

'We'll wait. Go.'

Simon looks to Jason for confirmation—apparently his word means more than mine—and leaves. As the screen door slams I slide into a chair and take off the scarf again.

'He'll be all right if he stays out of the way,' Jason says.

'And maybe the Rephaim won't be quite so quick to shift with him there.'

'Speaking of which . . . how did you learn how to do that?'

It's a simple question, but he watches me for a long moment. 'Why?'

'Because I need to learn and I want to know how you worked it out on your own.'

He picks at the corner of the table. 'Can't this wait? Rafa will back soon.'

'No . . . it can't.'

'You have to promise to stay calm and hear me out.'

'Jason, we haven't got all night! How did you work it out?'

He finally looks me in the eye. 'I didn't. Someone taught me.'

'Who?'

He swallows. 'You and Jude.'

Wait. 'What?'

'You and Jude taught me how to shift.'

I open my mouth. Close it. Try again. 'When?'

'Just before the turn of last century.'

I stare at him. 'Are you fucking kidding?'

'Let me explain—'

'You'd met me before?'

Jason nods, slowly. Wary. 'Our mothers were cousins.'

WE'RE NOT ALL THE SAME

'Just hear me out,' Jason says.

I sit back and gesture for him to go on.

'I had no idea there was anyone else like me until I met you and Jude.' He talks quickly. 'It wasn't long after I'd turned eighteen. I was mending nets on our jetty and you appeared in the shallows. I nearly fell in the water. You didn't even look around; you just started laughing and roughhousing each other. And then you saw me. I asked who you were and you said you were descended from angels and I shouldn't look upon you.'

'We told you what we were?'

'You were trying to scare me. It was your first shift outside the Sanctuary and you didn't mean to end up in the same place together. You wanted to enjoy the moment on your own. But then I blabbed my story—or at least the story my mother told me. Jude thought I was making it up to impress you. It was your idea to check the mark on my neck.' He pauses. 'I took you to meet Mamma. She lost her mind when she saw you. She threw herself at your feet, begging for forgiveness. She called you Ariela.'

I'm holding my breath. I let it out.

'I'd never heard of her—or you—before then. Ariela was her cousin. Your mother.'

I draw my knees up under my chin. Breathe.

'My mother wasn't alone when the Fallen came. Ariela was with her when *two* angels found them on the beach. Ariela came from another village, and when her father found out she was pregnant, he threw her out. Our village had already shunned Mamma for being pregnant without a husband, so Nonno, my grandfather, took in Ariela. Nobody knew he had two pregnant girls under his roof. He was a good man, but he never believed their story about angels. Until Nathaniel turned up.'

He breaks the moment and goes to the sink, pours a glass of water.

'We were about a month old then. Nonno said Nathaniel was dressed as a monk, asking at churches about unwed mothers needing absolution—'

I hold up a hand and he looks at me. 'Ariela didn't die giving birth?'

'No.' He drops his gaze. 'Nathaniel came looking for a mother and child. He found Ariela and her twins. By the time Nonno got to the room, Nathaniel had the babies and Ariela was dead. As soon as Nonno walked in, he vanished. Nathaniel never knew there was another woman and child.'

'Where were you?'

'My mother had taken me with her to pick lemons. She didn't know who Nathaniel was or why he came. Not until the two of you turned up eighteen years later and told us about the Sanctuary.'

Water drips from the tap into the sink. I watch the water gathering into droplets, then falling. Falling.

Nathaniel killed our mother. He *stole* us.

'The first time you shifted, you went back to where your life started. It was probably the same for everyone, it's just the others wouldn't have known it.'

His words finally register. 'Where were we born?'

'Monterosso al Mare.'

Italy.

I close my eyes. The memory of the day we ran up the hill in the vineyard, the day Jude told me he'd always look out for me. Whoever altered my memory wanted me to feel connected to the place where I was born.

'When we shift, I think we're drawn to locations where there are others like us. That's why you arrived near the jetty where I was, rather than in our house.'

I hug my shins. 'And we went back to Nathaniel? Even knowing he'd . . .' I can't say it.

'The Sanctuary was your home,' Jason says softly. 'And I'm not sure you really believed Mamma the first time. But you never told him about us.'

'How do you know?'

'Because he never came for me.' Jason gives me a small smile. 'You both kept coming back over the next few months. You were always supposed to be doing something else—you never told me what, and I never asked. I was just happy you came. It took a while, but you taught me to shift.'

I rest my chin on my knee. Jude and I were defying the Sanctuary a century ago. Why did we stay so long if we knew what Nathaniel had done? And why didn't I leave with Jude when he finally walked away all those years later?

Jason moves his glass on the table, smudging the ring of condensation. He sighs. 'It didn't last long. Mamma panicked. She trusted you and Jude, but she was terrified of Nathaniel. There was every chance he would find us one day if you kept coming, and she was afraid of what would happen to us when he did. So we got on a ship and went to New York.'

'Did we know where you went?'

'We were still a century or so away from mobile phones.'

'So, what? You haven't seen me since then?'

He straightens. 'Not exactly.'

'Don't fuck around, Jason—' I'm reaching to grab the front of his shirt when there's a gentle gust of air behind me and my stomach twists.

We're not alone anymore.

SKELETONS

Rafa is flanked by a huge guy and a caramel-skinned woman. They glance at each other, drop their duffel bags, and shift into fighter stances. Both are in loose black pants and T-shirts.

My brain is slow to change gears, still preoccupied with Jason. I get to my feet. I have no idea what history I have with these two. A heads up from Rafa would have been nice.

'This is Zak and Ez.' Rafa glances at Jason and me then back at Jason. He raises his eyebrows at me in a silent question, which I ignore. 'And that,' he says, gesturing to Jason, 'is the most elusive bastard on the planet.'

Zak and Ez give Jason a quick once-over but are more interested in me for the moment. Zak is at least half a head taller than Rafa, with shoulders almost as wide as a hellion's and skin so dark it shines. Unnerving pale blue eyes look out at me through a shock of curly black hair.

Ez is tall and slim with brown eyes and full lips. Silken hair hangs over one shoulder in a thick plait. She hasn't got a trace of makeup on, and still her skin is flawless—except for the four thick scars that start halfway down her left cheek and run the length of her neck to her collarbone.

'Hey,' I say, trying not to stare.

She tilts her head. 'You don't know us?' Her voice is beautiful.

I look from one to the other. 'No.'

'But you remember Jude?'

'Yeah.' I pause. 'Well, a version of him, anyway.'

Ez's eyes fall to the new scar on my neck. 'Can I see?'

I glance at Rafa, and he nods. She comes over, smelling like oranges and flowers. She keeps checking my face, like I might change my mind and take a swing at her.

'Daniel let a hellion drink from you?'

I nod.

She lets her breath out. 'What does that mean?'

'That he's a prick?' I say.

'You know you were once in love with him?'

'I think it's safe to say the love's gone.'

She turns to Rafa. 'Did you do this?'

'No, Ez, I really didn't.' He's still watching me closely,

a slight frown creasing his forehead. When Ez looks away, he mouths, 'What's going on?' I shake my head and that telltale muscle twitches in his jaw.

'Well, whoever did,' Ez says to Rafa, 'you're in their debt. And you.' She holds out her hand to Jason. 'Welcome to the circus, ah . . . ?'

'Jason.' He shakes her hand once, and lets go.

She offers him a slow smile. She is *beautiful*, scars or no scars.

'Was that always your name?'

'No.'

'Jason means healer, doesn't it? In the Greek—or is it Hebrew?'

'Both. How did you know Simon wasn't still here?'

Her smile falters. 'Who?'

'The barman,' Rafa says. 'We called in to my place on the way here, saw him ride past.'

Zak picks up the duffel bags and throws them on the table. They clatter. He unzips them and pulls out swords and knives, laying them side by side. 'You know how to use any of these?' he asks Jason. His voice is deep and gruff.

'No,' Jason says.

'We're not really using swords on each other, are we?' Ez asks Rafa.

He shrugs. 'Depends what they bring to the party. We're not going in unarmed.'

Zak grabs a curved sword like the one I used at the Sanctuary, only this one's in a leather scabbard. He makes sure I'm paying attention, and then tosses it to me. I catch it by the hilt. I slip the blade out and test its weight, again surprised by its familiarity.

'That was Jude's training katana,' Zak says.

The black leather straps around the hilt are scuffed, but the blade gleams so that I can see my face in it. I can't imagine my brother using it to slice someone open. *I* can't imagine using it against a person.

'Who do you fight with these?'

'Hellions, demons . . . the humans who worship them.' Rafa's not looking at me when he speaks. He knows something happened while he was gone. He rummages around in the bag and pulls out a hunting knife.

'And hellions are different to demons?'

'Your dreams were short on detail.' He slips the knife out of its sheath and checks one side then the other. 'Hellions are the attack dogs and demons are their masters.'

'Demons used to be angels, so they can take human form, like angels can,' Ez says. 'Hellions always look like hellions.'

I remember something from when I was in the cage.

'Who's Zarael?'

'Where'd you hear that name?' Rafa asks.

'The Sanctuary. Daisy mentioned him.'

'Zarael was hell's gatekeeper until the Fallen escaped. Then he was torn apart by his demon brothers, put back together and banished to the fringes of hell, along with his inner circle and pack of hell-turds. The only way they can get back in is if they deliver Semyaza and the two hundred in chains.' He glances down at my bare legs. 'You need to change.'

'Hang on, I'm not finished—'

'Do you want a crash course on demonology, or do you want to get your friend back?' Rafa repacks the weapons.

'Don't start acting like an arsehole again now you've got an audience.'

'Did you or did you not ask for my help?'

'I didn't realize it was a choice between saving Mags and understanding what's going on. Maybe if I'd known a little more, I would have made sure Maggie wasn't in danger in the first place.'

'Maybe she wouldn't have been in danger if you hadn't had your tongue down the barman's throat.'

'Oh, for fuck's sake, get over it.'

Ez smiles. 'This is just like the old days. I've actually missed this.'

Jason clears his throat. 'Speaking of Mags...' He gives me a meaningful look and then says to Rafa, 'Simon's gone to get maps and a four-wheel drive. He knows a back way—'

'I bet he does.'

I can't be bothered arguing with Rafa about Simon's involvement. I'm halfway across the kitchen when I remember I'm still holding the katana. I offer the hilt to Zak. He shakes his head, making his curls sway across his forehead.

'Keep it until we find yours.' Like we're talking about a tennis racquet.

'Could you look after it for now?' I hand it to him again, and this time he takes it.

In my room, I close the door and lean against it, waiting for the churning in my stomach to stop. Why didn't Jason tell me the whole story the night he dropped the bombshell? I can't stand that he knows more about my family history than I do. Or that Rafa was right about him hiding something. What else hasn't he told me?

There's a soft knock on my door.

'Gabe. Can I come in?' It's Ez.

'Sure.' I cross the room and sit on the bed, needing space for whatever this conversation is going to be.

Ez closes the door behind her, and spends a good minute checking out my room. I can't tell what she's thinking. I lean over and flick on the bedside lamp. Darkness isn't far away now.

Ez finishes her inventory of the room. 'You look . . . different.'

'How?' I'm still trying not to stare at her scar, although I'm sure mine's just as distracting.

'I don't know,' she says. 'Softer. It suits you.'

'I don't feel softer.'

She straightens the pile of books on my desk. 'Rafa says you've been here nearly a year? What's it like?'

'What's what like?'

'Living a normal life.'

'I wouldn't know. Nothing's felt normal since the accident.'

'But until we all showed up . . . You were happy, right?'

'You mean apart from the grief eating me from the inside out?'

She nods.

I think about it—about running on the beach, and Rick's, and laughing with Maggie. 'There have been moments. But only a year of my memory was actually real. The rest of my so-called normal life never happened.'

Ez sits down next to me. 'But what a gift.'

'I don't consider watching my brother lose his head in a car accident a gift.' I grab a pair of jeans from the pile on the desk and start to change. 'Whether it was real or not, I've had to get through every day since without him.' My voice cracks a little. 'And I know that in the *real* world we were apart for a decade, but that's not the life I remember. How could you call any of that a gift?'

She shifts on the bed so she can face me. 'It's a gift because you don't remember what it's like to be part of the Rephaim. To always have some demon or hell-spawn to fight. To be immortal but to never have a life of your own.'

'Isn't that why you left the Sanctuary—to get a life?' I pull on a navy T-shirt. Ironically, I don't own a lot of black. 'How's that working out?'

Ez gives me a tight smile. 'I'm living the dream.' She pauses then points to my hiking boots by the door. 'You'll want those.'

I sit on the floor to put them on.

'What did you mean about Rafa owing whoever changed my memories?'

'You really don't remember?'

I grit my teeth. 'No, and that's the last time I'm going to say it.'

She fiddles with her hair band, tightens it. 'You were meant to come with us when we left the Sanctuary, but at the last minute you changed your mind.'

'But I thought—didn't Rafa run off to be with Mya, and everyone else just followed?'

'Who told you that?'

'Daisy.'

Her laugh is short, cold. 'Of course she's still clinging to that lie. It's easier than the thought Jude left because he stopped believing Nathaniel's propaganda. Jude had a huge fight with Nathaniel. There had never been anything like it, and it forced everyone to take a side. You stood with us. Daisy didn't know what to do. She'd been in love with Jude for years—'

'What?' I interrupt. 'Are you sure?'

'Worst kept secret in the Sanctuary.'

'No, I mean the fight with Nathaniel. What was it over?'

Ez sits cross-legged on the bed, boots and all. 'Jude demanded that Nathaniel summon an archangel.'

'Why?'

'Nathaniel claims he's following orders from the Garrison—that they're the ones pulling our strings, guiding us towards some great destiny. Jude got tired of hearing it secondhand. He wanted to hear it from the source.'

'What happened?'

'Nathaniel refused. Said, "You don't summon the Host of Heaven," and Jude told him that if he didn't we were leaving.'

'But what did Jude think was going to happen if an archangel turned up?'

Ez leans back on her hands. 'If he didn't get struck down? He had a question or two. Like why we had to prove ourselves to a Garrison that's never shown any interest in us. Why we have to find the Fallen and hand them over.'

'What else would you do with them?'

'A few of us think that after a century and a half, we've earned the right to know our fathers.'

'And Nathaniel doesn't want that to happen?'

'He's scared we'll join forces with them. Betray him and the Garrison to keep our fathers out of hell. Of course, Mya has done nothing to dispel that myth.'

'Is that what she wants to happen?'

Ez gives the smallest of shrugs. 'I don't think Mya knows what she wants half the time.'

'I take it Nathaniel didn't summon an archangel.'

'No. And Jude left, along with everyone who supported him.'

I jam my feet into my boots. 'I supported him?'

'You did.'

'So why didn't I go?'

'To this day, none of us knows. Not even Jude knew. One minute you were all fired up, and the next you told us you were staying.'

I absorb that. 'So Jude was the reason everyone left. Not Mya?'

Ez sighs. 'Mya had quite an impact when Nathaniel brought her into the Sanctuary. She shook things up for sure, and there's no doubt she was a catalyst for what followed. But there was unrest in the ranks long before she came along. Mya has been blamed for the rift—and, believe me, she's quick to take the credit for it—but it wasn't that simple.'

'But Rafa and Mya were together when they left?' I wish this question wasn't so important.

'Yes, but you never cared whose bed he was in. You and he were never . . . you know. You were our best fighters. You bickered all the time, but you brought out the best in each other as warriors. Going into battle next to you turned him on more than any woman could.'

I give her a dubious look and she laughs. 'Maybe a slight exaggeration, but he really did love it.' Her smile fades. 'And you and Jude were inseparable. That's why it made no sense that you would take the opposite side to either one of them—let alone both. And then when they heard you'd become closer with Daniel . . .'

I finish tying my laces and drop my hands to the splintering floor. 'It's a mess, isn't it?'

She doesn't nod. She doesn't need to.

'It got worse after you and Jude disappeared last year. We thought he'd gone back to the Sanctuary to be with you. And when we heard you'd both died . . . Honestly, I thought Rafa was going to harm himself. He wouldn't talk to anyone for weeks. He drifted in and out of our operations, and then a few months ago he lost interest completely and stopped answering calls. We only knew he was still alive because he'd send Zak an occasional text.

When he told Zak about the possibility you'd resurfaced, there was no doubt he'd come looking for you—'

A fist bangs on the door. 'Gabe,' Rafa barks. 'Your boyfriend's here. Get your arse into gear.'

'Yeah.' I get to my feet. 'I'm the wind beneath his wings.'

WORLDS COLLIDE

Simon is standing in the kitchen near Jason, his eyes locked on Zak. He's put on a faded dark-green T-shirt and jeans. A map is open on the table, which Rafa is bent over.

Simon turns from Zak to take in Ez, and then me. I'm guessing no one's bothered with introductions.

'These are friends of Rafa's—Ez and Zak.'

He frowns. 'Sorry?'

Ez's face is turned away from Simon. He hasn't seen the scars yet. 'Esther and Zachariah,' she says.

'You don't look like an Esther.' There's a flush of red across his neck.

Rafa looks up from the map long enough to let me know he didn't miss Simon's reaction.

I ignore his smirk and double-check that my T-shirt is

still covering the bite mark, but it doesn't matter: Simon has spotted Ez's scars, and they've got his full attention.

'The barman has finally proven himself useful.' Rafa stabs a finger on the page. 'This track should get us close enough. As long as Pretty Boy doesn't have the same map, we've got a good chance of surprising those arse clowns.'

'Let's do it then.' I wish I was as confident as I sound.

Rafa turns to Simon. 'You got room for everyone in that rust bucket outside?'

'I just have to set up the back seat.'

'Now would be good.'

'I'll help him,' Zak says, and they leave together. He'll probably also have a quiet chat with Simon about staring at Ez's scars.

'How are we going to know which cabin they're in?' I shut the kitchen window.

'We'll know,' Rafa says.

'I thought you couldn't track each other.'

'We can't,' Ez answers for him. 'But if we get close to other Rephaim, we can usually sense them if they've shifted recently.'

'How?'

'It's hard to explain,' Ez says. 'A funny feeling in the chest, or the stomach.'

I remember that moment in the forest a few days ago, when I knew I wasn't alone. The day Rafa shadowed me through the trees. My body had known there was a threat before I saw him.

'We've got to get near enough to feel it,' Ez says, 'so we need at least a rough idea of where someone is.'

'How come Rafa didn't sense Jason was in town then, when he arrived?'

Ez frowns at Jason. 'Did you *drive* here?'

He gives a self-conscious shrug. 'Seemed less conspicuous.'

'How did Taya and Malachi find me?' I ask, but I already know the answer. 'Rafa was already here, shifting all over town.'

'Hey.' Rafa throws one of the bags of weapons over his shoulder. 'You're the one who put that story online, not me. I had no idea they'd followed me here. How was I to know the Sanctuary had nerds stalking me in cyberspace?'

Jason gets between us and grabs the other bag. 'Any chance we could discuss this later?'

'Good call,' Ez says, and she and Jason leave the kitchen side by side.

'For the record,' I say to Rafa, 'I wasn't blaming you for anything.'

'That's a refreshing change.' He doesn't look at me as we go down the hallway. 'You want to tell me what you and Goldilocks were talking about before I got back?'

'Not right now.'

I don't know what—if anything—I'll tell him, but I need time to get my head around it first. At the very least, to finish the conversation with Jason.

On the street, Simon and Zak are still fussing around in the back of the jeep. The sky is heavy purple now, and a few stars are already out over the water. I grab Rafa's T-shirt when he's a couple of steps down the stairs, and he turns to face me. We're at eye level. There's jasmine in the air, from the garden next door. A shout from the road.

'Look,' I whisper. 'Are you going to stay pissed off at me all night?'

His face is lit yellow by the light at the door. He doesn't say anything.

'I don't want to go back to the Sanctuary with Daniel.'

He still doesn't speak, and I can't read his expression.

'I mean, no question, the first priority is to get Mags, but the second is to keep me here, right?'

'That's the plan.'

I push a stray hair out of my face. 'But—'

'Gabe,' Rafa says, and I bite my lip. 'I *know*. I'll take care of it.' He leans closer. His T-shirt is twisted between my fingers. 'It's been a long time since you asked me for anything. I'm not going to fuck it up.'

'Any chance you could ease up on being an arsehole for a while as well?'

'That I can't promise.'

He makes no effort to move away.

'The bus is leaving, people!' Ez calls from the road.

'I'm scared,' I say.

I'm sure the old Gabe never said those words before going into battle, but I need Rafa to remember I'm not her.

'The last time you were scared, you separated a hell-turd from its head. I don't think fear's a bad thing for you at this point.'

'That's easy for you to say.' I let go of his shirt. His fingers slide around my elbow to keep me from moving past him.

'When it's happening,' he says, 'don't think. Just go with your instincts.'

I try to hang on to that thought. It's not only the fear of being dragged back to the Sanctuary that's scaring me.

What if I let everyone down?

THE HILLS ARE ALIVE . . .

It's a tight fit in the jeep. Simon is behind the wheel and Rafa is in the front with him. I'm between Ez and Jason, and Zak is wedged into the extra seat in the back, the weapons bags between his feet. They clattered when Rafa tossed them in and Simon pretended not to notice.

The guys weren't kidding when they called this a goat track. What started out as a wide gravel road soon turned to dirt, and then narrowed to two wheel ruts.

I grip the front seats, trying to keep my balance. The seatbelt is the only thing stopping me from launching into Rafa's or Simon's lap every time we come out of a dip and hit the next rise. Ez and Jason cling to the safety handles above their doors. Every now and then Zak grunts behind me.

'Any chance you could miss one or two of the potholes?' Rafa snaps.

Simon keeps his eyes on the road. 'Only if you want to take three hours getting there.'

We climb higher into the hinterland. Ez moves around to get comfortable. When she sees me looking she gives me a reassuring smile.

'Shit!' Rafa's voice is sharp. Simon slams on the brakes.

A wallaby is standing in the middle of the dirt track, eyes glassy in the bright headlights. Mesmerized, and measuring us. Simon sounds the horn, short and sharp. The wallaby blinks and hops away into the scrub. And we continue our rough, noisy ride up the mountain.

There's not much chance of conversation. It's actually a relief. Right now, all I'm thinking about is Maggie, and what I did in the cage—and how to do it again.

I'm looking out the window into the dark feathery forest, when Simon swears and jams on the brakes again.

Standing in the middle of the track are two guys in filthy shorts and blue tank tops. They've got shorn hair, long beards, and tattoos on just about every piece of exposed skin.

One is holding a shotgun and the other, a fence post.

'Who the fuck are they?' Rafa asks.

'The Butler boys. They must have a crop up here somewhere.'

I only know the Butlers by reputation—and the occasional glimpse of them hustling pool in the beer garden at the Imperial. They're the older brothers of at least two of the hoodie brigade I flipped off earlier today.

'Mick and Rusty,' Simon says. 'Mick's the big one with the gun.'

They both look pretty big to me.

'Let me handle this.' Simon cuts the engine. 'I went to school with Rusty.'

'Make it quick,' Rafa says.

Simon gets out, and the smell of eucalyptus and damp soil fills the jeep. He leaves the door open and walks as far as the bull bar.

'Zak, go,' Rafa says, his lips barely moving.

There's a click behind me and the faintest stirring of air as Zak shifts.

Mick shines a torch at Simon, making him shield his eyes. 'You lost, shit stain?' Mick's voice is flat and hard.

'Nah, mate,' Simon says. 'Just heading up the mountain.'

'Who ya got in there?' Mick moves the beam of light across the windshield. Rusty is beside him, eyes flicking from Simon to the jeep.

'Gaby and a few of her mates from down south.'

'Who the fuck's Gaby?'

'You know, the brunette who hangs out with Mags.'

Rusty peers at the windshield and finally speaks. 'The chick with the long legs and nice tits?'

'Yeah,' Simon says. 'We're taking a few of her mates up to the Retreat. Just doing a bit of bush-bashing on the way.'

'Rick know about that?' Rusty asks, grinning.

'No chance. He'd have my balls in a vice.'

Mick lifts the shotgun and I hold my breath. I'd been worried about Simon getting hurt by the Rephaim tonight—it hadn't crossed my mind he could get shot by a trigger-happy dope grower. But instead of leveling the barrel at Simon, Mick uses it to scratch the side of his rough head.

'You sure you haven't got pigs in there?' Mick rests the shotgun on his shoulder.

Simon shakes his head. 'Seriously, mate, I had no idea you had any *interests* up this far.'

He's playing this pretty cool. I guess working at Rick's has taught him a thing or two about dealing with testosterone-fueled meatheads.

'Get your mates out so I can see 'em,' Mick says.

For a few seconds, Simon doesn't move, and then he turns towards the jeep and signals for us to join him.

I unbuckle my seatbelt. 'Let's just do this so we can get going.'

Rafa grunts. 'If he points that rifle at me, it's going up his arse.'

We pile out of the jeep and take up positions either side of Simon. Rusty's gaze goes straight to me, but Mick scours all of us. The torchlight lingers on Ez.

He steps forward. 'What the fuck happened to your face?'

She levels her gaze at him. 'What the fuck happened to yours?'

It throws Mick for a second. He blinks, and then looks back to the rest of us. 'What's with all the black?'

'They're from the city,' Simon says.

'That'd be right.' Mick hawks up a wad of phlegm and spits it away from him with practiced efficiency. 'Cos we need more friggin' faggots dry-humping our chicks at your brother's pansy-arse bar. We can never have too many arseholes with money coming up here, can we, Rusty? Think we're all dense, don't they?' Mick taps the shotgun against his head.

Rusty shrugs. 'Simon's all right.' He points the fence-post at him. 'You wouldn't hang out with wankers, would you, mate?'

'Not if I could help it.'

Not quite a resounding endorsement.

'Present company excepted, of course,' I say, gesturing to the brothers. I know I should keep quiet, but we've got places to be.

Mick eyes me up and down. 'Your tits aren't that good,

love. You might wanna watch your mouth.'

He gets that I was being facetious. I'm impressed.

'So,' Mick says, shining the torch at Rafa. 'You wanna tell me what you cocksuckers are really doing in my back-yard?'

'Nope,' Rafa says. 'And if you're still blocking my path in another thirty seconds, I'm going to come over there and snap that fat neck of yours.'

Mick's eyes harden. 'What did you just say?'

'You heard me.'

Mick swings the gun off his shoulder and points the barrel at Rafa's head.

'Hey, mate, calm down.' Simon's hands come up in front of him.

'Fuck that,' Mick spits. 'Nobody talks to me like that.'

Zak materializes out of the darkness behind the brothers. Simon flinches, but Mick is so fixated on Rafa he doesn't notice. Rusty does though. He looks over his shoulder, just as Zak's hands flash up and crack the brothers' heads together.

They slump to the ground like wilting flowers.

'You took your time,' Rafa says to Zak. 'Another few seconds of listening to that and I would've had to rip his tongue out.'

Simon is looking from Zak to the Butler boys, jaw slack. 'How . . . ?'

Rafa ignores him. He and Zak drag the brothers off the track. They lean them against each other with their backs to a gum tree. Rafa pockets the shells out of the shotgun and leaves the empty weapon across Mick's thighs. Jason turns off the torch and sets it within Rusty's reach.

'You're just going to leave them here?' Simon says.

Rafa and Zak are already halfway to the car, so Ez goes over to him.

'That wasn't a hard hit. They won't be out long. We need to go before they come to because next time Zak won't be so gentle.'

Her hand is on his elbow, gently urging him forward.

'But . . .' Simon puts one foot in front of the other, his steps stilted. 'He just . . . appeared.'

Jason and I glance at each other.

'He's that good,' Ez says.

'But he just *appeared*.'

'Simon.' Ez lowers her voice. 'It's night. He's wearing dark clothes, and he's a beautiful black man. It all works to his advantage.'

Simon looks around at me. 'Didn't you see it?'

'No,' I lie. 'I was too busy watching what Mick was doing.'

We get Simon back in the driver's seat. He starts the car, but doesn't move. 'I know what I saw.'

'How about you just see the road?' Rafa says.

Simon stews for another second or two, then puts the car in gear.

'I know what I saw.'

IN THE NEIGHBORHOOD

Another half-hour of increasingly steep and winding track, and Simon swings the jeep into a clearing. He cuts the engine and the headlights. The forest slides back into darkness.

'Time to walk,' he says to nobody in particular.

Rafa opens the door. 'How far?'

'The Retreat's at the top of this ridge. We can't drive any further.'

I climb out and wait while the guys rummage about in the back of the jeep. The sky is low, smudged, the moon hidden behind clouds. My eyes adjust to the night quickly. The ridgeline looms over us, dark, crouching. The air is cooler up here, fresher than I expected.

'This friend of yours—she knows about us?' Ez asks me.

'She knows enough.'

'She's not going to have a meltdown if things get a little weird?'

'She'll be fine.'

I hope. I hope that shifting is the worst Maggie's experienced with Taya.

My pulse kicks up a notch.

The back door of the jeep slams and Simon's torch scans the group. The beam lingers on the duffel bags and then shifts beyond me, where a narrow track disappears into the trees. Pale light passes over palms, ferns, and the mottled trunks of old fig trees.

'Stay close to the torch.' Simon sets off. 'And watch where you put your feet.'

Jason falls into step with him. Zak repositions his duffel bag, and he and Ez follow.

I breathe in damp leaves and dark soil. This is it.

Rafa presses his palm on my lower back, moving me forward. 'Still good?' he asks.

'Yep,' I say, the lie almost convincing me. 'You feel the others yet?'

'We're not close enough.'

I pick my way over tree roots and on to a clear section of path. Rafa's hand falls away. 'What if Simon was wrong? What if this isn't the place?'

'Then Daniel needs to provide clearer directions.'

The track twists and turns, but I can see well enough without watching the beam up ahead.

'Maybe we should turn the torch off. We don't really need it.'

'You're right: we don't. Your barman does.'

'What? What makes you say—' I don't need to finish the sentence. I can make out each tree and shrub we're passing, even though the torch is well ahead of us. 'Oh.'

'Jude really was the smart one, wasn't he?' There's a smile in his voice.

'Shut up.'

The tension between my shoulders eases a little. If Rafa is being a smartarse, he can't be too worried about what's waiting for us at the end of the track.

It feels like we've been hiking uphill for about half an hour when Simon finally stops on a plateau. A gentle breeze rises from the valley. It cools the sheen of sweat on my neck. Pan Beach is far below, hugging the coastline, the town lights beautiful from here. Simon hunts around until he finds the beginning of a boardwalk, which disappears into the rain forest.

'The first cabin is a few hundred meters in,' Simon says, his voice low. 'There's a network of boardwalks through the forest. Stick to the map or you'll be wandering around for hours. I can come with you if you want—'

'Go back to town,' Rafa says.

'You planning on walking back?'

'Not your problem.'

'What about the Butlers?' I ask. I don't want Simon coming with us, but I also don't want him getting shot on the way down.

'Don't worry about me. You're the ones who need a getaway plan. Jason?'

Jason clears his throat. 'We'll be fine, seriously.'

'How? How are you going to be fine? You have to get Mags out without one of you getting hurt, and then you have to get off the mountain—'

'The less you know, the better,' Jason says.

'Don't give me that bullshit.'

'Trust me,' Jason says. 'It's not bullshit.'

Simon shifts his weight from one foot to the other. 'I want to see her when she's safe. I mean it.'

Rafa shrugs his duffel bag further onto his shoulder. 'Can we go now, or do you two need to hug first?'

'You're a dick, you know that? Here—' Simon thrusts a sheet of paper at him.

Ez laughs. 'He prides himself on it.'

Simon walks by me as he leaves. 'Be careful,' he says quietly. Then he heads along the trail without a backwards glance.

The sound of a zip pulls my attention to the board-walk. One of the duffel bags is open and Zak is handing out knives. Ez straps one to each of her upper arms. Rafa opens the other bag and passes out katanas to Zak and Ez. He hands Jude's to me.

'Any point in giving you one of these?' Rafa asks Jason.

'None at all.'

'Probably works better, anyway.'

'Does that mean you have a plan?'

Rafa laughs. 'Goldilocks, anyone would think you had no faith in me.' He re-zips the bag, scans the trees beside the boardwalk, and lobs it into the darkness. Then draws us into a circle.

'It's a bit thin on detail,' Jason says when Rafa's finished laying out what we're about to do.

'Got a better idea? No? Let's go then.'

We set off, Rafa now in the lead. I catch him in a few steps. 'Won't they feel us when we get close?'

'We didn't shift here, so maybe not. But if they do, they'll only know someone is coming. Not who, or how many.'

I keep the blade of the katana in front of me. 'The same goes for us too, though, doesn't it? We won't know how many of them there are either.'

'Daniel's not going to have an army up here. We can take them.'

We round a bend. My stomach dips, like I've stepped off the boardwalk into open space.

'Feel that?' Rafa asks me. 'You can stop worrying about us not being in the right place.'

He pulls out the paper Simon gave him. It's the mud map. I can just make out the markings Rafa's pointing to.

'The first cabin must be around the next bend,' he says. 'See how the path forks?'

We creep forward. I hear faint music before I see lights through the trees. Cabin isn't the right word: what's in front of us is an A-frame house, twice the size of our bungalow.

Rafa signals for us to leave the boardwalk. I look over the side. The forest floor is thick with ferns—it's hard to tell how far the drop is. He goes first, barely making a sound as he vaults over the rail. He lands in the waist-high ferns with a soft thud, keeping his feet. There's no way it's as easy as he made it look.

Zak and Ez go next, then Jason. He's not quite as agile as the others, but he's athletic and he lands with almost the same grace. I have no intention of impaling myself on Jude's sword, so I sit on the railing, swing my legs over, and drop to the ground.

We move through the ferns until we're beside the cabin. At the front is a wide deck that steps down to a grassy clearing with a picnic table and benches. Out back, French doors open onto a smaller deck and the forest is pressed close around it. The music is louder now, mellow

Spanish guitar. Maybe this isn't the right cabin. Maybe we're about to destroy someone's romantic weekend—

A figure moves into the open doorway and my heart jolts.

It's Taya.

Rafa waves us down, below the ferns.

I watch her from my new position. She's in regulation T-shirt and jeans, with her long hair pulled back in a slick ponytail. She's also armed, resting a sheathed sword across her shoulders as she wanders to the far side of the deck, scanning the forest.

Rafa nudges me to get my attention. Then he points to Jason, and then the house. Jason nods. Rafa holds up two fingers—*wait two minutes*—and moves off silently towards the front of the cabin.

Jason manages to stay still half that time, his breath shortening, and then crawls in the opposite direction. The rest of us stay put. I try to remember to breathe.

Rafa has doubled back to the boardwalk and now saunters onto the front deck, sword hanging loosely from his right hand. He bangs on the door. On the back deck, Taya's head whips around. She draws her katana and disappears inside. The music stops. I hear muffled voices.

Rafa waits, his shoulders loose. He grins when the door opens.

'*Buona sera*,' he says.

'Where's Gabe?' Taya's voice is flinty.

'Hanging out with the barman,' Rafa says, spinning the sword hilt in his hand. 'You told her to come at dawn. The new and improved Gabe apparently does what she's told.'

'What do you want?'

'To end this bullshit. Gabe's not going back to Daniel, so you may as well just hand over the blonde now.'

Taya steps out onto the deck, her sword in front of her. Her eyes graze the ferns where we're hiding. 'Who else did you bring?'

'For you and Malachi?' He laughs.

'You forget we can grab our guest and—' She snaps her fingers.

'Nathaniel's okay with you dragging that girl all over the world? Yeah, right. Just cut the crap and bring her out.' He looks past her, into the cabin. 'Ah, Malachi. How's the ball sack?'

A movement catches my eye. Jason, sneaking up to the back of the cabin while Taya and Malachi are busy at the front. I'm holding my breath.

He reaches the back door and slips inside.

Time stops. My heart bangs against my ribs. Above me, a green tree frog starts up its flat, repetitive call.

Jason just has to find Maggie, shift with her back here so we know he has her, and then we can all get out of here.

Something smashes inside the house.

'I *knew* it!' Taya says. She and Malachi race back into the cabin. Rafa shakes his head, glances over at our hiding spot, and follows them inside.

Beside me, Zak lets out his breath slowly. 'Guess it's plan B then.' He and Ez exchange a look and disappear, leaving me alone in the ferns.

IT'S GOOD TO SEE YOU

I stay put for about thirty seconds.

Then I slip forward, to the open window. Rafa's not going to like it, but what was the point of giving me a sword if he didn't want me to use it?

'So now you've got *two* human hostages.' Rafa's voice. 'Great work at keeping a low profile.'

I press my back against the cabin, one hand against the smooth wall, the other strangling the katana.

'He shouldn't be here.' Taya.

'He's her boyfriend. What did you think he was going to do?'

I hold my breath and peer between the timber shutters, my face in the shadows.

Maggie.

Drawing short breaths. Her brown eyes wide.

Taya has Maggie in front of her, the tip of her sword at Maggie's throat. Maggie's face is streaked with tears and her hands are bound tightly in front of her, but she doesn't seem to be hurt.

A guy I've never seen before is restraining Jason. He's tall, well built—as all the Rephaim seem to be—with cropped blond hair and light stubble on his jaw. They're in a large room with a bamboo lounge suite at one end and a wooden table at the other. A staircase winds up to a mezzanine level draped with mosquito nets. Maggie and her guard must have been upstairs when Jason went in.

There's no sign of Malachi. I bet that punch-happy prick is already back at the Sanctuary, raising the alarm.

Jason is so close to Maggie. Why doesn't he just lunge for her and shift? We'd factored in he might get caught. The plan can still work if he does something *right* now.

But he's frozen.

I should have seen this coming. Jason doesn't want to show them what he is. Maybe because he fears the Rephaim. Maybe because he's seen Maggie and realized she might not be quite so open-minded now about the offspring of the Fallen.

'This is on your head, Rafa. You brought him here,' Taya says.

Why haven't Ez and Zak shown themselves? If they're waiting for something, I should keep my head down too. But we'd agreed that if Jason's move didn't work, our next option was to fight. And as much as I don't want to use this sword, I'd rather do that than nothing. I need Maggie to know we've come for her. I need to see that fear leave her face. I need—

Sharp steel presses against my throat.

'You're early.'

Malachi. Fuck.

'I couldn't wait to see you.'

'I don't suppose you want to come back to the Sanctuary now, and save all the drama?'

'Um, no thanks.' My hand tightens on my sword.

He sighs. 'Come on, then.' He pulls me back from the window. 'Drop the weapon.'

I can't let him disarm me. I have to do something. I have to—

Don't think.

I duck sideways. Malachi's blade nicks my throat as I break his grip. I have time to get my balance and swing at his shoulder. He blocks the strike, and the impact reverberates up my arm. It hurts . . . and then that strength I felt in the cage pours back into me, like it's the most natural thing in the world.

I grab the hilt with two hands and swing again. Again

he blocks me, but this time he has to step back to absorb the blow.

'You got lucky in the cage.' He pushes me back.

I swing at his head. He blocks.

'Your technique is terrible,' he says. And yet he's not racing in to attack me.

Swing. Block.

'You're going to get hurt—'

In the light spilling from the cabin, I bring the blade down again, this time with one hand. He needs two hands to block the strike, leaving him wide open, and I punch him in the jaw.

He reels back. I press my throbbing knuckles against my thigh.

Malachi gives his jaw a quick rub, still backing away. 'But you're not . . .'

I shrug. 'I know.'

Daisy and Rafa might be on to something about residual memory in my body. But why is Malachi retreating? I'm holding my own against him, but he's still quicker.

Inside, Rafa curses and then Taya and Maggie materialize on the boardwalk behind Malachi, setting off a colony of fruit bats in the nearby trees. The screeching almost drowns Maggie out.

'Gaby!'

'Mags!'

Our eyes meet. In that fleeting moment, I try to convey everything I feel for her. Everything I'm prepared to do to save her. She lets out a small sob.

Taya glances into the house. Her face is bathed in soft light. 'Rafa's gone?'

Maggie's guard emerges, pinning Jason's arms behind him as he pushes him onto the deck. 'Yeah.'

Taya smiles. 'Wrong choice again, Gabe. When will you learn?'

I ignore her.

Rafa wouldn't give up that easily. I know the original plan has gone to shit, but he wouldn't leave me here. Would he?

Maggie's guard is staring at me.

'Now do you believe it's her?' Taya says to him.

His face breaks into a smile. 'Looking good for a dead woman, Gabe.'

Taya gives him a withering look. 'She has no idea who you are, Micah. Focus.'

In the moment of Taya turning to Micah, Maggie tries to run straight into the dark. Taya has her again almost at once. She grabs a handful of her hair, jerks her head back to expose her neck. The blade still hasn't broken skin, but another move from Maggie and she's going to bleed.

Her eyes are wild, begging me.

'Just put down that sword and come with us like a good

girl,' Taya says. 'Don't make me hurt you again.'

I risk a quick look at Jason. 'You okay?'

He stares at me, breathing way too fast. Is this an act, or has he really lost the plot? Maybe close contact with this many Rephaim was more than he was ready for.

'You made a deal,' Taya says. 'There was a time your word meant something.'

I move towards her. 'I'm pretty sure there was a time my friends didn't torture me either.'

I'm edging closer and she's watching every step. I don't know exactly what I'm going to do when I get to her, but I'm only going to get one shot at it.

The shadows on the deck beyond Taya shimmer.

'Oh, give me a break.'

Daniel steps into the light, flanked by four other Rephaim.

A PACK OF BASTARDS

'Rafa is nothing if not predictable.' Daniel stops beside Taya. Unarmed. He mustn't be planning on getting his hands dirty tonight. 'I knew he wouldn't be able to follow instructions.'

The guys with him are armed. Three are carrying shiny katanas, but the fourth is spinning a poleax.

A freaking *poleax*.

They all falter when they see me. The poleax stops moving.

Daniel glances over his shoulder. The fruit bats are quietening. 'Stay sharp,' he says.

The first to recover is a redhead with retro sideburns. 'Gabriella,' he says. 'I had to see it to believe it.'

Taya's still got Maggie. Micah is right beside her, sword

at Jason's throat. I'm badly outnumbered. I need time, for either Jason to get his arse into gear, or the others to come back.

'And who the hell are you?' I ask the redhead.

'Uriel,' he says slowly, like he doesn't quite believe I don't know him. Another one of the Five.

Daniel breaks in. 'You brought *him*?'

I watch Daniel as he studies Jason. Does he recognize him from the Sanctuary last night? Does he know what Jason is? He can't. He'd be making a bigger deal out of it.

'And you, Gabriella. You seemed surprised to see me. Did you think I wouldn't find out you'd arrived earlier than instructed?'

'I should have known Malachi would go running to you.'

'Malachi didn't desert his post.'

'Then how did you know I was here?'

Daniel almost smiles. 'Text message.'

Of course.

'Now, drop the weapon and come to me, and your two friends can leave.'

'Save your breath,' Taya says. 'She never intended to keep the deal.'

Daniel's eyebrows lift. 'Really? I'm disappointed.'

But clearly not surprised, given who he's brought with him.

'You had your chance to accept my offer when I was in Italy. You seriously think I'm going back with you for more cage time?'

'You set the terms of this exchange, and I intend to keep them.'

'Your word's worth about as much as mine at this point.'

I catch Jason's attention. He's not that far from Maggie. Any time now would be good . . .

Air stirs behind me. Why wasn't I watching my back?

'Just me,' Rafa says, before I can strike out. My heart gives two hard thumps and then settles back to racing.

'Where have you been?'

'Just waiting to see who Pretty Boy would turn up with.' He says it more to Daniel than me.

'Do you think you're good enough to take them?' Daniel gestures to the men around him.

'Sure.' Rafa stands shoulder to shoulder with me. 'Assuming you haven't enlisted another hell-turd. What the fuck were you thinking, keeping one of those things?'

'What happens at the Sanctuary is none of your concern, Rafael.' Daniel gives Rafa a dismissive once-over. 'You really think you're still good enough to take on this many disciplined soldiers?'

Rafa grins. 'I've got Gabe, remember?'

'I don't know if you've noticed, but that's not Gabe.'

'From what I hear, she's still got a few moves. I'll take my chances.'

'This is just a game to you, isn't it? Tell me, does Gabriella know your agenda?'

'What agenda would that be?'

'To use her to find the Fallen.'

Rafa gives a short laugh. 'That's your grand plan, not mine.'

'Are you telling me the Outcasts are no longer interested in the Fallen? I find that hard to believe.'

'I don't give a fuck what you believe.'

'Have you at least told her what Mya plans to do if the Fallen are found?'

'Not my problem.'

'You don't think she has a right to know?' Daniel's gaze locks on me. 'The people you have aligned with want to join the Fallen and make war on the Host of Heaven.'

I check Maggie. She's frozen, eyes vacant. Oh, please hang in there. I turn to Daniel.

'Firstly,' I say, 'I haven't aligned myself with anyone. And secondly, I've never met Mya and honestly couldn't give two shits about her, or her plans.'

A pitying smile. 'If only it was that simple. It's why you didn't leave with your brother, Gabriella. You could see Mya's path would only lead to death and destruction, and you'd be no better than the demons who hunt us. If the Fallen make war on the Host of Heaven, the battle will take place in this earthly realm, and it will be humans caught in the cross fire.'

'*Earthly realm*,' Rafa mimics. 'You say that like there are other realms you're familiar with. Have you found a way to other dimensions since we parted company? Have you seen a war between angels? No? It sounds to me like you've swallowed a fresh batch of Nathaniel's bullshit.'

The night shifts around us, loaded with violence and recrimination and fear. I need to focus, but it's not easy. It's one thing to come to terms with the fact I'm not entirely human. But angelic wars on earth?

'You think you've got all the answers,' Rafa continues, 'but as usual you've got no idea what's really going on.'

Daniel's lips twist. 'So, you're helping Gabriella for old time's sake? Not because her current situation might provide the only chance you'll ever have of bedding her?'

'*Bedding* her? For fuck's sake, Daniel, we're in the twenty-first century. Your wardrobe's caught up—don't you think it's time the rest of you did?'

'Stop this,' I snap. 'Maggie and Jason have nothing to do with any of this. Let them go.'

'He always intended this to be a fight,' Rafa says. 'That's why he made sure I knew you were coming here. Even

Daniel's not deluded enough to think you'd go back with him. This little scenario is about dragging you back to Nathaniel, unconscious, and inflicting as much pain as possible on me.'

Daniel's smile is thin. 'I didn't want any of this, but if you end up injured with no one to heal you, then so be it.'

The air moves behind me again.

'Everyone still getting along then?' Zak says, dropping into a fighter's stance beside Ez.

Daniel's nostrils flare. 'You think two extra swords will make a difference tonight?'

'If you play by the rules,' Ez says.

Daniel looks genuinely indignant. '*We* fight with honor. Can you say the same?'

'Everyone fights with honor until they're losing. And we rarely lose, Daniel.'

She's good. Was I ever that cool under pressure?

Rafa looks at me. 'Ready?'

I don't have time to say no before Daniel flicks his wrist and the four Rephaim who came with him charge us.

PARTY CRASHERS

Uriel picks me out. Taya shoves Maggie at Micah and runs at me too.

Rafa cuts her off, and I have time to see him block her first strike before I have more pressing issues of my own—the flash of steel at my right shoulder. I leap out of the way, but the tip of Uriel's sword catches me on the way through. It cuts through fabric and nicks my arm.

It stings, but there's no time to think.

I react before he's fully recovered from the follow-through, forcing him on the back foot. Uriel deflects the strike, and then punishes me with a hail of blows from every direction. It takes all my strength to block them. The fruit bats are screeching again but there's so much blood rushing in my ears I can barely hear them. Everything is noise. Our swords clash near the hilt, and he uses his momentum to push me back against the railing of the deck. His breath is hot on my face, thick with coffee and frustration.

'What are you doing with Rafa?' He's panting. 'And why are you fighting against us?'

Doesn't he know? 'Daniel thinks I'm lying about my memories'—I drag in more breath, my chest burning—'and thought feeding me to a hellion would help.'

Uriel winces, but of course this isn't news to him. I struggle against his crushing weight. He pushes back harder. 'You don't remember me?'

'No.'

'You seem to remember all my moves.'

He's braced his feet apart to pin me to the railing. It's all the invitation I need.

'Just luck,' I say, and slam my knee into his groin.

His legs buckle and he staggers sideways.

'Hamstring him!' Rafa shouts.

He's fending off Taya, Malachi, and another Rephaite, alternating between sword strikes, punches, and kicks. They're all moving so *fast*, but Rafa's holding his own, even outnumbered.

Hamstring something other than a hell-beast? Am I quick enough? What if Maggie sees? *Maggie.*

Taya left her to Micah. He's got Maggie and Jason.

I search the chaotic shadows for them.

In that brief moment, Uriel recovers and smashes the katana from my hand. It flies over the handrail into the ferns. Even he seems surprised at how easy it was. His sword's poised in the air . . . He doesn't bring it down. 'I can't,' he says, lowering the weapon. 'This is insane.'

I'm so focused on the lowering blade that I don't see his foot coming at me until his boot smashes into my jaw. And then I'm airborne.

The ferns don't break my fall.

All the breath goes out of me, and I lie there, absorbing the pain in my head and shoulder. I move my jaw from side to side. It throbs, but I don't think it's broken. My arm and neck are sticky with blood. I roll over, crawl along the ground, trying not to give myself away. I'm not slinking away: I want Jude's sword.

The fighting continues above me as I forage in the damp soil. My fingers touch leather and I grip the katana and climb to my feet, but the sight of what's happening on the deck stops me in my tracks.

The Rephaim are going to town on each other with swords and the poleax. It's a full-on brawl. Uriel and another guy are tag-teaming against Zak, but he's fast enough to protect himself, and Ez is confusing the guy with the poleax with a barrage of kicks.

Rafa has Taya and Malachi backed into the far corner

of the deck. He's got a sword in each hand now, swinging both with relentless efficiency. Taya is bleeding from her left eye and Malachi favors his right leg. I can't tear my eyes from Rafa. So much power and violence . . . Was I really like that? And was there ever a time when these people were on the same side? They're fighting each other with such intensity.

Daniel is watching it all from the doorway of the cabin, feet apart and arms folded, eyes flitting between the skirmishes and the point on the boardwalk where I disappeared. Through the railing, I can see one of Daniel's soldiers sprawled on the deck. I'm guessing it's his sword Rafa is now using in his double-handed assault. The injured Rephaite lifts his head, makes brief eye contact with Daniel, and disappears.

Across the deck, Maggie and Jason are sitting against the cabin, an arm's length apart. Micah is prowling back and forth in front of them, the tip of his sword close enough to be threatening. But he's only got one eye on them—he's more interested in the fighting. I only need to distract him, and possibly slap Jason, and we can get this plan back on track.

Daniel is the only one who notices when I climb back up over the handrail, and he seems more interested in what I'm going to do than in stopping me. My feet hit the deck and I take off, katana in hand.

Micah sees me, and waits, feet apart, tossing his sword from one hand to the other.

I'm halfway to him when a gun blast tears through the dark behind me. I turn and stumble. A second shot rings out, sending the fruit bats into a frenzy. The fighting on the deck stops and all heads turn to the boardwalk. The Rephaim each step away from their opponents, like this has been a training session and someone just called time-out. No one seems anxious, so I stay on my feet, halfway between the Rephaim and the cabin.

Three figures emerge out of the darkness, on the board-walk.

'What *the fuck* are you arse-wipes doing?' Mick Butler shouts, his shotgun pointed at the deck. The three of them are shoulder to shoulder: Mick and Rusty on one side— Rusty now toting a rifle—and Simon between them.

They've reached the edges of the light from the cabin. I can see the whites of Simon's eyes from here. Whatever he was expecting to catch us doing, this wasn't it.

'Hold position,' Daniel orders as he leaves the doorway, which I assume means: don't shift in front of the humans. He makes his way across the deck, shooting me a warning look as he passes. I follow anyway, and stop beside Rafa.

Simon spots me. His gaze drops to the katana and his mouth falls open. Then he tries to see past me. 'Mags! Mags, you here?'

'Shut the fuck up!' Mick turns on him and he takes a step back. Simon didn't orchestrate this surprise visit. This is all Mick's show.

Maggie is on her feet, her hands still tied. Jason struggles to join her, but Micah is right there, shoving him back to the deck, away from her.

'Simon, get out of here!' Maggie shouts.

Micah pushes her down, pressing the sword tip against her throat to stop her trying again. He gives her an apologetic smile. But all Simon sees is Maggie being manhandled, and he rushes forward.

'Get back here!' Mick bellows, but Simon only stops when Rafa blocks his path, swords held out either side of him.

'Not a smart move,' Rafa says.

Simon's gaze flicks between the swords. 'They had bikes. They found the jeep.' His voice cracks. 'And they had more ammo—'

'You should have taken a bullet before leading them here,' Rafa says.

'Oi!' Mick says. 'Got a gun here. You should be talking to me.'

'And I'm in charge,' Daniel says. 'So you should be talking to me.'

The Rephaim have split into two camps: Taya, Malachi, Uriel, and the others have fallen in behind Daniel; Zak and Ez are with Rafa and me. Micah holds his position at the cabin.

'So, what can we do for you?' Daniel asks Mick, all charm.

The noise in the trees is easing, which at least means Mick can stop shouting. 'First up, I wanna know why you faggots are up here playing ninjas. And second, I wanna take a piece out of him'—he points the shotgun at Rafa—'for this fucking egg on my head.'

Daniel spreads his hands wide on the deck railing. 'Please feel free to settle any score you may have.'

'Actually,' Zak says, holding up a hand, 'that was me.'

Mick's eyes narrow. 'Don't worry, big fella, you'll get your turn.'

Clearly he thinks two guns trump a dozen swords.

This could all go bad very quickly.

'What about Mags?' Rusty asks. He's trying to see beyond Daniel and his small army. 'Simon says you took her.'

'Which one is Simon?' Daniel asks.

Rusty waves his rifle in Simon's direction.

'That's the guy Gabe was all over,' Taya says through a fat lip. 'The barman.'

Daniel considers him. 'No one here is of any concern to you.'

'*Mags* is of concern to me.' Simon's voice is almost

steady. 'Let her go before I call the cops.'

'No cops,' Mick says, still a few meters away on the boardwalk. 'Listen, mate,' he says to Daniel. 'Give me five minutes with these two arseholes'—he gestures to Rafa and Zak—'and we'll be on our way with Maggie.'

Simon's attention is on my newly bruised face. Daniel doesn't miss his reaction.

'Don't worry about Gabriella, she can take care of herself.'

'Seems that way,' Simon says. 'I didn't know you could fight.' There's a hint of accusation in his voice.

'Me either.'

His gaze drops to my neck. 'Which one of these bastards hurt you last night?'

I use my free hand to cover the scar with my ponytail. 'You should be more worried about getting the Butlers out of here before someone gets killed.'

'What's with the swords? Who *are* these people?'

'We've got this. Now run along,' Rafa says. He's still between Simon and me, but has at least lowered his swords.

And then everything goes quiet. No cicadas. Not a peep from the fruit bats. Nothing. Not even a tree frog. Even Mick falls silent.

Rafa stares into the forest, beyond the clearing. One by one, the Rephaim turn away from the Butler boys and raise their weapons.

'What is it?' I say to Rafa.

He jerks his head for Simon to get behind him. Simon does it without arguing. 'Possibly a very large shit storm.'

Whatever's coming, it's not following the boardwalk. I've had enough surprises emerge out of the darkness tonight that nothing should shock me. But the Rephaim, who were trying to maim each other just minutes ago, are now standing side by side. Daniel has moved next to Rafa, and Rafa hasn't taken a swing at him. This can't be good.

Two tall figures appear between the trees. The ferns that reached my waist are at their thighs. The vegetation barely moves as they stride towards us. I let my breath out slowly. There's only two of them. We outnumber them.

And then two hellions lumber out of the darkness behind them.

TIME TO FACE YOUR DEMONS

My heart stops. I can't even form the question, but I already know the answer.

Daniel and Rafa step forward. They glance at each other, not speaking.

'Have you two reconciled? How touching.' The voice is deep and smoky, and comes from one of the two figures.

I force myself to keep breathing. Maybe if I'd never seen a hellion up close, I might mistake one for a bear in this light. A bear would be a truly bizarre sight in Pan Beach, but it would make more sense than a creature that shouldn't exist. Their chain mail glints . . . Oh, god, please don't let Maggie see them.

'What the fuck?' Mick says. Fortunately, nobody's interested in him right this second.

'Our boys here miss their brother.' The second voice is as deep as the first. 'We are here to collect our pet.'

Rafa speaks to Daniel without turning his head. 'This is why we don't play with hellions.'

'You're the one who shifted with Gabriella when she was covered in its blood.'

Rafa grinds his teeth. 'Yeah? Well, how'd they track us *here*?'

I almost grasp the significance of their exchange, and then the two figures step into the clearing near the picnic table and my mind goes blank.

There's a whimper behind me. I don't have to look to know it's Maggie.

The new arrivals are close enough in appearance to be twins. They must be male, from those voices, but from their faces it's hard to tell. They are pale and beautiful, with fine features and long white hair. There's something about the way they look that doesn't seem quite . . . real. And their eyes . . . The irises are on fire.

Demons.

Of course demons are real. If angels and hellions exist, then demons must too. It wasn't that long ago I thought hellions and demons were one and the same, and that I'd made them up.

I miss those days.

'And who are these queers?' There's the tiniest waver

in Mick's voice. Rusty shuffles behind him and stares bug-eyed at the hellions, now standing at their full height. They're taller than the demons, and both are sniffing the air like hunting dogs, smelling us.

Mick suddenly swings the barrel of his shotgun to point at the hellions. The movement catches the attention of the demons, who notice the Butlers for the first time.

'How thoughtful,' the first says. 'Snacks for our boys.'

'You will not touch these men,' Daniel says.

The demon smiles without a trace of warmth, showing perfect teeth. 'Of course, they prefer Nephilim blood.'

Daniel stiffens. 'We do not acknowledge that name.'

'That does not make it any less the truth.' The second demon gestures to himself. 'Any more than this appearance makes us human. You are the bastard children of the Fallen. You are Nephilim.'

'We transcend that label through our obedience to the Angelic Garrison. We are Rephaite.'

'You are Nathaniel's puppets,' the second demon says. 'As I have told you a thousand times.'

'And you have never had a thought Zarael didn't put in that abyss between your ears—'

'Are you serious?' Rafa says. 'You still have to have this argument *every* time before a fight? Who gives a crap what these rejects call us?'

He turns to Bel and Leon. 'Your pet's dead. So now

what? If you came to fight, we'd be spilling your filthy blood already.'

It's a mild evening, yet the demons are wearing flowing coats. Both have heavy swords hanging from their hips.

'There will only be a fight if you refuse to hand over the twin who has risen from the dead.'

My mouth goes completely dry.

The first demon is staring at me—at least I think he is. It's hard to tell with those flickering orange eyes. 'You were dead,' he says.

Beside me, Rafa moves a little closer. 'You say that like it's a fact.'

The demon's lips twist in what is possibly meant to be a smile. 'It is.'

'Obviously it's not. She's standing right here.'

'And a year ago she was dead.'

'How can you be so sure?'

The demon just keeps smiling.

'Bel, you sulphurous prick, how do you know?'

The demon, Bel, caresses the hilt of his sword with long spindly fingers. 'Because I put this blade through her neck.'

'Bullshit.'

Daniel has gone completely still. I'm waiting for him to say something, but whatever is going through his head, he keeps to himself.

Bel turns to his companion. 'Is it, Leon? Is it *bullshit*?'

Leon sweeps his long hair into one hand and brings it over his right shoulder. He looks bored. 'No, it is not. It was the highlight of my time trapped in this rotting realm.'

Blood pounds in my ears. 'Then how the fuck am I alive?'

Everyone on the deck stares at me. Either because I shouldn't be addressing the demons, or because they all want to know the answer.

Bel's fiery eyes bore into me. 'You are the only one who can answer that.'

'Haven't you heard?' My voice is too loud. 'A week ago, I didn't even know I wasn't human.'

Simon and the Butlers are right there, but I can't deal with that right now. I can't look at Simon. Or at Maggie.

'You do not remember your brother begging for your life?'

The night grinds down. It becomes darker, airless.

Did Jude and I take on these demons *on our own*? Is this pale demon responsible for the scar on my neck? And if Jude begged for my life, and I'm alive, does that mean he's dead?

I pry my lips apart. 'What happened to my brother?'

'Come with us, and we will show you.' It's Leon who makes the offer. Rafa's fingers dig into my arm.

'Where did this attack happen?' he asks.

Leon's impassive face finally shifts. 'You still do not

know?' He turns towards Daniel. 'Surely the Council of Five knew what they were doing? No? Dear me.'

Daniel still doesn't answer. What is *wrong* with him?

Next to the picnic table, the hellions are getting restless, shuffling from one foot to the other. The one beside Bel is drooling.

'So, the twins were acting without orders from either side,' Leon says. 'That is excellent news. Nathaniel's empire is continuing to crumble.'

'Leon!' Rafa snaps. 'How did you find them?'

Leon strokes his long hair. 'The same way we always find your half-breed kind. Through our skill and your laziness. Like tonight.'

'We tracked our hellion's blood to Patmos and then here, to that ripe little village down by the ocean,' Bel says.

'What happened to Jude?' Rafa is still holding on to my arm. It's starting to hurt.

Bel keeps drumming his fingers on his sword hilt. 'He is our prisoner.'

'Bullshit. You don't have Jude. And you thought Gabe was dead, which means you don't remember what happened to her either.'

'Oi!' Mick calls out. 'I'm gonna put a hole in your mate in the ugly suit if he takes another step towards me.'

The hellion is creeping closer to Mick, like a dog trying to sneak food.

Bel smiles. 'Oh, please, be my guest.'

'I mean it.'

The hellion takes another step, and another. Mick fires. The reverberation of the shotgun forces him back a step. The bullet penetrates the chain mail, but the hellion barely reacts. It snarls and keeps coming at him. It's still drooling.

'Stop!' Daniel shouts, but Mick uses the pump action to reload, and fires again.

'Come on!' he screams.

The hellion charges.

'Mick!' Rusty scrambles backwards. 'Move!'

Mick has time to reload one last time before the hellion smashes the shotgun from his hands and wraps him in a bear hug. The last thing I see before he and Rusty barrel over the handrail is the hellion sinking its razor-sharp teeth into Mick's tattooed neck.

I'M NOT SCARED . . .

Rafa takes one look at Daniel, tosses him his spare sword, and they disappear. One second they're on the deck, the next, they're down in the clearing. Bel is ready for them, blocking the first strike as soon as Rafa and Daniel materialize. The night explodes into violence.

There's no division among the Rephaim now—they move together as a single unit. Uriel and Ez go after the hell-spawn latched onto Mick. Zak and Malachi team up to attack Leon, and Taya and the other Rephaim circle the remaining hellion.

It's mesmerizing and terrifying.

And then I remember.

'Jason!'

He looks up from the chaos in the clearing.

'NOW!'

He doesn't have to be told twice.

Micah is watching the fighting, only half paying attention to Maggie. Even when he sees Jason dash to Maggie—hands untied—he doesn't react. He thinks he's got plenty of time.

Jason puts his arms around Maggie, says something in her ear, waits an agonizingly long second. And then they disappear.

Micah stares at the empty space, then up at me. I shrug. He shakes his head, and then bolts across the deck and vaults over the handrail into the fray.

'Gaby!'

Simon peers out the front door. In all the chaos, he's managed to get inside.

'Come on,' he says, gesturing wildly. 'We can get out the back.' He sticks his head out a little further. 'Where's Mags?'

'She got away with Jason.'

'Then let's go.' He grabs my wrist.

I glance back over my shoulder. I'd thought the fighting between the Rephaim had been full-on. But this . . . The demons are almost a blur, they move so fast, and the hellion—at least the one I can still see—is a lot more agile than the one I faced in the cage. And Maggie is safe now, so there's no reason to stay. And yet . . .

'You go,' I say to Simon, pulling loose from his grip.

'Are you insane? Come *on*!'

Jason appears behind him in the middle of the room, already moving before he's fully arrived. Simon turns to see what I'm looking at.

'What the . . .'

Jason doesn't break stride. He looks rattled. I guess Maggie didn't cope so well with the unexpected shift.

Simon backs away, hands out in front of him. 'Mate . . .' he says.

But Jason has him by the wrist—and they're gone.

Outside, Rafa and Daniel have forced Bel past the picnic table, towards the forest. The demon is fast and strong, but Rafa is almost his match. Daniel's no slouch either. They might despise each other, but they know how to fight together, tag-teaming, keeping the demon on the defensive.

Zak and Malachi aren't doing quite so well against Leon. The left sleeve of Malachi's shirt is shiny with blood, and when he next dodges a strike, I see a deep cut in his upper arm. Zak's still moving freely, but he's too big to be quick enough to take advantage if the demon drops his guard. What he needs is a third fighter.

I'm running down the stairs before I think about it.

I leap off the bottom step—and Micah cannons into me.

He's airborne, so I know it wasn't intentional. By the time we scramble to our feet, there are three more demons in the clearing.

Where did they come from? They're standing at the edge of the forest, swords hanging loosely from bony fingers, watching the clash with their fiery eyes. There's no way the Rephaim have the numbers to take them.

Taya is still trying to hamstring the hellion, but most of her efforts are focused on dodging its black talons. The hell-beast is herding her towards the new arrivals. She doesn't know what's behind her.

'Heads up!' Malachi shouts.

Taya glances over her shoulder. It's time enough for the hellion to reef the sword out of her hand and pounce on her. It sinks its teeth into her neck. Her scream is bone-chilling. Her body goes limp, paralyzed by the ferocity of the hellion's appetite. Pulling the life out of her with sickening efficiency.

After everything she's done to me, it should feel like payback.

It doesn't.

Malachi breaks away from his fight to charge the hellion. I'm right beside him. One of the newly arrived demons comes at us—quick and silent—and Malachi leaps around the hellion and Taya to meet him. That leaves me. I swing at the back of the hellion's legs as hard as I can.

The sword slices into its flesh. It drops to one knee and snarls. I jerk the blade out.

The beast throws Taya aside and slashes at me. I jump out of its reach, holding the katana with two hands now, waiting for the charge. The hellion hauls itself to its feet, favoring one leg. Taya's trying to get up, but all the fight's gone out of her. She slumps back to the ground.

'Get up!' I yell at her. 'I can't do this on my own!'

She nods in the direction of the forest. I risk a look, and see Micah leading another half-dozen Rephaim, armed with swords, knives, and maces. I'm really starting to like this guy.

'I've got your back,' a voice says behind me. It's Daisy, half-crouched, staring down the hellion. 'No way I was staying out of this one.'

I have time to see she's wielding two weird-looking skinny daggers before she flies through the air, wraps her legs around the hellion's waist and thrusts them in either side of its thick neck. The beast roars and digs its claws into her sides, trying to pry her off. It stumbles backwards and collapses to its knees, unable to bear the extra weight on its severed tendon.

Daisy pulls her weapons out of the hellion's neck and brings her fists down hard on its wrists.

I race in and smash the hellion in the side of the head with the sword hilt. It lets go of Daisy and swipes at me. I change my grip and bring the blade down on its forearm. Something drops to the grass with a dull thud. A clawed hand. The hellion's howling splits the air.

One of the demons swoops forward and grabs the hellion. They both disappear. I back up against the deck, catching my breath.

At least one of the guys who came with Daisy and Micah is already down, clutching his stomach. Daniel is shouting at him to shift, but the new guy seems not to hear him. Malachi is still fighting, but his whole arm is covered with blood now, and Zak is bleeding from his ear. There are flashes of movement in the forest beyond the boardwalk. Uriel and Ez must still be trying to bring down the hellion that bit Mick. Are the brothers still alive, or are they bleeding to death while half-angels and demons butcher each other?

Why are the Rephaim still here? Why hasn't Daniel called a retreat? Right now, he's fighting alongside Malachi, leaving Rafa on his own with Bel. Daisy's up again and racing at the nearest demon, her sides still torn and bloody.

I grab Taya by the arm and pull her out of the way. Her neck is punctured and her throat and shirt are slick with bright blood. Her eyes keep rolling back into her head.

'Shift!' I yell at her.

She tries to focus on me. 'Not without orders.'

'You'll bleed out.'

She shows me her teeth, also covered in blood. 'Doubt it.'

I can't leave her here. The first demon to get close enough will take her head. I position myself between her and the ongoing battle.

A demon materializes in front of me. It's more good luck than skill that I get my sword up to block the first strike. Daisy is next to me before he strikes again, and together we fend off an onslaught of blows. My arms feel like lead. Every cut on my body stings. Except, they're not just stinging. They're tingling—along with every other inch of my skin.

The clearing blazes with white-blue light.

'Enough.'

NOTHING LIKE A HOLLOW VICTORY

The voice cuts through the clashing swords. I dive away from the demon, turning my face from the blinding light. I hit the grass, and shield my eyes. What the . . . ?

The demon is silhouetted against the glare, turned away from its source. Daisy and I lash out at the back of his legs. Both blades strike flesh. The demon cries out—sounding so human my skin prickles—and then shifts.

I collapse back to the grass, panting. Exhausted. Relieved. And only then do I notice the fighting has stopped.

'Hold your position.' The voice is commanding, but not quite as sharp as before.

'Daisy?' I whisper between short breaths.

'It's Nathaniel.'

She hauls me to my feet. The white-blue light has softened, but the clearing is still lit up. The sky has vanished. Bel and Leon are at the edge of the forest, where they first appeared, a third demon with them. The other Rephaim are behind Nathaniel on the boardwalk, including Taya, who can't stand up. Daisy's grip leaves mine as soon as I'm steady, and I don't have time to look around for her before she appears with the others behind Nathaniel.

Rafa and Zak are in the clearing with me, and we're all that stands between the demons and the rest of the Rephaim.

I'm trying not to stare at Nathaniel—and failing.

He's a fallen angel.

He stands at the same height as the demons. And the white-blue light is coming from him. Not from something he's holding, but from *him*. Like an angel on a Christmas card. Except instead of robes or a tunic, he's wearing jeans and a shirt. His fair hair is cut shaggy against his chiseled face, and he's holding a sword that's throwing off as much light as he is.

I don't know what I was expecting him to look like, but this isn't it.

He's an angel. That makes him what? Thousands of years old, at least. And it sounds like he's raised the Rephaim like a high school principal, so I was expecting someone grim and authoritarian. Not a guy who could be a footballer on his way to a nightclub.

'The twin is no longer yours,' one of the demons says, shielding his flaming eyes, even though Nathaniel's light is not as blinding as it was. I think it's Bel, but now there are three of them side by side, it's hard to tell. 'We're taking her.'

I see Nathaniel's eyes. Where the demons' irises are orange, his flicker an icy blue. 'Why?'

'Because Zarael wants her.'

My heart stumbles.

'Belial, you know very well I don't care what Zarael wants.' Nathaniel's voice is as melodic as I remember it in the Sanctuary treatment room.

Bel's lip curls, revealing unnaturally white teeth. 'You will when he finds your brothers.'

The demon next to Bel—possibly Leon—raises the tip of his sword and licks blood from it. 'We have devised new torments for your return to the Pit, Nathaniel,' he says.

'The Fallen may well return to the Pit, but it will not be by your hand, Leonard. The Garrison will decide the fate of Semyaza and those who follow him, not a gutter rat like Zarael.'

Leon laughs. 'You cannot believe your fate is no longer tied to your brothers. Nothing you do in this realm changes what you are. Remember that.'

Daniel is rigid beside Nathaniel, his shirt skewed and face bleeding. It's the most crumpled I've seen him. None of the Rephaim are checking their wounds, or their wounded. They're tensed, weapons ready.

My attention drifts to Bel. He meets my gaze, and the skin on the back of my neck prickles. He smiles, and taps his sword hilt twice with his thumb. He and the other two disappear. I can't believe they're going to leave without—

A brightly lit figure materializes in front of me and shoves me backwards.

'Hold position!' Nathaniel shouts at his Rephaim, at the same time the three demons appear where I was just standing. He blocks their flashing swords.

Rafa and Zak close ranks around me, weapons ready.

Nathaniel is as quick as the demons. He moves like the laws of gravity don't apply to him, and his blazing sword, broader and heavier than any of ours, flashes so fast I can't see it, until it is buried in Bel's collarbone. The demon collapses under the weight of the blow and is still screaming when Nathaniel puts a boot on his chest and shoves him backwards, jerking the sword free.

The air around Nathaniel shimmers and brightens, and he starts to . . . *expand*. I stumble backwards and fall, but keep my eyes on that blazing shape. I blink. I'm starting to make out detail in the glare. It's not Nathaniel getting bigger, it's two massive wings unfurling on either side of him.

'GO!' one of the demons calls, his voice so loud I feel it in my ribcage.

A few seconds later, the wings are gone, along with the white-blue light. It takes a moment for my eyes to adjust. After the brilliance of Nathaniel's light, everything else is dark.

Rafa is beside me, breathing heavily and favoring one leg as he helps me up.

Nathaniel waits until he has Rafa's attention.

'There are humans here?' he asks him.

'Two idiots with guns,' Rafa says. 'Hell-turd bit one. Ez and Uri went after them.'

'Please call him Uriel, Rafael. You know he is a member of the Council of Five now.'

'Fights like it too.' Rafa's all attitude with Nathaniel, but he can't quite maintain eye contact.

'Do you not think you should find these humans?' Nathaniel asks.

Rafa straightens. 'I'm not the one—'

'I'll go,' Zak says before Rafa can finish. No doubt he's more concerned with helping Ez than stopping an argument between Rafa and Nathaniel. He jogs along the boardwalk and vaults over the rail. It's quiet again, and I can make out faint sounds of fighting, deeper in the trees.

Nathaniel signals for Micah to step forward.

'Please fetch the healers.'

The tall blond Rephaite disappears.

The other Rephaim haven't moved from their positions. Even Daisy stands waiting for orders, despite the fact she's bleeding heavily from her punctured sides.

Finally, the fallen angel turns his attention to me. I crane my neck to meet his gaze. Those flickering eyes, there's something strangely soothing about them. I have to remind myself he's sanctioned everything that's happened to me in recent days.

'They will not stop coming for you, Gabriella.'

'What just happened?' I ask. 'Why did they leave like that?'

Nathaniel regards me for a moment. 'Demons cannot stand to be in an angel's presence when we reveal ourselves in glory. In *full* glory, abyss sludge like Belial would combust at the mere sight of me. Sadly, I no longer wield that power.'

'But when you showed your wings—' I stop. Nathaniel has *wings*.

'It's enough to banish bottom-dwellers like Belial and Leonard.'

I dab at a cut on my face. 'Zarael is their, what, boss?'

'He is their lieutenant.'

'But didn't he manage to keep you chained up? How long were you down there?'

'Thousands of years.' He doesn't look away. 'There is

no glory in hell, so we were without weapons. That is no longer the case.'

Rafa is watching me closely, tense, like he's waiting for me to fall at Nathaniel's feet or something.

I take a long, deep breath. The air is heavy with eucalyptus. 'What would they have done to me?'

'Tortured you in ways you cannot imagine.' Nathaniel speaks without hesitation, bringing goosebumps to my arms.

'Because they think, like you do, that I know where the Fallen are?'

He doesn't answer.

'I thought demons were trapped in hell. Why are they in such a rush to go back? And if someone down there has the power to toss them out, why aren't they all running around up here?'

Nathaniel's gaze as he considers the question is unnerving. 'There is no simple answer,' he says at last. 'It is true that Lucifer and his followers are imprisoned in the Pit, but that doesn't mean they can't have influence in this realm.' He scans the silent forest for a moment. 'There are many types of demons, and it is more difficult for some than others to leave hell, but not impossible. There are portals, possession . . . You must remember, though, this world is a shadow playground for demons—one they can only experience in a limited physical form. It's not until the end of time that they will be able to fight the Angelic Garrison in their true form. In the meantime, they have their own dark kingdom in the abyss. It's the only home they know. And while they are in this world, they are vulnerable. Especially against my Rephaim.'

My fingers are wet with blood, and I wipe them on my clothes. 'But aren't demons just fallen angels too? What's the difference between them and'—I catch myself—'your brothers?'

It's Daniel who answers, still holding his position with the others. 'Demons fell because they believed they were equal to God. They grew arrogant and despised creation. The sin of the Fallen was that their profound love for God's creation was poisoned by lust. In every other way they were loyal Watchers and holy warriors.'

Nathaniel remains impassive. I can see where Daniel learned his emotional control.

'Gabriella,' the angel says, 'there's much you need to relearn, and you can only do that safely under my protection. Return with me and allow me to watch over you.'

I let out a startled laugh. 'Are you forgetting what happened the last time I was there?'

'Now that you have a hint of what we are up against, you must understand why we used certain methods to try to reclaim your memories. It did not work, and I give you my word it will not happen again.'

'What's the point? I can't give you what you want. One of your so-called bottom-dwelling demons just said he cut my head off. *He* knows more than I do. Maybe you should put your efforts into torturing him.'

A tiny crease appears between Nathaniel's eyebrows. 'Which one?'

'Bel,' Rafa says.

'Did he claim you were alone when this attack took place?'

'No. He said Jude was there. Begging for my life.'

Nathaniel looks to Daniel. 'Is this true?'

Daniel discreetly straightens his shirt. 'So Belial claimed.'

The darkness changes. Micah reappears on the deck with six new Rephaim. Like the others, they're in black, but they're not armed. They all do a double-take when they see me.

'Taya first,' Daniel says, and two of the women go to her.

'They're the healers?' I ask Rafa.

He nods. 'Soldiers not on rotation get healing duty.'

Of course. No down time at the Sanctuary.

Micah goes to Daisy. There's not much left of her black T-shirt. Her torso is smeared with clotting blood and grass. She puts her thumb and little finger up to her ear, and mouths, 'I'll call you.' Micah nods a farewell to me, and the two of them disappear.

'Look,' Rafa says, and I turn to see Ez and Zak coming along the boardwalk. Zak is carrying Mick and Ez has her fingers pressed to his bearded throat. In Zak's arms, Mick almost looks small. And he's so still.

'Can they shift to help him?'

'No,' Rafa says. 'That only works on us.'

Uriel is trailing behind them. He has Rusty over his shoulder and is swinging something big and gray in his left hand. Bile rises in my throat. It's a hellion head. Uriel tosses the macabre trophy to Malachi, who uses his good arm to catch it.

Rafa nods his head at the cabin and they take Mick and Rusty inside. We follow to see Zak laying Mick on the daybed. Ez takes her hand away to check on the wound. His neck is chewed up like it's been through a grinder. Blood seeps from multiple bites, so at least his heart's still beating. But he's a mess: his beard is matted and one eye is swollen. The blue tank top is soaked in blood.

I grab a tea towel from the kitchen and take over applying pressure on the wound. Ez checks Mick's side, gently probing for more damage.

'I think it's just the neck.'

'That's probably enough,' I say. Rusty is propped up in a chair at the dining table, his head lolled forward. 'How bad is he?'

Zak scoffs. 'Big hero fainted and smacked his head

against a tree going down. He'll survive. He's got nothing to worry about.'

'Except that his brother's been mauled by a hell monster.' I rearrange the tea towel to find a dry section and put pressure back on Mick's wound. 'He needs to get to a hospital.'

'We can treat him at the Sanctuary,' Daniel says, over my shoulder.

'Uh-uh.' I turn to face him and find Nathaniel has come inside too. 'There's a medical center in town,' I say. 'He's not going anywhere but there. Rusty's going too.'

Daniel doesn't need to argue for me to know he doesn't agree. 'What if he tries to explain how he got those injuries?'

'Who's going to believe them? Everyone in town knows what they do up here. They'll sound like the pair of stoners they are.' My muscles are aching now, and a slow throb has started in my cheek. 'Let's get Mick patched up. Right now, before he loses any more blood.'

'Enough of this,' Rafa says, stepping between Daniel and me. He signals for Ez to take over tea towel duty and sends Zak in Rusty's direction. 'Where's the medical center?'

As soon as I tell them, Zak and Ez shift with the Butlers.

'That was a mistake.' There's an edge to Daniel's voice I haven't heard before. He's about to lose his cool.

'This whole thing was a mistake,' Rafa says. 'So why don't you all piss off back to Italy and let us clean up your mess.'

'Do you really think you can keep Gabriella safe?'

'Not your problem.'

'But it is hers.'

Nathaniel doesn't interrupt their bickering. He's only interested in me.

'Gabriella,' he says quietly, 'Rafa is an exceptional fighter, but he alone can't hold back those who will come for you.'

I meet his eyes. 'Do you remember my mother? My *real* mother?'

He blinks. 'No.'

'Really?'

'Like all the other women my brothers seduced, she did not survive the birthing.'

I watch the lying, the smoothness of it.

'Every single one died?'

'Yes, Gabriella, all of them.'

I move to stand beside Rafa. 'I'm staying here.'

'In that *fishing* village down there?' Daniel says.

I straighten my spine but it's all bluff now. I've got nothing left. 'That *fishing* village is my home.'

'Gabriella.' Even Nathaniel's stillness demands attention. 'I understand how confusing this must be, so I will allow you some latitude. You may stay. For the moment.'

Like I need his permission.

'But I will assign Rephaim to watch over you.'

'No.'

'That is not negotiable.'

'Who?'

Nathaniel's lips curve a little. Possibly a hint of a smile. 'Taya and Malachi.'

'Fuck. Off.' I might not want Taya dead, but that doesn't mean I want her in Pan Beach either.

'Language, Gabriella.'

'They're injured,' I say. But, of course, they won't be for long. 'Well, they're sure as hell not staying with me.'

'They can look after themselves.'

I lean back against the table. I am so *tired*. I want to get cleaned up and fall into bed. But first, I need to see Maggie.

'I have to go.'

'As you wish.'

I turn to Rafa. 'Now?'

Rafa looks at Daniel when he answers. 'Sure.'

His hand slides around my hips. I think I see Daniel's nostrils flare before he gets himself under control.

'Come near my friends again and I'll cut your head off myself,' I say to him.

Daniel opens his mouth, as if to respond.

'Let's go.'

The cicadas start up again as I lean into Rafa, so anything Daniel may have said in parting is lost in their noise.

And then we're in that icy wind again. Rafa's arms are around me. Warm. Snug. His fingers in my hair, his heart beating against mine. Usually it's me clinging to him.

This time, he's holding me just as tight.

PRICE TO PAY

We find Jason alone at the bungalow, sitting at the table with his head in his hands. My heart misses a beat.

'Where's Maggie? Is she safe?'

He nods, not looking up.

'Where is she?'

'With Simon.'

I'm holding my breath. I let it out. 'But she's okay?'

'She's fine.'

'Why aren't you with her?'

He lifts his head. His blue eyes are exhausted. 'She doesn't want to be around any of *us* right now.'

'You just saved her.'

'I'm still not human.'

Rafa shakes his head, and mutters something I can't

catch. I push him out the way so I can sit down.

'What happened?' I lay the katana between us on the table.

'I asked her if she trusted me before we left the cabin. She said she did, and then I shifted with her. When we got here, she couldn't get away from me quickly enough.'

'Didn't you tell her you've never been a part of the Rephaim?' I ask.

'I didn't get a chance. She wanted me to go back and get Simon.'

'And then you let her walk out? After what just happened?'

Jason rubs his forehead. 'What else could I do? I wasn't going to force her to stay here with me.'

Rafa wanders over to the sink. 'Man up, Goldilocks. She's had a big couple of days.'

Coming from him, that's almost sensitive.

'Do you know where they went?' I ask.

Jason shrugs. 'Rick's, probably.'

So that's where we're going. I stand up as Zak and Ez walk through the door. They were polite enough to arrive in the hallway, on the off-chance we're not alone.

'Where's your friend?' Ez asks.

She's still covered in Mick's blood and is sporting a fading bruise on her cheek, above her scar. I touch my own face. The split skin has mended and my cheek is nowhere near as tender. Rafa must have healed me on the way here. He, on the other hand, is still bleeding from the shoulder.

'Gone out for a drink.'

'I don't blame her,' Ez says. 'I could go for one myself.'

'What happened with the Butlers?'

Ez rubs her right shoulder, and Zak absently begins to massage the muscle. 'We dropped them off at emergency,' he says. 'An ambulance pulled in as we got there. Ez told them we'd been hiking and found them in a gully. Then we got out of there.'

Rafa breathes out heavily. 'Those two are going to be a problem.'

'What do you want to do about it?'

'Nothing tonight.'

Zak nods. 'We might head back to Mexico for a few hours.'

I find the energy to stand up. 'Thanks, guys. I really appreciate what you did tonight. I know Mags does too.'

Ez is tired, but her smile reaches her eyes. 'It's just good to be on the same side again.' She gives me a quick hug.

Zak holds out his hand as if to shake mine, but when I reach for him, he hauls me to his huge chest and slaps me between the shoulder blades. 'Hang in there, kid. We've got your back.'

I'm glad they shift quickly, because I'm so tired and emotional right now I might cry. Again.

I pull myself together. 'Are we safe?' I ask Rafa.

'For a while. Nathaniel's backed off for tonight, and the demons won't come into town.'

'Why not?'

'They lost another hellion tonight and they'll think you're under Nathaniel's protection. They won't be in a hurry to face him again so soon. Not without reinforcements anyway.'

'I need to go to Rick's and see Mags. Will you come with me?'

'Sure.'

'And you?' I ask Jason.

'I can't take seeing that look in her eyes again tonight.'

'Jason—'

'I'm going to respect Maggie's wishes. I'll go back to the hotel so she can come home.'

'I'd rather you were here.'

The pencil that Simon used to draw the map is still on the table. He reaches for it and sets it to spin.

'I mean it,' I say. 'We've still got a few things to sort out.'

He looks at Rafa and then back at me. His shoulders sag. 'I'll go to the hotel and shower,' he says. 'Then I'll come back.'

'Tonight?'

He sighs. 'Tonight.' But makes no move to go.

I run my fingers through my hair and find the claw

marks on my scalp almost healed. The cuts on my neck and arm are pretty good too, no seeping blood. I clean myself up at the kitchen sink. My fingers linger on the hellion bite, and I look around for Maggie's scarf.

'Just wear your hair down,' Rafa says.

I take it out and let it fall to my collarbone, check myself in the reflection of the microwave. 'Got another plan?'

'It's fine.' Rafa turns me towards him and tousles the ends of my hair so it sits over the scar. 'It'll be fine.'

I grab a handful of tissues and gesture to his bleeding shoulder. He looks downs and shrugs. I gently dab at the wound. He watches me, his eyes dark in this light. Then he takes the bloodied tissues from me and tosses them into the bin. I catch Jason's attention one last time.

'See you back here in an hour.'

He nods.

'I don't care if Mags is talking to you or not. You and I are finishing that conversation.'

Rafa raises his eyebrows at me.

'Later,' I say and head down the hallway and out the front door.

DON'T FREAK OUT . . .

I pause at the top of the steps and lean on the post. The hill looks steeper than it did a few hours ago.

'Do you want to cheat?'

Rafa is so close I feel his breath on my neck. I lean against him. I feel his heartbeat as he wraps his arms around me, and then the deck is gone, and I'm crushed again by cold and noise. And then it's over. We're behind a recycling skip out the back of the bar, stale beer and rum in the air.

I disentangle myself from Rafa, surprised at how little dizziness I feel this time, and walk up the narrow alley between the bar and the neighboring shop. I straighten my clothes before I step out onto the street. And then I'm breathing in that wonderful salty air. The surf is rolling in beyond the lights and poincianas. Lorikeets still chatter in the trees. The hoodie brigade are laughing and smoking on a bench across the road. At least some things are constant. The smell of wood-fired pizza from Rick's kitchen reminds me I haven't eaten.

We move through the Tuesday night crowd outside the bar, weaving around stools and wine barrels. Maggie isn't at our usual window position. I push my way inside.

It's cheap sangria night, so there are plenty of girls lined up around the bar, and plenty of guys jostling to pay, including Jacques, the artist. He raises his wine glass and winks at me. It's hard to believe that only a few days ago he was the weirdest person I knew.

'—tore up by something. Deb reckons those huge feral cats are back.'

A snatch of conversation pulls me up short.

'Your sister's full of shit.'

'She bandaged him up, dickwad. I think she'd know.'

'What's Mick's say?'

'Dunno. He's still out of it. So's Rusty.'

'Dude, if there's something on the mountain big enough to take down those pricks, we're all fucked.'

I spot Maggie and Simon, huddled together at a table in the corner, near the jukebox. She's changed into jeans and a navy polo shirt, and her hair is tied back. She startles when she sees me, rises, as if to come and meet us, but then falters. By the time we reach her, she's just standing there, her arms wrapped around her chest.

'You okay?' I reach out and brush her arm.

When she flinches, Simon is straight up out of his chair. 'Get away from us before I call the cops. I should have called them already, but Mags said—'

'Calm down,' I say quietly.

'Calm down?' Simon eyes are unforgiving. 'Those *psychos* wanted you, not Mags. I can't believe you dragged her into this. It's all your—'

'Sit *down* and shut your mouth,' Rafa says.

Simon and Maggie drop back into their seats as if he's knocked them there. Rafa takes two chairs from a nearby table and we sit down.

'Those *psychos* locked Gabe in a cage with one of those monsters you saw tonight, so don't fucking whine about this being her fault.'

Maggie's face crumples when Rafa mentions the hellion.

'And you know that's true,' Rafa says to Simon, 'because you saw the marks on her neck this morning, didn't you?'

Simon doesn't answer, but Maggie is crying now. She finally looks at me. 'Oh, babe, is that true?'

I swallow the lump in my throat. 'I am *so* sorry, Mags. I had no idea they would grab you—'

She hugs me fiercely, burying her face in my neck. Her hair still smells of cherry blossom.

Tears leak down my cheeks. I'm crying in public. I don't care.

'What about Rusty and Mick?' Simon is less certain now.

'They're getting patched up,' Rafa says. 'They'll survive, if they keep their mouths shut. Same goes for you.'

The room contracts to me and Maggie and I pull back from her so I can see her. 'Did they hurt you? Did they do anything you didn't want them to?'

She shakes her head. 'Taya threatened to break my legs if I tried to escape, but she never laid a hand on me. None of them did.'

'Not even Malachi?'

She shakes her head again.

'Was anyone else at the cabin?'

'Just Micah, mostly. He seemed pretty stoked that you were alive. And then there was Daniel.' She gives me a sheepish smile and out of the corner of my eye I see Rafa roll his eyes and settle back to crowd-watching. 'He was very polite. He asked a lot of questions about you.'

'What sort of questions?'

'How we met, what you're like. If I'd ever seen you fight.' She shakes her head. 'I told him you had a temper but you didn't know how to fight—and then you turned up tonight swinging that sword . . . Those things, those hellions . . . they're what you dream about?' She shudders. 'They're hideous.'

'Yeah, I know.'

I'm not sure Simon can take any more talk about hellions. He's staring across the bar, eyes blank.

'Look, Mags, about Jason . . . He's been beside himself since Taya grabbed you.'

'Don't, Gaby. He had so many chances to tell us who he was, and he didn't.'

'He has his reasons. And he told me when it counted.'

'I don't care.' She looks away. 'That night on the couch at Rafa's, we talked about a lot of pretty intense stuff. And he said some things to me . . . If he meant them, then the least he owed me was the truth.'

I put a hand on her arm. She's trembling. 'He's never been a part of the Rephaim. Until tonight, none of the others knew he existed—not even Nathaniel. Especially Nathaniel. He risked all that to come get you.'

At Nathaniel's name, Rafa brings his boot up to rest on his knee. 'Poor little Goldilocks,' he says under his breath and taps the table to get Simon's attention. 'Hey, barkeep, any chance of a beer?'

Simon slowly focuses on him. Then he takes the last swig out of his own bottle. 'Only if you're buying.'

Rafa fishes notes out of his pocket and pushes them across the table. As soon as Simon is out of earshot, Rafa turns to Maggie. 'What did Daniel say to you?'

'What do you mean?'

'What did he say to make you so twitchy when we walked in?'

Maggie picks at her nails. I thought she was just freaked out by what she'd seen. It hadn't crossed my mind there was more to it.

'It's okay,' Rafa says. 'You can tell us.'

She finally looks up, at me rather than Rafa. 'Daniel said you'd done a deal with *demons*. He said you and Jude cared more about finding the Fallen than you did about protecting people like me. That if the Fallen got loose, millions of people would die.' She tears part of her nail free. 'And I know you don't remember what happened before you came here . . .'

I can only stare at her.

'Daniel doesn't believe Gabe made a deal with demons any more than I do.' Rafa knocks his knee against Maggie's. 'Pretty Boy was trying to scare you into spilling whatever secrets Gabe's told you. You can't trust a word that comes out of his mouth—'

'I know, I know,' Maggie says quickly. 'It's just, this is all so crazy.'

'No shit,' I say. I smile at her and she smiles back. Some of the tightness eases at the base of my skull. We might still be okay.

'I've got a theory,' Rafa says.

'Spill it.'

'Bel says he took your head. But you're still alive, and it's obvious he has no idea how that's possible. He says Jude begged for your life, but he definitely doesn't have him as a prisoner—or trophy—or we would've heard about it long before now.'

'Keep going.'

'You dream about scuffles Jude's had with hellions. You dream about me'—his mouth quirks—'and you knew about the Dark Thoughts blog. And the brother you remember is like some idealized version of Jude—'

'And then there's the Foo Fighters,' Maggie says.

Rafa frowns, and Maggie holds out her hand. 'Give me a dollar.'

He hands her the coin. She goes to the jukebox and picks a song. The single guitar note starts up as she sits back down. Maggie holds up a hand to stop Rafa interrupting. She watches me closely.

'Go on,' she says. 'You know it, don't you? But you didn't before.'

Of course I know the tune—Jude played it all the time, but I'd never paid attention to the lyrics. Except, of course, I know them by heart now.

Rafa is looking from me to Maggie. 'And?'

'Didn't Jude love these guys?'

'Holy shit.' Rafa is looking at me, but it's not me he's seeing.

'So? Rafa?'

'He must have had a hand in messing with your memories.'

I frown. 'Is that possible? I mean, could he do that?'

'No, but—'

'Then why say it?'

'Because it's the only thing that makes sense.'

'But that means he was still alive after I got hurt.' The muscles across my breastbone constrict. 'If he's been alive all this time, why haven't you heard from him? Why haven't I?'

'Maybe he's hurt. Maybe he's being held somewhere. Maybe he's in a coma.'

Or maybe we did something so bad, the only way Jude could protect me was by making me forget and then disappearing himself.

The song ends and in the quiet, Maggie says, 'Maybe he doesn't know who he is either.'

I watch this register on Rafa's face. The idea that Jude is out there somewhere, as defenseless as I was; the thought Jude might think I'm dead too. I feel like vomiting. Rafa looks the same way.

'That means he found a way to change your memories and then let someone change his,' Rafa says.

I want this to be true so badly, I can barely breathe.

'He couldn't do that alone . . .'

Rafa doesn't finish the sentence, but it needs to be said.

'It would involve doing a deal with someone who's not human, wouldn't it?'

Rafa grabs a coaster and taps it on the table in time with the new song grinding out of the jukebox. 'Nathaniel doesn't have that sort of power, so it can't be one of the Fallen, and the Garrison hates us, so it's not them. Demons definitely don't have the juice —and if Bel thinks he killed you, then maybe his memories about the attack have been messed with too.'

'Then who did it? And why?'

Simon is on his way back, carrying four beers by their necks.

Rafa leans in closer. 'That's what we're going to find out.'

I like the way he says 'we.' Like there's no option except the two of us doing this together. Maggie looks from me to Rafa and back again.

'What?' I say.

A small smile. 'Nothing.'

Simon puts the beers on the table a little too hard.

'What is it?' Maggie asks.

'Rick's jeep is still up the mountain.'

Rafa sighs. 'You want me to drop you back up there?'

Simon looks at him, a faint crease in his brow, and then his eyes widen when he realizes what Rafa's offering. 'I don't want anything from you—and sure as hell not *that*.'

'I agree.'

Rafa raises his eyebrows at me.

'I don't think anyone should be wandering up there alone any time soon. Simon came through for us tonight—'

'And now he's—'

'—and the least we can do is keep him out of strife with his brother.'

Rafa holds my gaze for a few seconds, and then pulls his phone out. He taps the screen, waits, and then says: 'Zak—one last favor.' He turns away, so I can't hear the rest of his conversation.

I grab my drink and down nearly half the bottle in three gulps. Beer has never tasted this good.

Simon watches me, fascination mixed with something else. Fear, maybe.

'What are you?' he says.

'Thirsty,' I say, and manage a tired smile.

His face softens, like it always does when I smile at him, but then the wall comes straight back up. 'You know what I mean.'

'Didn't Mags tell you?'

'I tried,' she says. 'He didn't want to know.'

'She can explain it when you're ready.' I tap Maggie's glass. 'Are you coming home tonight? I need to talk to Jason about a few things, so I told him to come back after he's cleaned up.'

'I don't know. I need time.'

Simon picks up the coaster Rafa was playing with and adds it to the neat stack in the middle of the table. 'Are we safe?' he asks.

'Yeah,' I say. 'It's over.'

Rafa ends the call as I finish my beer. 'Done,' he says.

'Good.' I stand up. 'I need to sleep.'

Maggie hugs me again.

'Please come home tonight,' I say, quietly. 'There's stuff I want to talk to you about.'

It's the best gift I have for her, and when she gives me one last squeeze, I know we're going to be okay.

THE THIRD WHEEL

Outside, Rafa turns right instead of left.

'I need to grab some fresh clothes,' he says.

'And we're walking?'

His face is lit by the glow of a restaurant. 'I thought you might prefer to stay on foot.' He stops. 'Are you still sore? Would you rather shift?'

'No, I'm okay.' I touch his shoulder and hold my finger to the light to see if he's still bleeding. 'You should have got Zak or Ez to fix that. Sorry I'm not more useful.'

'You were plenty useful tonight.' He moves off again and I fall into step.

'Listen.' I look down at the paved footpath. I want this to come out right. 'Thanks for everything tonight. I know you didn't have to do any of it.'

He laughs. 'Yeah, right. Like you would have let me off the hook if I'd walked away.' He glances at me. Something flickers in his face before he looks away. 'And, any excuse to cause a bit of chaos.'

'Well, either way, thanks. I don't know what I would have done without you.'

I wait for the smartarse comeback, but there's none. We walk in silence.

The fibro shack is in darkness. Rafa grabs the key from under one of the dead pot plants out front. He opens the door, flicks on the bare bulb overhead and heads for the bedroom.

'I won't be long,' he says, not looking at me.

I rub my eyes. I may as well freshen up while Rafa gets his gear together. I'm almost at the bathroom when he steps out of his room. Shirtless.

'Oh, sorry.' I step back, my cheeks hot. What is *wrong* with me? My eyes flick back to his bare torso. It's covered in bruises and welts. 'Rafa . . .' I nearly reach out and touch him. 'You need to get someone to heal those.'

Rafa closes the space between us. He searches my eyes, and then slides his fingers around my neck. My hands are on his chest, my fingertips pressing into him. His skin is warm. We watch each other, unblinking. And then his lips are on mine and it's like I remember—breath and heat. Only this time his kiss is slower, deeper. I mold myself against him. I've been waiting for this since he walked out of the bar that first night.

I'm not exhausted anymore.

My arms are around his neck, my fingers in his hair. I can't get enough. He presses me against the wall, his hand grazing my side to my hip. His lips are hungrier now. As are mine.

We only break apart for air, and then Rafa is nuzzling my neck, even the hellion scar near my collarbone. I make the smallest sound of pleasure and his mouth covers mine again. He pulls me to him and walks me backwards into his room, kissing me the whole way.

We're on the bed. My boots, shirt, and jeans come off, and his jeans are undone now and low on his hips. I'm not sure he's wearing anything under them. I can't keep track of the places he's touched and kissed me. My entire body thrums.

And then his hand slides up the inside of my bare thigh. All the way.

I gasp. I regret it as soon as the sound escapes me, but I've never been touched like this before, by hands so assured, so practiced.

His body stills and he stops kissing my throat. His heart is banging against his ribcage, and mine keeps pace with it. His hand lingers just inside my thigh.

'Do you want me to stop?'

I swallow. 'No. It's just . . .' I don't want to say it.

'Are you . . . Have you ever . . . ?'

'Does it matter?'

He watches me, wrestling with something. I don't look away. Just because I didn't want a drunken encounter in a backpackers' hostel doesn't mean I've been avoiding this moment. I wasn't ready. Until now.

'It's not a big deal.'

His breath is warm on my neck. 'Yeah, it is. It's a huge deal.' He slides his hand over my underwear and runs his palm across my bare stomach, the urgency already fading from his touch.

My hand has gone still on his back, but I slide it down to his hip now and gently move my thumb low on his abdomen, making a slow circle. 'It's my decision.'

Rafa closes his eyes. 'It's not just yours.'

'Who else's is it?'

'Gabe's. And she'd never forgive me.' He looks down at me, his green eyes serious. 'You think you're a virgin.'

Anger flares. 'I get it.' I try to roll away from him but he doesn't let me get far.

'Get what?' He pulls me back to him.

'You want Gabe. Not me.'

He traces a path down the length of my spine, resting his hand in the small of my back. 'Unless you're not paying attention, I think you can work out how much I want *you* right now.' He gives me a meaningful look, and I blush all over again.

'So why wouldn't *Gabe* forgive you?' I hate talking about myself in the third person, but I have to: she's not me.

His fingers lightly brush my skin. 'I told you,' he says, 'you and me, we haven't been on good terms for a long time. So if I took advantage of the fact you don't remember why, and then you got your memory back . . .' He gives me a grim smile. 'You'd probably make a coin purse out of my balls.'

'Nah,' I say lightly, like his rejection doesn't sting. 'I'd want something big enough to carry more than five-cent pieces.'

His smile slowly widens, and he draws me closer. 'Don't push your luck, *Gaby*. This resolve of mine is pretty fragile.'

'You could always tell me what you did, and I can decide for myself how pissed off I want to be.'

'What makes you think it was all me?' He's still playful, but there's a hint of warning in his tone.

'You know, you can't have it both ways.'

'Which ways would that be?'

'You can't make decisions for me based on what I might remember, and then punish me for what I don't.'

He laughs, deep and low in his chest. 'You still know how to complicate things, I'll give you that.'

'And you know how to avoid answering a question.'

'It's a long, complicated story—'

'So you keep saying.'

'—and we don't have time right now. Not if you want to talk to Goldilocks. And I for one want to hear what he's got to say. It's way past time I was in the loop.'

I rest my forehead on his chest and breathe in sandalwood and sweat.

I want to know what happened between Rafa and me in the past—there has to be more than what everyone's told me. But—

'Yeah, we need to go.'

His hand comes around to rest on my hip again, and then he pulls away and we're no longer touching. 'So, what's his story?'

I sigh. 'You're not going to like it.'

NOTHING STAYS BURIED

I tell Rafa everything Jason told me earlier tonight, sitting cross-legged on the bed—shirt back on and jeans close by. Rafa is leaning against the wall. He is quiet the whole time I'm talking. There's no interjection or sarcastic commentary. He just listens, occasionally looking away and grinding his jaw. I wait for him to call Jason a liar, or threaten to tear him apart. But when I'm finished, he stares past me.

'What are you thinking?' I ask at last.

Rafa doesn't look at me. 'I'm going for a shower.'

'That's it?'

He hunts around in a duffel bag on the floor and grabs a clean pair of jeans. 'Just give me a minute.' He goes to the bathroom.

And then I get it: this is a big deal for Rafa. For me, it was the latest in a long line of bombshells, but for him it's huge.

The shower starts up across the hall and I briefly wonder how well his resolve would hold if I walked in there now. But I'd never have the guts to do something like that. I put my jeans on.

He comes back into the room in a cloud of steam and apple shampoo, wearing only his jeans. He's rubbing his head with a towel, and when he stops his hair sticks up.

'I've got a question or two for that little fucker.' Rafa tosses the towel over the chair beside the bed.

My whole body relaxes. I much prefer Rafa being cocky or even childish: the pensive, silent version is too hard to read. He finishes getting dressed. 'Ready?'

I put my arm around him, ready for a quick shift, but he stands there for a moment, holding me. Two blocks away, the surf rolls in, and a car horn sounds somewhere on the esplanade. I feel every place his skin touches mine. He pulls me closer. And then we make the shift to the bungalow.

We turn up in the kitchen—no polite hallway arrivals for Rafa. My eyes are still shut, so I hear Jason's startled reaction: a cupboard thumping, and swearing.

'Goldilocks,' Rafa says.

I wait a second for my body to settle, nodding my

appreciation to Jason that he's come back. He's probably about to regret it. Jason is in fresh clothes, his hair in damp curls. The kettle is rumbling on the bench and he's holding a mug in one hand and a box of tea in the other.

'You want one?' he asks me.

Delaying this conversation is only going to make Rafa worse, so I blurt, 'I've told him everything.'

Jason takes a step back. 'Look, I realize you're probably angry—'

'Why would I be angry?' Rafa strolls over to the bench and runs his fingers over the handles sticking out of the knife block. 'Just because I've been lied to my whole life, my best friend didn't trust me, and you've played me for an idiot from the beginning—'

'I haven't played anyone,' Jason says, his voice tight. 'I didn't know if I could trust you. I still don't.'

Rafa pulls out one of the carving knives and checks the line of the blade. 'Let's say you're not completely full of shit. Let's say your mother didn't die, her cousin was Jude and Gabe's mother, and they found you. And let's say you've been hiding out all these years to avoid Nathaniel and the Sanctuary. Why have you crawled out of your hole now? What's your game?'

'I don't have a game—'

'Bullshit. Everyone's got a plan for the Fallen. What's yours? Hand them over to the Garrison or join them?'

Jason slams the mug down on the bench. 'Why does it have to be one or the other? We don't even know what happened to them. Shouldn't we find that out first?'

'You want a counseling session, Goldilocks? You want to sit on a couch and hold hands with your deadbeat dad and ask him why he abandoned you?'

'I want the truth,' Jason says. 'And I'd think you'd be a little interested in that yourself.'

Rafa puts the knife down. 'So, what, you've been looking for them all this time?'

'No, I've been learning everything I can about angels and demons, trying to understand what I am. I've read thousands of books, studied theology, visited dozens of sacred sites, and talked to just about every angel-obsessed *expert*—'

'But you never went to Nathaniel.'

'If he's got all the answers, why did Jude and the rest of you leave the Sanctuary?'

I think about all those books in Jude's room on Patmos. My brother's been searching for the same thing as Jason.

'For the minute,' I say, to stop their bickering, 'I'm more interested in the last time you saw me and Jude.'

Jason pulls a tea bag out of the box and takes a deep breath. 'I'll get to that, there are just a few things I need to tell you first so it'll make sense.'

'Like what?'

'Like the real reason my mother panicked and wanted to leave Italy after you and Jude found us.' He puts the bag in his cup and pours boiling water over it. 'She fell pregnant again.'

I frown. 'Who was the father?'

'Lucca, a fisherman from our village. He'd been in love with my mother for years. Always offering to make her respectable but she kept turning him down. That didn't stop her sleeping with him, though.' He gives a quick, tight smile. 'But Lucca was good to me, even though he knew I wasn't what you'd call normal. Anyway, when Mamma was carrying Arianna, she knew she was different too.'

'Different how?' Rafa asks.

'She said she could feel it.' Jason turns to me. 'And she fretted you or Jude would visit and see she was pregnant, and let something slip in front of Nathaniel. I mean, we knew Arianna wasn't going to be like me because Lucca was her father, but we shared the same womb. My mother thought there was a chance she'd still be special in some way and Nathaniel might come for her—and me. Lucca had family in New York, so Nonno sold our home and that's where we went.'

'And was she special?' I ask.

'On her third birthday, she told us there were devils in the apartment across the street. A week later it burned down. Arianna knew what I was before I ever tried to explain it to her. She had visions, premonitions—whatever you want to call them—about angels and demons, until she hit puberty. Then they stopped.'

'And then what?'

'We thought it was over. But years later she got married and had a daughter, Alessa, and she had the same gift.'

Rafa jams the knife back into the block. 'What the hell does any of this have to do with why you're here?'

'I'm getting there. In every generation of Arianna's descendents, the first-born daughter has had some form of the gift as a child. Some saw things before they happened, others dreamed about battles between angels and demons. I kept track of new births and when that first daughter arrived, I'd visit the family after a few years, introducing myself as a distant cousin. But every one of those girls already knew who I was as soon as they saw me—'

'So what!' Rafa's eyes flash. 'Get to the point.'

Jason squeezes his tea bag and puts it in the sink. 'The *point* is that the latest girl in Arianna's line doesn't have visions about angels and demons: she sees the offspring of the Fallen. She doesn't just know about me. She knows about every single one of us. Sees things that relate to us.' He looks back at me. 'It's the reason I made contact with you and Jude after all these years.'

'When?' I ask, already knowing the answer.

'A year ago.'

NO GOING BACK FROM HERE

'You know what happened to them?' Rafa's voice is low, frightening. 'You've known all this time?'

Jason backs away, his hands out in front of him. 'No—'

Rafa shifts and materializes a millisecond later. His hand is around Jason's throat and he slams him into the fridge. It rocks back with the force.

I grab Rafa by the arm. 'Let him finish!'

'I told you not to trust him.'

'Just let him finish. Rafa, please.'

He lets go.

Jason doubles over when his feet hit the floor. He coughs and rubs his throat. He shoots Rafa a filthy look, grabs his tea, and pulls up a chair at the table.

'The girl, Daniela, had a vision about you and Jude,'

Jason says to me. 'She wanted to tell you about it—warn you.'

Rafa prowls back and forth behind him, all fury and menace. 'What was the vision?'

'She wouldn't tell me, but it must have had something to do with the Fallen. There's no other reason she'd risk making contact with you.'

'So you went running to Gabe.'

He shakes his head. 'I had no intention of doing anything about it. Too dangerous.'

'For who, you? You are such a spineless—'

'For Dani. She's eleven.' Jason scratches at a chip on his cup. 'Like I was trying to explain, she has a link to us.'

Rafa stops behind Jason's chair. 'She what?'

'She meditates and can see where we are, where any of us are.'

'Do you know what Zarael would do if he could get his hands on her?'

'Yes,' Jason says slowly. 'That's why I wasn't going to let anyone anywhere near her.'

'What changed?' I ask.

'She wouldn't take no for an answer. I've never seen her so wound up. She kept on and on at me to get you and Jude, and I kept saying no—and then she showed me a number she found online for the monastery in Italy and threatened to call and ask for you . . . There was no way I was going to the Sanctuary, so I got her to track Jude instead.'

'And you went to him.'

He nods. 'I'm the reason you started talking again.'

I blink and lean against the bench. The kitchen walls contract towards me.

Rafa pulls up a chair beside Jason. 'Then what?'

'I took Gabe and Jude to see Dani. They stayed with us for a few days—'

'The kid lives with you?'

'No, with her mother, Maria. She was the first-born girl of her generation, so she already knew all about me, and the Fallen. She wasn't keen on you two coming into her home, but Dani convinced her it would be all right. And then'—he snaps his fingers—'the three of you disappeared.'

'Just like that?'

'One morning. Maria went ballistic. She turned the place upside down, screaming abuse at me until she found a note Dani stuck on the milk in the fridge. It said she was with you and Jude, and not to worry.' He gives a short, humorless laugh. 'Try telling that to a single mother whose only child has gone missing with a couple of half-angel bastards.' He tugs on his earlobe. 'Fifteen hours. That's how long I spent shifting all over the world. I had no idea where I was going or what I was looking for, but I couldn't just sit there.' He blows on his tea and takes a sip. 'And then Maria went into Dani's room for about the hundredth time and found her asleep in her bed.'

Jason pauses.

I know what's coming next.

'We didn't come back with her, did we?'

'No. And Dani couldn't remember where you went or what happened. She couldn't even remember the vision that started it all. That freaked her out. When she finally calmed down, she was able to meditate and look for you.'

'And?' I glance at Rafa. He's very still now.

'She couldn't find you. It was like you didn't exist anymore. The only thing that made sense was that you were both dead.'

Rafa stands up abruptly and Jason flinches, but he's only going to the fridge. He digs out two bottles of water, and hands one to me. It's cool against my palm.

'But Gabe wasn't dead, so how come this girl couldn't sense her?'

'I don't know.'

The light above me is too bright. The floor is unsteady under my feet. I sit down.

'You didn't see my short story online, did you?'

Jason turns his mug around on the table.

'Two days after you disappeared, Maria and Dani left town. She rang me a day later and said she had to keep Dani safe. She wouldn't tell me where they were, but said they'd stay in touch. I didn't hear from them again until a week ago. Dani had a vision of Rephaim coming here, to Pan Beach.' He turns to Rafa. 'She saw you watching someone in a forest. She had the same vision three times before she realized the woman was Gabe. It threw her because she still couldn't sense Gabe. She worked out the only reason she could see her at all was because you were here, looking at her.'

Rafa grabs Jason's cup to stop it moving. 'So Jude could be alive somewhere, but someone's hiding him, and your kid can't see him because he's not with other Rephaim?'

Jason nods. 'It's a possibility.'

I need air. I get up and open the window over the sink, letting the night breeze wash over me.

'So, you're here out of guilt?' I ask Jason, not turning around.

He doesn't answer straightaway. I'm about to check he's still in the kitchen when he says, 'I wanted to make sure Dani was right and you were alive. And when I saw you walk out of that library . . . let's just say my reaction was a little *emotional*.' He keeps going, even with my back to him. 'But I didn't know if you blamed me for whatever happened, so I kept my distance for a few days. The first time I walked by you in the street I was ready for you to drag me into an alley and break a few bones, but you had no idea who I was. It wasn't until Rafa turned up at the bar that I worked out you had no idea who *you* were either.'

I stare out at the endless night sky. 'Why did you stay?'

'How could I leave? We were friends, Gaby. You and Jude had every reason to turn your back on Dani and me a year ago. You didn't. And you didn't tell anyone else about us. So of course I stayed. I wanted to know what happened to you—'

'And if you found the Fallen,' Rafa says.

A sigh. 'And that. Obviously.'

I turn around. 'So what now?'

'We need to find Dani and Maria.'

'What's the point?' Rafa says. 'The kid can't see where Jude is.'

'But maybe being near Gaby will make a difference— help her see Jude, or even remember what happened.'

'You haven't found them in a year,' Rafa says. 'What makes you think we can? We start with the nurse in Melbourne.'

Jason looks to me. 'What nurse?'

'The one who told me I'd missed Jude's funeral.'

He purses his lips and nods.

'But,' I say, 'we've got other things to sort out too. We have to keep Mags safe. If we disappear, she'll be the first person Nathaniel's crew grabs—or Simon.'

A motorbike stops in front of our house. A few seconds later, it revs, then roars off. The front door opens and shuts, and then Maggie walks into the kitchen, shoulders straight and face composed. She doesn't acknowledge Jason.

'He okay?' I gesture to the street.

'Sort of.'

I tilt my head towards my room. 'Got a minute?'

Maggie's gaze skims across Jason and Rafa. 'Of course.'

I point at Jason, and then the couch. 'You can sleep there.'

'I'm paying for a perfectly good bed on the esplanade,' he says, watching Maggie walk down the hallway.

He's not going anywhere.

'What about you?' I ask Rafa.

He gives me a slow smile. 'We'll work something out.'

Does he think he's sleeping in my bed? How's that going to work? Heat spreads across my chest.

'Any chance you could organize something to eat in the meantime?'

His smile falters. 'Do I look like hired help?'

Jason sighs and stands up. 'We'll get it sorted. You two go talk.'

'Speak for yourself, Goldilocks.'

They're still bickering when I close my bedroom door. Maggie is perched on the bed. I open the window and smell the jasmine. I don't crowd her when I join her.

'Remember when the weirdest thing about me was that story?'

She manages a tiny laugh. 'Yeah . . .' The smile fades. 'Does this still hurt?' She gently touches my bruised cheek.

'A little.'

She pushes my hair aside to look at the bite on my shoulder. 'Oh, Gaby.'

'It's not so bad now,' I say. 'What about you? Are you all right?'

'I'm fine.' She sits back on the bed and crosses her legs.

I give her a dubious look.

'When I realized they weren't going to hurt me, I was more worried about you. I can't believe you went with Daniel to Italy.'

I pull my boots off. 'Yeah, well.'

'You want to talk about it?'

I don't, but it's what I promised her.

I prop myself up with two pillows and tell her everything.

'Oh my god, Gaby, you took my shift?'

I nudge her with my knee. 'Yeah, and Connie let me make coffee.'

'Get. Out.'

I laugh. 'No, *that* would be ridiculous.'

Maggie smiles, but it doesn't last. 'What about you?' she asks. 'How do you feel about being one of them?'

I could get away with dodging that question tonight, but I owe her more than that.

'I don't know.' My voice wavers. 'I've been beaten up, lied to, and heard a couple of different versions of who I am and what I've supposedly done. And . . .'

She squeezes my arm. 'What if Jude's really alive?'

'My heart stops every time I think about it.'

'Does it freak you out? The angel part?'

My laugh is short. 'Whatever I am, it doesn't feel very angelic.'

'Yeah, well, none of them are very angelic either,' Maggie says.

'Except Jason.'

Maggie glances away, straightens the blanket.

'Come on,' I say. 'He protects little girls, talks about his feelings, and likes to bake. He probably even helps old ladies across the street. And those curls . . .'

'Stop it.' She almost smiles.

'You know he cares about you. He wants you safe.'

She nods, still not looking up.

'Listen.' I tap one of her toes. 'I'll cut the head off the next bastard who comes near you. I'll do whatever it takes to keep you out of this.'

'I don't want you to keep me out of it,' Maggie says.

'I'm not putting you at risk again, Maggie.'

'I still have to live, Gaby. If Dad's death taught me anything, it's that life is short and you can't hide from pain.'

'Yeah, but—'

'I can't fight, and I can't shift, and I can't do any of the things your Rephaim can do, but I can be your friend. And don't tell me you don't need one—not after what I saw and heard tonight.'

I find a loose thread on the blanket and pull it free.

'I don't deserve your friendship.'

'Yeah, you do.'

My throat closes over and a tear slides down my cheek. I don't brush it away. 'God, I must be wrecked,' I say, my voice thick. 'I've never cried this much in my life.'

'Just shows you're human.'

I manage a strangled laugh, not sure if she means to be ironic or not.

There's a knock on the door. 'Dinner's up,' Jason says. 'It's Thai.'

Maggie stares at the wall as his footsteps fade. She sighs. 'Come on.'

I wipe my face. 'I'll be out in a minute. I need to change.' She gives me a quick hug, and leaves.

I pull on fresh clothes slowly, like I'm underwater. Then I go to close the window. Leaves rustle in the jacaranda tree and a bright moon shines down between its branches. Was it only a week ago I stood here after another dream, drenched in sweat, sobbing, and missing Jude so much I couldn't breathe?

Now there's a chance he's standing somewhere looking at the same moon. Is he thinking about me?

Who does he think I am?

Maybe we screwed up. Maybe we betrayed everyone close to us and deserved whatever happened to us.

I don't care.

What matters is that Jude might be alive. Not my Jude. Another Jude. But still my twin.

I sigh, pull the window in, and lock it.

And then I walk towards the voices in the kitchen.

ACKNOWLEDGMENTS

To my agent, Lyn Tranter: thank you for tirelessly championing my work and never pulling a punch. I'm eternally grateful to you on both counts. To Mandy Brett and Alison Arnold at Text: you both got *Shadows* from the start and your support is the reason this book has seen the light of day. 'Thank you' just doesn't seem enough.

To Alison again, as my editor: words can't describe my appreciation for your amazing talent or my gratitude for your passion for this story. You've challenged me, and helped make *Shadows* better than I could have ever hoped for. I can't wait to work with you on Book 2. (Oh, and Maggie says thanks—she'd be nowhere near as stylish and creative without you.)

Thanks to Text Publishing publicist extraordinaire Stephanie Stepan and the rest of the team at Text including Rights Manager Anne Beilby: what a pleasure it is to work with people who genuinely adore books and care about their authors.

Heartful thanks to Tundra Books Publisher Alison Morgan and Editorial Director Tara Walker for bringing the Rephaim to North America, and to Sylvia Chan, Val Capuani, and Dorothy Milne for all your respective efforts on this stunning edition of *Shadows*.

Thanks too, to the team Orion/Indigo in the United Kingdom (especially Jenny Glencross and Nina Douglas), particular for the gorgeous cover.

A huge thank you to friends who read the first draft of *Shadows* (most of you, in installments). Rebecca Cram (aka Place): I love that after more than twenty years of friendship, our conversations still range from human rights issues to Harry Potter. It's so appropriate you were the first person to read *Shadows*, and I love that I get to put your name in my book. Michelle Reid, Sarah Koch, Elise Dunlop, and Kate Bevan: your positive responses and constructive feedback were invaluable. You do realize that you have to read all early drafts of my books from now on, don't you?

To (Dr) Lee McGowan: Your advice on past manuscripts and those manic conversations over coffee made me want to be a better writer, so thank you. Thanks, too, to Louise Cusack, whose feedback on a previous manuscript five years ago helped my writing career move forward.

To Heather Scott: my friend, business partner, and collaborator in all things foodie, arty, and theater-y. Your beautiful friendship is as precious to me as your flourless chocolate cake. Thank you for all you bring to my life. Thanks, too, to your other half, Alex Milosevic: a good friend, a nifty barista, and one of the few people who can still bait me in an argument.

Humble thanks to Celia and Brent Southcombe, two people whose lives inspire me on a daily basis. Thank you for your unwavering support and belief. You are amazing people and I'm in awe of how you're changing the world.

So many people have been a part of my writing journey over many years, not the least of whom are Nicola and Troy Bishop, who have been there to celebrate every milestone (and drown every sorrow) with a bottle of red or two. Thanks, guys. Of course, the journey isn't over yet so keep those glasses handy. Likewise to Pam and Kevin Hall and the Weller family—thanks for all your support. And to my dear friend, Anna Mitchell: I wish you were here to see this dream finally become a reality. I know you'd be proud. I still miss you.

Thanks for the love and encouragement from my immediate and extended family, especially to Mum and Dad. (See, that misspent youth came to some use after all.) Apologies again, Mum, for the bad language in *Shadows* . . .

To my husband, Murray, who never stops believing in me, even when I doubt myself: thank you for letting me be me—and making me laugh when I take myself too seriously. I wouldn't have made it this far without you. Whatever the future holds, I'm okay with it as long as you're a part of it.

And God. Yes, I'm thanking God. I know it's overdone and clichéd, and I'm far from a poster child for organized religion. But I've seen enough, experienced enough and made enough mistakes to know I'm here by the grace (and good humor) of God.

Lastly, but certainly not least—thank you to everyone who reads *Shadows*. I hope you enjoy this opening install-ment to the *Rephaim* series, that it lets you escape from the other stuff in life for just a little while.

HAZE

LOVE. NIGHTMARES. ANGELS. WAR.

HAZE

PAULA WESTON

Designed by obroberts • Cover image © Eduardo Diaz/Arcangel Images

ISBN: 978-1-77049-550-0 • eBook: 978-1-77049-552-4

IN THE STILL OF THE NIGHT

I almost wish I still had the blood-soaked dream of the nightclub.

At least then I'd be asleep, not lying here in the dark chasing thoughts I'll never catch. The jacaranda tree outside is still in the warm night; the moon casts a slight shadow of its twisted branches against the wall.

It's the quiet moments like this that get me, when it's impossible to pretend I've got a grip on everything that's happened in the past week. In the daylight, in this bungalow, I can fool myself into thinking I still have control over my life. But here in the dark I know that's a lie. And my life already has too many lies. For a year I believed four things: that my twin brother died in a car accident; that nothing in my life would matter as much as that; that nothing in my life would matter as much as that;

that my violent dreams are not real; that my memories from before are so faded because I was badly hurt in the accident that killed Jude.

It turns out none of these things are true, and it's the truth that keeps me awake. The biggest truth of all: Jude might be alive.

The shadow shifts on the wall, sharpens, blurs. The ache comes back into my chest. The possibility that I'll see Jude again, the cruel hope of it, never fails to take the breath out of me.

A year of hurting and missing him.

A year of nightmares.

And now the truth. The impossible truth.

My eyes track to the mattress on the floor next to my bed; Rafa's boots are beside it. The TV is on in the lounge room, volume low, blue light flickering under my door. Through the thin walls I can hear Maggie stirring in her room. Jason might be in there with her, but chances are he's on the couch in the lounge room, ignoring Rafa or being ignored by Rafa, still thinking of ways to make amends for not telling her he's one of us. Maggie's forgiven me because I didn't know.

How is Maggie sleeping? Is she dreaming of demons? Or of the three Rephaim who held her hostage up the mountain to get to me? I wish I could undo Monday and Tuesday night. I wish I could remember what it is everyone wants me to remember. What Jude and I actually did a year ago. It's not that I don't want to.

I roll over in bed, stare at the silhouette of the old tree outside and the smattering of stars beyond it.

Rafa says we're safe for now, but given he's sleeping on my floor instead of in his own bed at the shack he can't really believe that.

Not that he spends all night on the floor.

I turn again, kick the sheet off. Pull it back over me again. God, I need to sleep.

The TV goes quiet in the other room. A few seconds later my door opens and closes, floorboards creak beside the bed.

Silence. I breathe as though I'm sleeping. I can feel him listening. And then a zip slides undone, clothes drop to the floor, and Rafa slips under the sheet with me. Warmth radiates from him. His movements are slow, careful. His breath soft on my skin.

Like last night, he doesn't touch me. The night before, Tuesday night—after the attack at the Retreat when we got Maggie back—I leaned against him when he settled behind me. As soon as our bodies touched he went straight back to the mattress on the floor. Shifted from my bed to his. It's one of the more annoying talents of the Rephaim—their ability to be somewhere else in the blink of an eye. He didn't say anything. No explanation. No smartarse comment.

So, since then, we don't touch and we don't talk and he stays. We've slept beside each other before—on the couch on Patmos, when Rafa told me who I was. *What* I was. Then he was teasing, testing me. This closeness is different. Almost restrained. There's no sign of this Rafa during daylight hours. I know he doesn't want to finish what we started in his bedroom, but why sleep in my bed if he doesn't want the temptation?

He gets comfortable behind me, so close I can almost feel him. Almost. A deep sigh shifts my hair, tickles my neck. I close my eyes.

He knows I'm not asleep; he has to. So is he testing me, or himself?

One week. That's how long it's taken to get this complicated. That's how long I've known Rafa. He's known me for a lot longer, but I don't remember it so it doesn't count. I don't remember anything that's true before I woke up in hospital a year ago. I don't remember anything about my life with the Rephaim.

I should roll over, say something. Talk about Jude. Talk about the Rephaim and what their next move will be. Demand to know what happened between Rafa and me—that other version of me—all those years ago. Ask him to tell me again what he knows about the fight that Jude and I had, and why we made up ten years later, and what it was we did a year ago that nearly killed me. But he doesn't have answers and I don't want him to leave my bed. I don't want to be alone with those other thoughts.

'Can you keep it down,' Rafa says. 'I can hear you thinking from here.'

Typical. He even breaks his own rules. Outside the stars disappear behind a bank of clouds.

'Gabe.'

I sigh. How many times do I have to tell him? I swear he calls me that other name just to get a reaction. I pull the sheet over my shoulders to my chin.

'*Gaby,*' he says. 'We can't put it off any longer' He still doesn't touch me.

'What?' I keep my back to him. I know what's coming next: the one thing guaranteed to keep me awake a while longer.

'Tomorrow we go to Melbourne and start looking for Jude.'

The Music
Library

The History of
Gospel Music

Other Books in this series include:

The Music Library

The History of Gospel Music

By Adam Woog

LUCENT BOOKS

An imprint of Thomson Gale, a part of The Thomson Corporation

THOMSON

GALE

Detroit • New York • San Francisco • San Diego • New Haven, Conn. • Waterville, Maine • London • Munich

Acknowledgments
Special thanks for research advice to Pastor Patrinell Wright, whose Total Experience Gospel
Choir has brightened the Seattle music scene for many years.

Dedication
To Kirsten, Rayahna, and Kaylene Honaker

© 2006 Thomson Gale, a part of The Thomson Corporation.

Thomson and Star Logo are trademarks and Gale and Lucent Books are registered trademarks used
herein under license.

For more information, contact
Lucent Books
27500 Drake Rd.
Farmington Hills, MI 48331-3535
Or you can visit our Internet site at http://www.gale.com

LIBRARY OF CONGRESS CATALOGING-IN-PUBLICATION DATA

Woog, Adam, 1953–
  The history of gospel music / by Adam Woog.
    p. cm. — (The music library)
  Includes bibliographical references and index.
  ISBN 1-59018-735-0 (hard cover : alk. paper)
  1. Gospel music—History and criticism—Juvenile literature. I. Title. II. Series: Music
library (San Diego, Calif.)
  ML3187.W66 2005
  782.25'4'09—dc22
                                                                          2005010358

Printed in the United States of America

• Contents •

• Foreword •

In the nineteenth century, English novelist Charles Kingsley wrote, "Music speaks straight to our hearts and spirits, to the very core and root of our souls. . . . Music soothes us, stirs us up . . . melts us to tears." As Kingsley stated, music is much more than just a pleasant arrangement of sounds. It is the resonance of emotion, a joyful noise, a human endeavor that can soothe the spirit or excite the soul. Musicians can also imitate the expressive palate of the earth, from the violent fury of a hurricane to the gentle flow of a babbling brook.

The word music is derived from the fabled Greek muses, the children of Apollo who ruled the realms of inspiration and imagination. Composers have long called upon the muses for help and insight. Music is not merely the result of emotions and pleasurable sensations, however.

Music is a discipline subject to formal study and analysis. It involves the juxtaposition of creative elements such as rhythm, melody, and harmony with intellectual aspects of composition, theory, and instrumentation. Like painters mixing red, blue, and yellow into thousands of colors, musicians blend these various elements to create classical symphonies, jazz improvisations, country ballads, and rock-and-roll tunes.

Throughout centuries of musical history, individual musical elements have been blended and modified in infinite ways. The resulting sounds may convey a whole range of moods, emotions, reactions, and messages. Music, then, is both an expression and reflection of human experience and emotion.

The foundations of modern musical styles were laid down by the first ancient musicians who used wood, rocks, animal skins—and their own bodies—to re-create the sounds of the natural world in which they lived. With their hands, their feet, and their very breath they ignited the passions of listeners and moved them to their feet. The dancing, in turn, had a mesmerizing and hypnotic effect that allowed people to transcend their worldly concerns. Through music they could achieve a level of shared experience that could not be found in other forms of communication. For this reason, music has always been part of religious endeavors, from ancient Egyptian religious ceremonies to modern Christian masses. And it has inspired dance movements from kings and queens spinning the minuet to punk rockers slamming together in a mosh pit.

By examining musical genres ranging from Western classical music to rock and roll, readers will find a new understanding of old music and develop an appreciation for new sounds. Books in Lucent's Music Library focus on the music, the musicians, the instruments, and on music's place in cultural history. The songs and artists examined may be easily found in the CD and sheet music collections of local libraries so that readers may study and enjoy the music covered in the books. Informative sidebars, annotated bibliographies, and complete indexes highlight the text in each volume and provide young readers with many opportunities for further discussion and research.

A Joyous Noise

Gospel music, you know, can't really be written down. You have to hear it and feel it.
—*Gospel singer Albertina Walker*

Gospel music is central to worship in African American churches. It is passionate song that praises and celebrates the spiritual messages of Christianity. It is thus a celebration of life as seen through the lens of one of the world's great religions.

Musically, gospel is one of the most important and influential of all the native-born American art forms. It has profoundly influenced the course of America's other great musical forms: blues, jazz, and rock and roll. In turn, these styles have dramatically influenced gospel as well.

Gospel is, at its core, joyous and uplifting music that inspires an ecstatic mood in both performer and listener, no matter where it is performed. When performers express these feelings, their audiences are similarly moved. The gospel sound is thus nearly universal; it attracts fans from around the world, from many religions and all walks of life. For years gospel was mostly confined to the black church, but its infectious enthusiasm, combined with its messages of love, hope, and equality, today strike responsive chords in millions of people in the wider world as well.

Slave Songs

Gospel is rousing music, but it is more than that. It is also a repository of history, reflecting the bittersweet story of black people in America. Its origin lies, in large part, in music that African slaves brought to America. In the eighteenth and nineteenth centuries, this music intermingled with the Christian hymns favored by white settlers. The results of this blend were songs called spirituals, composed by anonymous slaves.

Many spirituals were religious in nature. However, they also spoke directly and eloquently about the ordinary,

Vanessa Williams raises her arms as she sings with a gospel choir in a church in Hollywood.

everyday lives of the slaves. As such, they provide listeners today with a vivid picture of those times. Writing in 1925, the African American composer James Weldon Johnson commented,

> [T]he Spirituals taken as a whole contain a record and a revelation of the deeper thoughts and experiences of the Negro in this country for a period beginning three hundred years ago and covering two and a half centuries. If you wish to know what they are you will find them written more plainly in these songs than in any page of history.[1]

Gospel Develops

In the late nineteenth and early twentieth centuries, two forms of popular music—blues and jazz—began to mingle with the black community's religious music. These styles already shared many characteristics, including strong rhythms, improvisation, spirited interpretation, and blue, or flatted, notes. These characteristics were holdovers from African music, as gospel historian and performer Horace Clarence Boyer notes: "Blues and jazz employ the same materials that spiritual music employs—and in most cases in the same way. Because they come from the same wellspring, they are sisters and brothers under the beat."[2]

By the 1920s and 1930s, a new style of worship music called gospel was beginning to emerge from this crossbreeding of styles, and it quickly dominated black religious music. The gospel sound took many forms: Some

songs were slow, others rousing; some had simple words and melodies, others had complex structures. Some were sung by soloists, others by groups such as choirs or quartets. Primarily, gospel was vocal music. If there was instrumental accompaniment, it was typically sparse—usually just a guitar, piano, or piano/organ combination.

The new gospel style was also characterized by its close association with the fervent style of black preachers. Gospel developed a tradition in which many of its foremost singers also served as ministers (a tradition that persists today). The combination is a natural one, as the distinguished singer and minister Shirley Caesar remarks: "Music and preaching go together like ham and eggs."[3]

Baptist and Pentecostal

During the 1920s and 1930s, gospel roughly divided into two main styles. These two streams represented the main divisions of the black church: Baptist and Pentecostal. The Baptist denomination was the older and more established of the two, and its music reflected this status; it tended to rely on slow, sweet hymns performed in a dignified manner. In contrast, Pentecostal churches (also called Holiness or Sanctified churches) favored boisterous music delivered in a more demonstrative fashion.

The two styles were by no means exclusive; there was a fair amount of overlap. Many Baptist-raised singers, for instance, were deeply influenced by the expressiveness and strong rhythms of Pentecostal music. The legendary singer Mahalia Jackson once commented,

> We Baptists sing sweet [but when] these Holiness people tore into "I'm So Glad Jesus Lifted Me Up!" they came out with real jubilation. I say: Don't let the Devil steal the beat from the Lord! The Lord don't like us to act dead. If you feel it, tap your feet a little—dance to the glory of the Lord![4]

The Golden Age

Without losing its capacity to inspire joy, gospel continued to grow in the next decades. The period from the mid-1940s to the mid-1960s, often called the Golden Age of Gospel, saw gospel reaching new levels of sophistication. It also began to reach far beyond the tight-knit world of the black church to find new and enthusiastic audiences.

In the 1950s and 1960s, gospel also developed a social and political dimension. These were the years of the civil rights movement, when African Americans were struggling to obtain equality with whites in such arenas as voting rights and education. Gospel singers and civil rights activists frequently addressed many of the same issues, such as freedom and equality, and many gospel songs—renamed "freedom songs"—served to inspire the movement during its most difficult days.

Gospel today continues to profoundly influence popular music; blues, soul, and rock and roll would not exist in their present forms without it. Gospel itself is also still evolving, as new generations of singers absorb existing styles and adapt them to create their own music. And the audience for gospel continues to expand: it is still worship music, performed by and for the faithful at church, but it also appears in a variety of unlikely places, such as Broadway theatrical productions and advertisements.

Gospel music and its encouraging messages have touched millions of people over time. It continues to be a vigorous and inspiring music today. But the story of the music's development begins centuries ago, in the grim days of slavery.

Chapter One

The Roots of Gospel

Nobody knows the trouble I see
Nobody knows my sorrow
Nobody knows the trouble I see
Glory, hallelujah.
　　　— "Nobody Knows the Trouble
　　　I See," *anonymous spiritual*

It is impossible to determine exactly how many Africans were imported as slaves to the American colonies, but authoritative estimates vary from 1 million to 10 million. It is known, however, that the first slaves arrived in 1619; by 1750, their numbers stood at about two hundred thousand. Most were in the southern colonies, where massive numbers of workers were needed to harvest such labor-intensive crops as rice, tobacco, sugar, and cotton.

Slaves were considered nothing more than property, and had no rights. Their owners bought and sold them like cattle. They lived in wretched conditions and were routinely treated with cruelty—beaten, raped, and separated from their families. Masters could, in some cases, kill their slaves without fear of punishment, as the destruction of one's own property was legally considered one's own business.

These slaves had little to bring comfort to their bitter lives, but they did have music. The music persisted despite frequent efforts on the part of slave owners to extinguish traces of African culture from their slaves. It reflected a rich tradition brought from Africa and then passed down from generation to generation. Writer James H. Cone notes, "Through song they [the slaves] built new structures for existence in an alien land. The spirituals enabled blacks to retain a measure of African identity while living in the midst of American slavery, providing both the substance and the rhythm to cope with human servitude."[5]

Traditional Music

Music had always been an important part of the slaves' former lives in Africa. Singing, dancing, and drum-

A slave family on a Georgia plantation harvests cotton in this photo from the 1860s. Slaves often sang in the fields to help them cope with their harsh working conditions.

ming were integral to both daily routines and major events. Songs, typically invented especially for particular occasions, drew on a wide range of ideas and topics for their lyrics.

The songs brought to America from Africa also reflected many cultures. Africans sold into slavery in America came from a number of tribes and regions, particularly from the area that

"Nothing but Patience for This Life"

Nineteenth-century writer and abolitionist Thomas Wentworth Higginson was one of the first people to write extensively about black spirituals. This passage is from "Negro Spirituals," an article published in the Atlantic Monthly *magazine in June 1867, and is reprinted on a Web site maintained by the University of Virginia.*

Almost all their songs were thoroughly religious in their tone, however quaint their expression, and were in a minor key, both as to words and music. The attitude is always the same, and, as a commentary on the life of the race, is infinitely pathetic [melancholy]. Nothing but patience for this life, nothing but triumph in the next. Sometimes the present predominates, sometimes the future; but the combination is always implied.

today makes up Ghana, Senegal, Sierra Leone, and Guinea. Their music therefore represented a number of separate traditions, each with its own distinctive character. Nonetheless, the music slaves brought with them typically shared some general characteristics. For example, it strongly emphasized group singing and playing. African music typically used call-and-response patterns, in which a solo vocalist alternates lines with an "answering" chorus.

Slaves' music was also based firmly on strong rhythms, beats that were typically created with drums and hand claps. Often, musicians used many different rhythms at once, a technique called polyrhythm. Gospel historian Robert Darden writes about this elemental characteristic: "Among the richest of the lavish gifts Africa has given the world is rhythm. The beat. The sound of wood on wood, hand on hand. That indefinable pulse that sets blood to racing and toe to tapping."[6]

New and Old Songs

Slaves in the colonies did their best to maintain their musical traditions. However, they were typically not allowed to make music as they pleased. Slave owners often banned musical instruments, especially drums, among their slaves. This was because in Africa drums were frequently used to communicate over long distances; the slave owners feared that drums could be used to convey information about possible rebellion from one group to another. As a result, slaves in America usually had to make music using nothing more than their voices and "body percussion" such as hand claps, foot stomps, or knee slaps.

Despite these restrictions, slaves continued to make music, especially through song. They continued to invent songs to mark both large and small events in their lives. They passed these songs on to each other and to their children.

Passing on songs invariably meant changing them, adding variations or improvisations. Bits and pieces of old songs were joined together or refitted with new melodies or words. Even new songs underwent regular change, with each performer changing it slightly to create a new version. Over time, as new generations were born and old ones died out, the songs sung in African languages were forgotten and new songs were created and sung in English.

Because the songs were not written down, dozens or even hundreds of versions of a single basic song could exist. Familiar songs might be so altered by time or locale that they became essentially new compositions. Sometimes, a new interpretation proved more durable than the original. Thomas Wentworth Higginson, a white abolitionist who studied slave songs extensively, wrote in 1867, "They [the slave songs] often strayed into wholly new versions, which sometimes became popular, and entirely banished the others."[7]

A New Religion

The topics of these songs varied widely, and slaves sang them in many different contexts. Some were work songs. When slaves worked in the fields, the songs helped them pass the time, lifted their spirits, and allowed them to coordinate group activity (such as carrying a heavy load together). Songs were also frequently sung in the slave quarters. For example, mothers used songs to lull their babies to sleep. And, of course, people sang for the sheer enjoyment of singing.

One of the most important reasons, however, was as an expression of religious faith. The earliest songs reflected the beliefs the first slaves brought with them. Over time, however, these original ideas were gradually lost. In most cases, the lyrics were replaced with ones devoted to Christian beliefs.

Slaves were exposed to the Christian religions in a number of ways. White missionaries, mostly from the north and from the Baptist and Methodist denominations, were a primary source. These missionaries were devoted to converting non-Christians to their religion, since they believed this was the only way to save the converts' souls. Even when Christianity was not actively promoted, slaves were frequently compelled to attend their masters' worship services. Over time, many slaves accepted the ideas put forth there.

The songs featured in these services were typically psalms set to music and traditional hymns (sometimes called long-meter hymns because of their

Music from the Heart

This passage by Booker T. Washington, a major black leader of the early twentieth century, comments on the quality of spirituals. It is quoted in Robert Darden's People Get Ready! A New History of Black Gospel Music.

They breathe a child-like faith in a personal Father, and glow with the hope that the children of bondage will ultimately pass out of the wilderness of slavery into the land of freedom. In singing of a deliverance which they believed would surely come, with bodies swaying, with the enthusiasm born of a common experience and of a common hope, they lost sight for the moment of the auction block, of the separation of mother and child, of sister and brother. . . . The music of these songs goes to the heart because it comes from the heart.

---

slow tempo). These were slow and rather monotonous pieces, sung without instrumental accompaniment or harmony by black and white members of the congregation alike. Gradually, at least among the slaves, these European songs of worship began to mingle with African-derived songs. Darden writes, "At some point, as the first slaves were reluctantly exposed to Christianity . . . the songs [they sang] to their ancestors and African gods became the songs of Jesus and Moses."[8]

A Powerful Attraction

Some slaves were resistant to the new religion, at least initially. Even though Christianity is in theory based on a message of love, compassion, equality in God's eyes, and brotherhood, the slave owners, who mistreated and abused other humans, applied these principles only when it suited them. The double standard was certainly not lost on the slaves. As William Wells Brown, who was born a slave, recalled, "[We] regarded the religious profession of the whites around us as a farce, and our master and mistress . . . as mere hypocrites."[9]

Nonetheless, what they heard at church held a powerful attraction for many slaves. There were clear reasons for this attraction. The slaves were deeply moved by the stories found in the Bible and retold countless times by white preachers. Moses delivering the Jews from bondage, Joseph being sold into slavery by his brothers, Jonah regaining freedom because of his faith—

In 1860 a black preacher reads aloud from the Bible to a congregation of slaves and their masters on a South Carolina plantation.

these and other Bible stories had clear parallels in the lives of the slaves. The stories were retold in the lyrics of songs such as "Go Down, Moses":

Go down, Moses,
Way down in Egypt's land,
Tell old Pharaoh,
To let my people go.

Thus, despite the hypocrisy they saw around them, many slaves found sustenance and comfort in Christianity. Its promise of a better life to come in heaven held out clear hope for people who lived in wretched circumstances. Its assertion about the equality of all before God and its promise of redemption for those who sinned also appealed to the slaves. As a result, many slaves fervently embraced Christianity. African American choir director and composer Hall Johnson has noted,

> This new religion of the slaves was no Sunday religion. They needed it every day and every night. The gospel of Jesus, the Son of God, who had lived and died for men, even the lowliest, took hold of the imagination a strange and personal way, difficult to understand for the average Christian of the formal church. For them, He was not only King Jesus but also "massa Jesus" and even *my* Jesus. . . . [W]ith this powerful spiritual support, life took on new meaning, a new dimension. For now they *knew* with absolute, unshakeable faith, that somewhere, sometime—they would be FREE! And then the slaves began to sing—as they had never sung before.[10]

Jubilee Songs

Inspired by the basic Christian message and Bible stories, slaves began to create songs reflecting the religion's promise of a better life to come. The songs expressed the sorrows of the lives of slaves, but they also expressed their hopes for the future. These songs were thus bittersweet combinations of suffering and joy. James Weldon Johnson noted, "The Negro took complete refuge in Christianity, and the Spirituals were literally forged of sorrow in the heat of religious fervor."[11]

These songs had several names before they became known as spirituals. They were at first variously called corn ditties, cornfield ditties, or jubilee songs. The latter name was inspired by an ancient Hebrew law providing that each fifty-year period was followed by a "year of jubilee," when all slaves were to be set free.

Many jubilee songs had double meanings, speaking clearly of both religious salvation and freedom from slavery. The black abolitionist Frederick Douglass, himself a former slave who had escaped to freedom in the North, wrote about these songs, "A keen observer might have detected in our repeated singing of 'O Canaan, sweet Canaan, I am bound for the land of Canaan' something more than a hope of reaching heaven. We meant to reach the North and the North was our Canaan."[12]

In fact, some jubilee songs were coded messages that helped slaves escape and evade recapture. These songs were associated with the Underground Railroad, the network of antislavery whites and free blacks that helped slaves flee to the North. For example, the song titled "Follow the Drinking Gourd" instructed escapees to keep to a northerly heading by reading the stars—the "drinking gourd" was the Big Dipper, which pointed to the North Star.

Brush Arbor Meetings

Some slave owners encouraged their slaves to embrace Christianity, since its teachings also emphasize obedience

"Those Songs Still Follow Me"

These words from the 1845 autobiography of the distinguished black abolitionist Frederick Douglass, himself a former slave, describe his very personal reaction to spirituals. They are reprinted in Bernice Johnson Reagon's If You Don't Go, Don't Hinder Me: The African American Sacred Song Tradition.

They told a tale of woe, which was then altogether beyond my feeble comprehension; they were tones, loud, long, and deep; breathing the prayer and complaint of souls boiling over with the bitterest anguish. Every tone was a testimony against slavery, and a prayer to God for deliverance from chains. The hearing of those wild notes always depressed my spirit, and filled me with ineffable sadness. I have frequently found myself in tears while hearing them. The mere recurrence, even now, afflicts my spirit, and while I am writing these lines, my tears are falling. To those songs I trace my first glimmering conceptions of the dehumanizing character of slavery. I can never get rid of that conception. Those songs still follow me, to deepen my hatred of slavery, and quicken my sympathies for my brethren in bonds.

---

and acceptance of one's earthly fate, no matter how disagreeable. However, many did not allow slaves to hold their own services. There were several reasons for this. One was the need to maintain control; if slaves attended only white services, there was less chance that the gatherings would be used to plan rebellion. As a result, laws were commonly passed prohibiting slaves from holding their own religious celebrations. Typical of these was a Maryland law "to suppress tumultuous meetings of slaves on Sabbath and other holy days," while a Georgia law stated that "every slave which may be found at such a meeting may . . . immediately be corrected, without trial, by receiving on the bare back twenty-five stripes, with a whip, switch or cowskin."[13]

To counter this suppression, slaves frequently organized secret Christian worship sessions. Using covert signals and passwords, slaves would gather to pray in their own fashion. Because these meetings were typically held in wooded areas, far from prying eyes, they were known as brush arbor meetings.

A major element of these meetings was their music. A preacher typically led the singing there, but everyone joined in. Closely connected to the songs of a brush arbor meeting was a dance called the ring shout, a descendant of a common African dance. In its most basic form, the ring dance was a ring of people moving in single file around a central point as others sang, stamped their feet, and clapped their hands.

Camp Meetings

In the late 1700s and early 1800s, brush arbor meetings declined in popularity. Instead, black Christians (and many whites as well) were increasingly drawn to a relatively new type of worship called the camp meeting. Camp meetings were outgrowths of the Evangelical movement, a fervent branch of Christianity that stressed a highly personal relationship with God. Camp meetings were large gatherings, typically held in large tents erected in the countryside. They featured several days of continuous religious services and were a far cry from the reserved, conservative style of worship practiced by

Black and white Christians gather in a Connecticut town for a camp meeting, an outdoor worship service that typically featured music and singing.

Criticism of Black Camp Meeting Music

The earliest mention in print of a distinctive black religious music may have been this 1819 passage by John F. Watson, a white man who was critical of what he termed black "excesses" at Methodist camp meeting revivals. It is reprinted in "Spirituals, African American" by Toonari, on the Africanaonline Web site.

We have, too, a growing evil in the practice of singing in our places of public and societal worship, merry airs, adapted from old songs, to hymns . . . most frequently composed and first sung by the illiterate blacks of the society . . . [At camp meetings] in the blacks' quarter, the colored people get together, and sing for hours together, short scraps of disjointed affirmations, pledges, or prayers, lengthened out with long repetitive choruses. These are all sung in the merry-chorus manner of the southern harvest field, or husking frolic method of the slave blacks; and also very like the Indian dances. With every word so sung, they have a sinking on one or other leg of the body alternately, producing an audible sound of the feet at every step and as manifest as the steps of actual Negro dancing in Virginia, etc. If some in the meantime sit, they strike the sounds alternately on each thigh.

many early Americans. These newer services incorporated such lively elements as extended, semiextemporaneous sermons, boisterous music, and glossolalia. (Glossolalia is "speaking in tongues," when people uncontrollably utter unknown languages; Evangelical Christians believe this indicates possession by the Holy Spirit.)

The singing at camp meetings tended to be ebullient, and the most outgoing singers of all were slaves. A Swedish visitor to a camp meeting noted, "A magnificent choir! Most likely the sound proceeded from the black portion of the assembly, as their number was three times that of the whites, and their voices are naturally beautiful and pure."[14] It was not uncommon for a group of slaves at a meeting to sing all through the night—long after their white counterparts had

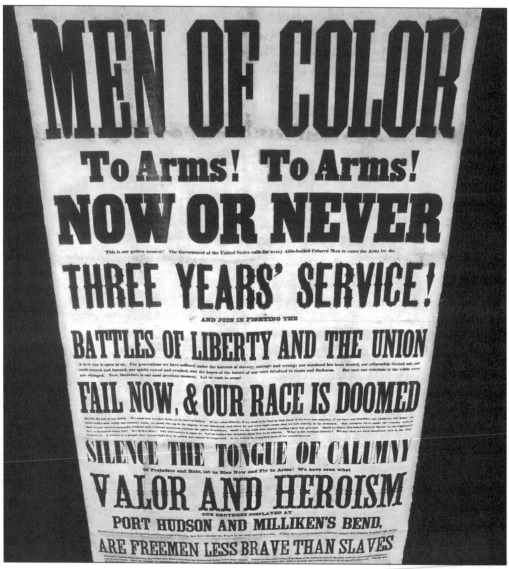

Posted by black abolitionists in Chicago, this poster urges black men to enlist in the Union army during the Civil War.

gone to bed. Another contemporary observer recalled that after an evening worship service, "at about half-past five the next morn . . . the hymns of the Negroes were still to be heard on all sides."[15]

Dr. Watts Hymns

As camp meetings grew in popularity, the lugubrious traditional European hymns used by earlier church groups in America fell from favor. Songs that reflected the more boisterous nature of the camp meetings replaced them. Boyer writes, "The fervent zeal [of Evangelical preachers and congregations] required a much livelier music than the slow, languorous long-meter hymns that were traditional."[16]

Especially popular for camp meetings were hymns written by an English minister, Dr. Isaac Watts. Many of his songs were slow in tempo, but they were catchy and easily memorized. The minister's compositions became so prevalent that virtually all religious songs of the period became known collectively as Dr. Watts hymns.

Slave congregations frequently adapted Dr. Watts's compositions for their own purposes. Singers might bend notes or add slurs, slides, and held tones to the basic melodies. Congregations as a group might change the melodies, altering them to reflect such characteristics of traditional African music as pentatonic (five-note) scales, blue notes, and melisma (a technique in which singers stretch one syllable over several notes).

Furthermore, black worshippers often changed the lyrics of these songs, adding extra choruses or verses or altering the words to suit the interests of a particular congregation. Musicologist Eileen Southern writes of these hymns, "Variation is so strong a factor . . . that changes are introduced into songs with each new performance. . . . [T]he melody of a song often serves chiefly as a vehicle for the text, and is constantly adjusted to fit, even as the singer extemporizes [improvises] from one verse to the next."[17]

In this way, European and African traditions began to merge significantly. The result was a very lively service indeed, as a visitor to a black worship service in 1820 noted:

> After sermon they began singing merrily, and continued, without stopping, one hour, till they became exhausted and breathless. "Oh! Come to Zion, come!" "Hallelujah, &c." And then "O won't you have my lovely bleeding *Jasus*," a thousand times repeated in full thundering chorus to the tune of "Fol de rol." While all the time they were clapping hands, shouting and jumping, and exclaiming, "Ah Lord! Good Lord! Give me *Jasus!* Amen."[18]

Slavery Ends

Meanwhile, as camp meetings and Dr. Watts hymns became more prevalent, the issue of slavery was becoming increasingly volatile in what was now the United States. All of the northern states had abolished slavery by 1804, but it continued to flourish in the South. The issue grew increasingly rancorous, upsetting the always delicate political balance between free and slave-owning states.

Slavery was a primary issue in the 1860 election that brought Abraham Lincoln to the presidency. It was also a major factor in the South's decision to secede from the Union, a decision that led to the Civil War. This bloody war finally ended in 1865 with the defeat of the South and the reunification of the country.

The end of the war marked the end of slavery, and millions of slaves were suddenly free. This was cause for great joy, of course, but a daunting set of interrelated social problems arose as well. Families needed to be reunited, jobs and homes had to be found, and millions of former slaves needed to be assimilated into mainstream American society. In such an environment, religious faith was a source of great sustenance for the African American community.

New Churches

One aspect of this situation was that former slaves, who had been denied the right to create their own churches, were now free to do so. Northern blacks, already free, were eager to establish missions in the South and transplant their already established denominations there. In addition, a number of white denominations, notably the Presbyterians and Episcopalians, sponsored missions aimed at former slaves. Furthermore, there were strong efforts in the South to create new, homegrown denominations.

The result was a dramatic explosion in the number and size of black churches across the South. Among those experiencing the most growth were transplants from the north, notably the African Methodist Episcopal (AME) Church and the African Methodist Episcopal Zion (AMEZ) Church. The AME Church, established in 1816, by the 1870s boasted a membership of nearly half a million. The AMEZ Church, founded in 1796, by

1870 included some two hundred thousand members.

Others were new denominations founded in the South specifically for former slaves. These included the Church of God in Christ (COGIC), founded in 1895 in Mississippi, and the Colored (now Christian) Methodist Episcopal (CME) Church, formed in 1870 in Tennessee. Meanwhile, the National Baptist Convention, the black-oriented branch of the Baptist Church, was founded in 1893 in Georgia; it soon became the largest black religious organization in the United States.

The proliferation of black churches in the decades after the Civil War virtually put an end to interracial worship groups. Although basic religious beliefs of black and white Christians remained largely parallel, the musical aspects of worship began to diverge. As writer Viv Broughton notes, "[B]lack Christians were forced into a separatism that was almost total. . . . [T]here was now minimal contact between black and white Christians and this was to have a profound effect on black religious music."[19]

Life Revolves Around the Church

Even after slavery ended, most political, cultural, and economic avenues were closed to black people. They were still the victims of vicious racism and discrimination on a daily basis. One of the few areas of society that was consistently open to them was the church.

It was natural, therefore, that for the typical black family, life revolved

These ministers and teachers at a 1901 conference belong to the African Methodist Episcopal Church, one of several black churches that emerged after the Civil War.

around church activities. In addition to formal worship services, churches typically organized activities such as picnics, sports events, travel, and, of course, musical gatherings. Church-related schools created a dramatic increase in literacy and in the number of black leaders, notably ministers. And, at least in the North, where the social climate for black people was more tolerant, churches were centers for political and civil rights activism.

Over the decades, new Christian denominations—some large, some tiny—continued to arise. Religious life for black Americans, especially in the South, became increasingly diverse. This variation created a dramatic contrast. Typically, churches in poor, rural areas tended to rely on hands-on worship, with boisterous singing and fervent preaching. In the cities, meanwhile,

where churchgoers tended to be better educated and more affluent, services tended to be more sedate.

This increasingly rich diversity was reflected in the diversity of musical styles. Broadly speaking, more conservative denominations, such as the AME Church, used standard Protestant hymns and sang them in a relatively sedate style. Black Baptists, meanwhile, continued to "raise" hymns in a more boisterous and outgoing fashion. Taken as a whole, black church music was developing into an emotional and highly distinctive form of music. Broughton notes, "Gradually, a recognisable body of songs emerged as the first folk music of black America—religious in character and pre-dating blues, jazz and gospel itself."[20] This "first folk music" would soon have a name: spirituals.

Chapter Two

The Birth of the Spiritual

Whatever their origins, whatever their structure, whatever their components—there can be no question in the minds and hearts of those who have heard them that in the Negro spirituals American folk art reaches its highest point.

> — *Musicologists Alan and John Lomax*

By the late nineteenth century, music written specifically for black churches had existed for years, and had sometimes been collected in songbooks. The earliest was probably a hymnal published in 1801, *A Collection of Spiritual Songs and Hymns Selected from Various Authors by Richard Allen, African Minister.* (Allen was a central figure in the founding of the African Methodist Episcopal Church.) This popular songbook drew primarily from the hymns of European composers such as Watts, though later editions added songs written by Allen himself and others.

Allen's hymnal did not include "folk" songs—that is, songs that had originated with slaves. The first collection of this sort was probably *Slave Songs of the United States*, an 1867 volume edited by William Francis Allen, Charles Pickard Ware, and Lucy McKim Garrison. It contained 136 songs collected from across the South, including the earliest known versions of such famous songs as "Michael, Row the Boat Ashore," and "Roll, Jordan, Roll." It may have been the first instance of a large-scale attempt to capture the songs of the slavery era on paper and preserve them.

Not Always Religious

These songs were primarily religious in nature. They inspired hope, expressed desire for forgiveness, and spoke of faith in a better life in the hereafter. Frederick Douglass, remembering his childhood in an 1845 autobiography, recalled, "They told a tale which was then altogether beyond my feeble comprehension; they were tones, loud, long, and deep, breathing the prayer and complaint of souls boiling over with the bitterest anguish. Every tone was a testimony against slavery, and a prayer to God for deliverance from chains."[21]

However, many spirituals were not overtly religious in their messages. Instead, they spoke of the daily lives of slaves. One example was "The Driver," about a cruel slave driver who abused his workers. Thomas Wentworth Higginson, the abolitionist and writer, heard "The Driver" sung near Beaufort, South Carolina, and spoke with the young laborer who had composed it. Higginson noted, "It will be observed that, although this song is quite secular in its character, its author yet called it a 'spiritual.' I heard but two songs among [the Negro community], at any time, to which they would not, perhaps, have given this generic name."[22]

Folk Songs with European Influence

Post-slavery, most African-Americans preferred not to sing these songs. No former slave, or child of a slave, wanted to be reminded of that hated

Richard Allen

era. However, the music did not die out. In fact, beginning in the early 1870s, jubilee songs surged in popularity as entertainment for white audiences.

In their new, written form, these songs were called spirituals, although it is unclear exactly when the word was first used in this context. The music was modified considerably. Spirituals retained the lyrics of the jubilee songs, but the rough edges of the originals were smoothed over with elements borrowed from European classical music, such as "correct" harmony, formal notation, and classical-style accompaniment.

A single group was responsible for sparking interest in spirituals: the Fisk Jubilee Singers from Fisk University, in Nashville, Tennessee. Founded in 1866, Fisk was one of the first institutions of higher learning specifically for African Americans.

As a private institution serving a population that could not generally afford to pay much in the way of tuition, Fisk faced lean budgets during its early years. In an effort to raise money, Fisk's musical director, George L. White, organized a choir to perform before white audiences. His group

The Fisk Jubilee Singers introduced spirituals to white people across the United States and had a strong influence on the development of gospel music.

originally included nine students—two separate quartets and a piano accompanist. All former slaves or children of slaves, the singers ranged in age from fifteen to twenty-five.

The Fisk Singers Set Out

The Fisk Jubilee Singers set out on their first concert tour in the fall of 1871. There were no guarantees that their fund-raising plan would be a success, or indeed that they would be heard at all. Broughton notes, "To set off on such a journey was an act of the very greatest faith. Though they had already presented concerts to local audiences . . . the wider American public had heard nothing of black music except minstrel novelties, and the little group had virtually no money with them other than the fare to their first stop—Cincinnati, Ohio."[23]

At first, the public and press did not receive the group favorably, even though they presented themselves in a dignified and professional manner and were skilled singers. Audiences seemed indifferent to the group's performances of sentimental ballads such as "Old Folks at Home" and patriotic anthems like "The Battle Hymn of the Republic." In an effort to try something different, White suggested adding spirituals to the repertoire.

The singers were reluctant at first, wanting no reminders of slavery days, but agreed to test the idea. To their surprise, the new material proved enormously popular. Hearing the songs performed in a serious, dignified style was a revelation to white audiences, who had mostly heard black music only in minstrel shows in which white singers and actors, made up with grotesque blackface, performed comic parodies of slave-era music.

"Gray-Haired Men Wept like Little Children"

The singers quickly made spirituals key parts of their programs. Musicologist Bernice Johnson Reagon notes that "the response to the music was phe-nomenal."[24] An early triumph came in 1872, when the Fisk singers were the sensation of a large-scale musical extravaganza, the World Peace Jubilee in Boston. They gained instant fame after they came to the rescue of a local black chorus.

The locals, who were untrained, were in disarray after their accompanying orchestra began playing in a key that was far too high. The well-trained Fisk singers, however, were able to sing the higher notes and joined in, saving

Embracing a New Faith

The black composer James Weldon Johnson, in this excerpt from his 1929 article "Negro Folk Songs and Spirituals," discusses why spirituals held great emotional power even years after slavery ended. Johnson's article is reprinted on the Document Records Web site.

There was at hand the precise religion for the condition in which [the slave] found himself thrust. Far from his native land and customs, despised by those among whom he lived, experiencing the pang of the separation of loved ones, knowing the hard lot of the slave, the Negro seized Christianity, the religion of compensations in the life to come for the ills suffered in the present existence, the religion that implied the hope that, in the next world, there would be a change in conditions, that he would be free from bondage. . . .

It is not possible to estimate the sustaining influence that the story of the trials and tribulations of the Jews, as related in the Old Testament, exerted upon the Negro. This story at once caught and fired the imaginations of the Negro bards [poets], and they sang their hungry listeners into a firm faith that, as God saved Daniel in the lion's den, so would He save them; as God delivered Israel out of bondage in Egypt, so would He deliver them.

the performance. According to J.B.T. Marsh, who wrote a history of the group, "The great audience was carried away with a whirlwind of delight. . . . Men threw their hats in the air and the Coliseum [where the performances were held] rang with cheers and shouts of, 'The Jubilees! The Jubilees forever!'"[25]

Soon, the Fisk singers were in demand across the United States and Europe. Their fund-raising scheme was wildly successful; after seven years of touring, they accumulated what for that era was an enormous sum—$150,000. This was more than enough to build Jubilee Hall, an imposing, six-story building that more than a century later is still a centerpiece of the Fisk University campus.

Along the way, the group accumulated many fans. According to one report, England's famously stoic Queen Victoria wept for joy after hearing them. Other admirers included President Ulysses S. Grant and author Mark Twain, who proclaimed, "In the Jubilees and their songs, America has produced the perfectest flower of the ages."[26]

Not all of the Fisk singers' fans were weeping royalty or gushing celebrities, however. The group also stirred many ordinary people. Dr. Theodore L. Cuyler, a New York minister, enthusiastically stated after a concert by the Fisk Singers at his church, "I never saw a cultivated Brooklyn assemblage so moved and melted under the magnetism of music before. The wild melodies of these emancipated slaves touched the fount of tears, and gray-haired men wept like little children."[27]

In the Wake of the Fisk Singers

The Fisk Jubilee Singers' success whetted the mainstream white audience's appetite for black spirituals. Plenty of performing ensembles were ready to oblige. Darden notes, "Everybody wanted in on the Jubilee phenomenon."[28] The Fisk singers thus had a dramatic influence on the course of gospel music.

Within two years of the Fisk singers' first tour, at least a dozen groups sprang up in imitation, usually bearing sound-alike names like the National Jubilee Singers and the Alabama Jubilee Singers. There was also a surge in the publication of black spirituals; typical was a volume called *The Jubilee Songs: As Sung by the Jubilee Singers*. Some of these books proved enduringly popular, going through many editions and selling in the thousands. One of them, published in 1874, marked the first known use of the word "gospel" in relation to music: *Gospel Songs*, by the prolific composer Philip Paul Bliss.

The proliferation of groups greatly increased the stature of black religious music. Then, around the turn of the twentieth century, a shift in how part of the black community worshipped—and, therefore, in how it made sacred music—helped change the music itself. The cause of this shift was the spectacular rise of a branch of Christianity called Pentecostalism.

Pentecostal preachers like Jack Johnson were boisterous and encouraged their congregants to participate vocally in the worship of God.

Fiery Services

Pentecostalism, also called the Holiness or Sanctified Church, was a relatively rowdy version of Christianity. Its worship services—musically and otherwise—were loud, outspoken, and lively. Such services were a sharp contrast to the worship traditions of the more established Baptist and AME churches, which favored a statelier, more dignified form of worship.

A notable center for early Pentecostal activity was the Azusa Street Revival in Los Angeles, California. This wildly popular Apostolic Faith Mission conducted three services a day, seven days a week. Azusa Street was not the first Pentecostal church, but it was the most influential, and its style of preaching and music making were models for Pentecostal activity around the country.

At Azusa Street and elsewhere, the preaching was far more exuberant than at AME and Baptist denominations. Some Pentecostal preachers were nationally famous for their fiery sermons; one such celebrity preacher was Reverend J.M. Gates of Atlanta, whose dozens of recorded sermons, with titles such as "Death's Black Train Is Coming," were perennial bestsellers.

But preachers were not the only ones who spoke out at Pentecostal services. Members of the congregation were also

"The Singing Filled His Ears"

Set in Chicago in the 1930s, Richard Wright's novel Native Son *is one of the seminal works of African American literature. In this excerpt, reprinted in Robert Darden's* People Get Ready! A New History of Black Gospel Music, *the book's main character, Bigger Thomas, encounters an emotional church service.*

The singing from the church vibrated through [Bigger], suffusing him with a mood of sensitive sorrow. He tried not to listen, but it seeped into his feelings, whispering of another way of life and death. . . . The singing filled his ears; it mocked his fear and loneliness, his deep yearning for a sense of wholeness. Its fullness contrasted so sharply with his hunger, its richness with his emptiness, that he recoiled from it while answering it.

encouraged to speak as the spirit moved them, encouraging the preacher or testifying to their own faith. This group participation led to services that could last for hours, with people shouting, fainting, and running up the aisles of the church.

Singing in the Spirit

Pentecostal music matched the preaching in liveliness, and typically came from a variety of sources. Some Pentecostal songs were either older hymns or newer songs written by people like Reverend Charles Price Jones, author of some one thousand compositions, including "Jesus Only," "I'm Happy with Jesus Alone," and "Where Shall I Be When the Last Trumpet Sounds." These were painstakingly written and arranged. Others, however, were "shouts" that were spontaneously composed by preachers or congregation members "in the spirit." These were far simpler in structure, usually nothing more than a line or two of poetry coupled with a simple repeated melody.

No matter the origin, Pentecostal songs were vigorous and passionate, with multiple rhythms and call-and-response choruses that involved the congregation as its members swayed, shouted, and clapped. Few who attended the services were trained singers, but all were encouraged to join in. This was certainly part of Pentecostalism's appeal, as Boyer notes: "[T]hey sang with such power and conviction that their singing became as much of an attraction to the services as were the doctrine and the practice."[29]

"Just like Being a Preacher"

Pentecostal congregations used whatever musical tools were at hand. Most churches used only percussion, while a few could afford a piano. (Pentecostals took their cue in this use of accompaniment from a passage in the Bible that exhorts worshippers to praise God "with the sound of the trumpet. . . . Let everything that hath breath praise the Lord."[30]) As a result, Boyer writes, Pentecostal services "were nothing less than ecstatic with forceful and jubilant singing, dramatic testimonies, hand clapping, foot stamping, and beating of drums, tambourines, and triangles (and pots, pans, and washboards when professional instruments were not available)."[31]

Many Pentecostal ministers were singers as well, and Pentecostal preachers were expected to be equally adept at both songs and sermons. The distinction between the two was often blurred, and their roles were often essentially the same, as singer Willie Johnson points out:

We're trying to deliver a message. It's a message to people about how God can heal you, how He can open doors for you, how He can make a way for you. How if you are burdened down you can be uplifted by song. If you've got trouble in your home or on the job, God can fix it. . . . That's just like being a preacher.[32]

Louis Armstrong, shown here in 1932, joined with other jazz and blues artists who incorporated sacred music into their own musical styles.

Moving Northward

The movement was especially strong in rural areas, but it also took root in America's cities. In large part, this was because of a major demographic shift in the early 1900s, when millions of blacks left the impoverished South in search of better jobs and living conditions. They gravitated in particular to the industrialized cities of the Midwest and Northeast; between 1910 and 1920, the black population of Chicago nearly doubled, while that of Detroit grew sixfold. Naturally, the worship practices and music of these migrants went with them.

The Pentecostal movement proved to be enduringly popular, and in the first decades of the twentieth century hundreds of churches, large and small, developed within it. The largest was the Church of God in Christ. Founded in Mississippi in 1895, by the 1920s COGIC claimed a membership in the hundreds of thousands. Its musical tradition was especially strong, and in the coming years many of gospel's top composers and performers would benefit from experience gained in COGIC church choirs.

Mingled Styles

As the Pentecostal Church and its brand of music was moving north and developing, so too were the most innovative and influential forms of black secular music—blues and jazz. By the 1920s, jazz pioneers like Louis Armstrong and King Oliver were exploring fertile new areas of improvisation and rhythm. Blues artists like Blind Lemon Jefferson and Ma Rainey were simi-

larly making the most of that music's expressive, earthy qualities. And sacred music was likewise changing; musicians like the legendary blind pianist-singer Arizona Dranes were developing their own passionate forms of music.

Whether in the South or the North, blues, jazz, and sacred music did not exist in isolation. The people who made and listened to one style often listened to and dabbled in another as well. Blues and jazz musicians typically had been brought up with church music, while those who were devoted to sacred music frequently had listened to blues and jazz (often in secret, since parents in devout families tried to protect their children from what they considered sinful music). The three musical styles, with their shared origins in the African American folk tradition, began to mingle and deeply influence each other.

Pentecostal musical styles, in particular, shared many characteristics with blues and jazz. All three genres, for instance, emphasized improvisation and blue notes—that is, the flatted third, fifth, and seventh notes of a scale. Pentecostal performers and composers also frequently used strong rhythms, such as syncopated ragtime rhythms. Furthermore, Pentecostal preacher-singers often accompanied themselves on pianos or guitars, the most commonly used instruments among blues and jazz musicians.

Although musicians in the three genres generally played different melodies, there were exceptions. This further blurred the line dividing sacred song from secular song. For example, the familiar jazz standard "When the Saints Go Marching In" originated in the Pentecostal church. Its lyrics refer to saints—believers who followed Jesus unquestioningly and therefore entered (went "marching in") to heaven.

"They Come out of the Same Soul"

Yet another instance of the sacred and secular blurring concerned the era's many itinerant street evangelists. These singers—who were often blind, since street performing was one of the few jobs a sightless black person could get—usually accompanied themselves on guitar. Often, their sound was indistinguishable from that of bluesmen of the period; only the religious lyrics set their songs apart. (Some street musicians, notably the Reverend Gary Davis, played *both* blues and sacred music, though Davis often made up new lyrics to reflect his religious leanings.)

Among the many sacred-music street singers of the era were Washington Phillips and Blind Mamie Forehand, but perhaps the street evangelist whose influence was most lasting was Blind Willie Johnson. His singing has been preserved on a handful of recordings, including "I Know His Blood Can Make Me Whole," "Dark Was the Night—Cold Was the Ground," and "Jesus Make Up My Dying Bed." Johnson's gruff, otherworldly vocals and haunting slide guitar have profoundly influenced several generations of blues musicians.

The connections between jazz, blues, and sacred music were clear to performers. Aaron "T-Bone" Walker, a pioneering blues guitarist, once commented, "The blues comes a lot from the church, too. The first time I ever heard a boogie-woogie piano was the first time I went to church."[33] According to another notable blues guitarist, Johnny Shines, "When you hear people singing hymns in church—these long, drawn out songs—that's the blues. Church music and the blues is all one and the same. They come out of the same soul, same heart, same body."[34]

"The Devil's Music"

Some musicians and fans approved of the cross-influences between sacred and secular music, and of the influences Pentecostal music had on Baptist and Methodist performance styles. These crosscurrents, they felt, made for a richer experience. Charlie Storey, a singer with New York's All-Stars Quartet, recalls,

Now, it used to be, when you walked into a Baptist church, you wouldn't see no shouting. . . . But then the Pentecostals got to having such a good time, feeling the Spirit and all—and some of the Pentecostals joined the Baptists, they might have a husband there, maybe a mother there. And the Pentecostals got the Baptist people to moving too. Sometimes you can't tell which is which.[35]

This is an advertising poster for the recordings of Blind Willie Johnson, a gospel singer and slide guitar virtuoso who performed on the streets of Texas.

Despite the clear connections between religious and secular music, the majority of black Baptists and Methodists heartily disapproved of blues and jazz. They denounced the genres as "the devil's music." They felt the music's rhythms and melodies were sinfully seductive, and were appalled by the explicitly sexual nature of blues and jazz lyrics.

To the pious, jazz was a music of wanton wickedness and the blues was the sound of despair. In contrast, spiritual music delivered a message of stability, hope, happiness, and love. About this contrast, Mahalia Jackson once commented, "Somebody singing blues is crying out of a pit. I'm singing out of the joy of my salvation."[36]

Far-reaching Influence

By the 1920s and 1930s, black sacred music was reaching even beyond blues and jazz in its influence. Early choirs, such as the Fisk Jubilee Singers, had been heavily influenced by the European classical tradition, borrowing methods of singing, accompaniment, and arranging vocal harmonies. Now, several white composers repaid the favor, borrowing from spirituals in an attempt to capture the energy and spirit of "that old time religion."

Probably the best known of these was the brilliant American composer George Gershwin. Gershwin gained fame for the dozens of show tunes he wrote with his brother Ira and others. However, Gershwin also produced several classically oriented compositions, notably his orchestral piece *Rhapsody in Blue* (1924) and his "folk opera" *Porgy and Bess* (1934). These pieces (and, to a lesser extent, Gershwin's pop songwriting) were strongly influenced by spirituals. For example, the song "Summertime" from *Porgy and Bess* sounds like a plaintive hymn, while "It Ain't Necessarily So" (also from *Porgy and Bess*) makes affectionate fun of Bible lessons.

An even earlier example is the Czech composer Antonin Dvorak. Dvorak's Ninth Symphony ("From the New World"), which premiered in 1893, made

Many religious blacks condemned Louis Armstrong, seen here in 1925 with members of his jazz band the Hot Five, for peddling the "devil's music."

clear use of African American folk melodies and themes. Dvorak noted that he considered spirituals "the most striking and appealing melodies that have yet been found on this side of the water . . . distinguished by unusual and subtle harmonies."[37]

These composers were not the only creative artists to pay homage to black church music. So did many artists associated with the Harlem Renaissance—a flowering of black literature, music, dance, and art that took place during the 1920s and 1930s in New York City's Harlem. For example, the lyrics and ideas contained in spirituals were woven throughout the writing of such notables as Langston Hughes and Zora Neale Hurston. Furthermore, African American singers of classical concert music, notably Paul Robeson and Marian Anderson, gave spirituals a prominent

Actor and singer Paul Robeson, who performed in George Gershwin's Porgy and Bess, *signs autographs in Paris.*

place in their repertoires.

This cross-fertilization of music would only grow stronger in the following decades. The stage was set for the development of a new, hybrid style of music. It was time for gospel to flower.

Chapter Three

The Flowering of Gospel

This new gospel music spoke . . . to the difficult life of being both black and Christian in the United States during the first . . . decades of the twentieth century.

— Horace Clarence Boyer,
The Golden Age of Gospel

No single person was responsible for creating gospel as it came into its own in the 1930s and 1940s. The new music was a collective endeavor, painstakingly crafted by many individuals. The result was the gospel sound—a fusion of the modern (jazz and blues) with the traditional (spirituals).

Fusing the Old and the New

This new music was distinctive in several ways. For one thing, the sound of gospel instrumentation was unique. It was characterized by a steady, rocking beat and sparse but robust accompaniment. (Typically, the instrumentation for gospel during this period was a single piano or a piano and organ playing together, with occasional use of other instruments such as percussion.) The rhythm and style of accompaniment both owed a strong debt to secular music. Gospel piano, for instance, was a richly emotional combination of rolling chords, ragtime syncopation, and other elements borrowed from jazz and blues.

Vocally, gospel was markedly different from older styles as well. As opposed to the group singing of previous times, solo singers with huge, expressive voices came into prominence. This trend encouraged increasing amounts of individual creativity, and singers grew adept at freely improvising additions to a song's basic melody, in the manner of an expert jazz musician. The result was high flying, crowd pleasing, and spirit raising.

Solo singers rose in prominence, but the group-singing tradition of the old spirituals was also alive. This came in the form of trios, quartets, and choirs,

Marie Collins of the Jubilee Singers sings a gospel song to piano accompaniment during a 1946 performance in London.

The gospel group The Golden Gate Quartet huddles around the microphone as they blend their sophisticated harmonies during a 1938 performance.

but with many additions and refinements. Perhaps chief among these was the development of vocal arrangements that featured rich harmonies. This was a sharp departure from the past, when complex harmony had often been ignored and unison singing (that is, all voices singing the same melody line) had been the norm.

Songwriting

As the music changed vocally and instrumentally, so did the craft of songwriting. Unlike the anonymous spirituals but similar to the later Dr. Watts hymns, gospel songs were *written down.* They had identifiable authors who composed the music and wrote the lyrics. These specialists crafted their songs to provide singers with what they sought most, such as opportunities to improvise on the basic rhythms and melodies.

The lyrics of gospel songs were markedly different from earlier spirituals. They resembled spirituals in stating a simple solution to a difficult problem (for example, any tragedy can be borne by trusting in God). However, the newer songs differed in that they used everyday language and concrete images or ideas from modern life. For example, the song "Jesus on the Mainline" made its point (that Jesus is always available and listening) by using a vivid image (the telephone) taken from technology that was then still fairly novel.

This mixture of new and old elements appealed to a wide, varied audience. Musicologist Paul Oliver notes, "The combination of a good tune, a structure which permitted the easy addition of new stanzas, [and lyrics that] related strongly to contemporary issues . . . combined to make many popular gospel songs acceptable to the different religious denominations."[38] Virtually all African American churches—Baptist, Pentecostal, and Methodist alike—eventually adopted the new sound.

A Pre-gospel Composer

This acceptance was not immediate, however; it took years for the gospel sound to catch on. A number of people had to pave the way before the music could fully come into its own. One of these pioneers was Dr. Charles Albert Tindley, a renowned Methodist minister and hymn writer from Philadelphia, Pennsylvania.

"The Greatest . . . Until I Came Along"

Composer Thomas A. Dorsey, in this quotation reprinted in Robert Darden's People Get Ready! A New History of Black Gospel Music, *pays his respects to his predecessor, pioneering pre-gospel composer Charles A. Tindley, and explains that Tindley's jazz-tinged style was popular with the gospel public.*

He was the greatest gospel songwriter—and this is not boasting—until I came along. I tried to do what Tindley did and that went along nicely, but it began to break off. I started putting a little of the beat into gospel that we had in Jazz. I also put in what we called the riff, or repetitive phrases. These songs sold three times as fast as those that went straight along on paper without riffs or repetition.

Born in 1851, Tindley was old enough to be writing in a period before gospel's full flowering; his most active period came in the last decades of the nineteenth century and the first decades of the twentieth. Nonetheless, he clearly wrote in a gospel style; his music combined a strong blues feeling with the traditional characteristics of Western hymns. Many of Tindley's compositions found a lasting place in the traditional gospel repertoire; songs such as "Stand By Me," "Leave It There," and "We'll Understand It Better By and By" would continue to be sung in the twenty-first century. This music was an important forerunner of what was to come, Reagon notes: "His compositions formed the base upon which the new Black gospel music was developed and influenced all the early gospel music composers."[39]

Miss Lucie

Another important pre-gospel figure was Lucie E. Campbell. Miss Lucie (as she was known) taught in the Memphis, Tennessee, public schools and never relied on music or other church-related activities for a living. Nonetheless, she was widely influential as a performer, music director, and composer.

Among her other accomplishments, Miss Lucie helped pioneer a role of authority for women in gospel. Her first song, "Something Within," written in 1919, is generally recognized as the first gospel song composed and published by a black woman. For decades,

Marian Anderson was a protégée of Miss Lucie, a key figure in the early days of gospel.

Campbell also served as a top officer of the National Baptist Convention. Since all singers and composers hoping to perform at this major annual conference were required to audition for her, Campbell's personal taste thus affected the direction of gospel music on a national level. The legendary singer Marian Anderson was only one of the performers she helped introduce to the gospel community.

Miss Lucie also set a high standard for showmanship. She was, by all accounts, an imposing and charismatic figure, especially when she appeared before an audience. The Reverend Charles Walker, who was both a minister and composer, recalled, "One of the great experiences at the National Baptist Convention was when Miss Lucie made her grand entrance on the stage. The people would come from miles around to see Miss Lucie strut. . . . The people would break out in a frenzy just at her entrance."[40]

Another Memphis Composer

Memphis was also home to another key figure of the period: Reverend William Herbert Brewster, for many years the pastor at Memphis's distinguished East Trigg Baptist Church. Brewster had, in musicians' terms, "big ears." That is, he readily absorbed music from Memphis's renowned jazz and blues scenes, as well as that of the city's Pentecostal churches (even though he was a Baptist). Brewster then incorporated these styles into his own music.

As gospel scholar Anthony Heilbut points out, these styles formed a powerful mix: "Not only did [Brewster] have the city's musical heritage to work from . . . but he was in immediate proximity to that powerhouse of gospel rhythms, the Church of God in Christ."[41] Furthermore, Brewster had a solid grounding in Western musical composition. The result was an unusually rich and varied style, Darden notes: "His music is theatrical and melodic, his lyrics are an uncanny blend of African-American idiom and his own vast reservoir of classical education."[42]

Brewster pioneered, among other things, the use of three-quarter or waltz time in gospel. Another distinguishing characteristic was his use of a technique called vamping. This approach, a holdover from African music (and a staple of blues and jazz), uses repeated musical or lyrical phrases to build tension and excitement. Among the two hundred–odd compositions Brewster wrote using such techniques were many pieces still familiar in the traditional gospel repertoire, including "Move On Up a Little Higher," "How I Got Over," and "Our God Is Able."

Gospel Pearls

Gradually, people active in the sacred music world began using the word "gospel" to describe the new compositions that were being created. The exact time the term was first used in this newer sense is difficult to determine. However, its widespread use can probably be dated to 1921. In that year, it

"There Had to Be a Feeling"

The Reverend A.W. Nix was a well-known preacher and singer of the 1930s. In comments reprinted in Viv Broughton's Black Gospel: An Illustrated History of the Gospel Sound, *Nix describes some of his feelings about gospel.*

This rhythm I had, I brought with me to gospel songs. I was a blues singer, and I carried that with me into the gospel songs. These songs were not just written. Something had to happen, something had to be done, there had to be a feeling. They weren't just printed and distributed. Somebody had to feel something, someone had to hand down light for mankind's pathway, smooth the road and the rugged way, give him courage, bring the Black man peace, joy and happiness. Gospel songs come from prayer, meditation, hard times and pain. But they are written out of divine memories, out of the feelings in your soul.

was used in the title of a popular collection of songs specifically created for black church congregations. This was *Gospel Pearls*, published by the National Baptist Convention and edited by a team led by Willa Townsend, a music professor at the now-defunct Roger Williams University in Tennessee.

Gospel Pearls was an important milestone in the development of the newer sounds of gospel music and their acceptance by the listening public. The songs it contained were mostly standard Protestant hymns written by white composers, as well as patriotic songs such as "Battle Hymn of the Republic." However, the book also spotlighted newer compositions, including Tind-ley's most famous song, "Stand By Me." Furthermore, the innovative gospel sound was evident even in the arrangements of old songs.

One reason *Gospel Pearls* was significant was that it conferred on newer compositions a degree of respectability. Its publication by the established and well-respected National Baptist Convention amounted to an important endorsement—a clear indication that the newer music was an accepted form of sacred song, on a par with established hymns. *Gospel Pearls* was welcomed by many denominations, and by the 1930s it was a familiar source of music to Baptist, Methodist, and Pentecostal congregations alike.

Professor Dorsey

Tindley, Campbell, and Brewster were just a few of the influential figures in gospel's early development and flowering. Many others also made important contributions. However, one figure stands above all of the others.

This was Thomas A. Dorsey, the acknowledged father of gospel. Professor Dorsey, as he was often called as a mark of respect, did not invent gospel, but he was without question its most important figure. Broughton asserts, "No-one has had a greater influence on gospel singing; no-one has been quite as prophetic; no-one spans the entire history of gospel music quite like Dorsey."[43]

Dorsey's influence was strong for several reasons. First of all, his compositions set the standard for the future of gospel's development. He was also a key figure in organizing gospel choirs throughout the country and introducing brilliant new singers to the public. Furthermore, Dorsey started one of the first publishing companies devoted exclusively to black gospel music, and he was the first to organize sacred concerts

A gospel quartet surrounds pianist and composer Thomas A. Dorsey, who helped popularize gospel with a global audience.

on a large scale outside of churches and revival meetings. Through all of these activities, Dorsey was thus instrumental in popularizing gospel, moving it out of the isolated church world and offering it to a wider audience than ever before.

Georgia Tom

Dorsey was born in 1899 in Villa Rica, Georgia, to a Baptist minister father and a church organist mother. The boy was a musical prodigy, and by the time the family moved to Atlanta in 1910 he was playing organ for his father's services. But Dorsey was pulled in another direction besides sacred music: he also listened—avidly, but in secret—to jazz and blues.

As a teen, Dorsey left Georgia in search of musical education and work, settling in Chicago by 1918. Speaking of himself and others who migrated to that thriving city, he recalled, "We went looking for money, man, good money."[44] Using the name Georgia Tom, Dorsey soon was well established in the commercial blues world, accompanying such top singers as Bessie Smith and Ma Rainey.

Despite his success with "the devil's music," however, the pull of the church was strong. Dorsey later recalled how, in 1921, he experienced a religious rebirth after hearing a stirring performance by a preacher-singer, the Reverend A.W. Nix: "He was great! He was powerful! He rocked that convention: shouts, moans, hollers, screaming. I said to myself, 'That's what I want to do.'"[45]

Forsaking the Blues

Dorsey joined Chicago's Pilgrim Baptist Church and began writing sacred songs. The songs provided little income, however, and he was forced to continue work as a bluesman. In 1928 Dorsey and guitarist/singer Tampa Red recorded "It's Tight Like That," one of the top-selling blues records of the year. The racy song gave Dorsey fame and money, but he suffered a bout of depression that same year and dropped out of the music scene for two years.

Blues singer and slide guitarist Tampa Red teamed up with Thomas A. Dorsey to record the risqué song "It's Tight Like That."

Dorsey's depression lifted after a minister told him that he would be healed if he used his music for God. The pianist accordingly devoted himself more to sacred music. However, the church community shunned Dorsey's efforts, rejecting the idea that a famous bluesman could write convincing religious songs: "Many times I walked through the snow from church to church until my feet were soaked. . . . I was very thankful to God for a good day when I had a dollar and a half in my pockets to take home to [wife] Nettie."[46]

Even personal appearances (with Dorsey accompanying various singers) were poorly received. Typical was the minister who promised Dorsey a spot in a Sunday morning service, then deliberately ended the meeting before he had his chance to perform. Dorsey recalled of such rejections, "I got thrown out of some of the best churches in them days."[47]

"Dorseys"

However, things began to change in the early 1930s. In 1932 one of his songs, "If You See My Savior," was warmly received at the National Baptist Convention. The positive publicity gave Dorsey the ability to establish a choir at a local church, Ebenezer Baptist. This talented, well-trained group specialized in Dorsey's compositions, and people came from all over the city to hear it. During this period, Dorsey also started a publishing house devoted to the sales of gospel sheet music.

He was composing all the while. Dorsey wrote roughly a thousand songs in his life, including such still-familiar classics as "(Take My Hand) Precious Lord" and "(There Will Be) Peace in the Valley." The church community's initial reluctance about these songs gradually faded, and they proved enormously popular—especially to the younger generation, who felt comfortable with both popular and religious music.

These fans liked Dorsey's sophisticated combination of stately Baptist hymns, Pentecostal-style fervor, and blues-tinged melodies. The blues, in fact, never completely left Dorsey. He once remarked, "Blues is a part of me, the way I play piano, the way I write. . . . I'm not ashamed of my blues. It's all the same talent, a beat is a beat whatever it is."[48] Meanwhile, Dorsey's simple but powerful lyrics held a special appeal. Boyer notes that Dorsey was "particularly skilled at writing songs that not only captured the hopes, fears, and aspirations of the poor and disenfranchised African Americans but also spoke to all people."[49]

As a result, Dorsey's compositions were increasingly performed in churches and private homes. He called these pieces gospel songs, but they were so pervasive, and their style so distinctive, that many people simply called them "Dorseys." Fans eagerly awaited the publication of the latest "Dorsey," and sheet music of his compositions became as commonplace in black Christians' homes and churches as the songbook *Gospel Pearls* had been a decade earlier.

Sallie Martin

Dorsey may have been a brilliant composer, but he was a poor businessman. Much of his success in business, as well as in organizing choruses, can be credited to his partner for a number of crucial years, a strong-willed singer and entrepreneur named Sallie Martin.

Born in Georgia in 1896, Martin moved to Chicago as a young married woman and joined the first chorus Dorsey organized. She soon began making her mark in the gospel community; though she could not read music and her voice was rough, Martin had a direct and personable style that audiences loved. Within a short time, she was a star of the chorus and was also managing the composer's sheet music sales. (Dorsey had been keeping no accounting, and stored his money in a drawer to which anyone had access.)

A shrewd organizer, Martin also helped Dorsey run his choir. He needed help; the group was so popular that it played to capacity crowds even after it shifted its base of operations to the larger Pilgrim Baptist Church. Dorsey and Martin then branched out, organizing similar choruses in cities and towns around the South and Midwest. These were linked under the banner of an organization Dorsey and Martin helped create, the National Convention of Gospel Choirs and Choruses.

Accompanying Gospel

The development of choirs specializing in the new styles favored by composers like Dorsey dramatically affected the growth of gospel. Along with this development came changes in the way gospel singers were accompanied. Two Chicago-based musicians played significant roles in this: Roberta Martin and Kenneth Morris. Together, they helped usher in what would become a seminal part of the gospel sound.

Martin (no relation to Sallie) was a noted singer, composer ("Try Jesus, He Satisfies"), choir director, and music publisher. She was also a gifted accompanist, with a rolling, swelling, warmly rich piano style built on the pioneering efforts of Arizona Dranes. Martin's style was so distinctive, and became so pervasive, that she is considered the founder of gospel piano.

Like many of his colleagues, Morris had multiple talents. He was a former jazz musician turned gospel accompanist, publisher, and composer ("Just a Closer Walk with Thee" and "Yes, God Is Real"). Perhaps Morris's most lasting contribution to gospel, however, was his pioneering use of the Hammond organ.

Morris began using the Hammond organ in 1939, combining it with the piano into a two-keyboard ensemble. The expressive Hammond organ soon became an inextricable part of the gospel sound, and the piano/organ combination was soon standard in churches all across the country. Boyer notes,

When the piano and Hammond organ were paired, they created the ideal accompaniment for gospel: one instrument would sustain tones while the other was rhythmically active; one instrument could affect the vibrato of the voice while the other instrument could be struck like the patting of feet; and one instrument could imitate a bass fiddle while the other instrument tinkled the highest keys like a harp being plucked.[50]

Tough to Make Money

While Dorsey and his colleagues were succeeding in building an audience for gospel music, the nation as a whole was experiencing serious troubles. A devastating economic slump known as the Great Depression had begun in 1929, and by the early 1930s, just as gospel was beginning to catch on, the country was deep in despair. Unemployment and homeless rates were skyrocketing, while industrial production and living standards were plummeting.

As difficult as this situation was for most people, it benefited gospel musicians. The government was sponsoring work programs and other policies to help people cope financially with the Depression, but no such program could provide them with spiritual solace. As a result, millions of people turned increasingly to religion, and, as always, they found that sacred music lifted them up and, at least for a while, lightened their burdens. As times got worse, gospel music, with its message of hope, surged in popularity.

Sister Rosetta Tharpe performs her unique gospel style, a combination of sacred music with jazz, at a New York City nightclub in 1940.

Gospel music's growth led to increased opportunities for musicians, and that gradually changed the sound and appearance of gospel. In years past, performers of sacred music had held day jobs and sang only in church on Sundays. Now, however, it was possible for the first time to become a professional or semiprofessional gospel performer. Singers and choirs were able to tour the gospel circuit, a loose affiliation of churches throughout the Midwest and South that sponsored sacred music concerts.

Even for the handful of performers who were popular on this circuit, however, making a living with gospel music was still an uncertain affair. The gospel circuit was, at best, a modest source of income. Even a celebrity and best-selling composer like Dorsey needed to occasionally moonlight throughout the Depression. (In his case, he played in blues clubs.)

Other Avenues of Income

In light of the chronic financial difficulties gospel performers faced, they were always eager to explore new sources of income besides live performance. One was the publication and sales of sheet music. Sheet music had been, for decades, the traditional big-money item in the music industry; in the days before the widespread availability of recorded music, virtually every middle-class home had a piano, and singing was a common form of entertainment among friends and family.

Every home and every church, therefore, needed lots of sheet music. Gospel was supporting perhaps half a

"The Way out of Darkness"

Composer Lucie Campbell's most famous song, "Something Within," was inspired by an incident she witnessed on a Memphis street. Campbell overheard a man try to pay Connie M. Rosamund, a blind sacred singer, five dollars to sing the blues, but Rosamund refused to perform nonsacred music. As Campbell later recalled (quoted in Luvenia A. George's "Campbell: Her Nurturing of Gospel Music," in We'll Understand It Better By and By: Pioneering African American Gospel Composers, edited by Bernice Johnson Reagon) the street singer stated, "No, I can't sing the blues for you or anybody else for five dollars or fifty dollars. I'm trying to be a Christian in this dark world, and I believe I've found the way out of darkness into light. I can't explain it, but it's something within me."

dozen publishing homes, and composers and publishers such as Dorsey and Martin were able to conduct a steady mail-order business. They could also directly sell their music at concerts, worship services, and meetings such as the annual Baptist and Pentecostal conventions.

Even for top composers, however, there were only modest amounts of money to be made, and profits were slight. The composers themselves typically received only $15 to $50 per song from the publisher, and were paid no royalties (although they retained the copyright). Of course, the motives of gospel composers were primarily spiritual, not monetary; Sallie Martin once remarked of their efforts, "They were songs written out of somebody's burden, not just to make money."[51]

Records

Another way for gospel performers to augment their income was through recordings, although this industry was still in its early years during the 1920s and 1930s. Recordings of sacred black music had been made since nearly the beginnings of the technology itself. In fact, the first black vocal music on record, in 1902, was an example of sacred music: a series of spirituals performed by a group called the Dinwiddie Colored Quartet.

As recording technology improved, from fragile glass and wax cylinders to sturdier and better-sounding 78 rpm records, the number of sacred-music recordings increased. In 1927, for instance, more than seventy recordings of male gospel quartets were issued.

Nonetheless, overall sales of recordings of sacred music remained relatively low. Records of spoken sermons by well-known preachers were far more popular among the black community. Furthermore, profits from records were still low overall, even lower than in the sheet music business.

Ushering in the Golden Age

The early obstacles to finding an audience for gospel music, and the continuing problem of making a living with it, limited gospel music's growth. However, by the end of the 1930s it was an increasingly popular musical genre. That growth continued through the next decade. Boyer notes that as of the end of World War II in 1945, "there were very few people in the African American community who had not heard gospel music."[52]

The music had changed dramatically from its tentative beginnings. As spirituals and jubilee singing had evolved into gospel, the sound of the music had greatly evolved. But it was changing in other ways as well, especially in its business aspects and its growing sense of professionalism. The stage was thus set for the era of the music's full flowering—the Golden Age of Gospel.

Chapter Four

The Golden Age of Gospel

Ever since Thomas Dorsey married off blues and spirituals to create gospel, the sights and sounds of black church music have influenced those of the devil and vice versa.

—*Viv Broughton,* Black Gospel: An Illustrated History of the Gospel Sound

The decades from the mid-1940s to the mid-1960s form the Golden Age of Gospel. During this fruitful period, the music—and those who performed it—reached a height of creativity and popularity. As gospel gained in popularity and became more creative, it also diversified into several distinct styles, including soloists, choirs, and small groups.

Jubilee Quartets

The dominant style—far and away the most popular during this period—was the male a cappella quartet. (A cappella singers perform without instrumental accompaniment.) It developed from barbershop singing, a tradition in which men gathered informally (often in barbershops) to sing both secular and religious songs.

The best known of the early gospel quartets was the Fisk Jubilee Quartet, formed in 1905 as an offshoot of Fisk University's renowned singers. It proved successful, sold millions of recordings, and inspired many similar jubilee quartets. Many of these were associated with African American universities, such as the Tuskegee Institute in Alabama and Wilberforce University in southern Ohio. Others were amateurs who sang for their own pleasure and for church services, revivals, and concerts. By 1925, formal and informal quartets were so common that composer James Weldon Johnson commented that one could "pick up four colored boys or young men anywhere and the chances are ninety out of a hundred that you have a quartet."[53]

The jubilee quartets' style reflected the relatively sedate traditions of Baptist

The rough-edged hard gospel sound of the Dixie Hummingbirds, shown here in 1955, propelled them to fame.

Strictly Business

The classic quartets worked extremely hard to perfect their tight harmonies. In this passage quoted in Viv Broughton's Black Gospel: An Illustrated History of the Gospel Sound, *Julius Cheeks of the Sensational Nightingales recalls the group's rehearsal:*

Our manager made us get up at eight or nine and we'd rehearse till lunchtime. Man, it was like gettin' out there plowin'. We'd hang a broom from the ceiling like a mike, and we sang all around it. After lunch, we'd get right back into rehearsal.

Quartets also typically set up stringent rules of conduct for themselves. These bylaws, reprinted in Horace Clarence Boyer's The Golden Age of Gospel, *reproduce some of the rules written up by the Fairfield Four in the 1940s:*

- Business meeting and rehearsal twice weekly. . . . All not present on time will be fined 50 cents, absent—$1.00.

- All discussions be made in meetings and not in public. Anyone caught arguing in public—$2.00.

- Members of quartet must be in church at all programs at 8:15 or be fined $1.00 without a lawful excuse.

- For members caught drinking within 8 hours of program—be fined $5.00.

- When in church any time during program no member should look at others, argue on stage or appear to look angry. Stage etiquette—no unnecessary talk, sitting out of order—if any clause be disobeyed—fined $1.50.

- Any member caught with alcohol on breath while on duty—be fined $2.50.

- Any member that doesn't respect members of group or any outside person—saints or sinners—be fined $5.00.

- Any member caught with chewing gum while in service—be fined $1.00.

- Each member fined $2.50 for the word G.D. and $1.00 for each additional offense.

- Any member that argues when fine is presented to be fined double.

worship. They sang mostly standard Protestant hymns, deviating little from the melody and maintaining even, tight, organlike harmonies. They typically had no individual lead singers; only occasional interjections such as "Yes, my Lord" broke their stately harmonizing.

Their demeanor was equally sedate. They dressed in formal clothes (typically tuxedos) and stood flat-footed and straight-backed, with little movement or facial expression. Alton Griffin of the Golden Crown Quartet recalled, "Most [singers] would stand with their hands behind their back. . . . They weren't emotional what-so-ever."[54]

Jefferson County and the Tidewater Region

By the 1920s, however, this dignified singing style was falling from favor, and a more demonstrative style emerged. Chicago, in many ways the primary center for gospel innovation, was not the wellspring of this new style. Instead, several regions of the South incubated it.

One of these was Jefferson County, Alabama, home to the cities of Birmingham, Bessemer, and Fairfield. Among the many pioneering groups from this area were the Foster Singers, the Ravizee Stagers, the Famous Blue Jay Singers, the Heavenly Gospel Singers, the Kings of Harmony, and the Four Great Wonders. The "Birmingham sound" they developed used the rich harmonies of jubilee quartets, but they also incorporated elements of jazz and ragtime. The result was characterized by precise timing, unusual harmonies, an element of improvisation, and a percussive, "pumping" bottom line maintained by the bass singer.

The Tidewater region of Virginia was another prominent center for quartets. As early as 1919, local groups like the Silver Leaf Quartet were perfecting a characteristically smooth style. Other prominent Tidewater groups included the Norfolk Jubilee Quartet, the Excelsior Quartet, the Harmonizing Four, and the Peerless Four. Norfolk was a particular hotbed of formal and informal singing sessions, as Thurmon Ruth of North Carolina's Selah Jubilee Singers recalled: "Norfolk, Virginia, that used to be a quartet town! I used to want to go to Norfolk because they told me that you could just be in bed at night and put your head out the window and guys would be on the corner blending, harmonizing."[55]

Innovations

The mellow, harmonically rich sounds of the Alabama and Virginia quartets served as a stylistic bridge from the earlier jubilee quartets to the still more innovative styles that were emerging. During this time, quartet singing spread throughout the South and Midwest and, in some ways, consolidated into a cohesive style; by the mid-1940s, the classic quartet sound was fully formed.

One aspect of this classic sound involved the lineup of voice ranges—typically two tenors, a baritone, and a bass. (Later, many groups had five or more members, typically adding a second baritone or tenor, but the genre was still referred to as "quartet singing.") This tenor/tenor/baritone/bass lineup was the same as that of the jubilee quartets, but the sound was markedly different—rougher and more emotional.

Several factors created this change in the sound of the quartets from the older jubilee style. One was that the newer quartets sang "from the chest," a more informal and "folksier" style than singing "from the head," which was favored by European-influenced performers. Quartet singers were also borrowing even more liberally from jazz and blues styles, scooping and sliding between notes.

Some quartets also revived the use of falsetto singing. Falsetto ("false soprano") refers to singing in the upper registers of the voice. Falsetto singing was often used in African traditional singing, and its revival in quartet singing added a tremendous excitement and emotional punch. Furthermore, the quartet sound expanded the dynamic range, capable of going from a whisper to a shout in a single song. And singers also dropped the flat-footed stance, emphasizing the music's rhythms by swaying together or quietly slapping their thighs.

In 1959 prominent gospel singer Clara Ward (center) performs in Leeds, England, with her group, the Ward Singers.

Lead Singers

One of the biggest changes in the quartet sound was the advent of a separate lead singer. This person (often, but not always, the second tenor) used the harmony created by other singers as a base from which to soar and improvise. Some lead singers had exceptionally sweet voices; others, with more aggressive and rougher voices, sang so-called hard gospel. In any case, according to the Reverend Edward Cook of the Mighty Gospel Giants, the lead singer had to have instincts that resembled those of a preacher:

> A good lead singer, he's what we call the gospel man, the Spirit getter. . . . He has to be smart. He has to know where to go to get the audience aroused. He has to know how to push the song, how to rev up the background, rev up the musicians. He's constantly thinking, he's constantly moving. He has a powerful voice. He's more of the preacher type, the shouting preacher type.[56]

To accompany the lead, quartets developed a technique sometimes called "clanka-lanka." The harmonizers strung nonsense syllables or phrases such as "Oh my Lord" together, rhythmically repeating them to form a base for the lead singer. Supporting a lead singer in this way was tough work, gospel scholar Ray Allen points out: "There is nothing unselfconscious or 'natural' about good gospel singing; it demands practice, precision, and discipline on the part of all group members."[57]

Another innovation was to augment the basic quartet lineup with a second lead singer; groups could thus maintain strong four-part harmony while leaving a lead singer free to improvise. It is difficult to determine which quartet first used this technique; some music historians single out the Soul Stirrers. Regardless of who first used it, this was an extremely important development, since it gave lead singers unprecedented room to add their personal stamps to the music. Heilbut asserts that the addition of a second lead "may have been the most revolutionary step in quartet history."[58]

Star Quartets

The techniques of quartet singing were at a high point of sophistication by the mid-1940s, and a number of groups used them to rise to prominence. For instance, the Swan Silvertones featured the beautiful falsetto vocals of the Reverend Claude Jeter.

Other groups specialized in hard gospel, a more aggressive style that emphasized power and strong emotion. Among the top "hard gospeleers" were the Five Blind Boys of Mississippi, the Five Blind Boys of Alabama, the Dixie Hummingbirds, and the Sensational Nightingales. The lead singers of hard gospel groups regularly whipped audiences into frenzies with flamboyant stage movements and vocal mannerisms like ecstatic moans, wails, screams, and falsetto shrieks. Hard gospel groups made no secret of their willingness to do whatever it took to put on a good show; as the Dixie Hummingbirds' Ira Tucker once commented, "I'm a firm believer in giving people something for their money."[59]

Another popular group of the era was the Golden Gate Quartet. Although not strictly a hard gospel group, it was renowned for inserting unusual sounds into its singing, such as imitations of trains, boats, and percussion instruments. The group was one of the first gospel quartets to broadcast on national radio, and a measure of its preeminence was its invitation to perform at Franklin Delano Roosevelt's 1941 presidential inaugural celebration.

Mahalia

Male quartets reached their peak of creativity and popularity during the Golden Age, but they were by no means the only groups on the scene. A number of all-female groups, for instance, included the Davis Sisters, the Harmonettes, and the Caravans. But perhaps the most familiar style during this period, after the male quartet, was the solo singer. During the Golden Age, a number of these brilliant soloists came to prominence, including Albertina Walker, Robert Anderson, Shirley Caesar, and Bessie Griffin. However, the most famous of them all was Mahalia Jackson.

Perhaps Jackson's greatest contribution to gospel was her widespread popularity. Using the new medium of television to strengthen her fan base around the world, Jackson became gospel's first superstar. She brought the music to unprecedented levels of popularity outside the black church; millions who had never heard or appreciated gospel before did so because of Jackson.

She had always had a stunning voice. Born in New Orleans in 1911, Jackson made her public singing debut at age four, and by age twelve she was a regular in her church's junior choir. Although raised a Baptist, she was strongly influenced by blues singers like Bessie Smith and Ma Rainey, whom she listened to in secret. Pentecostal meetings near her house also moved Jackson. She recalled,

Those [Pentecostal] people had no choir and no organ. They used the drum, the cymbal, the tambourine, and the steel triangle. Everybody in there sang and stomped their feet and sang with their whole bodies. They had a beat, a powerful beat, a rhythm we held on to from slavery days, and their music was so strong and expressive it used to bring tears to my eyes.[60]

A Skyrocketing Career

Jackson began her professional career after moving to Chicago in 1927. (She also owned and operated a beauty salon until her career took off.) The power and beauty of Jackson's voice attracted the attention of Dorsey, who hired her to demonstrate his songs; they remained a team, on and off, for many years.

Meanwhile, Jackson's solo career blossomed, and by 1946 she was singing full time. Her first hit record, 1948's "Move On Up a Little Higher," was also gospel's first million-seller, and within a few years she was gaining widespread exposure outside the church world. This included a weekly nationwide radio show, a prestigious French prize, and a hugely successful European tour. (Typical of the reaction on this tour was this comment from a British critic: "You need a heart of stone to remain unsmiling.")[61]

In America, Jackson was also attracting the attention of a wide mainstream (that is, white) audience. She made appearances on Ed Sullivan's top-rated TV

Considered the greatest gospel singer ever, Mahalia Jackson rose to prominence during the Golden Age of solo female singers.

variety show, sang in high-profile concerts at Carnegie Hall, and recorded for a major label, Columbia Records. Many longtime fans, however, were disappointed with the elaborate production but mediocre content of these recordings. Veteran record and concert producer John Hammond commented, "Columbia gave her the fancy accompaniments, and the choirs, but the wonderful drive and the looseness from the [early] recordings was missing."[62]

The Ward Singers

After Jackson, the next most prominent female gospel singer was Clara Ward, a native of Philadelphia. Her group, the Ward Singers, was a sensation when it debuted at the 1943 National Baptist Convention and continued to dazzle audiences for decades.

This combination of talent and showbiz glossiness was probably Ward's greatest contribution to the music's development. *Ebony* magazine noted in 1957 that she combined "the rhythmic genius of a jazz star, the emotional power of a great preacher and the flair of a sophisticated entertainer."[63] As such, she paved the way for the coming wave of gospel singers who would freely mix gospel with popular, entertaining music.

Ward and her singers were famous for lavish performances that included sequined gowns, flashy jewelry, and outrageous wigs. Even their mode of travel was showy—Cadillac limousines, with trailers for their costumes. But Ward, a difficult boss, could not keep the original group together. In 1958 its lead singer, Marion Williams, took several others with her when she formed a rival group, the Stars of Faith. Undaunted, Ward maintained her sometimes scandalous shows, which at one point included mock gospel routines in a Las Vegas nightclub.

Ward's penchant for show-business glitz angered some within the core gospel audience, but she was an undeniable inspiration to countless young performers. Many people devoted to gospel appreciated her efforts to expose a wide range of people to sacred music. One was singer and preacher James Cleveland, who noted, "I watched her carry gospel into many, many places where it hadn't been before and where it hasn't been since."[64]

On the Road

Life on the road, especially in the Deep South, was very hard for travelling gospel groups. In this excerpt from Viv Broughton's Black Gospel: An Illustrated History of the Gospel Sound, *the Reverend Isaac Ravizee, leader of the Ravizee Singers, recalls those days.*

One of our first trips was in Mississippi. Laurel, Hattiesburg, Picayune, Amory, Jackson, Mississippi. We went from there to Vicksburg and we left Vicksburg going to Monroe, Louisiana. Where we really got stranded was in a little old place called Bass Trap, Louisiana. There was a Baptist State Convention going on there and it was largely attended. There were some people from Mobile there, one of the ladies was Daisy Fisher. When she saw us in the yard she said, "Oh, here are the Ravizee Singers!" She went in and contacted the president of the State Convention and made a request to allow the Ravizees to sing. When we sung, we were stranded. We really didn't have any money and the car was broken down. When we got through singing they took up a collection of about $170. After we sang, the people were shouting and they heard it across the street at the church where the Women's Auxiliary of the Convention was meeting and they wanted to hear the Ravizee Singers too. So we went over there and it was almost pandemonium over there. They wanted to know how much the men raised and someone told them and they said, "We're going to beat them." And they gave us $200.

Sister Rosetta and Mother Smith

Another significant female soloist was the eccentric and utterly unique Sister Rosetta Tharpe. Tharpe was able to maintain a dual existence, combining hard-core gospel with saucy recordings of secular songs such as "I Want a Tall Skinny Papa" and appearances in nightclubs with jazz bands. Her shows were rousing combinations of infectious gospel, jokes, and rollicking blues, delivered with both religious passion and racy fun. One reviewer, summing up Sister Rosetta's appeal to even the most conservative listener, commented that she "could make a Republican Senator rock."[65]

In sharp contrast to Tharpe's outgoing style was the serene, graceful presence of Willie Mae Ford Smith. Mother Smith, as she was affectionately known, was raised in the Baptist Church but later joined a Pentecostal denomination. All her life, Smith's singing reflected both traditions, and she had no problem combining her Baptist heritage with a demonstrative, full-blooded Pentecostal style: "I'll sing with my hands, with my feet—when I got saved, my feet got saved, too. I believe we should use everything we got."[66]

As the longtime head of the Soloists Bureau of the National Convention of Gospel Choirs and Choruses, Smith trained dozens of talented singers. She also pioneered several techniques that became standard, such as the "song and sermonette" that inserted a five- or ten-minute spoken sermon into a song. And though she made relatively few recordings, the charismatic Smith made many personal appearances and routinely wreaked havoc in churches, as singer Zella Jackson Price recalled: "She was a *singer*. I've seen her walk out singing . . . on the way to her next appearance . . . and folks is just shoutin' everywhere, hats flyin' and carryin' on, just something terrible. She'd come in and just wreck all them buildings. That was Mother Smith, and she loved it."[67]

"Money . . . Was like a Bad Word"

In spite of all the developing professionalism within gospel, which gave it greater appeal to a nonreligious audience, the music remained a genre in which only a handful could earn more than living expenses. A few singers in the top echelon of professional gospel made good money during the Golden Age, but at the other end of the spectrum were thousands of performers who sang only around their hometowns on weekends. These semipro or amateur singers were in no way performing for the money; they did it strictly for love, typically holding day jobs and donating to their churches at least part of any money earned from singing. Charlie Storey recalled, "Back then, most groups sang for free. They'd come and help your church, and your church would come back and help their church. . . . Nobody said nothing about money in those days. When you spoke about some money, about getting paid, that was like a bad word—a curse word."[68]

In between these extremes were many professionals who eked out modest careers. These singers made their livings through hard and constant work; they occasionally recorded and relentlessly toured, crisscrossing the country on an expanded version of the early gospel circuit. Heilbut asserts that this was "both the toughest and most dangerous route in show business."[69]

Tours were typically made in secondhand cars (usually equipped with Maypop Tires—so named, performers joked, because they "may pop at any moment"). Even a battered old car was preferable to other methods of travel, however, especially in the South. With a car, at least, performers could avoid being relegated to the segregated sections of buses and trains, which were invariably dirty and overcrowded.

Worries on the Road

Touring singers faced many other problems, especially in the South. For instance, there was the difficulty of finding "colored" hotels and restaurants—establishments that catered to black travelers in what was then a part of the country that practiced strict segregation. Smaller towns sometimes lacked such facilities, in which case performers typically stayed and ate at the homes of local church members.

One reason that gospel singers earned relatively little was that gospel performances traditionally did not charge a set admission. A typical arrangement was that a group collected 60 percent of the "free will offer-ings"—that is, donations—taken in by the church or promoter sponsoring the show. Charging paid admission for gospel shows was not a common practice until the 1950s, and even then it was controversial, as many believed that people should not have to pay for what was, in their view, a religious service. Singer Vernella Kelly of the Faithful Harmonizers notes, "Well, a gospel program is a church service, it's not just something like a rock and roll concert. It's a church service, and you're going to worship—not just going to be seen or for a show or something like that. It's a religious service."[70]

Still, performers sometimes found themselves victimized by promoters with decidedly questionable ethics. An all-too-typical story concerns singer Alex Bradford, who was onstage—and had not yet been paid—when he realized he could not see the promoter anywhere. Bradford jumped offstage and found the man climbing out a window with the offering in hand.

To minimize such problems, many singers did their own promotion. They arrived in town early enough to put up signs and alert radio disc jockeys and ministers to upcoming appearances. Many groups also routinely arrived early enough to appear at Sunday services and sing a selection or two as advertisements for themselves. Even famous groups like the Swan Silvertones found promotion difficult, as Jeter recalled: "It was rough. It was just like nothin'. People had to put out handbills, posters, go through the city with

Acclaimed gospel singer Clara Ward mixed traditional gospel style with the glitz of the nightclub.

The audiences for these shows were frequently quiet and respectful. However, many performers encouraged boisterous audience response. In such a spontaneous atmosphere, singers could have a powerful impact. Parishioners, especially the women, would "get happy"—shaking their heads, shouting, and clapping their hands in response to the singing. Sometimes people got so excited that they fainted, and nurses were frequently on hand to attend to them.

Often, the enthusiasm of a gospel show was enhanced by friendly competition. It was common for several groups to appear in a single "extravaganza," each singing a short set and competing in "battles." Clarence Fountain, the lead singer of the Blind Boys of Alabama, recalled frequent competitions with Archie Brownlee, his counterpart from the Blind Boys of Mississippi: "Every night I had to battle it out with him. Who would the people like best? . . . At the end of the show we would come down the aisle, shake hands and collaborate together. That was really exciting. Archie, he could sing you to death."[72]

a sound truck. That's how we had to make it."[71]

Getting Happy

If properly promoted and attended, however, a gospel show could be a major social event. This was especially true in small towns that saw little in the way of special entertainment. A gospel concert was, first and foremost, a religious experience, but it was also a social occasion when one could see friends and show off one's best clothes.

Records and Radio

Nonstop touring kept gospel groups in the public eye. Increasingly cheap and available phonograph records also helped spread gospel. Dozens of small record labels, such as Savoy, Apollo, Atlantic, Specialty, and Peacock, recorded and distributed gospel artists. (However, the contracts performers typically signed were not lucrative. The standard pay was about $50 per record, with little if any chance of receiving additional money even if it became a hit.)

Another important avenue for popularizing gospel was radio, a medium that became widely available in the 1920s and exploded in popularity just before and during the Golden Age. Radio could make or break a group, since a spot on a national or regional program reached a broad swath of the public. For example, the Golden Gate Quartet's big break was being offered the chance to do a regular show on a Charlotte, North Carolina, station whose signal was powerful enough to reach the entire East Coast.

In radio's earliest years, stations aimed at black listeners had concentrated on jazz, blues, and dance music. Gospel was typically restricted to late-night or Sunday-morning time-slots. However, this began to change in the mid-1940s as gospel's popularity soared.

At that point, several stations began featuring it more prominently. Among them were WDIA in Memphis, WLIB in New York City, and WLAC in Nashville. WLAC was especially prominent because its strong signal could be heard for thousands of miles; the station had an estimated 8 to 12 million listeners during its prime in the early 1950s.

Sometimes gospel heard on the radio was previously recorded, but frequently it was performed live in a station's studios. During breaks in the music, announcers would pitch products for a wide variety of sponsors. According to Darden, these advertisements were for such diverse products as "baby chicks, hair pomade, recordings, garden seeds, choir robes and skin-lightening cream."[73]

The Line Blurs

Radio, records, and touring were all responsible for widening the audience for gospel during its Golden Age. High-profile concerts also played a role, notably a famous series of shows in New York City's Carnegie Hall, "From Spirituals to Swing," and the prestigious Newport (Rhode Island) Jazz Festivals of the 1950s. Thanks to these factors, the music reached far beyond the relatively small church community, to mainstream white audiences who loved the music even if they did not necessarily embrace the religious message it carried.

In a few short years, gospel had gone from being just one part of the black church's worship experience to being widely appreciated entertainment. At the same time, it graduated to a new level of professionalism. Boyer writes that "gospel moved from shabby store-front churches with a few untrained singers dressed in threadbare black or maroon choir robes to . . . extravagan-

"Their Pain and Their Joy Were Mine"

Writer James Baldwin, in an excerpt from his book The Fire Next Time, *describes the power a church service had on him. The excerpt is reprinted in Viv Broughton's* Black Gospel: An Illustrated History of the Gospel Sound.

There is no music like that music, no drama like the drama of the saints rejoicing, the sinners moaning, the tambourines racing, and all those voices coming together and crying holy unto the Lord. There is still, for me, no pathos quite like the pathos of those multi-coloured, worn, somehow triumphant and transfigured faces, speaking from the depths of a visible, tangible, continuing despair of the goodness of the Lord. I have never seen anything to equal the fire and excitement that sometimes, without warning, fills a church. . . . Nothing that has happened to me since, equals the power and the glory that I sometimes felt when, in the middle of a sermon, I knew that I was somehow, by some miracle, really carrying, as they said, "the Word"— when the church and I were one. Their pain and their joy were mine, and mine were theirs—they surrendered their pain and joy to me, I surrendered mine to them—and their cries of "Amen!" and "Hallelujah!" and "Yes Lord!" and "Praise His name!" and "Preach it, brother!" sustained and whipped on by solos until we all became equal, wringing wet, singing and dancing, in anguish and rejoicing, at the foot of the altar.

zas [featuring singers with] extraordinary control and nuance, dressed in blazing pastel gowns and bright suits."[74]

As elements of show business crept in, the line between sacred and popular music began to blur. Performers who had once sung only sacred music began to include nongospel songs in their repertoires. They increasingly injected elements of show-business polish into their performances. And popular songs began leaning heavily on the gospel sound—but with no overt references to religion. The stage was thus set for another major shift, as gospel began to mix even more dramatically with popular music.

Chapter Five

Gospel Evolves

*In all the great modern soul singers,
one hears echoes of the pioneer gospel
shouters.*

> — *Anthony Heilbut,*
> The Gospel Sound: Good News
> and Bad Times

In the 1960s, as the boundaries separating gospel from popular music
continued to blur, the styles
blended in new and sometimes controversial ways. For decades, popular music had influenced the gospel sound.
Now the tables were turning: gospel
was influencing pop.

In fact, the two were sometimes
so closely connected that it became
impossible to say exactly how one
style influenced the other. Indeed, except for lyrics, their sound could
sometimes seem interchangeable. Lou
Rawls, a gospel singer turned blues
and jazz star, once commented,
"Crossing over from gospel to pop
wasn't hard because it was just a matter of changing words."[75]

High-powered Shows

In the late 1940s and 1950s, a new
strain of black dance-oriented pop music emerged: rhythm and blues (R&B).
Earthy lyrics, impassioned vocals, elec-
trified instruments, bluesy melodies,
and, of course, a rockin' beat were
among R&B's chief traits, exemplified
by songs like Roy Brown's "Good
Rockin' Tonight," Ike Turner's "Rocket
88," and Amos Milburn's "Chicken
Shack Boogie."

R&B and gospel came to resemble
each other ever more closely. For one
thing, the visual presentation of both
styles made liberal use of theatrics and
showmanship. They also resembled
each other musically—that is, in the
way they sounded. R&B shared much
with hard gospel, the more aggressive
style favored by groups like the Blind
Boys of Mississippi and the Sensational Nightingales; this style was increasingly popular among gospel fans
as an alternative to the lighter, crooning
style of some quartets.

Ray Charles revolutionized American music by fusing the energy of hard gospel music with R&B sounds.

The appealing voice of gospel cross-over artist Sam Cooke, seen performing in 1960, attracted young white and black audiences.

The instrumental accompaniment for gospel was also influenced by the setup of a typical R&B band. Once, the standard gospel accompaniment had been only an organ or piano, possibly with percussion as well, and sometimes only percussion. Now a full rhythm section (guitar, keyboards, bass, and drums) was standard, an instrumental lineup borrowed from R&B.

The visual and musical similarities could easily be seen in concert. R&B shows were famous for their high-powered performances, and a show by a hard gospel singer was likewise an electrifying experience. Dorothy Love Coates—one of the few female hard gospel singers—typified this; as she sang, Coates moved her body, jumped up and down, and waved her arms wildly. She frequently walked into the audience in midperformance, and sometimes—overcome with the Holy Spirit—she became disoriented. Group members would have to leave the stage and lead her back. Meanwhile, the audience was, like Coates, "getting church"—standing up, swaying, crying, running up and down the aisles, and even fainting as the power of the music took hold.

Crossing Over

One way in which R&B and gospel did not resemble each other closely, however, was the financial arena. Even a charismatic and popular singer like Coates could make only a modest living by singing gospel. This was in sharp contrast to the world of R&B and other popular music, with its promise of big record sales, large concerts, and easy money. The temptation was strong for gospel singers to cross over to the more popular genre and reap these benefits.

Some, such as Clara Ward with her splashy shows, were eager to blur the line between pop and gospel

At Newport

When singers like Clara Ward and the Ward Singers appeared at the Newport Jazz Festival in 1957, it was a significant instance of the broadening of gospel's audience. Richard Gehman, music critic for Coronet *magazine, wrote about the Ward Singers's appearance. This excerpt is reprinted in Horace Clarence Boyer's* The Golden Age of Gospel.

They seemed nervous as they arranged themselves around a microphone and the woman at the piano, Clara Ward, played a few bars of introduction. They glanced at each other as though to muster strength. And then with a smiling placidity—they sang.

Rhythmic, high, clear, in perfect harmony they sang, the words in metered, driving cadence, underscored by piano. They began to clap their hands; and within seconds, hundreds in the audience were clapping with them. The singers threw back their heads and went into a second chorus, fervent and joyous. The voice of one [Marion Williams] soared above the others whose voices beat a counterpoint behind hers.

performance. Many hard-core performers, however, refused to cross over; there was still a strong stigma associated with performing what they continued to think of as the devil's music. Pop was, in the opinion of many, simply wicked. The gospel virtuoso Shirley Caesar once declared, "The U.S.A. doesn't have enough money to make me sing rock'n'roll!"[76] This attitude had been especially strong during the early part of the Golden Age. However, feelings began to soften by the mid-1950s. The time was ripe for a major gospel star to successfully make the leap to pop music.

That person was Sam Cooke, the lead singer for one of gospel's star groups, the Soul Stirrers. Gospel fans were outraged when Cooke abandoned sacred music, but his move proved wildly successful. It also profoundly changed the course of American popular music, paving the way for many more singers to come.

"The Young People Took Over"

Sam Cooke was born in Clarksdale, Mississippi, but grew up in Chicago. His father was a Baptist preacher, and young Sam sang in his father's church choir from an early age. Sam and his siblings also formed a group, the Singing Children, and as a teen he joined a well-regarded quartet, the Highway QCs. From there, he was recruited into the famed Soul Stirrers, already one of the top male quartets of the Golden Age of Gospel.

In 1951, while still a teen, Cooke became the Soul Stirrers's lead singer. Over the next few years, his performances brought the group to increasingly higher plateaus of fame. Cooke was blessed with a beautiful, supple, and highly distinctive light tenor, and he was also a gifted arranger and composer. Furthermore, his good looks and assured, charismatic stage manner helped him win over audiences wherever he sang.

In short, Sam Cooke was gospel's first teen idol. Because of him, young people began attending gospel shows in unprecedented numbers. Jesse Farley, a founding member of the Soul Stirrers, recalled, "In the old days, young people took seats six rows from the back, the old folks stayed up front. When Sam came on the scene, it reversed itself. The young people took over."[77]

"You Send Me"

Cooke may have been a gospel star, but he had ambitions far beyond its confines. Like Mahalia Jackson and other prominent gospel singers, he had always loved blues and jazz, and he had long incorporated elements of these styles into his singing. Now he began mounting an effort to develop the reverse—a pop style that incorporated elements of gospel. Within half a decade or so of becoming the Soul Stirrers's lead singer, he was emboldened to try his hand at recording secular music:

I was happy enough on the gospel trail and making myself a nice

Like Mothers and Babies in Church

David "Panama" Francis, the drummer on many of Ray Charles's classic soul recordings, explains in this passage about a certain rhythm Charles told him to play. The excerpt is from Portia K. Maultsby's "The Impact of Gospel Music on the Secular Music Industry," in We'll Understand It Better By and By: Pioneering African American Gospel Composers, *edited by Bernice Johnson Reagon.*

Ray was the one who told me to play with brushes like in the church and with a gospel feeling. All I played was straight quarter notes with brushes. If you remember, in the church, that was the way the mothers used to keep the babies quiet on their knees when they were singing; all they did was lift their foot and drop it—just a straight 4/4. . . . And they'd be patting the baby and it would go right back to sleep. And that's what I was playing on the drums in "Drown in My Own Tears."

living. . . . But the more I thought about the pop field the more interesting it became. . . . I wanted to do things for my family, and I wanted nice things of my own. Making a living was good enough, but what's wrong with doing better than that?[78]

Cooke knew that he might lose his core audience of gospel fans, and his first experiments in pop were cautious. He released his first R&B single in 1956 under an assumed name, Dale Cooke, partly to avoid offending his fans and partly to avoid a battle with the Soul Stirrers's record label (which was upset at Cooke's name being associated with R&B). This tentative first step was only moderately successful, but it was enough for him to part ways with the Soul Stirrers.

Cooke was then free to sign with a major label, RCA, under his own name. In 1957 his third single for them, "You Send Me," was a smash hit. It was only the first in a long string of classic hits, including "Cupid" and "Havin' a Party."

Predictably, however, many of Cooke's gospel fans saw his move as abandonment. To them, his story was a case of being fatally tempted by money. Cooke's former mentor in the Soul Stirrers, Rebert Harris, once commented, "It broke my heart when Sam went pop. He was so great and the church community loved him so much. [But] he came to me and told me they were offering him too much money and he just couldn't turn it down."[79]

More Crossovers

Cooke's success as a pop singer soon inspired others to partly or completely abandon sacred music. Gospel, popular though it was, had to compete for attention not only with fans but also many of its most gifted performers. Among the most prominent singers to abandon gospel were blues and jazz singers Johnny Adams, Lou Rawls, and Dinah Washington; rock and roll pioneer Little Richard; and R&B stars Johnny Taylor, Bobby Womack, and La Verne Baker.

Cissy Houston and Dionne Warwick (Whitney Houston's mother and cousin, respectively) left gospel to carve out successful careers in popular music. The Staple Singers (later the Staples) sang songs that combined elements of folk and gospel, such as "Will the Circle Be Unbroken." Several former gospel singers associated with Memphis's famous Stax/Volt label (including Wilson Pickett) and with Detroit's equally renowned Motown label (such as David Ruffin of the Temptations) also made the switch.

As might be expected, these singers initially met with bitter disappointment and fierce opposition from the gospel world. Some were shunned by their church communities or even disowned by their families. Bobby Womack, who had sung in a successful gospel group with his brothers before turning to R&B, recalls, "Our parents put us out of the house when we started singing pop music. My father said, 'You will not bring the devil here! If you gonna aim his pistol, I want him to know who to shoot.'"[80]

Undeterred, Womack and other singers of the era persevered in the pop field, bringing with them the passion and fire of gospel. Some were successful, others were not. Without a doubt, however, the most spectacular success stories concerned three especially powerful talents. Ray Charles, Aretha Franklin, and James Brown worked separately, but they had a common goal; together, they were the driving force behind a new style—soul music—that succeeded R&B and revolutionized the pop world.

The Genius of Soul

Ray Charles, nicknamed the Genius of Soul, was never a "professional" gospel singer, and he never formally recorded gospel music. Nonetheless, the emotion and pungency of the gospel sound underpinned all his music, and he did more than anyone else to merge it with more worldly music. Charles saw this mingling of styles as perfectly natural: "All music is related," he once remarked. "What you speak of as 'soul' in jazz is 'soul' in gospel music."[81]

Charles grew up singing in a Baptist church, lost his sight at an early age, and was a professional singer and pianist by fifteen. When he began recording in 1949, Charles's first efforts at jazzy pop were not very distinctive. However, he came into his own when he began recording for a New York R&B label, Atlantic Records, that encouraged the singer to develop a gospel-tinged style.

The results were unlike anything heard before. Charles's breakthrough single, 1955's "I've Got a Woman," combined a rolling gospel piano, a driving rhythm section, and impassioned vocals. The high-spirited earthiness of the song was brilliantly successful, both artistically and financially, and Charles followed it with many more, including "What'd I Say," "Lonely Avenue," and "Hit the Road, Jack."

The Queen of Soul

The second part of the soul triumvirate— Aretha Franklin, known to fans as the Queen of Soul—was born into gospel royalty. Her father was Reverend C. L. Franklin, a minister in Detroit, Michigan, with a national reputation for his stirring sermons. (He made over seventy best-selling recordings of them.) Franklin always acknowledged that her father's speeches deeply influenced how she sang: "Most of what I learned vocally came from him. He gave me a sense of timing in music and timing is important in everything."[82]

Reverend Franklin had friends throughout the gospel world, and as

The Queen of Soul, Aretha Franklin, graces the cover of Time *magazine in June 1968.*

a child Aretha sang informally with such regular houseguests as Mahalia Jackson, Sam Cooke, Marion Williams, and Clara Ward. She debuted at the age of twelve in her father's church, and by her teens had a voice powerful enough to stop a train; John Hammond, the veteran promoter, called her "an untutored genius, the best voice I've heard since [jazz legend] Billie Holiday."[83]

Her first record label, Columbia, tried to make her into a smooth nightclub singer, but the results were disappointing. Then Atlantic Records signed Franklin in 1966 and, as with Ray Charles, gave her artistic freedom. This meant letting her develop a unique fusion of pop and gospel; Franklin's producer, Jerry Wexler, recalled, "I took her to church, sat her down at the piano, let her be herself."[84]

The results paid off, beginning with "I Never Loved a Man"—a million-seller within weeks—and including such classics as "Respect," "Chain of Fools," and "Do Right Woman." Though the music she recorded was clearly pop, Franklin's voice and music remained so steeped in gospel that many observers feel she never truly left the church.

Long after her pop success was established, the singer made the connection explicit, returning to her gospel roots for a brilliant set of sacred music albums. Franklin has always acknowledged her debt to gospel, and the role it played in her fusion of styles. Accepting a Grammy Lifetime Achievement Award in 1994, she stated, "I want to first give thanks to God Almighty, and then to my father, the Reverend C. L. Franklin, for you all know where I'm from."[85]

The Godfather of Soul

The third giant of soul was James Brown, known as the Godfather of Soul (as well as "the hardest-working man in show business"). Raised in the Baptist church in Georgia, Brown had a wild youth and spent his early years in and out of reform school. He flirted with careers in baseball and boxing before turning to music full time.

Brown had a rough, intense voice that conveyed all the fervor and fire of a good Baptist minister. His particular gift lay in creating extended, multirhythmic instrumentals for his band, over which his remarkable voice could soar.

The singer's combination of R&B instrumental grooves, complex rhythms, and deeply gospel-tinged singing further strengthened the bridge that was being formed between gospel and popular black dance music. Brown also has profoundly influenced new generations of performers from a variety of other styles. Chrissie Hynde, leader of the rock group the Pretenders, once asserted, "There should be a statue of [Brown] in every park in America. He had the greatest influence of anyone in contemporary music."[86]

Freedom Songs

While Charles, Franklin, Brown, and their cohorts were using gospel to invent soul music in the late 1950s and

Combining hard gospel, R&B, and the beginnings of funk, James Brown, seen here onstage in 1968, is known as the Godfather of Soul.

Martin Luther King Jr. delivers his "I Have a Dream" speech in Washington, D.C., in 1963. Gospel music and freedom songs were an integral part of the civil rights struggle.

early 1960s, gospel music entered a new realm: it became a form of social commentary. This happened when gospel became closely associated with the civil rights movement, the epic struggle by black Americans to achieve equality with whites in such areas as education, job opportunities, and voting.

The civil rights movement was one of the most significant social and political events in American history, and gospel music was a natural fit to become its theme music. The movement as a whole was intimately connected with the black church, and many of its leaders, such as Martin Luther King Jr. and Jesse Jackson, were ministers. Churches were typically used as meeting places, and ministers routinely used their pulpits as springboards for spreading the word.

More generally, the movement's philosophy was built on the fundamentals of justice, freedom, racial pride, hope, and the overcoming of adversity. Gospel music, having blossomed from the old spirituals of slavery days, directly and eloquently addressed these same issues. King, the movement's key figure, once stated that gospel songs "are playing a vital role in our struggle. These songs give the people new courage and a sense of unity. I think they keep alive a faith, a radiant hope in the future, particularly in our most trying hours."[87]

Songs closely associated with the movement were called freedom songs. Their primary purposes were to give voice to important issues, inspire hope, and raise individual spirits during the movement's long struggle. However, sometimes the songs had more concrete applications as well. For example, during demonstrations in Birmingham, Alabama, in 1963, protesters faced potentially violent opposition from the city's police force. A local radio announcer and gospel show host, Erskine Faush, alerted protesters to police actions, in the hopes of avoiding the worst violence, by using certain songs during his broadcasts as coded messages.

"We Shall Overcome"

Among the most popular freedom songs were "We Shall Overcome," "Oh Freedom," "Kumbaya," "This Little Light of Mine," and "Eyes on the Prize." Some freedom songs were newly written works that were strongly influenced by old spirituals and gospel songs; others were older songs, often fitted with new lyrics. For example, in the old spiritual "Rockin' Jerusalem," the phrase "church gettin' higher" became "bail's gettin' higher," while "rockin' Jerusalem" became "prayin' in jail."

Singers frequently altered the lyrics of songs to reflect particular concerns. The new lyrics thus spoke to specific aspects of the civil rights struggle. For example, about Dorothy Love Coates, Heilbut notes, "Now when she sang in church, her moans were very specific. Not merely was this a 'mean old trouble land,' it was a place where 'our children can't go to decent schools.'"[88]

The most famous and frequently sung freedom song of all was "We Shall Overcome." It was adapted from a gospel hymn composed by Charles Tindley, "I'll Overcome Some Day." (It is likely that Tindley, in turn, based both the lyrics and melody of his song on an old spiritual, "I'll Be All Right.")

During the process of being passed down, this spiritual emerged from its original version with the words "I'll be all right/I'll be all right/I'll be all right someday/Deep in my heart/I do believe/I'll be all right someday." This was changed by Tindley to "I'll overcome . . ." and then adapted by civil rights workers to become its most famous version: "We shall overcome/We shall overcome/We shall overcome someday. . . ."

Protesters frequently added new lyrics to the song, such as "We will win our rights. . . ." The song in time became a touchstone and symbol for the entire movement. Reflecting on the significance of this seminal song, civil rights activist Wyatt Tee Walker commented:

> One cannot describe the vitality and emotion this one song evokes across the Southland. I have heard it sung in great mass meetings with a thousand voices singing as one; I've heard a half-dozen sing it softly behind the bars of the Hinds County Prison in Albany, Georgia; I've heard the students singing it as they were being dragged away to jail. It generates power that is indescribable.[89]

Gospel Outside the Church

Gospel songs were closely associated with the civil rights movement. They affected popular music by helping shape soul. Throughout the era, traditional gospel also remained popular with a core audience for its primary purpose—as a form of worship. Meanwhile, gospel also gained a few important footholds outside the church, the pop charts, and the picket line.

For example, it made an appearance on Broadway in the form of "Black Nativity: A Gospel Song-Play." Langston Hughes, the distinguished African American poet and writer, created this show by weaving a number of songs into a full-length theatrical performance that retold the story of the birth of Jesus. Two of gospel's brightest stars, singers Alex Bradford and Marion Williams, appeared in the play's original production. Despite initial skepticism, "Black Nativity" was a hit, running on Broadway for two years, enjoying an extended run in London, and touring Europe. It has also been revived regularly in many cities since.

Gospel showed up in other venues as well. A nationally broadcast television show, *TV Gospel Time*, ran for two seasons. A few top performers, including the Dixie Hummingbirds and the Soul Stirrers, appeared on *Hootenanny*, a popular TV show during the mid-1960s that capitalized on a boom in folk music. And the Apollo Theater, a legendary New York City venue, began

Spirituals and the Civil Rights Movement

In the mid-1950s, as the civil rights movement was under way, the great African American classical singer Paul Robeson made this statement, quoted in "Sweet Chariot: the Story of the Spirituals" on the Web Site of the Spirituals Project at the University of Denver.

T he power of spirit that our people have is intangible, but it is a great force that must be unleashed in the struggles of today.

A spirit of steadfast determination, exaltation in the face of trials—it is the very soul of our people that has been formed through the long and weary years of our march toward freedom. . . . That spirit lives in our people's songs—in the sublime grandeur of "Deep River," in the driving force of "Jacob's Ladder," in the militancy of "Joshua Fit the Battle of Jericho," and in the poignant beauty of all of our spirituals.

---

booking gospel in addition to its established roster of R&B and blues acts.

Some promoters and producers tried to mix gospel with commercial pop, but their efforts mostly were eccentric and poorly received. For example, there was a short-lived fad for gospel nightclubs, where waitresses dressed like angels and patrons drank liquor while listening to staged gospel shows. A style called pop gospel was also briefly hyped by the record industry; a Columbia Records executive stated hopefully in 1963, "It's the greatest groove since rock'n'roll. In a month or two, it'll be all over the charts."[90]

For better or worse, pop gospel never caught on. In fact, although traditional gospel retained its core audience, the music in any form did not achieve widespread acceptance beyond what it already had. Interest in gospel (as measured in concert and record sales) actually began to fade—perhaps because the civil rights movement was entering a phase of consolidating gains and the power of the freedom songs was dwindling as well. However, in the late 1960s a new style of presenting the music—the massed choir—successfully rekindled the gospel scene, updating the style and ringing in a new era in its development.

Chapter Six

Contemporary Gospel

Unlike other forms of music, gospel is . . . about more than just a song: It's inspiration.

— Contemporary gospel singer CeCe Winans

The massed choir dominated the period of gospel history that began in the late 1960s. As the name suggests, massed choirs assembled large numbers of singers to create a huge wall of sound. A musical director or conductor guided the various sections of this large group, in the same way a conductor directs a symphony orchestra, and often the choirs served as backdrops for soloists. Though the typical massed choir was in the forty- to fifty-person range, some incorporated several hundred singers. One choir, specially assembled for a gospel conference, boasted three thousand voices.

The concept of a large gospel choir was not new. A prominent early example was Wings over Jordan, the first full-time black choir in America. Wings over Jordan began in Cleveland, Ohio, in the mid-1930s—the era of choirs organized by Thomas Dorsey—and continued for many decades, becoming well known nationally for its weekly radio broadcasts. Despite the early presence of this and other choirs, however, the massed choir concept was not widely popular until the late 1960s.

"Oh Happy Day"

The era of the massed choir began in 1968 with a surprise radio hit. A San Francisco Bay–area ensemble, the Northern California State Youth Choir, recorded an album of gospel songs, but the group had only modest expectations for it. The choir hoped to sell five hundred copies and donate the profits to their church.

However, a disc jockey on an "underground," or alternative, FM radio station in the Bay Area began to feature one of the album's songs, "Oh Happy Day," a traditional Baptist hymn with

A group of university students in Iowa protests the Vietnam War in 1968. The late 1960s was a time of violence and social upheaval in the United States.

an infectious, inspiring arrangement by the choir's director, Edwin Hawkins. Unexpectedly, the song became a hit regionally; after radio stations outside the Bay Area began featuring it as well, the song was a smash hit nationally. Both the single of "Oh Happy Day" and the album it was taken from, *Let Us Go into the House of the Lord*, sold millions of copies, and the album won a Grammy Award.

The unexpected, massive success of "Oh Happy Day" may have been the result, at least in part, of events of the time. American society was in serious turmoil in 1968, polarized by the war the United States was pursuing in Vietnam, racial conflict, student unrest, and other issues. Some observers have argued that the up-tempo song, with its simple message of hope, soothed the spirits of people during those troubled times. In any case, it was a huge hit, and it touched off a renewed wave of popularity for gospel music.

James Cleveland

Hawkins never again achieved the overwhelming success of "Oh Happy Day." However, he and his extended

This 1960 promotional portrait of the James Cleveland Gospel Singers, features Cleveland (top) and organist Billy Preston (right).

family continued to be a significant presence on the gospel scene, particularly the newly popular sound of massed choirs. For example, Hawkins organized an internationally recognized annual music conference. Other family members, notably Walter Hawkins and Tramaine Hawkins, have forged outstanding gospel careers of their own as well.

The contemporary gospel movement was also strongly influenced by a number of other people. Prominent among them was James Cleveland, a Chicago-born, Los Angeles–based music director and pianist. Cleveland's contributions to the music included his sophisticated arrangements of traditional hymns, which gave the older songs a modern, jazzy feel. Cleveland's innovative arranging style was widely imitated and exerted a strong influence on the gospel sound of the 1960s and 1970s.

Cleveland was prolific and consistently popular as a performer, songwriter, and recording artist. He received many honors and awards during his career, including becoming the first gospel artist to receive a sidewalk star in the Hollywood Walk of Fame. One of the best known of the many albums he contributed to, meanwhile, was *Amazing Grace*, Aretha Franklin's brilliant return to her gospel roots, in which she was backed by Cleveland's Southern California Community Choir.

Another significant achievement for Cleveland was his role in organizing the Gospel Music Workshop of America (GMWA). This association, the largest of its kind, served (and still serves) as a modern version of Dorsey's groundbreaking organization, creating and linking massed choirs all over the country. The GMWA grew rapidly after its founding in 1967, and today boasts nearly thirty thousand members in some one hundred and fifty chapters in America and abroad. It also sponsors well-attended annual conventions and has served as a starting point for the careers of young artists such as Kirk Franklin and John P. Kee.

Soul Man

One of the most important figures in gospel during the 1970s was not part of the massed-choir movement. Al Green was—and still is—a performer with an eccentric and unusually intimate sound. As both a gifted singer and songwriter, Green infused his music with a double edge: his songs could be accepted equally as songs of religious, romantic, or sexual passion. With his overlapping, interdependent careers in the sacred and the secular, Green has helped gospel develop in yet another new and promising dimension.

Green grew up with gospel during his Arkansas childhood. He later recalled of the music he heard as a child, "It was put in my cornbread. . . . My mother and my father, they were Baptists. We were raised in the church, and we sang at home. I started when I was just a little peewee. I was just raised on the sound of Sam Cooke and the Soul Stirrers and the whole trip."[91]

Like so many other singers, Green began his career in church choirs and in a group with his siblings. And, like others before him, he was exiled as a teen from his family for secretly listening to blues and R&B. Working closely with a Memphis producer, Willie Mitchell, Green found fame and fortune as a soul singer; the hits they crafted together included "I'm So Tired of Being Alone," "I'm Still in Love with You," and "Call Me."

Green's music was sexy R&B, but it also contained strong religious references; it perfectly captured the push-pull emotions of a man caught up in both spiritual and earthly passion. Heilbut comments, "With a gospel singer's *chutzpah* [bold nerve], he would employ his voices—a limber falsetto, a breathless crooner, a growling preacher—in a three-way encounter, alternately exhilarating and schizoid."[92]

Green was a top soul man for years, but in the mid-1970s he experienced a spiritual reawakening. He became an ordained minister in Memphis and recorded primarily gospel, although with a light, airy touch that owed much to pop. In recent years, Green has returned to making occasional secular records, and his legendary status as a soul man has helped renew the public's appreciation of contemporary gospel as well.

Sounding More Commercial

Besides the continuing popularity of the massed choir and of variations such as Green's intimate style, gospel music's sound began to change in other ways. Notably, the traditional styles perfected during the Golden Age of Gospel fell out of favor in the 1970s. In their place came a sound that edged markedly closer than ever before to the slick sound of the era's pop music.

This sleeker, more commercial gospel was largely the result of a concerted effort on the part of record labels. Music industry executives wanted to attract wider audiences by making gospel's sound increasingly resemble the era's pop music, which relied heavily on sophisticated studio techniques and new technology. As a result, in the 1970s synthesizers largely replaced the Hammond organ, for decades the standard in gospel. The labels also encouraged performers to put on flashier shows and to tone down the overtly religious lyrics of their songs.

Some gospel singers were open to this commercialization of their music. For many, it was not much of a stretch;

after all, they were already experienced at putting on rousing live performances. Heilbut notes, "Gospel singers need an audience that shares their feelings and acknowledges their efforts in self-expression. The black church provides the best training in the world, and these singers have become the supreme showmen of our time."[93]

The new, highly commercial sound was epitomized by the Mighty Clouds of Joy. The veteran group jazzed up its sound with amplified instruments such as electric guitars and synthesizers. The group included in its repertoire secular songs with semireligious sentiments (such as Carole King's inspirational "You've Got a Friend"). It also made high-profile appearances with pop and rock acts such as Stevie Wonder and the Rolling Stones. In the opinion of Joe Ligon, the Clouds's founder and lead singer, this change from the group's established sound was for the better: "You have to mix your songs. Go traditional, then go contemporary. Traditional music will never die, because the church will never die."[94]

"Loves Me Like a Rock"

The Mighty Clouds of Joy were not the only gospel singers of the 1970s and 1980s to extend their boundaries. Another veteran group, the Dixie Hummingbirds, backed singer-songwriter Paul Simon on his 1973 recording of "Loves Me Like a Rock." Because this song was a big hit by an extremely popular musician, the Hummingbirds's classic quartet sound reached an

Singer Al Green, shown here in 1975, has enjoyed success with his unique musical style that combines gospel and soul.

The Future of Gospel

In this passage from his book The Golden Age of Gospel, *Horace Clarence Boyer comments on how gospel could continue to spread in the future.*

Like New Orleans traditional music (Dixieland), traditional gospel—the kind that Dorsey espoused—will survive as *one* type of gospel, for in the near future there will surely be many types of black gospel music. Like the blues, gospel will become part of the fabric of American music and will become synonymous with American music. It will be heard in elevators, over telephones, in department stores, movies, and commercials. But while it is being used for advertising and dancing, it will also be used for meditation and worship.

---

unusually wide audience. (This was not the first time traditional gospel had shown up in Simon's work; "Bridge over Troubled Water," released in 1970 while he was part of the duo Simon and Garfunkel, had been inspired by an old Swan Silvertones song: "I'll be a bridge over deep water if you trust in my name."[95])

Still another example of the commingling of gospel and pop was the vocal group Take 6. On the surface, Take 6 has many elements in common with the classic male gospel quartets. For one thing, the group sings almost exclusively a cappella. Also, it was formed when its members were students at a small religious college, just as so many of the old jubilee quartets had originally come together at African American colleges and universities.

However, the popular group sounds dramatically unlike the classic quartets. Its intricate, six-voice harmony sound owes relatively little to traditional gospel. Take 6 instead is more indebted to the highly stylized, carefully arranged jazz-pop vocal ensembles of the 1940s and 1950s, such as the Swingle Singers and the Hi-Los, as well as the more recent Manhattan Transfer.

"We're in the Music Ministry"

Not all gospel performers of this era changed their sound to fit a more commercial ideal. Singers like A1 Green and Andrae Crouch (who led a multiracial group called the Disciples), as well as choir directors like James Cleveland and Edwin Hawkins, continued to craft their own individual takes on the gospel sound. However, despite their different sounds, many performers of the era shared one important characteristic: an eagerness to perform anywhere and everywhere.

This was a marked change from the overall attitude of earlier years. There had been exceptions (notably Sister Rosetta Tharpe and Mahalia Jackson), but earlier gospel performers were in general reluctant to appear in secular concert settings (that is, appearances outside of church). These performers felt that, since their music was akin to a religious service, to perform it any place but in church would be improper.

By the 1970s, however, many prominent performers were happy to play in secular settings and for secular audiences. To these performers, singing outside of church was (and still is) an essential way to spread the message of Christianity. As Edwin Hawkins commented, "Anywhere there's a door open to take the Message in gospel song, we should do it. We're ministers of the Gospel, we're in the music *ministry*."[96]

"The Only Thing That Doesn't Change Is God"

Some performers active today continue to uphold the traditions of older styles of gospel—that is, styles such as quartet singing, piano-accompanied soloists, and massed choirs. However, gospel has hardly remained stagnant; in recent years it has continued to undergo changes. These changes are exemplified by exciting young artists who incorporate diverse styles, such as rap, rock, funk, and jazz, into their music.

Reverend James Cleveland, one of a number of gospel performers who consider themselves part of the music ministry, speaks at a convention in Miami in 1986.

These artists have their own individual musical visions. However, they also share a basic, common goal. They are attracting young audiences—their peers—to gospel by blending up-to-the-minute musical elements like rock and rap with more traditional styles. They are thus bringing gospel into current times without compromising its fundamental religious and spiritual messages. Yolanda Adams recognized the need for this modernization during her early apprenticeship as the lead singer for Houston's Southeast Inspirational Choir: "We were trying to make sure young people enjoyed gospel music, so we had really fresh beats and songs kids could sing along with when they heard them the first time. We were teen-agers; you wouldn't expect us to sing . . . like Mahalia Jackson sang in 1940."[97]

This decision—to reach younger audiences with a fresher approach to music—has been both natural and deliberate. Today's artists understand that gospel's sound can change with the times while still retaining its basic message. Adams comments,

> I've always believed that in spreading God's word, you should appeal to everybody—the oldsters, people who love pop music or jazz—everybody. And look at Thomas Dorsey. Everybody was saying, "Get him outta here!" because he was playing blues. We just have to understand that change comes. The only thing that doesn't change is God.[98]

Kirk Franklin

While an uncountable number of today's singers achieve only local or regional notice, as in past years, a handful have achieved widespread fame. One is Kirk Franklin. Franklin grew up poor in Texas, but was a child prodigy as a singer and pianist. At a young age he became the pianist for a gospel producer, Milton Biggham, directing his choir workshops around the Dallas/Forth Worth area.

Franklin's debut album, *Kirk Franklin and the Family,* was recorded with a seventeen-voice choir he formed; it contained the work that has become his signature song, "Why We Sing." Released in 1993, the album stayed on the Billboard Gospel Charts for a record-breaking one hundred weeks and won numerous awards. Subsequent albums, including *The Rebirth of Kirk Franklin,* have been equally successful; they have been artistically groundbreaking, reflecting the influences—including rock and funk—that have shaped Franklin's music as much as gospel has.

Franklin's success has been due in large part to his strengths as a composer and arranger. However, much of his success can also be attributed to his abilities as a charismatic performer. Even though the basic message of his music remains rooted in deeply traditional religious beliefs, Franklin in person can excite an audience as much as any rock or soul star does. He does this, in part, by incorporating such elements as dancers, lights, videos, and music with hypnotic, highly danceable rhythms. Mostly, however, the excitement is created by Franklin's own electrifying presence. In the words of one record company executive, "I've never seen a gospel artist get his clothes ripped off him at a show. It's his magnetism. People just seem to be very excited about this young man talking about the Lord."[99]

More New Stars of Gospel

Contemporary gospel's reigning queen is Yolanda Adams, a Texas native with a stunning voice (and equally stunning looks; she is a former model). Adams's music frequently includes hip-hop rhythms and other elements of current music. However, she is equally comfortable with more reflective, heartfelt songs that showcase her amazing voice playing off against traditional musical backdrops such as full orchestras and massed choirs.

As is the case with Kirk Franklin and others, one of Adams's most important contributions to gospel has been to dramatically widen its audience by attracting younger listeners. After several years of singing part-time around her home of Houston and recording for a

Role Models

In this quote from Janine Coveney's article "CeCe Winans' Modern Gospel" in Billboard *magazine, singer CeCe Winans reflects on the responsibilities of contemporary gospel stars.*

We need more positive artists, because music is a powerful tool. It can lift you up, or it can bring you down. It can encourage you to do the right thing, and it can encourage you to do the wrong thing. Especially our young people; I feel like they're in trouble. When you turn on the video channel and the radio. . . . you hear lyrics that are meant to do nothing else but destroy you and mess you up. And you can look at our young people and tell that it has that effect on them. So yes, I think gospel music is a positive, positive force for our community because it's simply good news. . . . Let's face it; young people like to see young people. They are persuaded by what they see on TV and what they hear. They're looking for role models. If they see this person up there [who is] emphasizing sex or violence, that's what our kids go out there and imitate. So I just wish more people, first of all, would take responsibility when [they're] on a platform.

Contemporary artists Yolanda Adams and Donnie McClurkin sing at the BET Awards in 2003. The two have helped attract a young audience to gospel.

small label, Adams signed with a major label, Elektra. The larger company's executives assured Adams that they would not change her music at all, only the size and scope of her audience. The company succeeded dramatically. Her album *Mountain High ... Valley Deep* debuted at number one on the Billboard gospel chart and won a Grammy Award. Subsequent albums have been equally successful, and have furthered the basic message Adams hopes to convey with her music—that "some person making a decision in [his or her] life will say, 'You know what? I do need to talk to God.'"[100]

A third singer who is proving to be influential in the development of contemporary gospel is Donnie McClurkin. Besides being blessed with an expressive voice and a gift for songwriting, McClurkin has a strong interest in exploring new and unusual venues for gospel. This was true even when he was a teen. To reach people outside the established circuit, McClurkin founded the New York Restoration Choir, a group that performed on city streets, in prisons, and in other nontraditional venues for gospel.

His work as a singer has led him to appear before presidents George H.W. Bush and Bill Clinton. Recent honors include a 2004 Grammy for his album *Donnie McClurkin ... Again* and a 2004 NAACP Image Award (presented by the prestigious organization to outstanding African American entertainers and leaders). McClurkin is also an ordained minister, with his own church on Long Island, in New York State. McClurkin sees his ministering as important a part of his life as singing, and a natural outgrowth of his interest in bringing gospel to an ever-widening audience. He comments, "Preaching is my passion, and music is a by-product of that. My church duties are first and foremost."[101]

Controversy

Midway through the first decade of the twenty-first century, many more talented singers have been garnering national attention with their own versions of contemporary gospel. Among the most prominent are Smokie Norful, Fred Hammond, Mary Mary (a female duo), John P. Kee, and BeBe and CeCe Winans (a brother-and-sister duo who are part of an extended family of gifted gospel musicians).

Sometimes, the newer sounds of gospel that these and other artists create can be controversial. This is especially true with the mixture of gospel with rap, since rap frequently includes obscenities and evokes violent images. In 2004 Kanye West, a top rapper and hip-hop producer, created an album, *The College Dropout,* parts of which had a strong religious message. However, *The College Dropout* was withdrawn from consideration for honors by the prestigious Stellar Gospel Music Awards. A nominating committee decided that the artist's use of profanity was not in the spirit of gospel.

West notes that the controversy over this decision was the effect he was looking for: "The fact they [the Stellar Gospel Music Awards] recognized it in the first place means that it had its impact. The message that God wanted me to deliver was made, and the people that it was supposed to help, it helped."[102] And despite the flap, West's best-selling album was eventually honored by the music industry; a song from the album, "Jesus Walks," won a Grammy Award in 2005.

Unlike West, some contemporary gospel performers prefer to avoid volatile images and words. They feel instead that gospel should offer listeners a meaningful alternative to the violence, misogyny, profanity, and bleakness that typifies rap. Singer Tramaine Hawkins comments, "What really concerns me is not so much the music [of rap] but the lyric content of what young people are hearing. It puts down women; it talks about violence; it is very negative. I feel that somebody has got to combat that."[103]

A Booming Business

Controversies aside, the success of new artists such as West, Adams, McClurkin, and Franklin has caused gospel's popularity to skyrocket. Gospel has grown explosively in recent years, both artistically and financially. This growth can be attributed to several factors. One is gospel's proven ability to change with the times. For decades, as musical tastes have changed, gospel has successfully adapted and attracted new generations of listeners.

But many observers have suggested that the surge in popularity has a deeper

reason, one created by more than its ability to connect with young people's taste for fresh rhythms and raps. These observers feel that much of gospel's recent popularity can be traced to the uncertainty of life in today's world. They argue that many people are finding a close connection with the message of hope and peace that gospel delivers. Singer Vickie Winans comments, "With [the terrorist attacks of] 9-11 and the war [in Iraq], people are looking for something to soothe their pain. They tend to go to church more where they can hear more songs that soothe them. That's why the awareness of gospel music has taken on such a greater power."[104]

Big Business

Whatever the reasons may be, in terms of sheer dollars gospel is bigger than ever and shows every sign of continuing to grow. Total revenues for the gospel music industry nearly tripled between 1980 and 1990. More recently, these figures have continued to increase—by more than 30 percent in the single year between 1995 and 1996, and another 30 percent between 1996 and 1997. The gospel music industry now accounts for hundreds of millions of dollars in business annually.

Other signs of continued popularity are everywhere. The cable TV network BET prominently features gospel. Dozens of gospel-oriented radio stations and Webcasts broadcast daily. In addition, there are numerous Web sites and monthly magazines devoted to gospel

Kanye West performs "Jesus Walks" during the 2005 Grammy Awards. West created controversy by mixing religious themes and rap in his music.

Entertaining and Edifying

In this excerpt from his book People Get Ready! A New History of Black Gospel Music, *Robert Darden comments on one of the many differences between secular and gospel artists.*

The dispute between traditional and contemporary, church and secular applications of gospel music is, as several artists suggested, as old as gospel itself. . . . Most popular entertainers need only be concerned with entertaining. Gospel artists must both entertain *and* edify [educate]. An offstage scandal can actually help a pop artist's career. Even the hint of a scandal can bring a promising career in gospel screeching to a halt.

music, such as *The Gospel Truth.* Several major recording companies maintain healthy gospel divisions, while smaller, independent gospel labels have skyrocketed in size and numbers. Furthermore, gospel's popularity is not limited to America; the music also has huge, enthusiastic followings in Europe, especially in Holland and Germany.

This explosive growth has inspired artists, producers, and music industry executives alike to work harder on spreading gospel's message of hope and redemption. Once, record company executives were reluctant to promote the relatively small genre of gospel, but now it is big enough to accommodate any number of new performers. Singer CeCe Winans comments, "Now that gospel acts can finally be counted on to sell platinum records, record companies are willing to invest in marketing campaigns to put more of us on the map. What we need are more young Christian artists out here."[105]

In the Future

Since its very beginnings, when anonymous slaves composed songs to ease their burdens and give themselves hope, black sacred music has proved itself unusually resilient and adaptive. It has been able to absorb new influences and, in turn, influence other musical styles.

In the coming years, gospel will no doubt continue to evolve in new and unexpected ways. At the same time, it will continue to spread its essential, unchanging message of hope, forgiveness, love, and peace. In the future, gospel will surely continue to be one of the most richly rewarding aspects of American religious music and culture.

• Notes •

Introduction: A Joyous Noise

1. Quoted in Robert Darden, *People Get Ready! A New History of Black Gospel Music*. New York: Continuum, 2004, p. 2.
2. Horace Clarence Boyer, *The Golden Age of Gospel*. Urbana: University of Illinois Press, 2000, p. 194.
3. Quoted in Darden, *People Get Ready!* p. 261.
4. Quoted in Viv Broughton, *Black Gospel: An Illustrated History of the Gospel Sound*. Poole, UK: Blandford Press, 1985, p. 53.

Chapter One:
The Roots of Gospel

5. James H. Cone, *The Spirituals and the Blues: An Interpretation*. New York: Seabury Press, 1972, p. 32.
6. Darden, *People Get Ready!* p. 1.
7. Thomas Wentworth Higginson, "Negro Spirituals," *Atlantic Monthly,* June 1867. http://xroads. virginia.edu/~hyper/twh/higg.html.
8. Darden, *People Get Ready!* p. 68.
9. Quoted in Darden, *People Get Ready!* p. 51.
10. Hall Johnson, "Notes on the Negro Spiritual," in *Readings in Black American Music,* ed. Elaine Southern. New York, Norton, 1971, p. 270.
11. James Weldon Johnson, "Negro Folk Songs and Spirituals," *Mentor,* February 1929. www.document records.com/content_show_ article.asp?id=189&offset=90.
12. Quoted in Paul Oliver, "Spirituals," in *The New Grove Gospel, Blues and Jazz,* by Paul Oliver, Max Harrison, and William Bolcom. New York: Norton, 1986, p. 12.
13. Quoted in Broughton, *Black Gospel,* p. 16.
14. Quoted in Eileen Southern, *The Music of Black Americans: A History.* New York: Norton, 1997, p. 84.
15. Quoted in Broughton, *Black Gospel,* p. 23.
16. Boyer, *The Golden Age of Gospel,* p. 6.
17. Southern, *The Music of Black Americans,* p. 185.
18. Quoted in Southern, *The Music of Black Americans,* p. 78.
19. Broughton, *Black Gospel,* p. 31.
20. Broughton, *Black Gospel,* p. 24.

Chapter Two:
The Birth of the Spiritual

21. Quoted in Bernice Johnson Reagon, "Pioneering African American Music Composers," in *We'll Understand It Better By and By: Pioneering African American Gospel Composers,* ed. Bernice Johnson Reagon. Washington, DC: Smithsonian Institution Press, 1992, p. 11.

22. Higginson, "Negro Spirituals."

23. Broughton, *Black Gospel,* p. 12.

24. Reagon, "Pioneering African American Music Composers," pp. 11–12.

25. Quoted in Southern, *The Music of Black Americans*, p. 229.

26. Quoted in Darden, *People Get Ready,* p. 110.

27. Quoted in Darden, *People Get Ready!* p. 117.

28. Darden, *People Get Ready!* p. 119.

29. Boyer, *The Golden Age of Gospel*, p. 17.

30. Quoted in Darden, *People Get Ready!* p. 140.

31. Boyer, *The Golden Age of Gospel*, p. 19.

32. Quoted in Ray Allen, *Singing in the Spirit: African-American Sacred Quartets in New York City.* Philadelphia: University of Pennsylvania Press, 1991, p. 175.

33. Quoted in Paul Oliver, *Songsters and Saints: Vocal Traditions on Race Records.* Cambridge: Cambridge University Press, 1984, p. 189.

34. Quoted in Broughton, *Black Gospel,* p. 32.

35. Quoted in Allen, *Singing in the Spirit,* pp. 34–35.

36. Quoted in Anthony Heilbut, *The Gospel Sound: Good News and Bad Times.* New York: Limelight Books, 1997, p. 299.

37. Quoted in Darden, *People Get Ready!* p. 129.

Chapter Three:
The Flowering of Gospel

38. Oliver, *Songsters and Saints,* p. 192.

39. Reagon, "Pioneering African American Music Composers," p. 14.

40. Reverend Charles Walker, "Lucie E. Campbell Williams," in *We'll Understand It Better By and By*, ed. Reagon, p. 126.

41. Anthony Heilbut, "'If I Fail, You Tell the World I Tried'—William Herbert Brewster on Record," in *We'll Understand It Better By and By*, ed. Reagon, p. 233.

42. Quoted in Darden, *People Get Ready!* p. 205.

43. Broughton, *Black Gospel,* p. 29.

44. Quoted in Broughton, *Black Gospel,* p. 36.

45. Quoted in Broughton, *Black Gospel,* p. 36.

46. Quoted in Michael W. Harris, *The Rise of Gospel Blues: The Music of Thomas Andrew Dorsey in the Urban Church.* New York: Oxford University Press, 1992, p. 129.

47. Quoted in Broughton, *Black Gospel,* p. 46.

48. Quoted in Heilbut, *The Gospel Sound,* pp. 21, 34.

49. Boyer, *The Golden Age of Gospel*, p. 61.

50. Boyer, *The Golden Age of Gospel*, p. 74.

51. Quoted in Heilbut, *The Gospel Sound,* p. xxvii.

52. Boyer, *The Golden Age of Gospel*, p. 49.

Chapter Four:
The Golden Age of Gospel

53. Quoted in Allen, *Singing in the Spirit,* pp. 2–3.

54. Quoted in Allen, *Singing in the Spirit,* p. 34.

55. Quoted in Darden, *People Get Ready!* p. 154.

56. Quoted in Allen, *Singing in the Spirit,* p. 147.

57. Allen, *Singing in the Spirit,* p. 151.

58. Heilbut, *The Gospel Sound,* p. 78.

59. Quoted in Heilbut, *The Gospel Sound,* p. 38.

60. Quoted in Boyer, *The Golden Age of Gospel,* pp. 83–85.

61. Quoted in Broughton, *Black Gospel,* p. 54.

62. Quoted in Darden, *People Get Ready!* p. 218.

63. Quoted in Darden, *People Get Ready!* pp. 207–208.

64. Quoted in Broughton, *Black Gospel,* p. 77.

65. Quoted in Darden, *People Get Ready!* p. 199.

66. Quoted in Darden, *People Get Ready!* p. 193.

67. Quoted in Darden, *People Get Ready!* p. 193.

68. Quoted in Allen, *Singing in the Spirit,* p. 78.

69. Heilbut, *The Gospel Sound,* pp. 256–57.

70. Quoted in Allen, *Singing in the Spirit,* p. 85.

71. Quoted in Broughton, *Black Gospel,* p. 66.

72. Quoted in "Blind Boys of Alabama," The Information and Entertainment Center. http://afgen.com/blindboy.html.

73. Quoted in Darden, *People Get Ready!* p. 224.

74. Boyer, *The Golden Age of Gospel,* p. 50.

Chapter Five: Gospel Evolves

75. Quoted in Portia K. Maultsby, "The Impact of Gospel Music on the Secular Music Industry," in *We'll Understand It Better By and By,* ed. Reagon, p. 19.

76. Quoted in Broughton, *Black Gospel,* p. 114.

77. Quoted in Broughton, *Black Gospel,* p. 95.

78. Quoted in Broughton, *Black Gospel,* p. 95.

79. Quoted in Darden, *People Get Ready!* pp. 231–32.

80. Quoted in Broughton, *Black Gospel,* p. 96.

81. Quoted in Broughton, *Black Gospel,* p. 101.

82. Quoted in Darden, *People Get Ready!* p. 247.

83. Quoted in Anthony DeCurtis and James Heinke, ed., *The Rolling Stone Illustrated History of Rock & Roll: The Definitive History of the Most Important Artists and Their Music.* New York: Random House, 1992, p. 334.

84. Quoted in Heilbut, *The Gospel Sound,* p. 277.

85. Quoted in Boyer, *The Golden Age of Gospel,* p. 129.

86. Quoted in Scott Cohen, *Yakety Yak.* New York: Simon & Schuster, 1994, p. 158.

87. Quoted in Darden, *People Get Ready!* p. 245.

88. Quoted in Heilbut, *The Gospel*

Sound, p. 165.

89. Quoted in Darden, *People Get Ready!* p. 251.

90. Quoted in Boyer, *The Golden Age of Gospel,* p. 189.

Chapter Six:
Contemporary Gospel

91. Quoted in Broughton, *Black Gospel,* p. 125.

92. Heilbut, *The Gospel Sound,* p. 321.

93. Heilbut, *The Gospel Sound,* pp. xii–xiv.

94. Quoted in Darden, *People Get Ready!* p. 286.

95. Quoted in Heilbut, *The Gospel Sound,* p. 120.

96. Quoted in Broughton, *Black Gospel,* p. 124.

97. Quoted in Darden, *People Get Ready!* p. 313.

98. Quoted in Darden, *People Get Ready!* p. 316.

99. Quoted in Darden, *People Get Ready,* p. 318.

100. Quoted in Darden, *People Get Ready!* p. 314.

101. Quoted in Darden, *People Get Ready!* p. 312.

102. Quoted in Steve Jones, "Kanye West Runs Away with 'Jesus Walks,' " USAToday.com, February 10, 2005. www.usatoday.com/life/music/news/2005-02-10-kanye-west-main_x.htm.

103. Quoted in Darden, *People Get Ready!* p. 303.

104. Quoted in Gail Mitchell and Deborah Evans Price, "Gospel's Big Steps into Mainstream," *Billboard,* March 6, 2004, p. 1.

105. Quoted in Deborah Gregory, "Earth Angels: Looking for Some Inspiration; Meet Three Divas of Contemporary Gospel," *Essence,* February 1, 1996.

• For Further Reading •

Books

Rose Blue and Corinne J. Naden, *The History of Gospel Music.* Philadelphia: Chelsea House, 2001. This brief history has some good photos and illustrations.

Sherry Sherrod Dupree and Herbert C. Dupree, *African-American Good News (Gospel) Music.* Washington, DC: Middle Atlantic Regional Press, 1993. This book's listings of gospel albums and singers are out of date, but it contains some wonderful publicity photos of performers both famous and obscure.

Vy Higginsen, *This Is My Song: A Collection of Gospel Music for the Family.* New York: Crown, 1995. A nicely illustrated collection of classic songs, with simple musical arrangements.

Barbara Kramer, *Mahalia Jackson: The Voice of Gospel and Civil Rights.* Berkeley Heights, NJ: Enslow, 2003. This biography looks at gospel music's first superstar.

Donnie McClurkin, *Eternal Victim, Eternal Victor.* Lanham, MD: Pneuma Life Publishing, 2001. An autobiography by the contemporary gospel star, including a frank discussion of his abusive childhood.

Roxanne Orgill, *Mahalia: A Life in Gospel Music.* Cambridge, MA: Candlewick Press, 2002. This biography of the famous singer is enlivened with many beautiful black and white photos.

David Ritz, *Ray Charles: Voice of Soul.* New York: Chelsea House, 1994. A good but outdated biography by the coauthor of the legendary singer's autobiography.

Silvia Anne Sheafer, *Aretha Franklin: Motown Superstar.* Springfield, NJ: Enslow, 1996. This biography of the Queen of Soul, who began her career as a gospel phenomenon, is well written, if somewhat out of date.

DVDs

Al Green: The Gospel According to Al Green, directed by Robert Mugge. New York: Winstar Home Entertainment, 2003. This DVD edition of a 1984 documentary focuses on the brilliant, eccentric singer who gave up his role as the premiere soul man of the 1970s to become a minister and gospel artist.

Say Amen, Somebody, directed by George T. Nierenberg. Carmel, CA: Xenon Studios/Pacific Arts, 2001. This DVD edition of a wonderful 1980 documentary features long interview/concert segments with Thomas A. Dorsey, Sallie Martin,

Mother Willie Mae Ford Smith, and many other key figures in gospel.

Web Sites

The International Gospel Music Hall of Fame and Museum. http://www.igmhf.org/. This reputable Web site is chock-full of biographical and other information about the world of gospel.

The Spirituals Project at the University of Denver, "Sweet Chariot: the Story of the Spirituals." http://ctl.du.edu/spirituals/Performing/robeson.cfm. This informative site is maintained by the Spirituals Project at the University of Denver Center for Teaching and Learning.

Thomas Wentworth Higginson, "Negro Spirituals," *Atlantic Monthly*, June 1867. http://xroads.virginia.edu/~hyper/twh/higg.html.

• Works Consulted •

Books

Ray Allen, *Singing in the Spirit: African-American Sacred Quartets in New York City.* Philadelphia: University of Pennsylvania Press, 1991. This is a scholarly text written by a professor of Music and American Studies.

Horace Clarence Boyer, *The Golden Age of Gospel.* Urbana: University of Illinois Press, 2000. A reprint of a 1995 book, this accessible volume was written by a professor of music and gospel performer.

Viv Broughton, *Black Gospel: An Illustrated History of the Gospel Sound.* Poole, UK: Blandford Press, 1985. This is an excellent short history written by a British musician and music historian.

Scott Cohen, *Yakety Yak.* New York: Simon & Schuster, 1994. A book of quotes from famous rockers.

James H. Cone, *The Spirituals and the Blues: An Interpretation.* New York: Seabury Press, 1972. A short, rather personal series of essays about the connection between gospel and blues.

Robert Darden, *People Get Ready! A New History of Black Gospel Music.* New York: Continuum, 2004. An extremely thorough history by a gospel expert who is also a professor of English at Baylor University.

Anthony DeCurtis and James Heinke, eds., *The Rolling Stone Illustrated History of Rock & Roll: The Definitive History of the Most Important Artists and Their Music,* 3rd ed. New York: Random House, 1992. A valuable resource, though this edition has been superseded by more recent updates.

Michael W. Harris, *The Rise of Gospel Blues: The Music of Thomas Andrew Dorsey in the Urban Church.* New York: Oxford University Press, 1992. This rather dry scholarly volume focuses on Dorsey's contributions to the music.

Anthony Heilbut, *The Gospel Sound: Good News and Bad Times.* New York: Limelight Books, 1997. An updated version of a classic book about gospel music, first published in 1971. It is not so much a straight history as a series of deeply appreciative essays.

Leon F. Litwack, *Trouble in Mind: Black Southerners in the Age of Jim Crow.* New York: Knopf, 1998. This volume by a specialist in African American and labor history contains a few passages on gospel music.

Paul Oliver, *Songsters and Saints: Vocal Traditions on Race Records.* Cambridge: Cambridge University

Press, 1984. A distinguished musicologist and scholar of the blues focuses here on how changes in African American vocal traditions were reflected in early recordings, including those of preachers and gospel singers.

Paul Oliver, Max Harrison, and William Bolcom, *The New Grove Gospel, Blues and Jazz, with Spiritual and Ragtime.* New York: Norton, 1986. An updated reprint of a standard reference text first published in 1980.

Robert Palmer, *Rock & Roll: An Unruly History.* New York: Harmony Books, 1995. This book by a prominent music journalist is not a straightforward history, but essential reading nonetheless for anyone interested in the subject.

Bernice Johnson Reagon, *If You Don't Go, Don't Hinder Me: The African American Sacred Song Tradition.* Lincoln, NE: University of Nebraska Press, 2001. A highly entertaining series of personal essays (first delivered as lectures) by a respected musicologist and singer.

———, ed., *We'll Understand It Better By and By: Pioneering African American Gospel Composers.* Washington, DC: Smithsonian Institution Press, 1992. Many of the essays about important innovators in gospel in this collection emphasize technical musicological analysis.

Eileen Southern, *The Music of Black Americans: A History.* New York: Norton, 1997. An updated reprint of a 1971 classic text—lengthy, scholarly, and extremely detailed.

———, ed., *Readings in Black American Music.* New York, Norton, 1971. This is a collection of fascinating pieces by a wide variety of commentators, tracing the history of black music from its earliest days in America.

Periodicals

Janine Coveney, "Cece Winans' Modern Gospel," *Billboard*, April 25, 1998.

Deborah Gregory, "Earth Angels: Looking for Some Inspiration; Meet Three Divas of Contemporary Gospel," *Essence*, February 1, 1996.

Gail Mitchell and Deborah Evans Price, "Gospel's Big Steps into Mainstream," *Billboard*, March 6, 2004.

Internet Resource

"Blind Boys of Alabama," The Information and Entertainment Center. http://afgen.com/blindboy.html.

James Weldon Johnson, "Negro Folk Songs and Spirituals," *Mentor*, February 1929. www.document-records.com/content_show_article.asp?id=189&offset=90.

Steve Jones, "Kanye West Runs Away with 'Jesus Walks,'" USAToday.com, February 10, 2005. www.usatoday.com/life/music/news/2005-02-10-kanye-west-main_x.htm.

Toonari, "Spirituals, African American," *Black American History: A History of Black People in the United States.* www.africanaonline.com/slavery_spirituals.htm.

• Index •

Gates, J.M., 32
Gehman, Richard, 71
George, Luvenia A., 52
Georgia Tom. *See* Dorsey, Thomas A.
Gershwin, George, 38
Gershwin, Ira, 38
Ghana, 14
glossolalia, 21
"Go Down, Moses" (song), 17
Golden Age of Gospel, 11, 54–67
Golden Age of Gospel, The (Boyer), 56, 71, 88
Golden Crown Quartet, 55
Golden Gate Quartet, 60, 66
"Good Rockin' Tonight" (song), 68
Gospel Music Workshop of America (GMWA), 85
Gospel Pearls (Townsend), 46
Gospel Songs (Bliss), 30
Gospel Sound: Good News and Bad Times (Heibut), 68
Gospel Truth (magazine), 96
Grammy Awards, 83, 93, 94
Grant, Ulysses S., 30
Great Depression, 51–52
Great Migration, 35
Green, Al, 85–86, 88
Griffin, Alton, 55
Griffin, Bessie, 60
group singing, 14, 40, 42
    see also choirs; quartets, male
Guinea, 14

Hammond, Fred, 93
Hammond, John, 61, 76
Hammond organs, 50–51
hard gospel, 59, 59–60, 68
Harlem Renaissance, 39
Harmonettes (musical group), 60
Harmonizing Four (musical group), 57
Harris, Rebert, 74
"Havin' a Party" (song), 73
Hawkins, Edwin, 83, 84, 88, 89
Hawkins, Tramaine, 84, 94
Hawkins, Walter, 84
Heavenly Gospel Singers (musical group), 55, 57
Heibut, Anthony, 45 ,59, 64, 68, 79, 85, 86
Higginson, Thomas Wentworth, 14, 15, 27
Highway QCs (musical group), 72

Hi-Los (musical group), 88
"Hit the Road, Jack" (song), 75
Holiday, Billie, 76
Hollywood Walk of Fame, 85
Hootenanny (TV series), 80
Houston, Cissy, 74
Houston, Whitney, 74
"How I Got Over" (song), 45
Hughes, Langston, 39, 80
Hurston, Zora Neale, 39
hymnals, 26
hymns
    Dr. Watts, 22–23
    traditional, 8, 15–16, 22, 46
Hynde, Chrissie, 76

If You Don't Go, Don't Hinder Me: The African American Sacred Song Tradition (Reagon), 19
"If You See My Savior" (song), 49
"I Know His Blood Can Make Me Whole" (song), 36
"I'll Be All Right" (song), 80
"I'm Happy with Jesus Alone" (song), 33
"Impact of Gospel Music on the Secular Music Industry" (Maultsby), 73
improvisation, 15, 23, 35, 40
"I'm So Tired of Being Alone" (song), 85
"I'm Still in Love with You" (song), 85
income
    from gospel music, 52–53, 62, 63–64
    from pop music, 71–74
    from R&B music, 71–72
"I Never Loved a Man" (song), 76
influence, musical
    mingled styles and, 35–36
    of gospel music, 11, 68, 72–73
    on contemporary gospel, 89–90
    on gospel music, 8, 45, 68, 70
    on white composers, 37–39
"It Ain't Necessarily So" (song), 38
"It's Tight Like That" (song), 48
"I've Got a Woman" (song), 75
"I Want a Tall Skinny Papa" (song), 63

Jackson, Jesse, 79
Jackson, Mahalia, 11, 37, 60–61, 76, 90
jazz, 8, 37, 88
    influence of, on gospel music, 10, 40, 58
    spirituals and, 35

• Picture Credits •

Cover: Getty Images

AP/Wide World Photos, 78, 92
© Bettmann/CORBIS, 13, 20, 27, 31, 38, 39, 44, 47, 48, 69, 83, 89
© CORBIS, 25
© Terry Cryer/CORBIS, 58
Getty Images, 17, 37, 41, 42, 51, 55, 65, 70, 75
© Gary Hershorn/Reuters/CORBIS, 95

Hulton Archive/Getty Images, 84
© Hulton-Deutsch Collections/CORBIS, 28
© Neal Preston/CORBIS, 9
© Profiles in History/CORBIS, 34
© Louie Psihoyos/CORBIS, 22
© Christian Simonpietri/Sygma/CORBIS, 77
© Underwood & Underwood/CORBIS, 61

• About the Author •

Adam Woog has written more than forty books for adults, teens, and children. For Lucent Books, he has explored such subjects as Louis Armstrong, Prohibition, Anne Frank, Elvis Presley, sweatshops, Amelia Earhart, and the New Deal. Woog lives with his wife and their daughter in his hometown, Seattle, Washington.